FIRST KISS

He turned the boat toward shore, sliding beneath a tree branch heavy with yellow jasmine flowers. Jenna folded her hands in her lap and turned her gaze to a pair of bright blue butterflies playing just above the surface of the water. They whirled madly, their wings blurring so that it was hard to tell which was which.

"They're mating," Alan said.

"That is the nature of butterflies," she replied.

"And men." He stowed the pole in the boat and sat down, letting the current draw them along. "Jenna," he whispered. "A kiss. That's all I want."

One kiss. Harmless, surely.

The kiss began gently, a butterfly-soft brushing of his lips over hers. Every nerve in her body came alive. When he claimed her mouth fully, she shuddered, wanting more. His mouth tasted like hot honey, mint, and male desire.

"One kiss," he murmured. "So, Jenna Llewellyn, did you like your first kiss?"

She shook her head and drew him closer . . .

TODAY'S HOTTEST READS
ARE TOMORROW'S SUPERSTARS

WENDY GARRETT

CAROLINA DAWN

ZEBRA BOOKS
KENSINGTON PUBLISHING CORP.

To my friend Christina,
sharpshooter in a hoop skirt

ZEBRA BOOKS are published by

Kensington Publishing Corp.
850 Third Avenue
New York, NY 10022

First Printing: October, 1994

Printed in the United States of America

Prologue

Roanna poled the flat-bottomed boat toward the island that nestled deep in the swamp, expecting to hear her daughter's pure, high voice raised in song to greet the new morning.

But instead of the tidy little cabin they shared, she saw a blackened shell. Wisps of smoke curled up from still-smoldering timbers to stain the cloudless early-morning sky. Her breath sobbed in her throat as she thrust the pole into the shallow water, driving the boat faster.

"Silvan," she called. "Silvan!"

Only the hum of insects answered her. A swarm of dragonflies darted ahead of her, their wings iridescent as they caught the dappled sunlight. Roanna would remember that sight forever. And she would never quite feel the same about dragonflies again.

The bow of the little vessel touched land. Gathering her skirts, she leaped out of the boat and began to search. She found her daughter behind the remains of the cabin. Her beautiful daughter Silvan had been brutally beaten, even more brutally used. Blood covered her loins, seeped out beneath the tattered remains of her shirt.

"Silvan," Roanna moaned. "Ah, Silvan."

The girl opened her eyes. "Mother. They . . . hurt me."

"I know. Let me help you. I can sew . . ." Her voice trailed off to nothingness as she lifted the blood-soaked shirt. Her heart seemed to stutter for a moment, shocked out of rhythm by horror.

Roanna took a deep breath, then another. "Who did this to you?"

"Orwell . . . Stepton." Pain laced Silvan's voice, dimming it. "His sons . . . and another man. I don't . . . know his name. They called . . . me . . . witch." She paused, drawing breath with a visible effort. "Take . . . care of Jenna. Tell her . . . I love . . . her." The last word turned into a sigh, and the light of life went out of her eyes.

Roanna pulled her daughter's limp body into her arms. Rocking back and forth in silent agony, she felt the tears flood down her face. "I'll take care of her, Silvan. I'll take care of them all."

She buried her daughter beside the cabin. Three days later, she left the island a changed woman. Her lustrous dark hair had turned completely white. Hate twisted her once-lovely face and burned like acid in the heart that had once been happy and generous.

It took her three days to walk out of the swamp, another two to reach Heronsgate. As she strode up the long drive toward the house, Orwell Stepton came racing up behind her on a huge black stallion. He reined in savagely. The horse reared, its iron-shod hooves barely missing Roanna's head.

Stepton fought to control his mount, but the horse continued to sidle and snort. Roanna stepped forward and lightly touched the animal's nose. It stood still, the whites of its eyes glinting in the moonlight.

"Who the devil are you?" Stepton growled.

"You killed a girl in the swamp, Orwell Stepton."

His brows drew down. "I killed no one."

"She named you. Lie to everyone else, lie to yourself, but here, tonight, do not dare lie to me."

"Very well, old woman. You can cry the news to the world, and no one will believe you. I'm the master of Heronsgate." His upper lip lifted in a sneer.

"Why?" she asked, forcing the words up through a throat that had gone tight with rage. "She was just a girl, a beautiful, gentle girl—"

"She cast spells on the cattle, sickening them. She bespelled the slaves, luring them away from their masters. Samuel Hatch followed her into the swamp, and he was swallowed up, never to be seen again. She was a witch. A witch!"

"No," Roanna said, smiling a smile that felt terrible and cold and feral. *"I* am the witch."

He drew back, shock spreading over his face. She stepped forward, grasping the horse's bridle.

"I curse you, Orwell Stepton," she hissed. "I curse your sons and your brothers and all the generations of your family. You will never live to see the fruits of your labors, and your dying will be such that you will beg Death to take you."

She saw him swallow and knew he believed. His eyes matched those of the horse, white-rimmed and frightened. Laughter bubbled up in her. It poured forth, a wild, lost sound that was terrible in its bitterness.

"You have no power over me, old woman!" he croaked.

The wind caught her hair, whipped it around her in a pale cloud. "Remember my face, murderer. I will stay in your memory, and I'll be with you when you dream, and when you die. I will call farewell as you make the journey to Hell. My name is Roanna. Remember me."

While he stared, frozen by superstitious fear, she slipped off into the darkness.

One

The little dog ran, yapping, into the morass of trees and vines that bordered the swamp.

"Boswell!" the girl cried, her short legs churning as she tried to catch up. Her white drawers flashed in the sunlight. "Boswell, come back!"

Jon grabbed her arm and dragged her to a halt. "Wait, Pudge. You know we're not allowed to go in there."

"I've got to get Boswell."

"We're not allowed."

Her bottom lip went out, and her delicate brows contracted in a scowl. "I want Boswell. An' my name is Elizabeth. Pudge is a baby name, and I'm six. And I want *Boswell!*" The last word was punctuated with a stamp of her foot.

The barking grew fainter. Jon glanced over his shoulder, where Heronsgate's chimneys were just visible. This forbidden journey—bringing his sister on this trip into the edge of the swamp—had turned into a disaster.

"Hurry, let's go," Beth cried.

"Do be quiet, Pudge, while I figure out what to do," he said from his vast, lofty tower of nine years. Then he sighed. "Can you keep a secret?"

"Of course!"

"It's a very big secret, and you can't tell anyone. Promise?"

"Not even Dorcas?"

"Especially not Dorcas. She'll tell Father for certain, and then we'll never get to play here again."

Her eyes grew wide. "I promise."

"Come along."

He led her to his secret place. Holding her hand, he helped her walk across a fallen tree that bridged the land and the water. He raised his finger to his lips, reminding her of the promise, then lay flat upon the log and parted the bushes at the far end. Beth gasped as he pulled the small, flat-bottomed boat out from its hiding place.

"Ooooh, Father would *never* allow you to keep that," she said.

"I know." He looked with pride on the tiny, battered craft for which he'd traded his silver whistle. The sound of Boswell's yapping floated on the quiet summer air, and he jumped down into the boat. "Come on, Pudge," he said, holding his arms out.

She jumped into them, trusting her big brother as she always had. He retrieved his pole from beneath the tree, then pushed off into the sluggish current.

"Can you hear him?" she asked.

He stilled for a moment, then pointed northwest, toward the interior of the swamp. "That way."

They followed that faint bark for an hour or so. Clouds moved into the sky, building up higher and darker. Jon poled onward through a hushed, expectant twilight. Soon the rain began to fall. It spattered on the leaves, whipped a thousand tiny froth-points on the dark water.

Lightning speared across the sky just overhead, followed by a tremendous clap of thunder that made Beth cry out in fright. The rain started coming down in earnest, blinding sheets of it. Wind slashed it into Jon's face.

The boat hit something under the water, tearing the pole from his grasp and hurling him flat. The little vessel spun madly as he pulled his sister into his arms.

"I'm scared, I'm scared!" she sobbed.

"Don't," he said, holding her tighter. "I've got you."

The world seemed to have turned all to water. Water and wind and lightning rending the darkness, only to disappear again amid the crashing of thunder. Beth buried her face against Jon's chest, and he held her with one arm and braced them both in the boat with his feet and his free hand.

There were times when he was sure they were about to die, times when the boat shuddered and tilted, times when lightning stabbed down into the forest, splitting trees and branches with terrifying crashes. But the storm finally ended, or rather, muttered off to belabor another part of the marsh.

A few last bouts of rain spattered Jon's face. The wind died, leaving the boat drifting slowly and peacefully. The sun peeked out of the clouds. He sat up. Brushing the wet hair back from his forehead, he looked around. Water turned the tree trunks black, dripped in golden beads from the heavy coil of vines. But the bright glory soon faded as dusk crept through the swamp. Mist came with the darkness, swirling across the water like a pale, delicate shroud.

"Do you think Boswell's all right?" Beth whispered.

"I'm sure of it. Dogs know what to do, even an idiot dog like Boswell."

"I want to go home." Her bottom lip quivered.

He put his arm around her shoulders and tried to ignore the water that seemed to be seeping through the floor of the boat.

"Jon?"

"Yes?"

"I'm standing in water."

"I know, Pudge. I think there's a hole in the boat."

She started to cry, noisy hiccoughs that seemed to echo through the trees. "I want Father. I want Dorcas. An' I want to go *home!*"

"Shhh, Pudge. Everything's—" He broke off, staring open-mouthed at a pale shape that seemed to materialize out of the mist.

"Noooo," Beth moaned. "Is it a ghost?"

It drifted closer and closer, and finally Jon could make out the form of a woman. She was slender and tall, and her hair drifted like moonlight around her. Her eyes were the pale, clear green of new leaves, her face smooth and very beautiful.

She smiled. Jon felt his chest tighten with something he didn't understand. But he did know he couldn't look away from her and that he'd do whatever she wanted.

"Hello, children," she said.

Once the storm passed, Alan Langston strode across the wet lawn, surveying the property that had become his so recently and unexpectedly. The house had none of the elegance of his father's estate in Braxbury, but it was well built and solid, with a wide porch and graceful white columns, the tall windows to catch every breeze.

Heronsgate. It was beautiful, nestled in a rich, green land. And most of all, it was his. He never questioned the luck that had made him heir to his American cousin's fortune. As a second son, he'd accepted the gift of providence and been grateful for it. If only Helena could have seen it. If only she'd lived to come to America with him, if only she hadn't made that trip to St. John Walford, if only . . .

"If only," he said. "Your life is full of if onlys, Alan my lad."

"Mr. Langston! Oh, Mr. Langston!"

The nanny's voice shattered his reverie. A welcome interruption, actually. He turned to see her standing on the porch, her long face creased with exertion and annoyance.

"Yes, Dorcas?" he called.

"What have you done with the children?"

"I haven't seen them since before the storm. Aren't they with you?"

"Jon said they were going to find you."

"I was off in the east fields," Alan said. "Jon knew that."

She clapped her hands sharply. "Drat that boy! He's gone haring off on one of his so-called adventures."

"You should be accustomed to that," he said with some amusement. Dorcas tried, but it would take an army of nannies to keep Jon in the traces. The boy possessed the full measure of the Langston scapegrace wildness, a quality much more enjoyable for the sons than the fathers who had to raise them.

"I know what you're thinking," she said. "But this time he's taken Beth with him. I'm worried, sir. With that horrible swamp on our very doorstep, bears and snakes and God knows what else—"

"When did you see them last?" For the first time,

Alan felt a stirring of concern. Jon knew better than to take his sister too far from the house. Didn't he?

"Since just before the storm."

"Before—" His concern crystallized into alarm. "Three hours! Where the devil could they have gone?"

"I've searched the house, the barn and all the outbuildings. No one's seen them. Surely he wouldn't have taken her into town."

"Not Jon. Town's far too tame for his taste."

A high-pitched bark brought Alan swinging around to see Beth's dog come running from the stand of trees bordering the swamp. Alan summoned the animal with a whistle. Boswell, his white and black coat covered with a thick layer of mud, came with lolling tongue to sit at the man's feet.

"Where did you get so muddy?" Alan asked.

Heedless of his white lawn shirt, he bent and scooped the dog into his arms. A familiar smell clung to the animal's coat. Mud soaked Alan's shirt, seeped through to lay a cold hand upon his heart.

"What's the matter?" Dorcas asked. "Oh, sir, your face—"

"They've gone into the swamp."

The nanny gasped. "No."

Alan set the dog down. As he straightened, his gaze settled on the house he'd been admiring such a short time ago. The long rays of the setting sun gilded its white flanks and cast sparks on the copper windvane on the roof. But he saw no beauty in it now, only fear and the knowledge that if something had happened to his children this, and everything else, would have no meaning for him.

"Find me Mr. Tate," he said. "And find me a boat."

A short time later, Alan stepped down into one of the

small, flat-bottomed boats that were used to navigate the swamp. He slashed a hatchet deep into the rail and hung a lantern from its handle.

As he reached to untie the craft, John Tate, his overseer, grasped the rope.

"Let me go with you, sir."

"I need you to organize the search."

"Then wait until I get more men—"

"They're—my children, John," he said. "And they may not have the time."

The overseer heaved a sigh. "Sir. You don't know the swamp. Stay to the river, or you might not come out again."

Alan nodded, his gaze already focused on the mist-shrouded dimness beyond the trees. He pushed off, spreading his legs to balance his weight evenly, and poled out into the current.

"Remember!" Tate called. "Stay to the river!"

Alan searched for an hour, then another. He called out at intervals, until his voice grew hoarse from shouting. As though mocking him, the swamp remained silent but for the drone of insects and the occasional raucous scream of a wildcat. He drove himself to exhaustion and beyond, because his children were out there and he could do nothing else.

He almost missed the half-submerged boat that had nudged itself beneath the bole of a fallen tree. He might not have seen it at all except for the pink hair ribbon caught on the rail.

"Beth," he rasped. "Jon. Oh, God, don't let it be!"

He slid over the side of the boat and swam to the tangle of branches, making his way through with a savage disregard for his own hide. Fear hammered in his brain, fear of what he might find, and what he might not.

The little boat was empty. He dove deep, swimming through the treacherous maze of branches, searching blindly with his hands and heart for . . . anything . . . that might have been caught under the branches. Finally, with his overtaxed lungs screaming for air, he returned to the surface.

"This won't happen," he panted, laying his cheek on the boat's rail. "I won't let it happen."

He reached for the ribbon. Something lashed out of the dark water, fastening on his arm just below the elbow. A snake, his rational mind told him. But his being had centered on the ribbon that might be all he'd ever have of his daughter. Almost carelessly, he slung the reptile off and grasped the slender strip of satin.

When he emerged from beneath the tree, he saw his own boat drifting around the curve of the river. Unreachable. He shook the wet hair out of his eyes, then tied Beth's ribbon around his arm just over the snake bite. With a galvanic thrust of muscles, he pulled himself up out of the water and onto the spongy land.

His children needed him. He'd find them. If he walked until he died and afterward, he'd find them.

Two

Jenna leaned on her pole and regarded her two small passengers. "What shall I call you?" she asked.

"I'm Jonathan Langston," the boy said. "And this is my sister Elizabeth."

"Beth," the girl offered.

"You're English."

He nodded "Can you take us home, please?"

"All the way to England?" Jenna studied him, saw his initial confusion fade as he realized she'd been jesting.

"You're very pretty," he said.

"Me?" With an adult she would have been embarrassed. But under the child's direct, guileless gaze, she merely tossed her hair back over her shoulder and smiled. "What do you know about pretty, little man?"

"Hah. Lots of pretty ladies come to see Father."

She raised her brows. "And does he like them?"

"I s'pose," Beth said. "But *I* don't, 'specially that Miranda Carrew. She's just silly, the way she always bends down so Father can see her buzzums."

"Buz . . . oh," Jenna said, repressing a laugh. "Bosoms."

"Anyway, she's not nearly as pretty as Mama."

Jenna's brows went higher. The boy flushed crimson and hastened to explain.

"Mother died, you see. When Beth was two."

"Ah," Jenna said, more gently than before. "I do see. My mother died when I was five."

"How old are you now?" Jon asked.

"Twenty-five. It seems a great age to you, I'm sure."

He shook his head. "Father's thirty."

"He takes care of us now that Mama's gone," Beth said.

On a sudden impulse, Jenna went down on one knee and held out both her hands. The children each laid their hands upon her outstretched palms, a gesture of trust and kinship that brought a curious stretch to her heart.

"I'd better get you two home," she said. "Where do—"

Then a flash of light caught her gaze and she straightened.

"What is it?" Jon asked.

"Lights. See them?"

Beth clapped her hands. "It must be Father! He's come for us."

"Shhh," Jenna said. "Lights can be many things here in the swamp, from foxfire to the glow of lightning-struck peat."

Another light flickered into existence, then another and another. They moved steadily, following the path of the river. They were no phenomenon of the marsh, then, but lanterns. The sound of human voices drifted on the sultry breeze, an alien intrusion in the swamp.

"I can hear voices," he said.

Jenna nodded. "Call to them."

"Hallo!" he cried, cupping his hands around his mouth. "Hallooo! Father, is that you?"

"Jon?" The answering shout was joyous. "Did you hear that, men? We've found them!"

"That sounds like Mr. Tate, our overseer," Jonathan said. "Beth, we're going home!"

For a moment more, Jenna watched those lights, listened to the voices. They made her shudder. Townsmen. The same brutes who'd killed her mother, who came into the swamp to cut timber and dig their canals. Burning, destroying, always destroying—they had no regard for the swamp or the animals that lived in it, no perception of the beauty and power of the natural forces there.

She could go no further—for the price of her life, no further. "You're safe now," she said, poling the boat toward a tree that hung far out over the water. "Just stay with the current and you'll meet your friends."

"You're leaving?" Jon asked. His small, sharp-featured face tautened with surprise and a sudden loss. "Oh, but you must come. Father will want to thank you."

"I think not. Goodbye, my young friends."

"But we don't even know your name!"

Jenna picked up her pack and slung it over her shoulder. As the boat passed beneath the tree, she sprang upward into the moss-shrouded branches. She crouched there, hidden from sight, and watched the boat and its cargo fade away into the mist.

"When will I see you again?" Beth called.

There was a plaintiveness about the child's voice that tugged at her heart. She almost answered. Then reason took over, and she clamped her teeth against the words. True, her life was a lonely one. But loneliness was much better than what would be her fate at the townsmen's hands.

She retreated into the depths of the swamp, making her way with the sureness of one born and bred there. An owl flew overhead on silent wings, so close that she could feel the wind of its passage. A pair of raccoons waddled past, and a swarm of bats darted through the trees past them.

Jenna lifted her head. She'd lived here all her life; she belonged here. She lived and breathed the rhythm of the swamp, knew its dangers and its beauties.

And something was wrong.

All the animals were moving in the same direction—away from something. Her moccasins made no sound on the soft ground as she made her way toward whatever had frightened the beasts. She found it a few hundred yards further on: a print, left by a booted foot.

"A man," she murmured. "A townsman. And on foot. Is he mad?"

She found a second footprint, then a third, and realized the man had been staggering. "Drunk or ill," she said, bending to touch the water that had welled into the last bootprint. "Well, whoever you may be, I'd better find you before you kill yourself."

She followed that wavering trail, losing it in one of the numerous pools of amber water but picking it up again on the other side. One mile, two. The footprints became still more erratic, revealing the steady deterioration of the man who'd made them. But he kept going, beyond her expectations, beyond what she could have imagined.

Admiration bloomed in her, grew with every step. There came a time when she almost thought he could go on forever, a titanic struggle beyond human limitations. But she did find him, eventually, lying face down amid the wreckage of the brush he'd torn down in his fall. His fine clothes were muddy and torn, even the leather riding boots scarred by rocks and thorns. She rolled him over carefully.

Her breath caught at the sheer masculine beauty of him. The planes of his face were well-defined, his chin strong, his eyebrows flaring dark arches above his eyes. His lashes were thick and dark and beautiful, his lips a firm, sensual mold. She brushed the hair back from his forehead, noting that it was black and slightly wavy and passed like thick silk through her fingers.

Then he groaned softly, and she shook off the strange reverie. This man needed help. Her help. Expertly, she checked him for injuries. She found a nasty-looking gash in the big muscle of his left thigh, but it shouldn't have been enough to bring a big, determined man down. Then she noticed the small double puncture in the skin of his forearm.

"Ah, I see," she said.

"Got to reach . . . can't . . ." he muttered.

Even now, he tried to get his feet under him. Judging from the extent of his delirium, he'd been bitten several hours ago. She couldn't imagine what had kept him going this long.

"Stop," she said, putting one hand on his chest to restrain him. "Lie still and let me help you."

His head moved from side to side fretfully. "Have . . . to walk. Have to . . ." He bumped his injured arm and pain washed over his face.

"Lie still," she ordered.

Either her tone or the pain made him obey. Gently, she slid the point of her knife up his shirtsleeve, slitting it to the shoulder. He'd tied a scrap of filthy fabric just over the bite, a futile attempt to keep the venom from entering his body. His arm had swollen, and the rag cut painfully into the flesh. She reached out with the knife to cut it from him.

His hand shot out, imprisoning her wrist. She twisted her arm, vainly trying to break a grip that should have been weak but numbed her arm to the elbow.

He opened his eyes. They were indigo, deep and wild as a stormy midnight sky. Jenna felt as though she'd fallen into them, body and soul whirled away into the chaos of his being. Deep, deeper, far and farther still, until she felt she'd never come out again.

"Beth," he muttered. "My son. Jonathan."

His voice released Jenna from her strange paralysis. Of course. He'd fought hard for Beth and Jon, harder than she'd ever seen a man fight. "Your children are safe. Do you hear me? They're safe."

"Safe," he whispered.

His breath went out in a rush. He let go of her wrist, his hand falling to his side as though all the strength had gone out of him. Those remarkable eyes closed.

Jenna sat back on her heels, brushing stray curls of hair back from her forehead. Now she understood what had driven him to stumble forward when another man would have fallen, to keep going when his body only wanted to give up.

She felt a kinship for him. Strange and unwelcome it was, this heart-bond with a townsman. And a fancy one at that. But even had she been the sort of person to walk away from someone who needed her help, his courage would have bought her kindness. As it was, she was determined to save him.

"I will," she said. For the children, and for him.

Moving him would be impossible; he outweighed her by many pounds. So the fight for his life would be waged there, with the things she could find and make and her knowledge. She opened her pack and took out the small iron pot and the dried herbs and rolled strips of fabric she always carried with her.

She started a fire and set a pot of water to boil. While the fire hissed against the wet iron, she moved to tend the gash in his thigh. Her hands trembled inexplicably as she pulled off his boots and unbuttoned his trousers, inexplicably because she'd tended many men as a healer, seen many men as Nature had made them.

But for some reason, this man was different. She tried to avert her gaze as she slid his trousers down and off, but it kept straying back to him. A beautiful man, truly, long-limbed and lean, with hard muscles beneath the skin. His chest was heavily furred, arching deep and powerful, his waist spare, tapering to slim hips and strong thighs. The sight of his maleness brought a flush to her cheeks.

"Dolt," she muttered. "As if you've never seen a naked man before."

True. But they'd been patients. Broken bones, fevers, cuts and swellings and bleeding, whipped backs. She'd tended them with all the knowledge and gentleness she possessed. Not once had she experienced this desire to stroke her hands along a man's skin, to touch, to feel the prickle of hair and the hardness of muscle against her palms. It confused and frightened her just a little.

She draped the remains of his shirt across his naked loins, then set to work sewing the cut on his thigh. He moved once while she sewed, restlessly, but didn't wake. As she bent to cut the thread with her teeth, she inhaled the fine masculine scent of him. Musk and mint, the faint trace of expensive cologne—it seemed to settle in her flesh, a brand by which she'd always remember him.

The water had begun to boil. She pulled the pot away from the flames and measured powdered snakeroot into it. Once the herb had a chance to steep, she scooped out a cupful and raised his head so that he could drink.

At first he lay limply, but as the taste registered, his eyes came open and he tried to push her hand away.

"Drink," she said. "If you want to live, drink."

"Tastes . . . awful," he muttered.

"Do you want to see your children again?"

He choked the contents of the cup down. It only lasted a moment but long enough for him to swallow the contents of the cup. Then his eyes drifted closed as the fever took him again. Jenna gently laid him flat and began assessing his lesser injuries.

Cuts and scratches crisscrossed his skin. She brewed an infusion of witch hazel and began to bathe him, gently running the wet cloth along his arms and chest and down his long legs. The heat of his fevered skin burned through the fabric.

Not wanting to let him sleep on the damp ground, she gathered Spanish moss into a bed and half-lifted, half-coaxed him onto it. His fever grew hotter as the night went on, until she began to think she might lose him after all. But she wouldn't give up. She fought the fever as he'd fought the swamp—doggedly, determinedly, refusing to think of anything but winning.

She made him drink more snakeroot infusion, then tea made from the root of the swamp willow. Again and again she forced him to drink, sometimes getting only a few drops down his throat, sometimes more.

"Fight," she murmured. "You will live if you fight."

His eyes opened suddenly. They were clear and rational, as though he'd pushed the delirium aside for a moment by sheer force of will. "I have no intention of dying," he said.

She believed him. Staring into those fathomless indigo depths and seeing the determination there, she believed that Death could not take him if he willed it otherwise. Then his eyes closed, releasing her from the strange fascination which had held her. She became aware of a sharp clicking noise. After a moment, she realized his teeth were chattering.

"Damn," he muttered.

"It's the fever," she said, instinctively knowing that he hated his own weakness.

His jaw clenched as he tried to control the shivering. With a soft, exasperated sound, she slid down onto the bed beside him. He moved closer, as though greedy for the warmth. Moved by an impulse she didn't understand but which was too imperative to ignore, she slipped her arm around his waist.

"What's your name?" he murmured blurrily.

"Jenna Llewellyn."

"Sounds like . . . wind singing in the trees." He touched her hair. "So pale. Like quicksilver. And cool." Turning toward her, he nuzzled into the curve of her neck and shoulder. His breath was hot against her skin, and his hand curled into the thick, tumbled mass of her hair as though it belonged to him. "You smell like honeysuckle."

Jenna pulled her hair away from him. "Go to sleep. The fever's taken hold of your senses."

"Not the fever," he said. "You. You've . . . you touch my soul."

"Oh, Lord, I'd better get you some more snakeroot," she said, sitting up away from him.

"I don't want any more snakeroot."

"But—"

Jenna found herself flat on her back, looking up into

dark, dreamy eyes that glittered with fever and something else that set her heart racing. She didn't understand why he affected her so powerfully or how a simple healing had turned into something profound and disturbing. He was only a man, after all.

"Let me up," she said, forcing herself to speak calmly. "You're going to hurt yourself."

"I feel like I've known you forever." His gaze turned inward, and he seemed almost surprised by what he found. "Like I've been looking for you forever."

She drew her breath in sharply, unaccountably moved by his words and the look on his face. His eyelashes were thick and long, his lean jaw shadowed by a burgeoning growth of beard. Pain etched brackets on either side of his mouth, but otherwise he showed no sign of it.

"Let me up," she whispered.

"I can't."

He ran his fingertips along the curve of her cheek and down her jawline, brushed gently along her full lips. She caught her eyes drifting closed and forced them open again. Strange, this uncommon lassitude, this inability to control her own reactions. There was great danger in the sweetness of his touch, and the magic that must have been birthed in the moonlight and coiling mist. She should get up. She should. But she only lay staring at him, wondering what would be next.

"You're beautiful," he said, his thumb making small, restless circles on her bottom lip.

"And you're delirious."

"Yes, I think I am."

"Lie down!" she whispered.

To her astonishment, he obeyed. But his capitulation did not mean freedom for her; indeed, his weight lay half over her, pinning her even more securely to the moss bed. She tried not to look at him, for that way lay danger. But her gaze, of its own volition, sought his. She was caught. Caught and held by his heat, by the inevitability in his eyes.

Her awareness of the world faded, leaving her in a warm velvet haze. The sensations were so achingly beautiful that she held onto them longer than was necessary. Longer than was prudent. *A moment. A heartbeat more, and I'll stop him.*

His hand splayed out over her hip, then moved slowly up the side of her body. She gasped at the unexpected touch. When he encountered the gentle swell of her ribs, she knew she should stop him. When his hand drifted further, across the full curve of her breast, she knew she should be outraged. And when he caressed—lightly, oh so lightly—the sensitive pout of her nipple, she knew she should be afraid. But there was nothing lascivious about his touch. It was almost . . . reverential. So she lay silent and still, breath suspended, body tingling with sensations she'd never felt before.

"Helena," he muttered.

Reason flooded back in a stinging rush, and Jenna deftly slid out of his embrace. The night air felt cool and remote after sharing the intimate heat of him.

"Helena," he said again.

Jenna realized that he hadn't been touching her; he'd been caressing the woman of his fantasy. That soft, reverent touch, so hot, so disturbingly welcome . . . it hadn't been for her at all. She felt like a thief.

She turned away sharply, blaming herself for what had happened, not him. He had the excuse of delirium. She'd known better, or should have. Ah, but it had been so

achingly lovely. Illusion that it was, it seemed as though
it had been made for her. Crafted in her soul and brought
to life by this man, this stranger with the warm, gentle
hands and eyes of midnight sky.

Idiot, she thought. *To let yourself become bespelled
like that by a man who isn't rational. He doesn't even
know who you are!*

At least he seemed quieter now, the shivering less profound. She didn't dare touch him again. Not just now,
with the memory of his touch running like foxfire
through her body. So she sat down with her back against
a tree trunk and watched him, trying to understand why
he had moved her so deeply.

"You're only a man," she murmured. "Flesh and bone
and blood. No magic. No spell of the moonlight or the
mist."

The muscles of his arms and chest rippled as he rolled
over onto his side. His hair, longer than convention dic-
tated, fell in a dark fan across the rugged plane of his
cheek. Her hands trembled with the desire to brush it
back. Ah, sweet, treacherous magic! She resisted it,
clenching her fists.

Those beautiful indigo eyes met hers again, stirringly,
then drifted closed. She watched him sleep, her gaze
fixed on the rise and fall of that powerful chest. Suddenly
realizing that she'd begun to breathe in time with him,
she forced herself to a different rhythm. Her hands unclenched, her fingers spreading out over her knees.

"Only a man," she said again.

Three

Alan fought his way up through layers of unconsciousness. Fever lay hot in his body, underscored by pain. It urged him to sleep, to heal, but he ignored it, stubbornly clawing his way to wakefulness.

He opened his eyes to full morning light—or at least what passed for it here in the swamp. Overhead, tree branches twined into a green canopy strung with lush ivy and bearded with Spanish moss.

"Where the hell am I?" he muttered.

Raising his head, he took stock of his condition. Someone had obviously tended his wounds and quite expertly.

It hadn't been a dream then. His memories of last night were vague and disjointed, but he remembered being told that his children were safe. And, for some inexplicable reason, the scent of honeysuckle. With a hiss of indrawn breath, he flexed the snake-bitten arm.

"I wouldn't move that arm much if I were you."

The voice was female, low and soft. He remembered it from the night before, from his dreams. Propping himself on his good arm, he sat up and looked at its owner.

His gaze traveled the length of her, pausing momentarily at the three fish that hung on a cord from her hand, then moving on to more interesting territory. She was lovely, tall and slender but with a woman's curves beneath the mud-stained white gown. Her skin looked like mother of pearl in this muted light. She'd pulled her marvelous ash-blonde hair into a thick braid that hung below her waist, but a riot of curls had escaped to frame her face.

Hers was an unworldly beauty. He'd never seen eyes like hers —clear green like the new leaves of spring, yet fathomless with depths it might take a man's lifetime to explore.

"Artemis," he murmured. "Come to succor the wanderer in her realm."

Jenna lifted her chin, stung by his overbold appraisal. "That Goddess wasn't overfond of men," she said. "Likely she'd have called you intruder and turned you into a stag."

"You know the fable then?"

"Are you so surprised?" Her chin went higher. "Knowledge is not restricted to townsmen."

Ah, pride, he thought, admiring the haughty lift of her head. "I was trying to give you a compliment."

She blushed, suddenly and riotously, like an untried girl. It stirred him immeasurably, that rush of innocence. It made him want to probe the mystery of her, to learn her secrets and her desires and to make himself part of them.

"You *did* tell me my children are safe," he said.

She nodded, still caught by his eyes.

"Was it you who found them and brought them out of this accursed mudhole?"

Her bemusement shattered. His words underscored the differences between them: townsman and swamp rat, cultured Englishman and a woman his friends would call witch.

"This isn't a mudhole," she said. "Nor is it accursed. This is my home."

"Excuse me for being unappreciative, but just now I fail to see its charms."

Was that humor in his eyes? It disconcerted her, for of all the responses he might have made, a jest was the least expected. She didn't know how to deal with it, or with him.

She crouched, striking sparks into a pile of dry moss with flint and steel. A moment later, a plume of smoke spiraled up and tiny flames licked hungrily at the tinder.

"My name is Alan Langston," he said.

"Jenna Llewellyn."

She found herself holding her breath again, waiting for him to say again that her name sounded like wind singing in the trees. But that had been the fever talking, not him. Strangely, she felt bereft.

"You tended me all night?" he asked.

She looked up, a slanting flash of green eyes beneath arching golden-brown brows. "You slept two nights and a day."

"Two nights?" he repeated, astonished. "Then I—"

"Nearly died. Yes."

"You tended me all that time?"

She merely nodded, preferring not to talk about the many cups of snakeroot she'd forced down him, the constant bathing to bring his fever down, or especially the many times he'd called out to the woman named Helena.

"I owe you my life," he said.

Jenna returned her attention to the fire, adding twigs and dried leaves to the smoldering tinder. "I tended your fever, townsman, but your living or dying was in God's hands, not mine."

"Is this humility, or merely an unwillingness to accept a townsman's gratitude?"

Her brows drew downward. His gratitude would be short-lived if he knew who she was. "It's reality," she countered.

"And my children?"

"What about them?"

"You saved them, too."

"Why do you think that?"

He smiled. "Because you knew they were safe. Thank you, Jenna Llewellyn. For their lives and mine."

She felt hemmed in, pressured. Evidently he was the kind of man who never took no for an answer, who never gave up until he got what he wanted. Another shiver went up her spine, and this one had nothing to do with anticipation. His sort of gratitude came with bonds, and if she accepted the one, she had to accept the other. So she merely shrugged, refusing both.

"Do you feel well enough to eat something this morning, Mr. Langston?"

He sighed, sensing her withdrawal even as his fascination deepened. He'd never met anyone like her. And he intended to know her better, much better. "Alan," he corrected, smiling.

Jenna found her breath coming shallowly; that smile was wry and sensuous, blatantly male, and had the most curious effect on her. Warmth ran through her veins like sweet, hot wine, then pooled in the depths of her body.

"I'd like my trousers back," he said.

Just a few innocent words, she knew. But they made her overly aware of his nakedness and tightened her chest even more. She retrieved his pants and boots and tossed them to him, then turned her back and busied herself with the fire. She spitted the fish and set them over the flames to cook.

"I sent word into town," she said without turning. "So that your children will know you're safe."

"Dare I thank you?"

"Dare I accept?"

"Touché," he murmured, admiring the sweet curve of her hips and derriere. "Tell me, Jenna Llewellyn, do you always wear white while traipsing about the swamp?"

"What?" She blinked, disconcerted by the sudden change in subject. Then she looked down. "Oh, the dress. It was my mother's. I was just . . . dabbling in a bit of nostalgia when I heard a little girl crying to go home. And I certainly didn't expect to have to track a lost townsman through the scurf."

"Scurf?"

"The ground." She twitched one of the fish away from the fire and slid the fragrant, steaming meat onto a plate made of bark. "Are you dressed?"

"Yes, although the shirt is beyond wearing."

She turned, expecting to be relieved that he was covered. But the tight-fitting trousers only made his hips seem leaner, his shoulders broader. His chest was thick with muscle, his waist slim and taut. With that overlong black hair and those bold indigo eyes, he looked more like a pirate than a soft Englishman.

"Eat," she said.

He obeyed. But his gaze remained on her, disturbingly, and she felt as though he'd read every thought in her head. "Is it all townsmen you dislike or just certain ones?" he asked.

"I didn't realize it was so obvious."

"You've hardly been subtle."

"I dislike you all," she said, her voice revealing more of her anger than she would have liked. But he'd pressed for her answer, and by God, she'd give him one. "You come onto the land like a plague, and you destroy everything you touch."

"And yet you went to the rescue of two lost children and tended me for two nights and a day."

"Some would call me a fool for it."

"Not I." He settled back onto his elbows, watching her. Her distrust of others hadn't affected the generosity of her soul, but there was a shadow in her eyes that shouldn't have been there. "Why do you live here?"

"This is my home."

"This is a swamp."

She picked up a piece of fish and nibbled at it delicately. "This," she gestured up at the looming trees, "is the edge of the cedar forest. I think this section is what gave Dismal its name."

He looked up. The branches were festooned with fungi and mistletoe and hung with the ubiquitous Spanish moss. Sunlight filtered through only dimly here.

"Did you know there's a black gum forest deep in Dismal's heart?" she continued. "The water there is so dark it's nearly black. And then there's the Green Sea—"

"Sea?" he asked, startled.

She nodded. "It's a vast stretch of green cane twice as tall as a man. How many swamps can boast a sea?"

"Fascinating," he said, and he didn't mean the swamp.

The green of her eyes deepened, and for a moment he thought he saw the forest reflected there. So badly did he wish that it had been he, not the trees, reflected there that his breath caught in his throat. *Go slowly, lad. She's as fey and shy as a deer and twice as wild.*

But it seemed as though he'd been caught up in a whirlwind. He desired her with an intensity that made his hands tremble and shook him to the depths of his soul. Somehow she'd stoked a fire inside him, a fire that tasted like honeysuckle and burned hotter than anything he'd known before. To a man who'd always considered himself secure and self-contained, it was a very disconcerting feeling. He set the rude plate aside lest she see the trembling of his hands.

Instantly alert, Jenna left the fire and went to bend over him. "Are you feeling unwell?" she asked, reaching to put her hand on his forehead.

"No," he said hoarsely, his gaze dropping to the lovely double curve of her mouth.

"Your arm, then. Is it hurting?"

He grasped her wrist and drew her hand down so that it rested on his cheek. Jenna drew her breath in sharply, stirred by the contact that had begun as a healing touch but had turned into something very different. She could feel the lean hardness of his jaw, the prickle of his whiskers against her palm.

"You *do* smell like honeysuckle," he murmured.

"It's the fever," she said, more to herself than to him. "I'd better brew some more—"

"Damn the fever," he growled.

He pulled her toward him, overbalancing her, and they sprawled together onto the moss bed. Shock raced through her as she felt the line of his aroused manhood against her belly. But with the shock came a spreading, molten heat.

Her mind struggled to control the welter of unwelcome sensations. She braced herself on her arms, trying to prop herself away from him. He only smiled, holding her with apparent ease.

"Let me up," she gasped. "You're—"

"Delirious?" he supplied. "I was once, but now I know exactly what I'm doing."

"Let me up!"

"Just a kiss," he said. "That's all I want."

Just a kiss. Jenna didn't think it was that simple—for him or for her. Panic shrilled along her nerves, crying for flight, even as her treacherous body urged her to stay.

"Do you ask . . ." she paused, trying to wriggle free, "a kiss of every woman you meet?"

"Actually, no. But you're not any woman." His eyes slitted almost closed. "And if you don't stop wriggling around like that, I won't be responsible for what might happen."

Jenna stilled instantly, her heartbeat pounding frantically in her ears. "Don't," she said.

"Just a kiss. I have to know whether you taste like honeysuckle, too."

She knew she should refuse. But that smoldering heat within her whispered sweet, warm things into her mind, urging recklessness. Had it been this way for Mother? she wondered. Had she been carried away by curiosity, perhaps, or merely the touch of a man's hand? One kiss. Harmless, surely. She'd wondered many times about this mystery of men and women; one kiss and she'd satisfy her curiosity and earn her freedom as well.

"If I kiss you," she whispered, "will you let me go?"

"If you want me to."

Of course she would. Jenna bent her head, pressing her lips to his for a moment. There, she thought. It's done. And it wasn't dangerous at all.

"That wasn't a kiss," he said.

She blinked in surprise. "But I watched—"

"Observation doesn't give one knowledge of the true process," he said, smiling up at her with eyes that had turned brilliant with laughter and coiling desire. "Too many things are hidden."

"Hidden? I don't understand."

"You can't watch a kiss. It has to be felt. And shared." He stroked his thumb along the curve of her bottom lip. Jenna shivered, overwhelmed by the sudden drenching rush of sensation.

"Do you like that?" he asked, knowing the answer.

"I—" She broke off, gasping as he did it again.

His hand spread out over the back of her head, both cradling and imprisoning her. It was a heavily male gesture, possessive and strangely tender at once. Jenna couldn't stop watching the firm line of his mouth. Wondering how he'd feel, how he'd taste. Oh, he'd been right about observation not giving one a true idea of what a kiss was like; it was this, the rushing sensations, the shivering sweep of anticipation and the wonderful, frightening feeling of being possessed. *That* magic began in his eyes and hands and ended deep in the core of her.

He drew her down. Jenna's world narrowed to his mouth. Her eyes drifted closed, which surprised her; she'd wanted to watch. But she'd become wrapped in something too powerful to be controlled. It surged through her like a river swelled by hard spring rains, and the only sensible thing to do was to let it run its course.

But a moment later, when he claimed her mouth at last, she knew she'd underestimated the dangers of the bargain. The kiss began gently, a butterfly-soft brushing of his lips over hers. Then he nibbled at her bottom lip.

Every nerve in her body came alive, and her heartbeat shot even higher.

"Ah," he murmured, a pleased sound. "Do you like that, too?"

Jenna couldn't have answered; he'd begun kissing the corners of her mouth, and her attention couldn't have been diverted had the sky fallen around her in blue glass shards. When his tongue lightly traced the line between her top and bottom lip, she sighed.

"Part your lips," he whispered.

Mindlessly, she obeyed. And gasped again in exquisite pleasure as he claimed her mouth fully. His tongue slipped inside, exploring the sensitive insides of her lips, then delving deep. She shuddered, wanting this, wanting more.

Hesitantly at first, then with greater boldness, she followed his lead. His mouth tasted like hot honey, mint and male desire all rolled together.

Alan groaned, sliding his hands down her back to her waist. She felt like fire beneath his palms, burning hotter than he would have believed. She did taste like honeysuckle. And passion, he thought, plumbing the depths of her mouth. He knew he'd been the first man to kiss her, the first to awaken her to that smoldering sensuality. It excited him immeasurably. And yet it was not all passion; his heart ached with a strange tenderness for her. It was a new feeling, one he didn't understand.

He wanted her, body and soul. Wanted her more than any woman he'd ever known. But she wasn't his to take. This moment, this kiss had been stolen, a moment of magic carved out of the shroud of reality. Exquisite. Finite. He didn't want it to end. He wanted to hold her like this forever, and he wanted so very much more.

It took every shred of self-control he possessed to

break the kiss. He did it slowly, lingeringly, releasing her a fraction of an inch of a time. Every moment hurt. Then she looked at him, bewildered and shattered and lovely, and he thought he'd die of it.

"One kiss," he said. *"If* you want me to stop."

Jenna took a deep breath, slowly rising out of the haze of desire that had submerged her mind and her will. She had to stop now or not at all. "Yes," she said, her mind forcing the words past lips that wanted only to be kissed again. "I want you to stop."

"A pity," he said. "There's so much more."

She was acutely aware of the hardness of him beneath her, the barely-leashed passion that burned in his eyes. Shaken by the power of what had happened between them, she could only stare.

"So, Jenna Llewellyn. Did you like your first kiss?" he whispered.

Too much. Ah, too much. But she'd come back to herself, and that was a question she refused to answer. It would be so easy to slip back into that mindless sensation, and much too dangerous.

"It was . . . interesting."

Her answer startled him into laughter. He spread his hands out across the small of her back, feeling her heat and the smooth line of the muscles that ran along her spine. He ached with the need to dip lower, to the sweet curves below. With an effort of will, he controlled it. "To describe a kiss as 'interesting' is not the best way to stroke a man's pride," he said. "Perhaps we should experiment further."

Jenna wanted to. Feared to. "I think not."

Alan looked up at her, seeing his reflection in her eyes at last. It was almost his undoing. "If there's any mercy in you," he rasped, pulling his hands from her with an effort, "you'll get up."

With a flush heating her cheeks, Jenna scrambled to her feet. He made no attempt to hide his blatant arousal, but lay looking up at her with eyes molten with desire. Her limbs felt oddly weak and liquid.

"So, that was a kiss," she said, then blushed again.

"That was a hell of a kiss, Jenna Llewellyn. One that makes a man burn for more."

Jenna turned away, both disturbed and intrigued by the intensity of his desire and hers. "If you're well enough to think about your manhood instead of your snakebite, you're well enough for me to take you out of the swamp."

"Are you so anxious to be rid of me?"

"What purpose would it serve to keep you here? You're a townsman, I'm . . . what I am, and it's unlikely that we'll ever meet again."

His jaw hardened. "Do you truly believe that?"

"Yes."

"Look at me and say that."

She turned slowly, drawn by the inevitability of his voice. Determination lit his eyes and something that looked like destiny. Both frightened her. Her breath caught in her throat.

"You see?" he said. "We're bound to meet again. Your heart knows."

A far-off sound tore her attention from him. A baleful sound, one which was much too familiar. She spun, a smooth, lithe movement, and grabbed her pack.

Alan stared at her in surprise. Then he heard the sound that had caught her attention—a long, low baying. "Dogs?" he asked.

"Slave dogs."

Bending, Jenna slashed the hem of her gown, then tore the skirt all the way around to her knees. She felt a momentary regret for the final ruin of her mother's dress, but it was remote in the urgency of her task.

"Wait," Alan said, rolling off the bed. "Where are you going?"

"Stay here." With a flash of white muslin and smooth limbs, she was gone.

"Jenna!" he shouted.

The hum of insects was his only answer.

Four

The baying of the hounds seemed to roll through the swamp, a mournful and terrifying sound that rang of the imminence of a man's death. Jenna ran as fast as the terrain allowed, praying that she'd be in time.

She blamed herself. If she hadn't spent two nights nursing Alan Langston, she would have been more alert to what was going on in her swamp. If she hadn't let him bemuse her with his words and kiss, she would have heard the dogs sooner.

"Bemuse!" she panted. "Stupefy, more likely!"

The baying grew louder and more menacing as she got nearer. Suddenly she changed direction, drawn by the crashing of brush a short distance ahead of the dogs.

She saw the hunted man at last. His face was contorted with effort, and his feet moved heavily, as though fueled with his heart's blood. Sweat beaded his mahogany skin. Cuts and scratches and a welter of insect bites showed that his flight had been long and desperate.

Jenna stepped into view. "Come!" she called, gesturing urgently. "This way."

Evidently he'd heard of her, for he obeyed instantly. She wasn't surprised; many of the escaped slaves who came into Dismal knew to ask help of the witch.

"They're close," he gasped.

"Go!" Jenna swung into step behind him, reaching into her pack for the sack of pepper and bitter herbs she kept there.

She strewed handfuls of the pungent stuff across their trail, making certain it sifted over the brush as well. The smell of it hung heavily in the still, humid air and even at this distance made the eyes water.

"They got my body scent," the man said.

"They won't be smelling anything but this for a quarter of an hour." She flung another handful across their trail, then moved ahead of him to lead the way.

A moment later, the baying stopped. Jenna glanced over her shoulder at the man and grinned. His answering smile was broad, and his footsteps firmed. She knew his strength had been renewed by success. Hers, too; for a moment, it felt as though her feet didn't touch the ground. They ran until the noise faded behind them and the swamp's normal sounds returned. Surrounded only by the hum of insects, they felt safe enough to slow to a walk.

"What's your name?" she asked.

"I be Nathan, ma'am. And grateful. They said to find you if I could, that you help anybody that comes in the swamp."

"Usually the people I help are a bit farther ahead of the dogs than you, Nathan."

"I been runnin' two days straight, but I wasn't going to give up. I figured I'd run 'til I died."

Jenna had found a man like him, a man who wanted freedom so badly he'd run until his heart burst. She'd buried him deep in the swamp and planted holly on his grave. "Where are you headed?" she asked.

"Anywhere but Georgia," he said. "I been whipped for the last time."

"I don't think so, *boy.*" The man's voice slapped at them.

Its owner stepped out from a stand of black adder trees. Buckskins covered his tall, lanky frame, and his eyes glittered like hard blue glass in a seamed, weathered face. He held a flintlock rifle in his hands.

Jenna took a half-step to her left but stopped when the man swung his weapon to point straight at her face. Behind her, the fugitive let out his breath in a groan.

"That's right, boy," the newcomer said, showing tobacco-stained teeth in a smile. "You goin' right back to the master's whip."

Swamp rat, Jenna thought, then reconsidered. A rat would have scorned claiming this man as kin. A few of his kind prowled the Dismal, predators of everything and everyone.

"Now ain't this my lucky day," he said. "I catch me a slave who's gonna get me a twenty-dollar re-ward, and I catch me a witch along with him. Yes, indeedy, a real lucky day."

"Who are you?" she asked.

"Jonas Rafferty. Mebbe you've heard of me."

Her nostrils flared. The name Rafferty was indeed known among the runaways. Rumor held him to be a cruel man, a man who held no respect for the pain of others. Looking into his flat, emotionless eyes, she believed every word. "You're a slave hunter," she spat. "Are those your dogs back there?"

"Nah. You did me a favor stoppin' them hounds, witch; fer a moment, I thought the competition were goin' to beat me to it." His grin widened. "We ain't heerd much of you since pore old Orwell died. Some folks said you was gone, but I knowed better because I seen too many slaves come into this swamp and not come out agin. You don't hurt runaway slaves none, just good, God-fearing white folks."

"Do you mean Orwell Stepton?" she asked. "What makes you think he was either good or God-fearing?"

He chuckled, his gaze traveling down her body with insulting slowness. "Do you know that a man kin do anything to a witch, and nobody's goin' to call him nothin' but a hero. You and me's goin' to have a nice, long talk about that."

Nathan moved to stand beside Jenna. "You got to kill me first."

"I don't got to kill you, boy," the slave hunter said. "All I got to do is shoot you somewheres where it'll hurt real bad and heal real quick. And then I git to take you back to your master and pocket my re-ward."

A man hurtled out of the brush beside the slave hunter. Jenna got a single, incredulous glimpse of Alan's blazing indigo eyes and flying black hair as he leaped upon Rafferty and tore the flintlock from his hands.

Roaring in surprise and rage, Rafferty turned on his attacker. His fist connected with Alan's cheek, sending him staggering backward. The moment's respite gave the slave hunter time to draw his knife.

With a cry that echoed the clear, high tones of a hunting eagle, Jenna leaped upon his back. His arms windmilled frantically as he fought to maintain his balance. Then he flung himself backward, slamming her brutally against the bole of a tree. Sparks jagged across her vision. Gasping for breath, she sank to the ground.

Rafferty spun around, his lip lifted in a snarl. "I'm goin' to—"

The last word ended in a squawk as Alan's hands wrapped around his neck. He lifted the slave hunter clear off the ground. The man's feet flailed as his breath was cut off. Nathan bent to pick up the fallen knife.

Without letting go of Rafferty, Alan glanced over at Jenna. "Are you all right?"

"Yes. Just a little shaken." She pushed herself to a sitting position.

Alan let the slave hunter dangle a moment longer, then slowly lowered him to the ground. Rafferty collapsed to his knees. With swift efficiency, Alan pulled the rawhide lacings off the man's boots and bound his wrists together.

"Watch him," he told Nathan.

He strode to Jenna, his brows a black slash of concern across his face. Her breath caught in her chest as she watched him come. He looked dark and savage, his eyes burning sapphire, his jaw as hard-set as granite. Muscles rippled along his arms and chest as he crouched in front of her.

"That was a bad knock you took," he said. "Are you sure you're all right?"

"Yes, of course," she said.

"Liar."

Ignoring her protest, he ran his hands down her arms and legs in a search for broken bones. The warmth and gentleness of his touch made her even more breathless.

She pushed his hands away, repressing a groan as she rose to her feet. Her back had been scraped raw by the rough tree bark, but she wasn't about to tell him. The way he looked right now, he'd either kill Rafferty right here and now or strip her to tend the injury. Perhaps both.

"You see?" she said. "I'm no worse for wear."

He stood up, reaching out to brush a stray lock of hair back from her face. "Do you always leap headfirst into knife fights?"

"Only unequal ones," she said. Her gaze drifted downward, noting the spreading crimson stain on his trousers. "You've torn your cut open."

"It's nothing," he said. But pain etched grooves on either side of his mouth, and she suspected he'd pay a heavy price for this exertion. "Now we have to see about getting this vermin to justice."

Rafferty started to laugh, a hoarse, harsh sound that brought them both around to stare at him. He dragged his forearm across his mouth, wiping the blood away. "You redcoat bastard," he snarled. "I ain't breakin' the law. *You* are."

Alan's brows went up. "Indeed?"

"In-deed." Rafferty jabbed his thumb toward Nathan. "This slave's run away from his rightful master, and *she* be helpin' him."

Alan glanced up at Nathan. "Is that true?"

Wordlessly, Nathan turned and pulled up his shirt. His back was seamed with white whip-scars, some as wide as a man's thumb. Several were half-healed, the new flesh still pink and delicate.

"I ain't going back," he said. "No man's goin' to whip me again."

Jenna watched Alan closely, but his eyes betrayed nothing of what was going on in his mind. His face might have been carved from stone.

"I know who you are," Rafferty said. "And you ought to know better than to interfere in this. If you be the law-abidin' man folks thinks you be, turn and walk away now. I kin take care of these two."

"The Langstons have always obeyed the law."

Rafferty grinned. "That's what I thought you'd say."

"However," Alan said, "I owe this woman my life, and she seems to want to keep Nathan out of your hands."

"You let him go, you're damn well finished around here," Rafferty spat.

Fury finally got the better of Jenna. "And who's going to tell them? You? You won't get the chance if I drop you into a smoldering peat bog."

"I think I can handle this without further violence," Alan said, adding sotto voce, "little savage."

Jenna stiffened. "I won't let him take Nathan back to be whipped again, or worse."

"Trust me," Alan whispered. "Please."

Of all the responses he could have made, that was surely the least expected. She looked into his eyes, and it almost felt as though her soul leaped out to dive into those dark blue depths. Slowly, she nodded.

He smiled at her, and for a moment she felt as though she'd been bathed in fire. The warmth persisted even after he turned back to Rafferty.

"While Miss Llewellyn's very direct approach has merit," he said, his mouth quirking in a smile, "I think I can offer an alternative. Who is your master, Nathan?"

"Was," Nathan said. "My master *was* Mr. Zebulon Bryant of Talleyville, Georgia."

Alan nodded. "As a law-abiding man, I can't countenance your running away—"

"I won't go back. I'll die first."

"—so we'll have to see that your former master gets paid," Alan continued. "I'll send him a letter stating the situation, and a draft for the full value of your services."

Nathan's hands fell to his sides. "You're freeing me?"

"Not I. Miss Llewellyn. Do you know where you're going?"

"I got me a map." The big man looked at the slave hunter, disgust plain on his face. "My son tried runnin'. He got caught an' brought back. It was his second time, so the master cut the tendons in his legs. But he remembered. He told me about you, Miz Llewellyn. Said to trust the lady with moonlight hair if'n I was lucky enough to find you."

Moonlight hair, Alan thought. A description as beautiful and fey as the woman herself. He wanted to free it from that confining braid and comb his fingers through the platinum silk heaviness of it. It took an effort of will to keep from touching her.

"Go on," he said to Nathan. "And good luck to you."

The big man nodded, a gesture of respect that had nothing of servitude in it. Then he slipped into the tangle of vines and was gone.

Jenna looked up at Alan. She'd never felt this way before, never knew herself capable of such tenderness. For the first time, she wished she'd been brought up like other girls so that she'd be better equipped to deal with these powerful new feelings.

"Thank you," she said softly.

Alan stared into her eyes, watching the heat rise amid the bewilderment. She's a true innocent, he thought, untouched by the emotions shared by men and women. And yet she burned like a flame. Sensual. Moonlight pale but with the sun's glory inside. He took a sharp breath, shaken by his own reaction to her.

"You bastard." Rafferty's coarse voice jarred Alan out of his reverie. "You ain't stopped me. I'll be on his trail soon enough."

Alan grinned, a wolfish smile that belonged more to

a pirate than a civilized man. "I expect you're right. I'll just have to make sure that trail is very cold."

"You ain't got the . . . hey!" Surprise replaced the scorn in his voice as Alan grabbed him by the back of his shirt and dragged him to the nearest tree.

"What the hell are you doing?" he demanded.

"Buying some time." With quick, practiced motions, Alan tied the slave hunter to the tree. "Have you ever been to sea, Mr. Rafferty?"

"I was born right here. Never had need to go elsewhere."

"Ah. Well, I was a seafaring man for several years, first on other men's ships, then on my own. I'm rather good at knots. This is a reef knot. If you use your head, you'll be able to work yourself free. Eventually."

"You bastard," Rafferty snarled. "Pompous English bastard!"

Alan straightened. Holding his hand out to Jenna, he said, "Come, Jenna. Let's leave the man to his labors."

She swung her pack over her shoulder. As her palm slid into his, she felt as though she'd come home. His fingers closed over hers, a gesture rife with possession. She drew in a deep breath, feeling the weight of something powerful and inevitable.

It took an effort of will for her to pull her hand from his. She led him north, toward the spot where she'd stored another boat. Her nostrils flared as she caught his scent—pine and musk and man, with an exotic touch of the yellow jasmine he'd run through on his way here. Had she been blind, she would have known his presence.

Behind them, Rafferty's curses rose on the air. Jenna tried not to hear them. He carried such ugliness with him, such malice, that he seemed to blacken everything around him. Every step gave her more distance and purer air. Fifty yards, a hundred; soon she'd put him aside entirely.

Then, suddenly, surprisingly, the slave trader began to laugh. Jenna stopped, drawing Alan to a halt beside her.

"Has he lost his wits?" she asked.

"If he ever had any."

"I know you can hear me, witch," Rafferty shouted. "You like that pretty Englishman, do you? Why don't you ask him where he lives?" A moment's pause, then he began again. His voice rang with hate and triumph. "I'll tell you, witch. He's the master of Heronsgate, that's what!"

Her hands went numb. Heronsgate. *Heronsgate.*

She took a deep breath, trying to hold onto a world that had gone terribly wrong. Her heart, which had begun to open like a delicate flower, shriveled away from the horrible reality.

"You . . . bought Heronsgate?" Her gaze skittered here and there, anywhere but on Alan. She couldn't bear to see the warmth in those indigo eyes, couldn't bear the inevitable leap of her heart.

"No," he said. "The Steptons were cousins. I inherited the property after Orwell died."

Blood enemies, she thought. Because of who they were and what they were, only enmity could exist between them. And like the Steptons, he was cursed. Roanna had forged that destiny in hate and in the blood of her murdered daughter; father and sons, brother, nephews, cousins—all cursed by the Llewellyns. Roanna and Jenna, the infamous witches of the Dismal Swamp.

She forced herself to move forward steadily. One step, then another, then two more. Behind her walked a man with endless indigo eyes, a man who smelled of pine and musk, a man whose hands touched her with such gentleness and power. He'd hate her if he knew.

They walked a quarter of a mile more. For a moment she thought she'd carried it off. Then he asked, "What's the matter, Jenna?"

"No." She didn't stop, didn't turn, knowing the lie would show on her face. She'd never been able to lie well.

"Why did Rafferty think the mention of Heronsgate would bother you?"

"I . . . don't know."

He grasped her arm and swung her around to face him. As he did, his hand grazed her scraped back, and she couldn't repress a hiss of pain.

"You're hurt!" Concern roughened his voice.

"It's nothing," she protested. "Truly, it's nothing."

He ignored her. Taking her by the hand, he dragged her over to a fallen log and pushed her down upon it. Before she could think of another protest, he turned her around and started unbuttoning her dress.

"Why didn't you say something?" he demanded.

"I . . ." Her voice trailed off, and she didn't have the power to make it go again.

Her bodice loosened dangerously. She spread her hands over it, preserving her modesty. Her cheeks flamed. She could feel the brush of his hands across her shoulder blades as he spread the back of her dress open.

The air hit her scraped skin, and she drew her breath in with a hiss of pain.

"Good Lord, woman," he said. "Why didn't you tell me?"

She craned to look over her shoulder. "It's only a scrape."

"He might have broken your ribs."

"But he didn't," she said.

Alan drew in his breath sharply. Rage burned in his chest at the sight of the raw, red scrapes marking her satin skin. He'd always considered himself a civilized man, but the sight of that wound made his hands itch to throttle Rafferty again.

"I should have killed him when I had the chance," he growled.

Surprised by the savagery in his voice, Jenna glanced over her shoulder at him. His mouth had thinned to a grim line, and his eyes glittered with sheer male aggressiveness. He looked quite dangerous. Why? Because she'd been hurt. The thought sent a shiver fluttering up her spine.

If he knew the truth, he'd despise you.

She pulled her pack open. Taking out a wooden vial, she unstoppered it and handed it to Alan. "Just rub this on," she said.

He sniffed its contents, finding the scent strange and sharp but not unpleasant. "What is it?"

"It's a lotion made from the bark of the witch hazel tree."

"You know a great deal about these," he sniffed again, "country medicines."

Of course. I'm a witch. Aloud she only said, "There are no doctors in the Dismal Swamp. But nature provides what is needed—if you know where to look."

The lotion felt cool on her skin, his hands hot. She closed her eyes as the now-familiar reaction swept through her body. It shouldn't be so. They were enemies. By blood and violence, bitter enemies. But she didn't feel bitter just now; with his hands stroking so gently, so tenderly, she felt only a rush of liquid heat that seemed to settle in a rich pool at her core.

"Does that hurt?" he asked.

"No," she murmured, drifting on a tide of sultry sensation. "It doesn't hurt."

Alan could see only the curve of her cheek and the long sweep of gold-tipped lashes. But he didn't need to see her face to know that the magic had returned; she'd softened, her muscles relaxing as though her body were moulding to his hands. His own body had tightened, a man's response, a man's desire. He wanted her so badly he ached with it.

He finished tending her wound. It would have taken more will than he possessed, however, to lift his hands from her. Instead, he moved closer, stroking upward to her shoulders. It seemed as though his very flesh had become attuned to her; his fingertips registered the satiny warmth of her skin, the smooth curve of her shoulders and the delicate line of her collarbone beneath his fingers.

Her bodice slipped down another inch, and he could see the beginning swell of her breasts. It was all he could do to not cup those sweet mounds in his hands. And then he saw her nipples pout, twin points of arousal clearly visible through the fabric of her dress. His heart pounded, and desire beat heavily through his veins.

"Jenna," he murmured, a mere breath of air against her ear. "You burn beneath my hands."

She opened her eyes, but doing so didn't release her from the well of sensation into which she'd fallen. His chest pressed so close against her back that she could almost feel the beat of his heart, and his big hands were spread out over her shoulders, his fingers stroking the skin with a touch that was incredibly arousing. The muslin of the dress felt rough and unwelcome against her over-sensitive nipples.

Of their own volition, her hands let the bodice slip another inch. She heard the sharp inhalation of his breath, felt his heartbeat surge higher. Her own pulse seemed to chatter in her ears.

His hands moved over her slowly, a caress that was still chaste but which stoked a need in her that was anything but innocent. She pressed her legs together, holding it in, knowing only he could assuage it. She ached with it, yearned to know its completion.

And it was wrong. With this man, with the legacy of hatred that stood between them, it was terribly wrong.

Her mind knew. But her heart—and her body—wanted nothing more than for this to last forever. She closed her eyes again, willing the world to go away for another exquisite moment.

"You're so beautiful," he whispered. "You look like an angel, but you feel like a woman."

Angel. That's what Roanna had called the daughter she had lost. Silvan, with her quicksilver eyes and the voice that made the birds go silent with envy. Sweet, laughing Silvan, who'd been abandoned by the man she'd loved and then so brutally murdered by Orwell Stepton and his cohorts.

Jenna drew in her breath as Alan's hands strayed downward, his fingertips stroking along the upper curves of her breasts. If she didn't stop this now, she wasn't going to be able to stop. Desire swirled through her veins, urging her to silence.

Suddenly her grandmother's voice rang through her mind. "Remember what they did to Silvan!" it cried. "You're a witch. Like me, like your mother. Let a townsman use you, he'll cast you aside like yesterday's spoiled meat."

Jenna sighed, regretting the reality that intruded into the lovely spell Alan had cast over her. "Stop," she said, her voice trembling with the effort of saying it. "This has gone far enough."

Alan closed his eyes. Every instinct, every inch of his body clamored for him to continue, to brush her protests aside and drown her uncertainty in passion. He could do it; her response to him was too genuine, too powerful to deny him if he seduced her.

But he didn't want seduction. He wanted her to *give* herself. Freely. With joy. So he took his hands from her, closed them into fists so he wouldn't touch her again.

"I wouldn't hurt you," he said.

She ducked her head. "We come from two different worlds, you and I."

"There's magic between us, Jenna. You feel it as much as I." He reached out, lifting a stray curl from her cheek with his forefinger. "The woman with moonlight hair," he said. "I wish I'd been the one to say it first."

Ah, exquisite temptation, Jenna thought. She shook her head, denying him, denying herself. She felt stripped bare, her soul as naked as her back. Reaching behind her, she fumbled with the buttons of her gown.

Alex brushed her hands aside. "I'll do it," he said, his voice harsh with frustration.

The moment he finished, she got to her feet. The sooner she got him out of her swamp, the sooner she could forget him. But a small voice at the back of her mind called her liar; she had the feeling she'd remember his touch, his scent, and the heat of his desire for the rest of her life.

"This isn't finished," he said, echoing that unwelcome voice.

"It has to be."

"It will never be."

She turned away, unable to bear the desire in his eyes. "Come. I have a boat hidden a mile or so away."

Thrusting her supplies back into her pack, she swung it over her shoulder and started north again. Even had she not heard his footsteps behind her, she would have known he was there; her body was as aware of his presence as if he'd been tied to her. Perhaps it had become her curse, this over-awareness of her blood enemy.

"How long will it take us to get to Heronsgate by boat?" he asked.

She glanced upward, gauging the position of the sun. "One full day, perhaps more."

"We'll be together tonight, and perhaps one more night."

"So?"

"The nights can be long. And very warm."

She refused to answer.

"No matter how fast you run, you can't escape yourself," he said. "Deny your feelings, deny your own womanhood, but they won't go away."

His deep voice felt like a caress. She reached for her grandmother's admonitions, held them close.

"No, they won't go away," she retorted. "But *you* will."

He laughed softly. There was humor in it but also a steely note of determination. This wasn't a man who gave up easily, or at all. She remembered his fight to save his children, the struggle that had gone beyond endurance and the weakness of his body, and shivered.

A night, perhaps two. Dread settled like a cold weight in her chest.

Five

Jenna glanced over her shoulder at Alan. Strain taut-ened his face and etched lines around his mouth, but she knew he'd never admit it.

"Why don't we take a short rest?" she asked.

"We're almost there, aren't we?"

"Almost. But I want to tend that cut on your leg be-fore—"

"You can tend it all you want in the boat."

It was the same answer he'd given her for the past hour. She glanced back at him again. His jaw was set, and his chest heaved as though he'd run the entire dis-tance. Sheer stubbornness kept him moving, as though he knew as well as she that once he stopped he might not get started again.

She pushed onward, inwardly chastising herself for ad-miring the man so much. A tenacious man, her enemy.

"How do you walk so lightly atop this damned quag-mire?" he panted. "You look almost as though you float above it."

"I've lived here all my life," she said. "The Dismal is not a terrible place, but living at peace in it requires a person to adapt to *its* ways, not the other way around."

She paused to lift a tangle of vines out of the path, motioning with her free hand for him to go past her. His arm brushed her breast as he did, and the brief contact left her tingling. Awareness lit his eyes, dispelling the exhaustion for a moment, and she knew the touch had affected him as powerfully as it had her.

He turned toward her, and for a moment his broad chest seemed to encompass all the world. She watched, fascinated, the play of muscles beneath the skin, the intriguing line of hair that arrowed downward over his hard-ridged abdomen to disappear beneath the waistband of his trousers. Her gaze drifted lower to the thick bulge of his manhood, which had risen as though divining her thoughts.

Remembering what he'd looked like naked, she felt an answering rush of heat in her core. Her mind conjured up a stunning, irresistible picture of him aroused, that sweep of black hair falling over the stark angle of his cheek, passion smoldering in his midnight eyes as he leaned forward to kiss her.

So compelling was the vision that she reached out and laid her hand flat upon his chest. The fine, curling hairs prickled her palm, and the flat male nipple hardened beneath her fingers. His pulse beat against her, through her, coaxing her heart to the same rhythm.

"If you don't stop looking at me like that," he said hoarsely, "I'll take you here and now."

"I . . . thought you were a gentleman." Speaking was surprisingly difficult.

"With you, I'm only a man."

So simple, she thought. And so very complicated. She shouldn't feel this way, shouldn't react this way. Her gaze rose to his mouth. It was a man's mouth, firm and determined, but with a sensual curve to the bottom lip that struck sparks to her soul. Desire coiled through her veins like thick, hot honey.

Then a woodpecker hammered loudly on a nearby tree trunk, snatching her back to reality. Only a man, he'd said. But he was also her enemy.

"Come," she said, turning away. "We'd better get moving."

Alan followed her, his surging passion only slightly abated. Just watching her aroused him. Her back was straight and slim, her legs, exposed to the knees by the ragged white dress, were long and shapely. His gaze lingered on her narrow waist, the flaring curve of her hips.

He wasn't sure why she affected him so powerfully. Certainly she was lovely. But he'd met many lovely women since Helena had died, and none had reached his heart in any way. Many had been well schooled in *amour*, perfumed and pretty and eager. But Jenna, wild, fey creature that she was, touched something in him no other had. Perhaps it was her very artlessness that enchanted him so.

His gaze drifted downward to her bare calves, noting the smooth female muscles beneath skin that almost seemed to gleam with a light of its own, the slim ankles, the dress that swung with every stride to reveal tantalizing glimpses of still more skin. Lovely. She moved with such grace, as though only lightly fettered by the bonds of earth. It made him want to claim her, hold her, to tie her to *him* and him alone. Strange. He'd always thought himself a civilized man, one who had iron control over his temper and emotions. But these past days had stripped that surety away; he felt as primitive as any savage, driven by instinct instead of intellect. It wasn't a comfortable feeling.

"How do you find your way through this waste?" he asked, hoping for some distraction to his thoughts.

"How do you find your way around Heronsgate?"

"Lord, woman. Even if I couldn't see the length and breadth of the place, there are barns and outbuildings, not to mention a great, sprawling beast of a house."

Jenna smiled, inordinately pleased by the image he'd drawn. "I, too, have landmarks, only they're made by God, not man. Do you see that tall oak over to the west, the one that looks like something took a bite out of its crown?"

He glanced up, startlement on his face. "Yes."

"And there to the northeast, the loblolly pine with the lightning scar down its side?"

"I see it."

"Look around you. Really *look*. Landmarks are all around." She pointed south. "If I walk for half a day in that direction, I'll come to a great gum tree that's slowly dying. Its crown is half bare, and one of the dead branches looks like a great blackened pitchfork. Turn west from there, and I'll reach the river that runs near Heronsgate."

"And when the gum is completely dead?"

"Then it will fall, taking the vines and creepers with it, and it will leave a mark that even a townsman could see."

"In time, the vines will cover even that."

"True. But then I'll find another landmark. The swamp is a place of great bounty and beauty for those who live by its rules." She pointed to the trunk of an oak, where the bark had curled into the face of a wizened man. "This marks the way to the river. The boat is just ahead."

She slipped through a tangle of cassina bushes and stepped out onto the river bank. The murky green water flowed in a current as slow and lazy as the summer heat. Just ahead, a tree had fallen into the river. Its bark had been stripped away by the water, leaving a bone-white skeleton above the surface. Jenna stepped out onto the trunk, balancing easily as she made her way toward the crown. Bending, she untied the boat she kept hidden amid the branches, letting the current nudge it out and into the shore.

"Do you keep boats all over the swamp?" Alan asked.

"Not all over," she said, putting a deliberate chill into her voice. She didn't want to give away just how close they were to the little cabin that was her home.

He smiled at her, his gaze curious. But he didn't press, instead climbing down into the boat and steadying it with the pole. He held out his hand to help her in, but she avoided it, not daring a return to that smoldering sensuality. She jumped lithely into the craft.

She reached for the pole, but he pulled it away. "It's your turn to rest."

"You don't know where you're going," she said.

His smile turned mocking. "Downstream would be the logical choice, since even I know the rivers flow out of the swamp and not in."

Jenna opened her mouth to protest, but closed it hastily when his gaze dropped to her lips. She turned away from the sudden flare of heat in his eyes. Taking her place in the boat's square bow, she sat down and tucked her legs beneath her.

He poled the craft out to the center of the stream, then tucked the pole inside and let the boat drift lazily along amid the fallen leaves and skittering waterbugs. With a sigh that seemed to come from his toes, he settled in the stern.

"You see, my lovely wood sprite, I didn't overtax myself," he said.

Jenna was not about to respond either to his teasing tone or to that provocative "my." "Let me tend that cut," she said, taking her pack with her as she went to kneel beside him.

He peered down at the wound. "It's almost stopped bleeding."

"It still needs tending." Slipping her knife out of the sheath, she slit his trouser leg from knee to thigh.

"Those were my favorite trousers," he said.

She looked up at him. He grinned at her, a wicked, wanton smile that made her bones turn to water. Thoroughly irritated at herself for letting him affect her so, she sat back on her heels and scowled at him. "Better to lose the trousers than the leg."

"Bluntly said. Have you cut off a man's leg before?"

"No." Seeing the challenge in his eyes, she lifted her chin in a defiant gesture. No Llewellyn had ever turned away from a challenge. "Fingers and toes, yes, and once a man's arm. But I'd do it if I had to."

"You're an astonishing creature," he said. A moment later, he added, "You amputated a man's arm?"

"Rot had set in. It was that or let him die."

Alan stared at her, truly astonished. Or rather, astonished again. She was unlike any woman he'd ever met. A strange ache settled into his chest, a pain unconnected with her gentle probing of his wound.

"I'll have to sew it up again," she said. "Otherwise it will bleed every time you try to walk."

"Go ahead."

"It will hurt."

He smiled again. "It hurts now."

She moved his leg so that it lay across her lap. Alan

watched her work, those slim white hands moving with the ease of long practice.

"Needle and thread," he said, raising his brows. "How very modern."

"I traded wild honey for the needle. There are some who don't mind trading with . . ." She broke off. Almost, she'd said "trading with the witch." But that would have begun a discussion she had no intention of having with him, so she went on to other things. "The thread comes from the stem of the bitterroot plant. Indians have used it for centuries for thread, fishnet, and clothing."

"More bounty from the swamp?"

She glanced up. "The needle is a convenience, nothing more. I could live here my whole life with nothing more than what the land provides."

Lightly, he traced the whorl of an errant curl with his forefinger. "Don't you ever wish for some of the things civilization has to offer?"

"Such as?"

"Pretty gowns and music, for example."

"I don't care a whit for clothes." She put her head to one side, debating whether or not to tell him more. But his eyes compelled her. "But once I passed near a house and heard music. It was very beautiful. It sounded something like this." She hummed a few bars.

"Ah," he said. "Mozart's *The Magic Flute*. Truly music to stir the soul. If you like music, you'll like dancing. Have you ever danced, Jenna?"

"No."

"It can be nice," he said. "With the right partner."

His voice was as intimate as his eyes, and Jenna knew he wasn't talking only about dancing. She'd never missed the outside world. Never, that is, until Alan Langston had come into hers. He made her yearn for things she'd never thought about, things she could never have.

She ducked her head and started sewing the cut. He drew in his breath sharply, but his leg remained rock-steady beneath her hands.

"Sorry," she said. "This will only take a few moments. There. And now a little witch hazel lotion—"

"Bloody damn!" he hissed.

"—to help the healing. I've found wounds fester less often when washed with witch hazel lotion twice a day."

He took a deep breath, then another. "You wouldn't have a bottle of brandy in that bag, would you?"

"If I did, I'd use it for healing and not swilling."

"My dear young lady, one does *not* swill brandy."

Startled, she looked up into his eyes. They were full of such irrepressible humor that, enemy or not, she threw back her head and laughed.

His hands clamped on her shoulders. Reflexively, her own hands came up to push him away. Then she stilled, imprisoned more by the raging desire in his eyes than by his grip. He pulled her closer. His eyes had gone slumbrous and hot, and she knew he was about to kiss her.

Panic swept through her, giving her the strength to pull away. Grabbing her pack, she retreated to her seat in the bow.

"Are you afraid of me?" he asked.

"Of course not."

His smile was knowing and more than a little cynical. A man accustomed to women, she thought, and accustomed to his own effect on them. Remembering his son's artless statement about the ladies who flocked around Heronsgate, she pressed her lips together in a full, hot sweep of annoyance. She wasn't about to join the ranks of his admirers.

"Who is Helena?" she asked, astonishing herself. Never in her wildest imaginings would she have expected to ask such a question. It seemed to hang in the air between them, unbidden and unwanted. If she could have taken it back, she would have.

His face closed, a swift hardening of jaw and eye. "Where did you hear that name?"

"You called out to her in your delirium," she said.

With a sigh, he rubbed his hand over his face. "Helena was my wife. She died three years ago. It was very sudden, a riding accident."

"I'm sorry," Jenna said. "You haven't stopped mourning her."

"We grew up together, Helena and I. It was only natural to assume we'd be together forever."

"Did you love her?" That, too, astonished her.

"Do you always pry like this?"

She retreated from the bitter-sounding rejection, curving her legs beneath her and staring silently out into the trees.

"I'm sorry," he said after a moment.

"It was not my place to ask."

"True. But I was overly harsh, and that you didn't deserve."

It occurred to her that he still hadn't answered the question. But she'd gotten control of her wayward tongue, and held it. The only sounds were those of the Dismal: the gentle splash of a fish jumping, the drone of insects, the sough of the wind in the trees.

She watched his eyelids droop and the rise and fall of his chest deepen. Exhaustion had finally caught up with him, then. Good. She felt too vulnerable with him, as though her natural concealment of self had become stretched so thin it was transparent.

Why do you care whether or not he loved his wife? she asked herself. *Why do you care if he loves her still?*

Her grandmother had taught her only to hate the outside world, to hate even more Stepton and all his kin. Roanna would have quietly poisoned this man—mistletoe, perhaps—and even more quietly have dumped him in the river. And Heronsgate would be without a master again.

The witch's curse.

Jenna rose, soundlessly bending over her enemy. His face, even in sleep, was sharp-planed and determined. A hard man, she thought. And for all his precise manners and speech, one with a certain amount of ruthlessness. But one could say that about many of the men who'd come to America to carve their futures out of the virgin land.

No matter how hard she looked, she could find no trace of the cruelty that had brought Orwell Stepton to his doom.

Gently, she laid her hand on his forehead. His skin was cool, however; she could detect no trace of fever. Of their own volition, her fingers slid down to his cheek, lingered for a moment on the hair-roughened skin.

"You shouldn't have come here," she whispered.

But she didn't know whether she spoke for him or for herself. With an effort of will, she pulled her hand away from him and went back to her seat. Curling her legs up beneath her, she pillowed her head against the prow and closed her eyes. She'd slept only fitfully the past two nights, and in only moments she found herself drifting off into a dappled haze.

Tomorrow, he'd be out of her life forever. She'd go

back to her former rhythm of existence, and in time would forget to think about him at all. Yes, that's how it would be.

Alan woke with a start. The sounds of the swamp were hushed in this moment when the night bowed to the day. He glanced around, disoriented for a moment, then spotted Jenna in the stern. She poled the boat with smooth, steady movements.

Mist swirled around the boat, first concealing, then revealing her slim form. Her face seemed almost to glow in the muted light. She looked as cool and unreachable as Artemis herself, a goddess to be admired, pursued, but never possessed.

He wanted her. In one glorious flood of desire, he knew he'd never rest until he'd had her.

"Jenna—"

"Shhh. Look." Slowly, she lifted one arm and pointed toward the shore.

He turned. There, on the riverbank, stood a doe and her half-grown fawn. They made their way to the water with an exquisite grace that reminded him somehow of Jenna. Dew glistened like liquid diamonds on their flanks. The fawn bent to drink. The doe stood guard for a moment, ears raised alertly, then lowered her head to the stream.

Despite the beauty of the scene, Alan found his gaze drawn to Jenna. She stood watching the deer, her face soft with tenderness. He was shaken by the sudden, volcanic desire for her to look at *him* like that. To touch him and not as a healer.

Suddenly the doe looked up, straight at Jenna. For a moment they stared at one another, deer and woman.

Alan saw a likeness between them that went beyond the differences of species. Both were wild and woods-born, both belonged to the swamp. Then the doe sprang away, the fawn following her as though bound by a thread. The flare of their white tails disappeared into the mist.

"Beautiful," Alan murmured, and he didn't mean the deer. "Why don't you rest? I'll pole for a while."

"I'm not one to sit and do nothing."

"Neither am I."

She glanced down at him. "It's my boat."

"Aye-aye, Captain."

Alex had no intention of letting her work; but she looked so lovely standing there, the morning breeze stirring the pale curls that framed her face, that he didn't want her to move until he fixed the memory of her in his mind. Then, with a suddenness that took his breath away, dawn came. Everything turned golden. Even her hair turned from moonlight to bronze, and her skin glowed like rich cream in the dappled light.

"Why did you ask me if I loved Helena?" he asked.

"It was . . . mere curiosity," she said.

"An odd question for 'mere' curiosity."

Jenna felt her cheeks flame and bent her head to hide it. "I'm not accustomed to drawing-room conversations. I daresay a great many of my questions would seem strange to a townsman."

"Why do I hear an insult when you call me that?"

"Your neighbors would call me worse things."

"Swamp rat, you mean?"

"For one."

"Jenna, believe me when I say this: no man with half an eye in his head would ever call you a rat."

She smiled a bit grimly, wondering what he'd think

when he learned the truth about Jenna Llewellyn. *Why don't you tell him now? Because you like to see the admiration in his eyes. You like the desire, and you know it can't last. Once he knows, it will all be gone.*

"Why did you come to America?" she asked.

"I'm the second son of an earldom that has more name than money. I made my fortune at sea and lost the bulk of it in paying my brother's gambling debts."

"Was this before Helena died?"

"No, thank God. She was a gentle woman, unused to coping with adversity." Strange, he thought, how Jenna seemed able to walk in and out of the holy of holies of his heart, and it didn't seem to hurt overmuch. He glanced at her hands, lax now in her lap, the fingers long and graceful despite the callouses and broken nails that bespoke her active life. A gentle touch, even with a man's soul.

It occurred to him that Helena wouldn't have liked it here. She'd hated discomfort of any kind, and the heat, the insects, and the lack of amenities would have been a torment for her. But the thought seemed disloyal, so he pushed it away.

"The family fortune," Jenna prompted.

"Right. Since there is no such thing as a Langston fortune, and since I couldn't go back to sea with two young children to raise, inheriting Heronsgate was like a gift from Heaven itself."

"Why?"

"Land, Jenna." He held his hand out, slowly closing it into a fist. "I've craved it all my life, knowing I wasn't going to be able to stay at Langston Hall after my father died. Land to hold, to keep, to pass on to my children.

That's why I came to America. And that is why I will hold what I have with every bit of strength I possess."

His words held power and passion and sent a shiver rushing up her spine. "There are things that cannot be held. Should not be held."

"Not to me."

He stood up and reached for the pole. Jenna retained her grip. With a smile that had more than a hint of wickedness in it, he pulled the pole—and her—back against his body. Jenna let go, preferring to lose this battle than to be drawn so close to him.

"Sit down," he said, triumph sparking his eyes. "If you want to do something, why don't you catch us some fish for breakfast?"

"With perhaps some hemlock for seasoning?"

"I doubt you'd poison me after all the trouble you've gone through keeping me alive."

"That was before I got to know you," she said.

"If you get to know me still better," he said, his voice a caress, "you may want to do other things besides poison me."

She jerked her pack open and peered inside, more to hide her flaming cheeks than to find anything. "In a few hours, sir, you'll be gone. 'Tis unlikely we'll ever set eyes on one another again."

"Ah, Jenna." The smile left his eyes, and she saw again the steely determination that had kept him moving when another man would have given up. "If you think that's true, you're only fooling yourself."

She lifted her chin defiantly. "Is that a threat?"

"Only a promise."

Turning her back on him, she dropped hook and line

into the water. Something touched her back with invisible, chill hands; it felt ominously like destiny.

Never, she thought. The only destiny she could share with Alan Langston was that of enmity. Sworn enemies, the master of Heronsgate and the witch.

Six

Jenna watched Alan as he poled the boat forward. Sweat shone on his chest and arms, delineating the smooth ripple of muscle as he moved.

"You're staring," he said.

"I'm just wondering how a man came to be so stubborn."

He grinned. "Born that way, I suppose."

"Master of the manor, born and bred?" There was more tartness in her voice than she would have liked. But then, from the moment he'd thrown off the fever, he'd pressed her temper and her serenity.

"It seems to bother you," he said. "Why?"

"It doesn't bother me," she replied. "I just find it strange that a man can go through life expecting to get his way in everything."

His dark blue gaze turned speculative. "But that is the nature of men, Jenna. Just as it's the nature of women to be possessed."

"Not I," she said with absolute conviction.

"Even you," he said with matching surety.

She retreated into silence, returning to the basket she was plaiting from supple reeds. It was comforting, this task, one her hands knew of their own accord.

Alan cocked his head to one side. "More bounty from the swamp."

"Just something to do with hands left idle too long."

He turned the boat toward shore, sliding beneath a tree branch heavy with yellow jasmine vines. Reaching up, he plucked a handful of bright blossoms. He let them fall into the basket, a shower of gold brighter than any Midas could have conjured.

One blossom caught on the edge of the basket; with a duchess's aplomb, she pulled it free and tucked it over her ear. He drew in his breath sharply, caught by a sudden, powerful sweep of desire.

"You're very beautiful," he said.

"You've the tongue of an experienced flatterer, Mr. Langston."

"Only when it's so richly deserved."

She scowled, irritated by the thought of him giving pretty compliments to other women—especially Miranda Carrew with the bosoms so flagrantly offered to him. "Indeed. And how do I compare to the ladies who flock to Heronsgate to play coy with its new master? Do they have elegant bonnets like mine, perhaps?" She held out her hands, palm out. "Are their callouses as lovely, their gowns as soiled?"

"I doubt any of them could cut off a man's arm," he said, choosing lightness because his temper had begun to spark.

"Indeed," she said.

"Indeed," he replied.

Unsure whether she'd won that round or not, Jenna retreated into silence. She folded her hands in her lap and turned her gaze to a pair of bright blue butterflies that played just above the surface of the water. They whirled madly, their wings blurring so that it was hard to tell which was which.

"They're mating," Alan said.

"That is the nature of butterflies," she replied, refusing to be intimidated.

"And men."

The butterflies danced. As they dipped down toward the dark water, a huge bass leaped out of the water, caught them both in its mouth, then splashed back with its prize.

Alan watched the rapidly spreading ripples that marked the fish's passage, then glanced up at Jenna. "Dangerous thing, mating."

"Especially for the unwary," she said.

"I'll be ever on my guard."

"A wise choice."

He stowed the pole in the boat and sat down, letting the current draw them along. "If I'd had that exchange with a lady in a drawing room, I would have interpreted it as a clever play at seduction."

"Don't make the mistake of judging me by your drawing-room rules," she said.

He smiled, his gaze resting on her mouth. "I wouldn't dream of it. If those other ladies of whom you speak are well-groomed housecats, then you're a very lovely, very untamed lady cougar."

"That intrigues you?" she asked, baiting him.

"Of course. I have the feeling the taming of a lady cougar would be a most enjoyable thing."

Ah! she thought. He'd fallen into the trap. "I would expect a slave owner to think in terms of taming. Such sport, is it, in taking something free and breaking it to your will?"

Alan drew a deep breath, ready to retort. Then he let it out slowly and said, "You're deliberately starting an argument, and I don't intend to oblige you."

He was right, and that only annoyed her more. She had started an argument; somehow, anger seemed safer than the emotions that stole into her heart whenever she looked at him. She didn't want his compliments, his admiration or his passion.

"I did not try to start an argument," she said, illogically.

"Yes, you did. And furthermore . . ." he began, then swore as he slapped at his chest, then again at the side of his neck. "What the devil are these things?"

"Yellow flies," Jenna said. "This is the time of year when they swarm the thickest."

He glanced up at her, his dark brows lowered. "Why aren't they bothering you, then?"

Jenna opened her pack and pulled out a jar of salve. "Here," she said, holding it out to him. "Spread this on your skin. It will keep the insects away."

He didn't reach for it. "You'll have to do my back."

Jenna clenched her teeth. He'd caught her neatly, putting her in the position of having to touch him. She didn't want to. Her body's reaction to him was too powerful, too dangerous. But refusing would not only give her away, it would cause him no small amount of satisfaction.

"Very well," she said. "Turn around."

He obeyed. His back was broad, tapering downward to his narrow waist. Muscles coiled beneath the skin as he shifted position, and his dark hair fanned like heavy silk across the back of his neck. Jenna wanted to bury her fingers in that thick darkness; instead, she unstoppered the little pot and scooped out a dollop of translucent white salve.

Her hands moved of their own accord, smoothing across his heavy shoulders, over the ridges of his ribs, then tracing the deep groove of his spine. His skin warmed beneath her palms, and the heat seemed to spread upward along her arms. The clean, sharp odor of the salve hung in the air. Mixed with the male scent of musk and leather, it was a heady thing. Something hot and sweet settled in her body, making her breasts tingle and her belly tighten. Her breathing quickened.

He didn't speak, didn't move. If he had, she might have thrown off the molten spell that had claimed her. But his stillness only fed the mood, and she continued to slide her palms over his back. Shoulders, sides, ribs, a smooth slide from neck to waist with her thumbs tracing his spine.

Alan closed his eyes, striving for control. Her hands were pure magic, her touch gentle and sensual at the same time. She was close enough that he could smell the honeysuckle-sweet fragrance of her skin. So naive, so virginal, so incredibly seductive. He'd deliberately maneuvered her into this, wanting only to be touched by her again, but he'd called up something powerful and primal, something he wasn't sure he had the strength to control. She didn't know what she was doing to him; had she realized the extent of his arousal, she'd have run from him in terror.

"Jenna—" he began.

She stopped, and he nearly groaned with the loss. He swiveled to face her. "Do the rest," he whispered, his words a command despite the softness of his voice.

Jenna looked deeply into his eyes. They raged with desire, a need so wild that it called to her own untamed heart, making her reckless, reckless. She wanted only this moment, this brief, precious time when the rest of the world fell away and there was only the two of them.

Without looking away from him, she dipped her fingers into the pot and scooped out another dollop of salve. As she smoothed it over the broad sweep of his chest, she felt his heartbeat throb frantically beneath her hands. Slowly, slowly, she ran her palms down the hard-ridged plane of his abdomen, then up again, more slowly still, to the strong column of his throat. Unable to stop, unable to think, she stroked downward again. And up, her hands spreading out across his skin in a pure caress.

He groaned, a deep male sound that sent her pulse racing still higher. His hands closed over her wrists, tugged. She found herself pressed against him, his legs enclosing her, straining her against the hard bulge of his manhood.

Flee! A small, sane corner of her mind screamed. *This is madness!*

But she was caught, trapped by those blazing midnight eyes and by her own treacherous desire. Her body flowed with heat, a liquid flame that settled deep inside and turned her whole being molten.

She arched her back as he slid his hand up her spine and into her hair. His fingers spread out, cupping her head in a gesture both tender and possessive. Helpless, she watched his mouth descend toward her. Desire swept along her veins, pooled in her belly. Of their own accord, her lips parted to welcome him.

His kiss was scorching, demanding, almost savage with a hunger barely held in check. Pure possession. He seemed intent on devastation, first probing deeply, then retreating, drawing her into mindless response. She heard his ragged breathing, felt his legs tighten around her, and knew the full sweep of a woman's triumph.

He bit softly at her lips, drinking in her sighs, then slid his mouth downward to her throat. Jenna arched her back. With a muttered exclamation of need, he slid her higher against his body. She gasped as his mouth closed over her nipple, wet heat enclosing her through the fabric of her dress. Pleasure ran white-hot from that point, bringing a strange yearning tightness in her female core. She closed her legs tightly around it lest she lose this new, wonderful feeling. He moved to her other nipple, suckling, his tongue circling in a delving motion that made her hips move in unconscious response.

She moaned softly as he returned to her mouth. He ran his hand down her waist to the flaring curve of her buttock, a slow, hot caress that made her breathing run as ragged as his. Then he lifted her leg up and over his hip, pressing her feminine mound against the straining ridge of his maleness. Jenna trembled, feeling him so close, so hard, and only the thin cotton of her pantaloons between them. A cold shaft of fear speared through the haze of passion.

"I have to have you," he rasped. "Now, Jenna."

She stiffened, pushing frantically against his chest. "Let me go!"

"What the bloody hell?" His hands clamped her shoulders, holding her against him.

Panic claimed her. She twisted in his grasp, hurting herself. Still cursing, he wrapped his arms around her and trapped her against his body.

"Stop it," he said, his voice harsh. "I'm not going to hurt you."

"Don't touch me," she panted. "Please, don't—"

"I'm not going to take you against your will," he snarled, frustration a razor-edged blade stabbing through him. "What the hell is wrong? A moment ago you were all fire in my arms."

She closed her eyes. Reality had come back with a vengeance; this was her enemy, sworn so on her mother's blood. It would have been a cursed coupling, one they both would have soon regretted. "I didn't expect . . . everything just happened so fast. I've never felt that way . . . I didn't have a chance to think—"

"It was magic between us, Jenna."

"Let me go."

Her voice had sunk to a whisper. Alan pushed the wild clamor of his body into abeyance. He studied her face, wishing he could make her understand what to him was so very clear. "There is nothing wrong with what we share."

She opened her eyes. "In a short time, you'll be back at Heronsgate and I'll return to the swamp."

"It doesn't have to be that way."

"But it does," she said.

He released her, his body aching with what had gone unfinished between them. She retreated to the bow, curling her legs beneath her and staring out into the forest. He could tell by the faint tremble in her hand that her outward serenity was just a pose. God, he wanted her! An hour, a day, a week—long enough to drown himself in her and not come up again until he was sated. The scent of her lingered on his hands, an exotic trace of honeysuckle and woman, a piquant memory of what might have been.

"This isn't finished," he said. "Not for me and not for you."

Stung, she lifted her chin defiantly. "It was my fault for not controlling things better. But it *is* finished."

"Your lips are swollen from my kisses." His voice was silken and deep, almost as potent a caress as his hands.

Jenna reached up to touch her mouth, then instantly regretted the action; it brought back memories she'd rather have ignored. She saw that he was watching her, a smile playing at the corners of his mouth. But it was the desire in his eyes that disturbed her the most. It raged like wildfire in those dark blue depths, calling to something equally hot, equally primal inside her.

It can never be. She turned away from it, fixing her gaze on the water instead. As the frantic beating of her heart slowed, she became aware of a human voice ahead, calling, calling, then waiting to see if there was a response. She stilled, every sense tuned to the intruder in her swamp.

Coldness filled her heart as she realized what the man was shouting. She turned back to Alan. "He's searching for you," she said. "Calling you Master."

He grimaced, still unused to this American custom of slaves and masters. It reminded him of the many things he had yet to do at Heronsgate, the changes he had to make while trying not to disorder the lives of those who depended on him. He cocked his head, listening to the voice, and said, "That's Ben, I think."

Jenna started to rise to her feet, but he leaned forward and grasped her wrist. "Come with me."

"Your slave will see that you get out."

"I want you to come to Heronsgate with me."

"That would be madness for both of us. This," she swept her hand to indicate the tiny world bounded by the sides of the boat, "isn't real. And the illusion would end the moment you stepped out onto Heronsgate land."

Perhaps, he thought. But he wanted her. He didn't

know how his desire for her had grown so powerful or why. God knows he should've been happy with what he already had: two children he adored and a plantation on which to build his future. Still, he desired this fey, beautiful woman with the fathomless eyes the color of new leaves and hair like spun moonlight.

"I want you to come with me," he said.

She twisted her arm in an unsuccessful bid for freedom. "We don't always get what we want."

"I do."

Her eyes narrowed. "That's because you *own* the people you live with. But I have a choice."

"Do you think you'll be able to run back into the swamp and forget what happened between us? Do you think I'd allow it?"

"Allow! Haven't you learned that the only ruler here is the Dismal?"

"I learned only the lesson of the passion between us. Can you forget it? It sings in your blood, Jenna. Just as it sings in mine."

He rose to his feet, pulling her up with him. Jenna gasped as his arm slid around her waist, drawing her against his body. Desire darkened his eyes, but the tenderness had gone. Instead, she saw raw need, the frustration of a man who wanted and could not have, and the determination to see that change. Her heart beat wildly with fear. Fear of him, fear of her inability to resist him.

"Jenna—" he began.

Then she saw his gaze shift to a point behind her. His grasp loosened, and she pulled away. Turning, she saw a small, flat-bottomed boat much like hers move around a curve in the river. A man poled it steadily against the gentle current, sweat gleaming on his dark skin.

"Master Alan!" he called. "Thank the Lord I found you!"

"Hello, Ben." With a sigh that seemed to come from his toes, Alan picked up the pole and moved his own craft forward. The two boats bumped gently, then drifted slowly downstream and toward shore.

"Come across, Master Alan," Ben said, jabbing his pole deep to anchor both craft.

Alan jumped over to the man's boat. "Are my children well?"

"Yes, suh. Fat and sassy an' as full of themselves as always. They . . ." His voice trailed off as his gaze went to Jenna.

Ben stared at her for a long, frozen moment. Then he bowed.

Alan felt his jaw drop. That hadn't been a bow given in politeness. No, it had been a deep bow, one that bespoke great respect—and homage. *As though she were a queen,* Alan thought, completely astounded.

He whirled toward Jenna, only to find an empty boat bobbing on the gentle water.

Cursing, he scanned the shore, the trees, everywhere she might have gone. And found nothing. It seemed as though she'd vanished into thin air.

"Where is she?" he demanded.

"She went back to the swamp, suh."

Alan's throat tightened. She'd gone. Without a word, a touch, without giving him a chance to convince her to stay. "You knew her."

"I knows *of* her." His dark face held the remains of awe. "I never thought t'see her. The Lady."

"What did you call her?"

"The White Lady, suh."

"Tell me about her."

Ben's eyes shuttered. "I don' know nothin'."

"I doubt that, my good man. You knew her on sight."

"Everybody knows the White Lady. My own father tole me about her when I was just a chile sittin' on his knee."

Alan studied him, noting the liberal sprinkle of gray hairs amid the dark. "How old are you, Ben?"

"Nigh forty, suh."

"Jenna is obviously in her early twenties."

"Yes, suh."

"So she can't possibly be the White Lady your father told you about, could she?"

"No, suh."

But as he looked into the man's eyes, Alan knew he believed otherwise. He'd spoken to protect Jenna. Interesting. More than interesting.

Something in the water caught his gaze: the reed basket, the yellow blossoms it had held floating on the surface around it. He reached for it but was able to catch only a single blossom.

"Ready to go, suh?" Ben asked.

"Yes," he said. "And bring the other boat."

"But it belongs to—"

"Bring it."

"Yes, suh."

Ben tied Jenna's boat to the stern of his own, then poled both craft downstream. Alan sat against the bow, wincing against the pain of his injured leg. He brushed the flower across his lips. Over and over, the petals as smooth as a woman's skin. Strangely enough, it didn't smell like jasmine. Alan closed his eyes, breathing deeply. Perhaps it was his imagination, or perhaps the last, lingering remains of his fever. Whichever, he couldn't shake the scent of honeysuckle.

"Father, Father!"

Alan strode across Heronsgate's lawn toward the two small figures hurtling toward him. Beth's short legs flashed as she ran, and the afternoon sunlight struck mahogany sparks in Jon's brown hair. The most welcome sight in the world. Alan reached them in a rush, scooping them into his arms and holding them close.

"Are you all right?" he demanded after a long, heart-stretching embrace.

"Oh, yes," Beth said. "The beautiful fairy found us."

Wood sprite, he thought. For a moment, he almost thought he smelled honeysuckle. "She found me, too. I suppose it was a lucky day for the Langstons when she happened upon us." Movement caught his eye, and he looked up to see Miranda Carrew coming across the lawn toward him. "I didn't know we had company."

Jon glanced over his shoulder. "She's been here every day since you've been gone. Said she wanted to comfort us."

"That was kind of her."

"She just wants to show you her buzums," Beth said.

"Ah . . ." With an effort, Alan swallowed a laugh. "Let's not talk about it right now, sweeting."

"But Father, she's going to bend over—"

"Shhh," he admonished as Miranda came into hearing distance. She did indeed take every opportunity to show him her "buzums," something he hadn't minded overmuch until now. In fact, he wouldn't have minded taking her as his next mistress; with her lush figure and much-displayed sensuality, she might have proved interesting. But now she seemed a bit too lush, her tawny hair too carefully coiffed, and he detected a trace of calculation in those aquamarine eyes of hers.

His mind conjured a vision of another woman, one slim and graceful, whose passion was as clear and deep as her eyes, and whose hands were as exciting as they were capable. Miranda just didn't compare. Perhaps no one could. Jenna was, after all, unique.

"Hello, Miranda," he said.

"Alan, darling! We've been so worried about you," she murmured, enveloping him in a waft of perfume as she flung her arms around his neck. "They said you were alive, but you never know whether to believe—"

"Obviously, I'm safe and sound." Gently, he extricated himself from her embrace. "And now I'd like nothing more than a nice, hot bath and a shave."

"What happened to your arm?" Jon asked, pointing to the still-swollen flesh of Alan's right forearm.

"A snake bit me," he said. "If she hadn't found me when she had, and if she hadn't known exactly what to do, I wouldn't be standing here today."

"She?" Miranda echoed. "Who?"

"The fairy lady," Beth said.

Miranda glanced down at the child, incomprehension in her face. "What are you talking about?"

"We told you," Jon said.

"I thought it a child's fanciful tale," she snapped.

"Jenna Llewellyn is quite real, I assure you," Alan said.

"Llewellyn?" Miranda's head snapped up, and her eyes grew round. "She said her name was Llewellyn?"

"Is something wrong?" Alan asked.

Miranda began to laugh. "You haven't heard? Gracious, Alan, you really *don't* pay attention to local gossip, do you?"

"Explain."

"It will be a pleasure," she murmured. "You see, the Llewellyns have lived in the swamp since this area was settled. They've been a pest and pestilence since anyone can remember, from the first to the last. Everyone fears them."

Alan remembered the look on Ben's face as the man bowed to Jenna. It had been reverence, not fear. "What do you mean?"

"Jenna Llewellyn is a witch."

"She's a fairy!" Beth cried, fury sparking in her deep blue eyes. "She saved us, an' she's a fairy!"

"Witch," Miranda said with obvious relish. "Like her mother and grandmother before her. The Llewellyns have hounded the good people here, blighting the crops and sickening our livestock with their evil spells, frightening the poor loggers half out of their wits. Sometimes slaves run into the swamp and are never found again. Some say the witch eats them."

"Enough!" Alan snapped.

Beth began to cry. "You're wrong, you're wrong!"

"Am I?" Arms akimbo, Miranda swung around to Alan. "The witch cursed the Steptons. A few years later, Ewell and Farleigh were killed when their carriage ran off the road, and a few years after that, Orwell himself fell ill with a disease as mysterious as it was horrible."

Alan drew his breath in sharply. Putting one hand on each child's shoulder, he said, "Go on up to the house. I want to talk to Miss Carrew alone."

"Don't believe her, Father!" Beth cried, tears running down her cheeks in a sudden flood.

"Jon, take your sister to the house," Alan said.

"Come on, Pudge." The boy took Beth's hand and pulled her, still sobbing, toward the house.

Alan turned back to Miranda. "Was there a need to frighten the children with this?"

"Perhaps I spoke in haste," she said, moving closer. She took a deep breath, almost lifting her bounteous breasts out of the deeply decolleté bodice. "But I had to warn you. I wanted you to listen. The witch is dangerous."

"Jenna saved my life and those of my children."

Her eyelids drifted to half-mast. "Is she as beautiful as they say?"

"Yes." Again, he caught that elusive trace of honeysuckle.

"So is a viper. But it's as deadly as it is beautiful, and so is this Llewellyn creature." She put her hands flat on his chest. "Shall I tell you about this curse?"

"Do I have a choice?"

She smiled. "The witch cursed Orwell Stepton. Cursed his sons, his brothers, and his brothers' sons. Any of his family who come to be masters of Heronsgate are to die horribly."

"What?"

"That's right, Alan. You, too, are cursed."

"But she saved my life."

Slowly, Miranda slid her hands up his chest and clasped them around his neck. "If she did, it was only to preserve you for a worse death than a mere snakebite."

"That's ignorant superstition."

"Is that so?" Anger tautened her face, making it look petulant and mean. "You want her. I can see it in your eyes when you speak of her. Do you wonder why, Alan? Don't you think a witch can bespell a man as easily as she does the crops and the cattle? Think of it: what sport it would be to ensnare the heart of the master of Heronsgate, to make him yearn, to hold him in thrall while she waits for the curse to take him as it took all the others?"

Alan pulled free of her. "You're mad. There's no such thing as a witch. Or a curse."

"It took Orwell six months to die, and that was far too long. No one could help him, nor could anyone determine the nature of his affliction. Near the end, his pain was so terrible that he begged his friends to kill him to end the misery. Not one of them dared; he died alone, in screaming torment."

"Why didn't they dare?"

"Because the witch had decreed his end, and they were afraid they'd share his fate if they interfered."

"Bloody hell!" Alan exploded. "There's no such thing as witches or curses!"

"Perhaps not," she called after him. "But what if you're wrong?"

Superstition, he thought as he strode toward the house. *Just because the Llewellyns were different from the rest, these townsfolk branded them as witches.* He didn't know how this legacy of hatred had begun, but it was past time for it to end.

But one burning question nagged at his mind, and no amount of rational thought could drive it away: Why hadn't Jenna told him? She knew who he was, knew the consequences of their meeting.

Perhaps he should ask her.

Seven

Jenna watched her grandmother's hands as the old woman ground yarrow root into a paste. Age had withered those hands and laid a dusting of brown spots upon the once flawless skin. Her hair had been pure white for as long as Jenna could remember; braided now, when unbound it fell well below her knees.

Emotion tightened Jenna's throat. Roanna had raised her, loved her in a rather grim way, taught her about herbs and healing, and sung to her on the autumn nights when the great storms raged through the Dismal. And Jenna loved her back, this woman who'd been mother, father, grandmother, teacher, companion. The Llewellyns. Witches. Ostracized by their own kind, welcomed only by the Dismal.

It had never bothered Jenna before. But then she'd met Alan Langston, and he'd made her feel things she'd never felt before: the loneliness of her life, curiosity about the world outside, and most of all, the power of a woman's desire.

She looked around at the island that had been her home all her childhood. The tiny cabin had been created out of the things the Dismal provided—cypress logs and thatch of tough marsh grass—it sat like a natural outgrowth among the trees. Racks held drying herbs, and

the ground bloomed with a kaleidoscope of summer
flowers. The pale parasols of Queen Anne's lace bobbed
majestically above a golden dusting of swamp butter-
cups, amid which were sprinkled vivid splashes of crimson bee balm and the regal purple of spiderwort. When
she'd left here to build her own home in the swamp,
she'd used the same materials, the same simplicity and
grace of design.

Beautiful, she thought. *Serene, beautiful, and isolated.*
For the first time in her life she questioned the assump-
tion that serenity came from isolation and beauty only
from nature. And all because of the man named Langston, who was her enemy.

With a sigh, she sat down at her grandmother's feet.
"Tell me about my mother."

"Again?" the old woman asked without looking up
from her task. "Ahhhh, very well, child. You look much
like her, for all her hair was dark and yours light. The
two of you have the same graceful step, the same beauty,
the same compassionate heart. But you're fiercer than
she was, my Jenna. Stronger. I always worried what
would happen to Silvan when I was gone but not you."

Jenna didn't want to think of that. Pulling her knees
up against her chest, she wrapped her arms around them.
She knew this story by heart but never tired of its telling.

"Silvan could sing like the angels," Roanna continued.
"The birds themselves would hush so they could listen
to her. She was but sixteen when she met the trapper
Rene Broussard and fell in love. He was not a man to
stay in one place long, however, and left her behind when
he moved on. She didn't sing again until you were born.
You became her joy."

"I dream about her sometimes. I hear her singing so

clearly that I'm sure all I have to do is turn around to see her. But when I do. I can never see her face." Jenna sighed. "I feel so lonely those nights."

"You can thank Orwell Stepton for that loneliness."

Jenna fell silent. She knew this part of the story as well as the rest, Roanna taking her to see the heart of the swamp the day the townsmen came on their mission of murder.

"I cursed him," Roanna said, her face seamed and drawn by the memories. "Him and all his kin. To the end of time, I'll hate those of his blood."

Kin, Jenna thought. Alan Langston. Jon. Beth. Innocent inheritors of Orwell's legacy. Alan. Ah, Alan. Her flesh remembered the feel of his hands, her mouth the taste of his kiss.

Roanna looked at her at last, and the illusion of age-born weakness vanished. Time could wither her body, but nothing could dim the indomitable will that lit her fierce black eyes. "Something is bothering you, child."

"There's a new master at Heronsgate."

The old woman let her breath out in a long sigh. "Stepton blood?"

"Cousins."

Roanna's face hardened, her jaw settling into a line Jenna knew well. Her eyes turned cold, implacable. "So."

"Grandmother, the new owner is no Orwell Stepton. He . . . seems an honorable man, come here from England to build a future for himself."

"You met him?"

Jenna nodded. "I found him wandering in the swamp. delirious from snakebite—"

"Hah! You saved him then. Should've left him where you found him."

"This isn't a subject for jesting."

"Who said I was jesting?" Roanna glared at Jenna from beneath mothwing brows. "If Stepton blood runs in his veins, he's doomed, just like the rest of them."

Jenna remembered the children's faces, so innocent, so trusting. The little girl had eyes just like Alan's, so deep a blue it was almost black. "Grandmother, he has two children."

"Ah, children. Too bad, then." With a sigh, Roanna laid her hand on her granddaughter's head. "There is nothing I can do. The curse has been spoken, laid with your murdered mother's blood."

"But you spoke the curse; you can lift it."

"It was made in hate, forged in your mother's blood. Even if I wanted to, I haven't the power to revoke it. And I don't want to; those animals took my daughter from me, my Silvan, and I rejoice to see justice done."

"Justice was done with the Steptons. But what justice can there be in the deaths of an innocent man and two children?"

Something new came into the old woman's eyes, and it looked almost like fear. She grabbed Jenna's chin and turned her face up into the light. "Did he take you?"

"No," Jenna said. *But he touched me. He touched my heart, and perhaps even my soul.*

Some of the tension went out of Roanna's face. "Thank God!"

"Grandmother—"

"Silence!" The old woman's hands dropped to Jenna's shoulders. Her fingers dug into the flesh painfully. "You must never love a man. Any man, and especially that one."

"But why?"

"Because he will destroy you. It is our fate, women such as us. Rene Broussard took your mother's love thoughtlessly, as though it was his due. She paid a high price for it."

"By having a child?"

"By bringing herself to the attention of men like Stepton, who thought that since one had had the witch, she'd be fair game for them all."

"Alan isn't like that."

Roanna shook her head. "I should have schooled you in the ways of men earlier, my girl. Let me begin my answer with a question: How is it you can find your way in the swamp whether it is day, night, clear or fog or storm?"

"I don't know the way of it," Jenna said. "But I always seem to know where I am."

"That's instinct, bred into the Llewellyns since the time we walked the shrouded Welsh mountains. When Silvan gave her love to a man, she came to trust what couldn't be trusted, and to mistrust her instincts. It cost her her life. Now tell me, Jenna. What does your heart tell you about this new master of Heronsgate?"

"That he is a strong man and," she glanced away, "that he makes my blood sing."

"And what do your instincts tell you?"

"To be afraid of the recklessness he stirs in me."

"Ah." Satisfaction lightened Roanna's voice. "Listen to your instincts, my girl, for they will never fail you. His destiny is already set, and no human being can interfere. You'll forget him soon enough."

Forget him. The memory of Alan's face bloomed in her mind. Passion tautened his lean, aquiline features and raged in the depths of his indigo eyes. She could almost feel his hands on her back, a possessive, sensual touch, almost feel his mouth claiming hers. Her body came alive. Desire raced through her veins like sweet, dark honey and pooled in the depths of her womanhood. Powerful. Compelling.

Forget him. Wisdom, perhaps. Impossible, more than likely.

"When does the hate stop, Grandmother?"

Roanna picked up the pestle again and resumed grinding. "Never. There were four of them who killed my Silvan that day. Four. The curse took three, but there is someone out there who carries her blood on his soul."

"It's been twenty years," Jenna said. "He could have died long ago."

The old woman shook her head. "I would know. He belongs to me, that one, and if the curse must take fifty to get him, I'll be content."

"But—"

"You weren't there that day, girl! I've never told you what they did to your mother, for it is too terrible to be spoken. And I won't. You dream of loneliness and your mother's songs; I don't want you having the dreams *I* have."

Jenna saw the old woman's pain. But it wasn't as dark as the black hatred that made her seem bigger than she was. "Why must it be this way?"

"Because Orwell Stepton felt like killing a witch one day. For sport. And because there will always be men like him. Stay in the swamp, Jenna. It is the only protection you have."

Jenna nodded, believing. But it seemed as though a cord connected her to Alan, to the outside.

Alan waited three weeks before going back into the swamp. Every night he'd been tormented with long, feverish dreams of a woman with pale hair and vivid green eyes. She wrapped him in a silken net of desire, a pleasure so sharp he'd cry out with it. And then he'd awaken to an empty bed and empty arms and bedding churned into a wild tangle.

He had to see her again. Witch, angel, savior, or enchantress, he had to see her. He had to look into her eyes and know the truth. His friends had tried to dissuade him, and Dorcas had cried as though she expected never to see him again. Only Jon and Beth agreed; they, too, wanted to see the "beautiful fairy" again.

"I used to be a practical man," he told the trees, and they nodded as though in agreement.

He thrust the pole deep, pushed the boat along with a powerful sweep of his arms. Two days ago, he'd found the great gum with a branch that looked like a blackened pitchfork. Now he searched for a lightning-scarred loblolly pine and a tall oak that looked as though some great beast had taken a bite out of its crown.

"Hah!" he said, spotting first the pine and then the oak. "If I can find my way across the ocean, I can find my way through this bloody swamp. With the help of a wood sprite's landmarks, of course."

A few minutes later he came to the fallen tree beneath which Jenna had hidden her boat. Now came the tricky part. Mooring his boat among the whitened branches, he walked along the trunk with a seaman's sure stride to the spongy land beyond.

He closed his eyes, needing his other senses more than sight just now. His ears caught the gentle lapping of the water behind him, the drone of insects and the faint rustle of a small animal moving through the sedge. His nose caught the sharp odor of pine, the heavy, mingled scents of summer's full bloom. And faintly, the piquant tang of wood smoke.

It could be anyone's fire. But somehow he didn't think so. His passage here had been so sure that he couldn't imagine finding anyone but Jenna at the end.

He followed that faint scent, tracking it to a place where a webbing of shallow creeklets webbed the land. Reeds grew thickly here in water turned orange-yellow from the leaching of juniper and cypress trees. A few hundred yards ahead, he saw the small, green hump of an island. Nestled amid the trees was a tiny hut, in good repair despite the rude materials that had been used to build it. Smoke rose from a small fire a few yards in front of it. He moved forward, jumping across the streams when he could, wading across when he could not.

Jenna came around the corner of the hut. Her hair was unbound, gleaming like pale silk in the ruddy afternoon light as she bent to pick something up from the ground. Alan's gaze moved lower, taking in the trousers that hugged the sweet curve of her hips. Desire tautened his body.

He found himself walking toward her, his feet taking him forward before his mind had quite ordered it.

She whirled, her eyes wide in startlement. "You!"

"Yes," he said. "Me." With a swift dart of surprise,

he saw that she cradled a white egret in her arms. It lay peacefully in her grasp, not even protesting the bandage and splint upon its right wing. "So you heal animals as well as men."

Jenna's mind was awhirl with emotions: surprise, chagrin, disquietude, but overwhelming them all was a glorious bright blaze of happiness at seeing him again. Then she saw the hard glitter of suspicion in his eyes and knew that someone had told him about the Llewellyns.

"Some might say that animals are more deserving than men," she said. It was a challenge, and she saw awareness of it come into his face.

"Are you a witch?"

She met his gaze levelly. "Some call me that."

"Is that what you call yourself?"

She lifted one shoulder, let it fall. "I prefer Jenna."

"Was it you who cursed the Steptons?"

"No."

"Who, then?"

Jenna set the egret back on the ground. It stalked away into the reeds, searching for fish. " 'Twas my grandmother. Did they tell you *why* she cursed Orwell Stepton?"

He shook his head.

"He raped and murdered my mother, he and his two sons."

Alan sighed, wondering when men would ever learn tolerance. "I'm sorry, Jenna."

"It was a long time ago."

"Then why is there a shadow in your eyes?" he asked, tipping her face up.

"Because she was my mother." His sympathy was an almost palpable thing, releasing a tumble of words from her. "My grandmother had been branded a witch; towns-men had nothing to offer her except a rope. And Stepton was the master of Heronsgate, a rich man with great influence in the community. He laughed when my grand-mother confronted him with his crime. Laughed! With her daughter's blood still on her hands, Grandmother cursed him."

"Does she still live, your grandmother?"

Fear hammered at her heart; no one must know Roanna still lived, no one! The old woman moved slowly now, her joints stiffened by seventy years of use, and she'd be easy prey.

"My grandmother died years ago," Jenna said. Nec-essary as the lie was, it still left a foul taste in the back of her throat.

Alan studied her. If malice toward him or his lurked behind those clear green eyes, he couldn't see it. Ah, but he wanted to believe her so very badly. His hands ached with the need to touch her, his body to possess her. To plumb her depths, to know her mind, her heart and all the mysteries of her spirit.

Jenna watched as the icy intensity left his eyes, re-vealing the smolder of desire. Warmth stole through her limbs.

"How did you find me?" she asked.

He smiled, that same roguish grin she kept seeing every night in her dreams. "I knew you wouldn't leave a boat just anywhere and so decided you had to have some kind of habitation nearby. So I came by way of a pitchfork gum, a lopsided oak and a lightning-struck pine. And a bit of wood smoke."

"I'll have to be more careful in giving landmarks out willy-nilly to strangers."

"I'm no stranger, Jenna."

His voice was a caress and so were his eyes. To hide her own reaction, she turned toward the fire. "It's nearly dark. I'd better take you back to your boat."

"Do I have to pretend illness or injury for you to offer the hospitality of your evening meal?"

Startled, she looked up at him. "You can't stay here."

"We have much to talk about, you and I."

"Such as?"

"Witches and healers and runaway slaves."

Alarm ran in an icy tide through her veins. "I don't want you here."

"But I am here," he said. "And I don't intend to leave yet."

"You're a most annoying man."

"Does that mean mistletoe tea for me tonight?"

"Don't tempt me." She drew herself up, gazing directly into his eyes. "That is only one of many ways I know of dealing with annoying men."

Alan's reaction was instantaneous, illogical, and too powerful to resist. He grasped her by the shoulders, his fingers spread wide with hot possession. "What men?" he asked in a voice gone deadly quiet.

Jenna stared into his eyes, read danger there. Something wild and defiant bloomed in her. "What right do you have to pry into my life?"

He pulled her up against the rock hardness of his chest. As she hung suspended, pinned by his hands and the blazing male jealousy in his eyes, she knew the first glimmerings of fear. But stubborn Llewellyn pride kept her from showing it, or from giving in.

"Don't play games with me, Jenna," he growled. "I'm not a docile man."

"And I'm not a docile woman," she said, digging her nails into the fabric of the shirt covering his shoulders.

"There's one sure way of getting an answer to my question."

Fury narrowed her eyes. "Ah, yes. Defilement is a family trait, is it not?"

Her words swept over him like a gout of ice water. Gently, he lowered her to the ground. "You hit hard, Jenna. And low."

"And you're an ill-tempered man who pokes his nose where it isn't welcome."

He studied her, noting the high color in her cheeks, the outrage that turned her eyes the color of jade. "That wasn't ill temper; it was jealousy. The fact that you provoked a man in the clutches of that green demon betrays just how innocent you are. Another woman would have known better."

"By another woman, you mean the one who makes a habit of bending over to show you her bosom?"

He stared at her for a moment, then threw his head back and laughed. "Beth and her 'buzums,' " he said when he'd gotten his breath back. "Has she told the entire world?"

"I wouldn't know," Jenna snapped.

"Ah, so you have a touch of the green demon, too," he said, his voice going silken. "Then you should have compassion, my lovely wood sprite, and forgive me my transgression."

She started to shake her head, but he caught her chin in his hand and stopped her.

"Please," he said.

Ah, those indigo eyes, she thought. They were as beguiling as those of the Devil himself. Her anger flowed away, replaced by a sweet, treacherous warmth.

"Are you going to invite me to dinner now?" he asked.

She sighed, wishing she were stronger. " 'Tis only fish and vegetables."

"Ah, but the company is sublime," he said.

"Pretty words. You should save them for the bosoms."

"Touché." So many of the women of the *ton* were simpering, vacuous, and amoral. His wife had been a gentle soul who never argued and never, ever challenged her husband. Jenna, with her tart naiveté and penetrating wit, inflamed his mind as well as his body.

"Sit down over there," she said, pointing to a tree stump near the fire.

"Surely I can make myself useful somehow."

She looked him up and down, doubt plain on her face. His amusement grew.

"There are cups and plates in the hut, if you'd like to fetch them," she said. "And a jug of elderberry wine."

Alan, who had become accustomed to the finest wines in Europe at his father's table, repressed a shudder. But he would have endured much more than elderberry wine to remain in his wood sprite's company.

The inside of the hut was painfully spare. A table and a three-legged stool were the only furnishings, unless one counted the pallet upon the floor. For a moment he hated the stark utility of Jenna's life; such beauty as hers should be surrounded with fine things, not grubbing in the muck of the swamp.

"Why do you stay here?" he murmured, trying to understand the strange, lovely woman who'd turned his life upside down.

He looked around the hut again, trying to see it with

her eyes. For all its spareness, it was clean and airy. Dried flowers hung from the ceiling, adding a ghost of floral fragrance to the scent of cedar. A shelf upon the far wall held two wooden plates and a pair of wooden cups. He lifted them down to admire the handiwork that had gone into their creation. The inside surfaces were satin-smooth, the outer carved with a lovely design of leaves and flowers, then stained a beautiful red-gold. He didn't need to ask to know that Jenna had made them.

"Don't forget the wine," she called from outside.

"Fortune should so smile upon me," he muttered.

He spotted the jug on the floor beneath the table. It was an ugly thing, and didn't belong here. A gift, perhaps, from some grateful patient. Absurdly, it annoyed him that there was a whole segment of her life he knew nothing about.

"Fool!" he growled under his breath. "And getting more foolish by the moment." Grasping the jug by its neck, he carried it and the dishes outside.

Jenna was crouched by the fire, scraping the coals to one side with a blackened stick. Then she scooped the hot sand away with a piece of bark, revealing a long parcel that had been wrapped in leaves. Pulling it out, she slit the covering, letting out a steam that smelled deliciously of dinner.

Alan smiled down at her. The glow of the coals made her skin look like warm cream and cast copper glints in her pale hair. "Shall I bring the table out?" he asked. "We can pretend the island an elegant dining room, the cicadas our symphony, and the stars our chandelier."

Jenna looked up, captivated by the image he presented. "I'd like that," she said.

So they feasted there beneath the dark velvet sky. Alan

hardly tasted the bream or the strange, starchy vegetables she told him were the roots of bull-nettle and morning glory. His senses were too full of her, sight and sound and scent, for him to register anything else.

Jenna accepted the night for what it was, a brief interlude in the passage of her life. In the morning, he'd be gone. But for now, as she listened to his tales of balls and dancing and the glitter of London, she could let her imagination transport her to the world outside.

"But it's so complicated," she said when he'd finished. "A lady can flutter her fan this way but not that. One can wear only a certain thing at certain times. Truly, don't these people have anything better to do with their time than to think up silly rules?"

Alan drew his breath in sharply, thinking how quickly and effectively she had just let the air out of an entire society. "I suppose they don't. I have to admit that here, beneath this sky, all that seems damned trivial." He took a draught of the vile wine, finishing the entire cup with a shudder.

He watched her, enchanted by the way her eyes sparkled and most especially by the tiny dimple that appeared at the corner of her mouth.

Jenna saw his eyes darken, watched the passion in them burn hotter by the moment. Quicksilver heat slid through her veins, a honey rush of desire to match his.

Unable to control herself, she dropped her gaze lower, to his mouth. And lower still, to the vee of his open shirt, where she could see the beginnings of his chest hair. Then she glanced at his hands. They clutched the cup with white-knuckled force, causing the tendons to stand out clearly beneath the skin. Her pulse fluttered madly. She had to do something, anything, to break this seething tension.

"More wine?" she asked.

"Yes," he said, his voice harsh.

His throat moved as he swallowed, a fascinating play of muscles beneath the skin. She wanted to press her lips to the strong column of his neck, to run her hands down the length of his arms and gentle those taut hands.

Oh, no. It couldn't be. It could never be. Separate lives, separate worlds, separate destinies. And still she watched him. Wanted him. Wished, for one searing moment, that she could forget who he was.

With an effort of will, she brought her careening emotions under control. "I . . . It's time we got some sleep," she said.

His jaw tightened. "I suppose you're right."

"You can sleep there, under the pine. It's dry. I sleep there myself when the weather's nice like this."

"Thank you."

"Well, good night."

Alan watched her go into the hut, then propped his elbows on the table and rested his head in his hands. His body raged with a need so powerful he shook with it. He took a deep breath, searching for control, then another. Then he reached for the wine jug.

"It's a hell of a thing when a man can't find a decent brew in which to drown his sorrows," he muttered, pouring another cup.

Eight

Alan drifted upward through layers of sleep, drawn by the scent of honeysuckle. He'd fallen asleep here at the table, his head pillowed on his arms, his hand still wrapped around his empty cup. He'd found no surcease. Now, in the silvery half-light just before dawn, he felt as though he'd spent half the night in Heaven, half in Hell.

He stiffened suddenly as he caught sight of something pale at the far end of the island. Then he realized that the paleness was Jenna's hair, unbound as he loved to see it. Moving slowly and silently, he got up and walked toward her.

She sat on the trunk of a tree, combing her hair with long, smooth strokes. Loose, it coiled down her back in a mass of long curls that seemed to catch the predawn glow and cast it back again with a light of its own. The breeze lifted shining strands and fanned them out around her.

The scene was incredibly erotic. He wanted to sink his hands into that pale, satin cascade, to rub it across his skin and bury his face in the fragrant thickness of it. Sweat broke out on his brow.

Her hands moved with languid grace as she combed that marvelous hair. She rose to her feet, shaking the heavy mane back from her face. It fell down below her hips in a shining cascade of curls. Alan sighed, imagining her naked beneath it. There would be tantalizing glimpses of warm female skin beneath the moonlight strands, sweet, curved flesh that promised incredible delight.

No woman had ever affected him like this, set up storms of lust in his body and tenderness in his heart. Lust, he could deal with; the Miranda Carrews in this world were easily seduced, even more easily forgotten. But there was only one Jenna.

And he wanted her. Wanted her with an intensity that set his whole body thrumming.

He must have made some sound, for she turned abruptly and looked at him. She looked as fey and frightened as a startled doe, and he couldn't find the words to reassure her. Just now he felt as primitive and savage as any beast of the forest, and it was all he could do to hold himself in check.

"Why are you staring at me like that?" she asked.

"I've never seen hair so beautiful," he said, his chest tight with the desire to touch it.

Jenna saw the coiled tautness in him. Frightened by it, she rose and hastily pulled her hair back. Here in the silent half-dawn, she felt too vulnerable.

"No," he said. "Don't bind it."

She stopped, frozen by the raw need in his eyes. He stepped closer.

"What are you doing?" she gasped.

His face was starkly beautiful in the moonlight, the sharp planes of his cheekbones casting knife-edged shadows across his cheeks. "Just let your hair hang free, Jenna. I want to look at it. I want to look at you."

His gaze was so consuming that she felt as though she stood naked before him. Heat blossomed inside her, making her breasts ache. Even her skin seemed too sensitive; she shivered in the warm summer breeze.

"I—" she began.

"Shhh." He reached out to her. "Don't say anything."

Jenna heard him but saw only the raging need in his eyes. He looked like a man possessed as he lifted a single lock of her hair and let it run through his fingers. A simple caress but one made exquisitely sensual because his eyes were anything but chaste as he did it. Jenna sighed, aching for what it could be.

His fingertips drifted across her face and along her throat, then moved lower. Her nipples tautened, as though begging for more. Her eyes drifted closed as the upwelling arousal surged through her body.

"Don't," she said. "Please, don't."

"I won't hurt you, Jenna."

"You can't help but hurt me."

His chest heaved as though he'd been running, and a firestorm of passion raged in his eyes. "You feel what I feel," he said. "A desire like this only grows more powerful when denied. I should know; I've thought of little else the past three weeks."

Desire. Yes, she felt it. And like him, the memory of it had haunted her dreams and her waking hours. It made her want things she'd never wanted before, made her reckless and discontented when she'd known such serenity. Desire. She denied it, lifted her chin in a defiant bid to drive it away.

"We're enemies, you and I," she said.

"Why?"

"Because we are who we are, and it's our destiny to be."

He dropped his hand, closed it into a fist to keep from touching her. "I decide my destiny. No one else."

"Did you make your children come into the swamp? Did you make that snake bite you?"

"Those are incidents. I chart the course of my life the same way I used to chart a path across the ocean. It's a matter of choice."

She shook her head.

"Yes," he said. "You chose to save two lost children. You chose to save a man you considered your enemy. And by making those choices, you've changed the course of your life. And mine."

Turning on her heel, she walked away along the edge of the island. Her mind was spinning with confusion. Why had this man come into her life? How had he gained the power to command her body's responses and corrupt her will?

She heard his footsteps as he came up behind her. His hands hovered above her shoulders as though he wanted to spin her around, but he didn't touch her. She was glad; she felt brittle, as though she'd shatter into a thousand pieces in his grasp.

"Do you know what my children call you?" he asked. "They call you the 'beautiful fairy'."

She drew in her breath sharply. "They'll learn the word 'witch' soon enough."

"They saw no evil in you," he said. "And neither do I."

"What do you want from me?" she whispered.

"I want you to come back to Heronsgate with me."

"Why?"

"Because I don't believe in witches or curses, and I want everyone to see that you're no more or less than the lovely healer who saved my life."

She laughed, a bitter sound with no humor in it. "You're wasting your time."

"Then come because Jon wants to show you how well he can fish and Beth wants you to hear her sing 'Lady Greensleeves'."

"Why do they want to see me?"

"Because they like you, Jenna. They want to be friends."

"And you?" she asked. "Do you also want to be friends?"

"I'd be a liar if I said I didn't want to be much more than that," he murmured, his mouth so close that his breath stirred the hair over her ear.

She shivered at the beguilement in his voice. Surely no woman had ever been tempted so. Almost, she swayed back against the man who should be her enemy.

"Come back with me," Alan murmured.

Ah, sweet temptation! But perhaps the temptation might run both ways; if he left Heronsgate, he might elude the curse. And his safety had become important to her. Important enough to follow him when her instincts urged her to run.

"If I go back with you," she raised her hand to forestall his inevitable comment, "for a day or two, will you promise to listen to me with an open mind?"

"Obviously you have something to say that you expect me to disagree with."

"I expect you to disagree with anything that goes against your wishes," she said, perhaps too tartly.

"True."

There was no penitence in the admission and much laughter in his eyes. Jenna's pulse stuttered even as she firmed her will against the urgings of her wayward body. "There is something else you must do," she said.

"Yes, my lovely wood sprite?"

"Promise not to touch me."

Alan narrowed his eyes. She was asking much, perhaps more than he had the strength to give. "I'm only flesh and blood, Jenna."

"You are also a man of your word," she said, tilting her head back to meet his gaze directly. "Aren't you?"

"I am."

"Then give me your word that you won't touch me."

The breeze blew a lock of her hair across the back of his hand, a touch so erotic that he had to close his eyes against the violent sweep of arousal. *Damn. Bloody damn.* "That's quite a sweeping promise, Jenna. Can I not take your arm to keep you from falling?"

"You know what I mean."

"Do I?"

Jenna let her breath out in a sharp sound of exasperation. "Then you must promise not to touch me . . . as a man touches a woman."

"In desire?" he asked, his voice turning soft and sultry. "No caresses that make you sigh, no kisses to make our blood burn, our hearts and bodies meld together in passion's fires?"

His words brought a sweeping rush of memory. She fought it, even as desire spread through her limbs in a sweet, hot current. "Yes," she whispered. "That."

"I promise," he said, willing to give almost anything to take her back to Heronsgate with him. But even as he gave his word, he had the feeling it would cost him dearly. "Unless you tell me otherwise," he added.

Her golden-brown eyelashes cast fan-shaped shadows

across her cheeks. The lovely double curve of her mouth drew his gaze irresistibly, and he burned to taste those lips again.

"That will not happen," she said.

"Are you sure?"

"Of course. Are you sure you can keep your promise?"

He smiled. *I vow to have you, Jenna Llewellyn. Somehow, I'll convince you to free me from that stupid, bloody promise, and then we shall see.*

"I'm a man of my word," he said.

Heronsgate gleamed brightly in the sun as Jenna walked up the lawn toward it. She had always looked upon this place with hatred, as though it held the soul of the man who'd murdered her mother. But now, with Alan striding beside her and the shrieks of playing children coming from the open windows, it seemed merely a house.

Alan held his arm out to her. She looked at him, startled, and he smiled at her.

"It's courtesy for a gentleman to escort a lady in," he said.

She tucked her hand into the crook of his arm, unsure whether she felt more a fool for letting him bind her into his conventions or for letting her nervousness show.

He led her up the stairs and into the foyer. A wide staircase lay just ahead, its banisters polished to a mahogany gleam. A stained glass window cast multicolored shards of light upon the wide oak planks of the floor and sparked scintillant gleams in the crystal chandelier overhead.

A full-length looking glass dominated the far wall. Jenna stared at their reflection, noting that despite Alan's ragged clothing, his brooding aristocratic looks made him seem like a king come home to his castle. She looked like what she was: a swamp rat come to rub elbows with the high and mighty.

"She's here, she's here!" Beth shrieked.

A moment later Jenna heard a frantic clatter of footsteps on the upper landing. The children hove into sight, plunging down the stairs like a pair of wildcats.

"Jon! Beth!" A woman cried from upstairs. "Your manners!"

The boy slid down a pair of steps, then caught himself and continued down with more decorum. Beth, however, brushed past him and ran straight to Jenna.

"Hullo," she said. "You're even prettier in the sunlight." Suddenly she turned toward her father, arms akimbo. "See, Father? She's wearing trousers. Why can't I wear trousers?"

Alan smiled down at her. "She's a wood sprite, sweetling. If you were a wood sprite, then you could wear trousers, too. But you're a mere mortal and thus constrained by the conventions of society."

"What did he say?" the child asked.

Jon reached the bottom of the stairs. "He said you can't wear trousers."

"Hello, little man," Jenna said, grinning.

"I caught a catfish yesterday."

"Did you indeed? Did you eat him?"

"Mr. Tate said they're no good for eating. I threw him back in the river."

"Mr. Tate?"

"No, silly. The catfish."

Jenna nodded. "A true hunter takes only what he needs. But one day I'll have to cook you a proper catfish so you'll know them for the delicacy they are."

Beth tugged on the end of Jenna's shirt. "Lift me up, please."

With a laugh, Jenna lifted the child into her arms and swept her high and hard so that her petticoats swirled riotously. "How is that, Miss Elizabeth?"

"Again!" the child commanded breathlessly.

"Enough," Alan said. "Do you think Jenna is some sort of horse for you to ride?"

"No," she replied gravely. "But you are."

Plucking her out of Jenna's arms, he swung her onto his own shoulder. "Let's show our guest her room."

Jon took Jenna by the hand and led her up the stairs. Alan followed, watching how easily his children talked to her. They hardly knew her, but obviously a bond had been forged during those few hours they'd spent with her. And it was equally obvious she was quite fond of them in return; in fact, it piqued him no end that she seemed much more at ease with his children than with him.

"It's a lovely room," Jon told her. "Beth and I picked it out for you."

Jenna let him pull her down the hall and into a nearby doorway. The bedroom was bright and airy with tall windows and a high ceiling. An enormous fireplace dominated the north wall, flanked by a pair of green brocade armchairs. The lofty armoire was reflected in the looking glass on the opposite wall, and a pretty rose matting covered the floor. The color was matched in the draperies and the coverlet on the four-poster bed. Jenna eyed the latter a bit suspiciously; she'd never slept in a bed before, and this one looked rather like it would swallow her up the moment she got near it.

"Come see the view," Jon urged.

She joined him at the window. It was quite a lovely scene, with the neat squares of human cultivation on the left and the wild beauty of the swamp on the right. But also very strange. So many buildings, so many people. For a moment the yearning to be home made her chest tighten.

"Dorcas!" Beth called to someone out in the hallway. "Come meet our fairy."

A woman came in, to be introduced as Dorcas Browne, the nanny. She was tall and spare, her hair almost completely gray. Her face had a faintly equine look to it, and her mouth, which would have been full and pleasant in repose, was drawn into a thin line of disapproval. With her suspicious eyes, erect carriage, and fine clothing, she was very intimidating.

"What is a nanny?" Jenna asked.

Dorcas stared in obvious astonishment. Alan stepped forward, taking Jenna's hand in his and leading her forward. "Dorcas takes care of Jon and Beth for me and does a wonderful job of it."

"They're very nice children, Dorcas," Jenna said, deciding the woman was some sort of relative. "But of course you know that."

Dorcas inclined her head regally. "Thank you, miss."

Jenna saw real love in the glance the woman turned on her charges. Ah, now she understood the nanny's suspicion: the witch had come into the house no doubt to do something awful to the children and their father. She sighed; this wouldn't be the last time she'd have to face this.

"Have you lived with the family long?" she asked in an attempt to ease the tension.

"Thirty-odd years, miss. I've cared for the children since they were born, and long ago, I was nurse to Mrs. Langston." It was spoken with pride.

"We consider Dorcas a member of our family," Alan said.

Jenna turned to him, confused. "Why wouldn't you?"

"Because . . ." Alan sighed, unable to find the right words to explain the relationship between master and servant to her. She wouldn't understand, and he doubted she'd approve if she did.

"It's nearly time for dinner," Dorcas said. "Beth, Jon, go wash up, if you please. And quietly!" she called after them. "Don't go haring about like a pair of savages!"

Alan reached out to touch Jenna's shoulder, then remembered his promise. He curled his fingers into his palm. "Why don't you show Jenna the gown, Dorcas?"

The nanny's mouth went even tighter. Turning, she opened the armoire and lifted down a lovely dress just the color of new leaves. The skirt hung in long, loose folds from the high waist, and the sleeves and tiny bodice were edged in creamy lace.

"I was fortunate to find fabric just the color of your eyes," Alan said.

She stood silently for a moment, considering the implications of his gift. "You were very sure of yourself."

"If you hadn't come back with me, I would have found a way to bring it to you. After all, I owed you a gown, since you ruined your other one tracking me through the swamp. And the Langstons always pay their debts."

"So do Llewellyns."

He inclined his head. "Of course I had to go from memory as to height and size, and it may need some adjustment to be perfect. What do you think, Dorcas?"

She inspected Jenna. "I'd say you had a very good memory for detail, sir," she said, her voice curt and inflectionless.

Realization swept through Jenna, bringing with it a hot flood of embarrassment. The nanny thought she'd come here to be Alan's mistress or perhaps had already taken that role. Oh, Jenna knew about mistresses; wasn't she herself the child of just such a union?

"Dorcas," Alan said, "tomorrow I want you to take Jenna into town and make arrangements to have more clothing made for her. I think she'd be stunning in sapphire satin, and I have a personal fondness for white. And we'll need undergarments—"

"No!" Jenna said. "Thank you."

"Why not?" he asked.

"I won't be here that long. And," her chin lifted in that gesture of defiance he was coming to know very well, "my own clothes suit me just fine."

Alan studied her. She looked like a goddess standing there in the streaming afternoon sunlight, Aphrodite clad in men's clothes but no less beautiful for it. "Please?"

"I think you've been pleased far too much in your life, Mr. Langston. I'll keep my own things."

"Why are you being so stubborn?"

"Why are you?"

He raked his hands through his hair. After all the trouble he'd gone through enticing her here, this sudden obstinacy was most unwelcome. A number of courses of action occurred to him, none of which she'd like, and certainly none of which fell within the bounds of his damned promise. "It's only a dress, Jenna."

"Then why is it so important to you?" she asked with calm unreasonableness.

Dorcas, who'd been looking from one to the other and back again, stepped forward. "Why don't you go freshen up for dinner, sir? You could use a clean shirt yourself."

He swung around to her, eyes narrowed, then took a deep breath as he realized she could handle this situation much better than he. Damn, but he'd been an inch away from throwing stubborn Miss Llewellyn down on the bed and stripping her naked. Now *that* would have been a hell of a breach of his promise.

"I'll see you at dinner," he said, turning on his heel and striding from the room.

"Now, Miss—" Dorcas began.

"Why did you interfere?"

"Because someone had to."

"I don't mind fighting with him," Jenna said.

The corners of Dorcas's mouth twitched. "I can see that, miss."

Jenna turned back to the window. The sun had sunk low on the western horizon, painting the sky in brilliant colors. Mist had already begun to rise in the swamp and in an hour or two would begin to creep out over the land. She wished it would wrap her up and carry her back home. "It's going to be a foggy night," she said.

"How do you know?" Dorcas asked.

Jenna glanced over her shoulder at the other woman. Dorcas's gaze was challenging, and something hard and hot rose in her, urging her to meet it. "We witches always know these things."

The nanny regarded Jenna levelly. "Indeed. Well, miss, I don't know if I believe in witches any more than Mr. Langston does."

That surprising statement brought Jenna around to face the nanny. "Then why are you so suspicious of me?"

Dorcas took a seat in one of the armchairs beside the fireplace. "Mr. Langston has been quite lonely since my Helena's death. It isn't that he's been without female companionship; a man like him attracts the ladies like bees to honey. But none has caught his interest for more than a . . . well, shall we speak plainly, Miss Llewellyn?"

"I know no other way."

"Good. Mr. Langston has had dalliances since his wife's death, of course. They never last. He has always been a man ruled more by his head than his heart, and he knows very well he'll never find anyone to compare with Helena."

Jenna was surprised by how much that hurt. "I want nothing from him, from you, or from those children."

"Then why did you come?"

"I want to convince him to leave."

The nanny's brows rose. "You must be joking."

"He told you about the curse?" When the older woman nodded, Jenna continued. "The only hope is for him to leave this place, he and the children. If there is no master at Heronsgate, then there will be no curse."

"He'll never give up this plantation. In all his life, Alan Langston has never run from anything. And what he wants, he holds."

Jenna swallowed, her throat gone suddenly tight. "I have to try."

"Are you sure that's the only reason you came?"

"Of course."

"Hmmm. Do you know why he brought you here?"

Jenna shrugged. "He thinks to prove to his neighbors that there is no such thing as a witch or a curse."

"You're not nearly as intelligent as I think you are if

you believe that. Mr. Langston seems quite taken with
you—"

"It's only gratitude," Jenna said.

Waving the words away, Dorcas continued. "Men, you
know, can be fooled in their judgments of women by
their own, ah, desires, but children seem to be able to
tell the dross from the gold. Jon and Beth like you very
much. Because of that, I will suspend my judgment of
you until I see more."

Jenna drew herself up with quiet dignity. "You have
no right to judge me."

"Perhaps not. But I shall anyway. In the meantime,
however, why don't we all try to get along during your
visit?"

"Which means wear the dress?"

"Very good, Miss Llewellyn. And as I realize you'd
rather not go into town, may I suggest we compromise
and have the dressmaker come here?"

The woman's gaze was direct and very honest. Jenna
met it, respected it and her. "I made him promise not to
touch me," she said.

"That was wise. It would never do."

Jenna's mind agreed. But her heart, however, cried out
in protest. Landowner, witch, townsman, swamp rat—all
that vanished when they touched. The prudent thing
would be to walk back into the swamp and never come
back, but Jenna found nothing prudent inside her. She
couldn't walk away until she knew why these powerful
new feelings consumed her, or why her enemy was the
one who'd brought them to life within her.

Besides, she had the promise. And that made her safe.

"I'll wear the dress," she said. "Tomorrow we'll discuss the issue of the dressmaker."

"Agreed. But you should know that Mr. Langston is accustomed to getting his way."

"Then it's time that he learned something new," Jenna said.

Dorcas smiled for the first time. "I believe I'd like to see that. I wish you luck, Miss Llewellyn."

Nine

Jenna struggled futilely with the long silk evening glove. Her work-roughened hands caught the delicate fabric, and she was afraid she'd ruin the dratted things completely if she pulled too hard.

A knock sounded at the door. She looked up, hoping it was the maid come back to help. "Come in," she called, accidentally knocking the box of hairpins off the dressing table. With a muttered imprecation, she bent to pick them up.

Alan swung the door open. His eyes widened at the sight of Jenna, her skirts hiked above her knees, rooting around on the floor amid scattered hairpins. She hadn't donned stockings or shoes yet, and the sight of her bare skin rocked him to his core. It astonished him that such a seemingly innocent thing could be so staggeringly erotic.

He drew a deep breath and was startled by it because he hadn't been aware he'd been holding it. "Looking for something?"

Jenna sprang to her feet with a lithe movement a tigress would have envied. "Oh!" she gasped. "I thought you were—"

"The maid? Where is Maisie, anyway?"

"I let her leave. I think she was afraid of me."

Alan's pulse stuttered as he looked at her. Her hair had been wound into a knot at the top of her head, but exquisite little curls had escaped confinement to frame her face. The green of her dress made her skin glow like fine ivory and accented the green-crystal clearness of her eyes. Her breasts, as full and white as he'd imagined, thrust enticingly against the bodice. Enough of those sweet curves were displayed by the decolleté neckline to make his heart race, and it took an effort of will to keep from pulling her to him and kissing her senseless.

"You're beautiful," he said.

"Empty flattery," she retorted breathlessly.

"Give me your hand."

Startled, she just stared at him. He smiled at her a bit crookedly and said, "I only asked for your hand, no matter how delectable the rest of you may be."

It was the smile and not the words that prompted her to place her hand in his. His fingers closed over hers, a gesture rife with possessiveness despite the gentleness of his touch. She shivered, partly from fear, partly from the burgeoning warmth inside her.

He led her to the looking glass, turning her so that she stood facing it. She looked, not at her reflection but at his. The candlelight caught the planes and angles of his face, making him seem as stark and predatory as an eagle. If either of them were beautiful, she thought, surely it was he. His brooding aquiline looks were accented by the dark coat, long in back but cut away in the front to show a white brocade waistcoat, and by the snowy cravat and shirt. His trousers hugged the muscular length of his legs. But it was the flaring desire in his eyes that caught her the most, caught her and sent a tidal wave of response crashing through her.

"I . . . feel very foolish," she said, too breathlessly.

"Why?"

"Dressing like this," she swept her hand down at the fall of soft green silk, "is like powdering and perfuming the livestock."

"That's the most idiotic thing I've ever heard," he said. "Look at yourself, Jenna."

She obeyed, unable to resist the command in his voice.

He stepped behind her, a dark foil to her reflection. "What do you see?"

"A foolish girl trying to be something she's not."

"Has no one ever told you how beautiful you are?" His voice was as intense as his eyes.

"Only a drunken boatman once, hoping I'd give him a tumble in the bushes. Somehow, I doubted his judgment."

His gaze was drawn to the sweet curve of her shoulder. He brushed his hand just above her skin, triumph rushing through him as he saw her eyelids lower in response. "And what did you do to him?" he murmured.

"I turned him into a toad."

Alan drew in a deep breath, unsure whether he was more annoyed at her baiting him or at the thought of some drunken sod trying to seduce her. But he controlled himself, admirably he thought. "I've got a present for you."

Doubt tightened Jenna's throat. "I don't think—" she began, then broke off abruptly when she saw him take a spray of honeysuckle blossoms out of his pocket. Their scent rose sweetly upon the air.

No other offering could have disarmed her so or made her feel more at home. She smiled at him in shy thanks.

"Wear it in your hair," he said.

She sat down at the dressing table and pinned the flowers just at her temple. The funnel-shaped blossoms made a bright yellow splash against her pale hair.

"How is this?" she asked.

"Perfect"

"Thank you," she said, reaching up to touch the flowers with a gentle finger. "For a moment, I was afraid—"

"That I'd bought you a jeweled bauble?"

She looked away, blushing again. "Yes."

"If I could have captured the moonlight in a stone, I would have bought it for you. Nothing less would do."

Their gazes caught, held. Again, he felt that sweeping, unexpected tenderness for her. And desire. Ah, yes. He wanted her with everything that made him a man. In the most primitive and powerful way, he wanted to possess her totally. His soul burned for her nearly as much as his body did, and here he was, a few paces from heaven, and honor-bound not to touch her.

Jenna turned away from his searing gaze. Desperate to find some occupation, she picked up the gloves and made another futile attempt to put them on.

"Shall I act as ladies' maid?" he asked.

Jenna's nostrils flared. She felt the dangerous tension in the room, but it was an exquisite sort of danger, more intriguing than frightening. "Are you good at it?"

"I'm good at a number of things."

"Gloves?"

"That's a start."

Reaching up, Jenna touched the honeysuckle blooms once more. "Very well. I think it would be easier wrestling a pair of water rattlesnakes than putting these things on."

"I'll have to touch you. Will you allow it?"

She looked up, straight into his burning midnight eyes. "If you behave yourself."

"I was raised a gentleman," he said.

"As you said before," she reminded him, "there are times when you're only a man."

Alan saw the feminine awareness of power in her eyes. *She's enjoying this.* Ah, but such a game was a two-edged sword, and he had more experience in it than she. "Better the gloves," he said, "than the stockings."

The thought was a most provocative one and sent molten heat coursing through her veins. Held silent by the searing image in her mind, she rose and brought the gloves to him.

He rolled one carefully to the wrist and held it out for her to insert her hand. "There's an art to donning evening gloves," he said.

"An art I'll have little use for," she replied.

"True. All you have to do is come to me. Any time you need me." He smoothed the glove over her wrist, slowly, slowly, then upward along her forearm. Her skin was warm and smoother than the silk of the glove.

His pulse began to beat in a swift, hard rhythm. He'd never felt like this, never wanted a woman so profoundly. It wouldn't have been so bad if she hadn't wanted him in return. But to see the flare of need in her eyes and be barred from loving her was almost more than flesh and blood could bear. He took a deep, shuddering breath, fighting for control.

She looked lost, her eyes swimming with hot desire. Sweet, sensual Jenna—afraid of love, yet snared by her own passionate nature.

He reached her elbow, his knuckles grazing the sensitive spot inside. His gaze drifted to her throat, where the pulse throbbed visibly beneath the delicate skin. He slowed the movement of his hands as he slid the glove in place just over her elbow. Then he ran his cupped hand along the underside of her arm, ostensibly to smooth the wrinkles out of the silk but really to prolong the exquisite contact between them.

"How does that feel?" he whispered.

Jenna stared at him, so wrapped in the sensual cloud of desire that she didn't understand his question.

He smiled. "The glove. It's not too tight, is it?"

"Oh. No, it's fine."

"Then shall we move on to the other?"

She nodded. His hands were so gentle, so very warm as he began slipping the other glove onto her arm. Sensation sparkled along her skin, making it so sensitive that it seemed to burn wherever he touched her. The heat spread and deepened, sinking straight to her core. Without her willing it, her eyes drifted closed.

His hands left her. Bereft, she opened her eyes. He stood in front of her, so close that a scant inch separated them. She could feel his heat, feel the surging torrent of his need.

A muscle throbbed at the corner of his jaw, and his brows drew together as though something hurt him. Her gaze moved downward along the length of his body, and she saw the long, thick line of his arousal stretching the front of his trousers. The sight should have terrified her; instead, it only increased the hot, liquid flow deep inside her.

"Shall we begin on the stockings now?" he asked softly.

A flush heated her cheeks painfully, even as her body reacted to the thought of those big, lean hands skimming up her calves, smoothing the silk stockings over her thighs oh, so slowly . . . With an effort, she pulled her wandering thoughts back to order.

"No," she said. "No stockings."

"Why not?"

"The shoes . . ." She paused for a moment, drawing a tight breath, "the shoes don't fit."

"Are you sure?"

She knew he wasn't talking about shoes or stockings or anything but the passion coursing between them. "I'm sure." Oh, it was a lie, another lie, but as necessary as the first.

"Why do you torment me, and torment yourself? Just admit it once, this magic between us, and set yourself free."

She closed her eyes against the hot, importuning blue of his gaze. "I am the witch. Magic is my province, after all."

"Jenna—"

"No. No more. I made a mistake letting you touch me tonight; this was my fault, and I'll make sure it doesn't happen again."

Turning on her heel, she walked toward the door. He caught up with her, of course, his long strides easily out-distancing hers.

"It was my fault as much as yours," he said. "I asked permission, did I not?"

"Why did you?"

"I couldn't help myself," he said with no contrition in his voice at all. "I am, after all, cursed."

He smiled down at her, and she felt her heart contract with sudden bittersweet pain. Why, of all the men in the world, did this one affect her so?

Alan saw the capitulation in her eyes. "Truce?" he asked, offering his arm again.

"Truce," she said, accepting his escort. "But no more gloves."

"Of course," he replied, knowing very well he'd find another way.

He led her toward the stairs, enveloped in the scent of honeysuckle and woman. It brought his desire to a peak again in a single, sweeping rush.

No matter what she said, he knew the truth of it. He'd seen passion in her eyes. Shared, exquisite, powerful. He hadn't the strength to resist it, and neither did she.

Someday, somehow, she would come to him.

Dorcas and the children were waiting in the dining room when Jenna and Alan arrived.

"Oh, you look pretty!" Beth said. "Did Father allow you to come without shoes and stockings? He never allows me to go without shoes and stockings."

Jenna flushed, painfully aware of Dorcas's cool, assessing gaze. Taking her hand from Alan's arm, she moved forward into the room. "It's only that my slippers didn't fit, sweetling."

"Well, come sit down. I'm very hungry."

Jon rose, pulling out the chair between his and his sister's. Jenna couldn't help but smile.

"Thank you, little man," she said, taking the proffered seat.

Alan would have preferred to have her beside him, but this way gave him an excellent view of her profile. Reward enough, perhaps. His gaze focused on her gloved hand, and his blood warmed at the memory of putting it on her. He'd never see gloves in quite the same way again; gloves and honeysuckle had become synonymous with Jenna, and passion.

Opal, the cook, came in with a tray. It contained a golden-brown roasted chicken surrounded with potatoes and onions and plump butterbeans. Two house servants followed her, bearing platters of cheeses, bread, and fresh figs from Heronsgate trees.

"Jenna, this is Opal, our cook, and a real jewel she is," Alan said. "Maisie is her daughter. And these are Ulysses and Enos, who take good care of us."

Jenna nodded. The two men had the same fear in their eyes as did the girl Maisie—fear of the witch. But the cook's dark gaze held knowledge, one woman to another, of the White Lady's work.

"Pleased t'meet you, Miss Jenna," Opal said. "We're happy to have you."

"Thank you," Jenna murmured.

The servants moved around the table, serving as they did at every meal, but Alan sensed a subtle difference tonight. It was as though the focus had changed, shifting from the family to Jenna. He watched with interest as the choicest portions of chicken and the ripest figs ended up on her plate.

Jenna didn't seem to notice; she watched the slaves as they worked, and a sadness came into her eyes. Alan knew that if she could, she would have taken them all away to freedom.

So let her. You haven't been a slaveowner long enough to learn to like it. But he couldn't, at least not until he found a way that would hurt neither Heronsgate nor the people themselves. Certainly he couldn't absolve himself of that responsibility just to put joy in a pretty woman's eyes.

Opal gave the table one last, encompassing glance, then shooed her helpers out before her. The children immediately turned to their guest.

"When can we go fishing, Jenna?" Jon asked. "Tonight?"

"Not tonight," Alan said firmly.

Jenna smiled down at the boy. "How about tomorrow just before dawn?"

"Won't the fish be sleeping?"

"Oh, no. They're very active then, when the rest of the world is hushed and quiet."

"Children, your food is getting cold," Dorcas said.

Taking that as her own admonishment, Jenna turned her attention to the meal. She watched how the others ate, fork in one hand, knife in the other, and followed their example.

Alan saw how she observed, understood, and so quickly adapted. He knew she was nervous. She shouldn't have been; she had a natural grace of movement and regality of carriage that would do in His Majesty's court itself. And even as he watched her, his mind wandered to those lovely bare feet of hers below the table and what it would feel like to have her long, long legs wrap around him.

Lost in his carnal imaginings, he ate without tasting, drank without feeling the wine. He didn't need liquor; Jenna was more of an intoxicant than anything created by man. She laughed with his children, and he could feel her lilting voice like a physical touch on his skin.

"Is everyone ready for dessert?" Dorcas asked, her practical British voice spearing through his reverie.

"What is it?" Jon asked.

"Blackberry pie, I believe." The nanny tugged the bell pull, and a moment later Opal and her helpers appeared, cleared the table, then set slices of still-warm pie at each place.

"I've never had pie before," Jenna said.

"Truly?" Dorcas asked.

Jenna spread her hands. "Even if I was able to obtain flour, lard, and sugar all at the same time, I have no oven."

"Good heavens!" The nanny stared at her. "Then eat up, miss. It's a crime not to have experienced blackberry pie."

Alan watched Jenna take a bite. At first she looked surprised. Then wonder spread over her face, and she took another bite.

"Oh, it's wonderful," she said.

His attention narrowed to her mouth, where a drop of berry syrup clung to the ripe, ruby flesh. The tip of her tongue darted out to lick the sweetness away, leaving her lips glistening with enticement. He nearly groaned at the sight. His own appetite gone, he pushed his plate away.

Finally, Dorcas rose, beckoning Jon and Beth up with her. "It's time to get ready for bed, children."

"Just a little while longer?" Beth pleaded.

"One more piece of pie?" Jon echoed in the same wheedling tone of voice.

Jenna smiled, even as the thought occurred to her that having one's way seemed to be a fact of life with all the Langstons. "We're to be up early in the morning, remember?"

"Come on now," Dorcas said, clapping her hands. "I'll come tuck you in, but we must hurry so that I can have tea with your father and Miss Llewellyn."

"Jenna and I don't mind if you stay with them," Alan said.

Panic laid its icy touch on Jenna's heart. She didn't trust herself to be alone with him and didn't trust him with that look in his eyes. Silently, she looked pleadingly at the nanny, hoping the woman would see the message she was trying to convey.

Dorcas's mouth softened just a bit. "I couldn't possibly leave you and the young lady unchaperoned, sir. After all, we have her reputation to consider."

Alan sighed, capitulating only because he was so sure his time would come. "Come give me a kiss, children."

They obeyed, then ran to Jenna and kissed her, too. She laughed, not minding that they left sticky spots of blackberry pie on her cheeks.

"G'night, Jenna," Beth murmured, planting still another messy kiss on her cheek.

"Good night, sweet. Good night, little man."

Giggling, they ran out of the room.

"I'll be down in a moment," Dorcas said. "I've arranged for tea to be served in the study."

She followed her charges, leaving Jenna alone with Alan. He leaned back in his chair, regarding her from beneath his lashes. Suddenly nervous, she clasped her hands in her lap and stared down at them.

"You didn't finish your wine," he said.

"I'm not accustomed to drinking wine."

His voice went lower, becoming much too intimate for comfort. "You've got blackberry syrup on your face," he said. "Would you like me to take it off for you?"

"No, thank you."

"Are you sure?"

She lifted her chin, suddenly irritated at him but more

at herself for letting him do this to her. Dipping the corner of her napkin into her water glass, she scrubbed her face clean. "Your servants—Opal and the others—are they slaves or freedmen?"

Alan sighed; he'd known this question was coming. "They were part of the Heronsgate estate."

"Ah, yes," she said. "Like the furniture."

"People can never be compared with furniture," he said, "as you very well know."

"But they can be owned."

"That is obvious," he said, picking up his wine glass and taking a sip. "Let me ask you something, Jenna. If one of my people ran away into the Dismal, would you help him or her to escape?"

"I help anyone who needs it."

"Even when it's against the law?"

She pushed her chair back and got up. "Townsmen's laws mean nothing to me."

"So you make your own?"

"Yes."

He smiled, rising so that their eyes were on a level. "One of them being, as you so colorfully described to Jonas Rafferty, to drop transgressors into smoldering peat?"

"Perhaps."

"Would you have done it if I hadn't been there?"

"Perhaps."

"I don't believe you. I don't think you've hurt anyone in your life."

"You're the one who called me a savage."

"That's because I feel very primitive around you."

His eyes had gone dark with desire, and Jenna's pulse began to flutter with dread and excitement.

Opal thrust her head into the room. "Tea, suh, is in the drawin' room."

"We'll be right there," Alan said.

The woman withdrew. With a sigh that came from deep inside, he turned back to Jenna. "The world conspires against me."

"You should take it as a sign," she said.

He cocked his head to one side, considering that, then grinned. "The only sign I believe in is the invitation in your eyes."

"It's very easy to misread things you want to see in other people's eyes," she countered.

He moved close, still not touching her, but near enough that her skin registered his heat. Her gaze dropped to his mouth. She stared at the firm, curving lips that were slightly parted now, her mind awash with the memories of his kiss.

Temptation ran hot, imperative fingers up her spine.

"Don't be afraid of me," he murmured. "I want only to please you. Anything you want, you have only to ask."

I only want the loneliness to end. I want friendship. Even as one part of her mind spoke those thoughts, another part realized how incomplete they were. He'd set up a whirlwind of feelings inside her, an aching tumble of emotions that frightened her with their importunities. She, daughter of the swamp, had no right to feel those things. Not with him. Not with any townsman.

Then with whom? her heart cried.

Footsteps sounded in the hallway outside. They gave her the strength to step away from him. "Our tea will be getting cold," she said.

"Damn the tea," Alan growled.

Dorcas appeared in the doorway, her stolid gaze taking

in the scene. Jenna felt the heat of a blush rise into her cheeks; despite the fact that she and Alan were standing several paces apart, she was sure her confusion and desire were written upon her face.

"Are the children in bed already?" Alan asked. Frustration coiled his hands into fists, and it was all he could do to keep himself from ordering Dorcas from the room and tossing Jenna's skirts up whether she wanted him or not.

"The prospect of fishing on the morrow gave them incentive to hurry," Dorcas said. "Well, Miss Llewellyn, would you like to learn the proper English way of serving tea?"

"I'd love to," she said, grateful for the escape.

"I've had brandy brought in for you, sir," the nanny said. "I expect you'd rather have that."

"Indubitably," he muttered, his gaze still riveted on Jenna's lovely face. "It seems to be the only fate allowed me."

Ten

"I've got one, I've got one!" Jon cried, jerking the line hard to set the hook.

"Easy," Jenna said, stilling the frantic movements of his hands. "Keep a steady pressure or you'll lose him."

She glanced over her shoulder at Dorcas, who was gamely helping Beth put a worm on a hook. The nanny had no doubt come to make sure the witch didn't spirit away her charges. Now, with her hair half down and her gown spotted with water and grass stains and even less savory things, she actually looked as though she were having a good time.

"He's huge," Jon panted. "Have you ever seen one so big?"

"I've seen the Grandaddy Catfish himself." Jenna pulled line in hand over hand. "When we're done, I'll tell you the story. Keep him to the left or you'll snag on that submerged log over there."

The line bucked as the fish darted left, straight toward the log. Jon muttered something that Jenna didn't quite catch but which brought Dorcas swinging around with indignation plain on her face.

"He's gone under!" the boy cried.

"Best to cut the line—"

"But he's the biggest ever!"

Jenna tilted his face up. His face was flushed, freckles dusting his short nose. Disappointment shadowed his soot-gray eyes, and determination firmed his childish jaw into one that looked much like his father's.

"Is it that important to you, little man?"

He shook his head, but she could see that it was. With a sigh, she tied the ribbons of the bonnet Dorcas had insisted she wear, then bent and rolled her trouser legs up to her knees. Dorcas made a small sound of distress.

"Keep the line taut," Jenna told the boy. "Don't start pulling him in until I tell you."

Arms akimbo, she surveyed the trees, noting that the branches of one particular oak hung far out over the water. She climbed the tree easily, then made her way onto the branch nearest the log.

"Do be careful!" Dorcas called.

Jenna eased out along the branch. It gave under her weight, a precarious springboard that dipped closer to the water with every inch she moved. Carefully, she slid first one foot, then another, onto the log, making sure the support below was adequate before letting go of the branch. Her feet slithered for a moment on the moss-covered wood, then gained purchase.

Bending, she drew the line around the end of the snag. "All right, Jon. Pull him in," she called.

The boy worked quickly, at the end giving a tremendous heave of the pole that slung the fish high out of the water and onto the bank. He hurled himself upon his flapping captive.

Jenna laughed. "Hold him, little man, before he gets away, " she called, while Beth shrieked with delight and Dorcas tried to separate the tangle of boy and line and flopping catfish.

Her laugh stopped abruptly when she saw Alan step through the tangle of cassina that screened the river from the house. He paused to hold the branches aside, and a moment later a woman ducked beneath his outstretched arm and stepped upon the riverbank.

A beautiful woman. Her tawny hair caught the sun in a whirl of gold, her figure was lush, well-rounded, her eyes the turquoise of the sea at dawn. She tucked her hand into the crook of Alan's arm, gazing up at him with sultry invitation. Miranda Carrew, no doubt. The "buzums" were indeed freely displayed, twin mounds of jiggling white flesh precariously contained in the tiny bodice of her yellow silk gown.

Jenna felt suddenly cold inside. How easily Alan had forgotten his heated blandishments of the night before. A new day, a new woman.

So you've learned a new lesson in the ways of men. Remember it the next time he whispers sweet flatteries in your ear.

He hadn't noticed her yet, out there in the river. She watched him grin as he disengaged his arm from the woman's grasp and went to his son's aid. Plucking the boy from his struggling captive, he subdued the fish and held it up.

"He's enormous," he said, turning the catfish this way and that. "Good work, son."

"Jenna helped."

"Indeed? And where is Jenna?"

Jon pointed out into the river. "There."

Alan turned, and felt his jaw drop in astonishment. For one incredulous moment, he thought Jenna stood *atop* the water. Then he realized that she was standing on a submerged log and let his breath out in a sigh of relief.

"What are you doing out there?" he called.

"Jon's line was snagged," she said. Peevishly. She wished she could take it back; she'd never been peevish in her life.

Alan smiled, enjoying the sight—and situation—immensely. He hadn't welcomed Miranda's uninvited presence, but then he'd decided to bring her down here in the hope of putting some fire under his wood sprite's delectable tail. Judging from the flare in her green eyes and the pique in her voice, he'd done it. His gaze traveled the slender curves of Jenna's trouser-clad body. A staid little bonnet shaded her face, a plebeian contrast to the elegant beauty below. Her legs were bare to the knee, her smooth pale skin glistening with water. He had no idea how she'd made it out to that log without swimming, but he was certain she'd have to ask for his help to get back to shore.

"Who is that?" Miranda asked, her voice even more peeved than Jenna's.

"That," Alan said, "is a wood sprite. Jenna, say hello to Miranda Carrew."

"Hello," she said, wondering if he had deliberately avoided using her surname. Perhaps, she thought, he didn't want his lady love thinking he'd befriended the witch.

Miranda ignored her. Leaning close to Alan, she pressed her bountiful breasts against his arm. "It's terribly hot out here, Alan. And besides, Mother is probably wondering what happened to us. Let's go back to the house."

"Not now, Miranda. I couldn't leave a lady in such an . . . interesting position."

Miranda looked Jenna up and down, her aquamarine eyes contemptuous. "I suppose not."

"Well, Jenna, you've got yourself in a fix this time,"

Alan said, disengaging himself from Miranda's clinging hands.

Jenna studied him, seeing the self-satisfaction in his face. Oh, the rogue! He thought she'd have to ask him to carry her back to shore. Her eyes narrowed. He'd have to carry that hot-eyed townswoman but not Jenna Llewellyn.

"I'm not having any trouble," she said.

He grinned. "No?"

"No."

Suddenly Dorcas screamed. Jenna jerked in surprise, her feet slithering across the mossy log, then steadied herself.

"A snake!" the nanny shrieked. "Jenna! Behind you!"

Jenna glanced over her shoulder. A long shape slid through the water toward her, sinuous and graceful. She almost slipped again as she heard Alan shout. Turning, she saw him plunge down the bank and into the water, swimming toward her with smooth, powerful strokes.

Then she pivoted, bent, and plucked the snake out of the water. Miranda and Dorcas screamed.

Alan reached the log, ready to do battle. As he shook his wet hair out of his eyes, however, he saw Jenna balanced securely, the snake coiling and twisting in her grasp. She looked down at him with inscrutable green eyes.

"It's only a water snake," she said. "Perfectly harmless."

It took a moment for his heart to start beating again. He put his feet down and found himself able to stand. With his feet in muck and water lapping his shoulders, he gave rein to a fury born more of relief than anything else.

"Put the bloody snake down," he snarled. "And come off that log."

"I don't take orders from you," she said, her own temper lighting.

"Don't test me, Jenna. I'll—"

"You'll what?" She smiled at him, a malicious female smile, and his anger went up another notch. "Beat me? You can't touch me unless I allow it, remember?"

He set his feet more firmly. Grasping a projection on the log, he gritted his teeth and heaved upward with all his strength. For a moment the log resisted, then shuddered and rolled.

Jenna struggled for balance. Consternation mixed with admiration as she realized Alan had managed to lift the tremendous weight of water-logged wood. Then her feet went out from under her and she tumbled backward into the river. Her arms went up and out, flinging the snake high into the air, and she heard another chorus of shrieks from the shore.

Green dimness closed over her head, and she plunged through a froth of bubbles. She touched bottom gently, then swam back to the surface.

She expected to find Alan waiting for her. Instead, she saw him step onto shore to be set upon by a sobbing Miranda. Dorcas patted the hysterical girl's back.

"It came straight at me!" she wailed. "Great, disgusting . . . oh, Alan, I was so frightened."

She started to sag, and Alan lifted her into his arms. Jenna watched the possessive curve of Miranda's fingers on his shoulders as he carried her up to the house.

Jenna felt suddenly empty, as though the ducking had leached all emotion out of her. She swam to shore. As she emerged, dripping, Jon and Beth came running to her.

"What a snake!" the boy said. "You should have seen her run when that blighter came sailing through the air!"

"Poor thing," Jenna murmured.

Jon's jaw dropped. "You don't mean *her?*"

"No," she said. "I meant the snake."

Beth clapped her hand over her mouth. But a giggle squeezed out around her fingers, and Jon's face was a study in pure, unholy joy.

Jenna tried not to laugh, truly she did. But she couldn't help herself. The three of them laughed until the tears ran down their cheeks. Finally, they collapsed on the ground, arms wound around one another in exquisite shared merriment.

Arms akimbo, Dorcas came to stand over them. Jenna looked up at her, gasping for breath.

"It was an accident, Dorcas, I promise," she said.

The nanny's mouth twitched. "Indeed." Clapping her hands briskly, she said, "Time to go in, children. Beth, you carry the poles, please, and be wary of the hooks. Jon, you bring that great beast of a fish you caught."

"I want to eat him," Jon said.

"We will all eat him," Jenna said. She got to her feet and wrung water out of her clothing. "Thank you for the warning, Dorcas."

The older woman inclined her head. "For a harmless snake, it certainly gave us all a fright. Poor Miranda. I fear she came straight out of her hairpins."

"Or her bodice," Jenna murmured.

To her surprise, Dorcas smiled. "I must admit," she said, "this is turning out to be a most interesting day."

"What do you mean?"

"Oh, nothing, really." The nanny turned away and began helping Beth wind up the lines. "Miss Carrew and her mother will be staying for tea, I hear. Unless, of course, the young woman is completely undone by the shock."

Remembering the way Miranda's hands had clutched Alan's shoulders, Jenna said, "She'll recover enough for tea."

"I expect she will."

A few minutes later they headed back to Heronsgate. A knot formed in Jenna's stomach and grew larger and tighter the closer she got to the house.

It wasn't because of the way Miranda Carrew looked at Alan, as though she'd like to devour him. No. It was the fear of seeing him return that look. She didn't understand herself or the feelings raging inside her. Yet they were powerful, these feelings, powerful and disturbing because she didn't know what caused them. It seemed as though Alan had seeped into her like a fever. Her soul shook with it, and she was very much afraid. Bitterroot tea wouldn't cure this fever, nor infusion of swamp willow or Everlasting.

The time had come for her to go. Life at Heronsgate had just become too complicated for her and dangerous because she lacked the skills to deal with it. Better to return to the life she understood.

"Jenna, tell us the story of the Grandaddy Catfish," Jon begged.

She nodded, glad of the diversion. "There's a part of the swamp where the cedar grows tall. It's a dim and mysterious place, where even the wind is hushed. Mistletoe and Spanish moss hang from the branches, and strange fungi grow thick on the tree trunks."

Beth's eyes grew wide. "Is it a bad place?"

"No, dear." Jenna cupped the child's delicate cheek in

her palm. "It's just strange. A place becomes what you expect of it, good or bad or otherwise."

"Have you ever been there?"

"Oh, many times. I find it a place of great beauty, and have never once been afraid there."

They reached the house. Jenna sat down on the top step of the wide, airy porch. The children settled down beside her, Jon cradling his great fish in his lap. Dorcas eased down on the step below, moving the fish's tail aside with perfect aplomb.

"Now," Jenna said, "back to the tale of Grandaddy Catfish. Once, many years ago, there were trails in the swamp and any who knew the way of the woods could travel freely there. These men knew the land, respected it, and were welcome. Then a trapper by the name of Jacques Lebeaux traveled deep into the cedar swamp. He was a cynical man, this Frenchman; he liked to say that nothing frightened him, nothing surprised him. The farther he went into the swamp, the larger the catfish he caught. He'd never eaten so well. This was a good thing, he thought, and every day he moved closer to the heart of the swamp."

"But he became greedy and began catching more than he could eat. And still he moved on, catching ever larger fish for the sport of it. Finally, he reached the center of the swamp. It was very still, hushed and breathless as a church. The sun did not reach the ground there, and the water lay as dark as midnight beneath the trees. Even at midday, owls glided overhead on silent pale wings."

The children's eyes were wide, their faces rapt. Jenna paused for breath, then continued.

"Jacques poled his boat to the spot where the water was darkest. There, he dropped his line. Triumph filled him, for he knew that here would be the greatest catch of all. Something nudged his line, tugged a bit as though teasing at the bait. Then he felt it jerk as the hook sunk home. He pulled, hand over hand, his muscles straining. It must be enormous, he thought, pulling and pulling. This one he'd take back to civilization with him for all to see and marvel."

"And then a head broke the surface, and Jacques cried out in terror. It was as long as his boat, and wider, the whiskers as thick as his wrist."

"Ooooh," Beth gasped.

"Then he looked into its eyes, and his fear vanished. For those eyes were filled, not with anger, but with great sadness. And then the fish spoke. 'O man,' it said, 'I have been generous with you and your kind. I allow you to catch and eat my children, for that is the way of nature. But you have taken food when you were not hungry, thus depriving others. This cannot be. So you and your kind are no longer welcome here.'

"And then Jacques Lebeaux found himself suddenly at the edge of the cedar swamp. All the trails had vanished, and to this day that part of the Dismal remains a trackless waste. Legend says that the great fish still lives in the dark, silent heart of the swamp, protecting it."

Beth heaved a deep sigh. "I'd like to meet him."

"Do you think he'd mind me eating my fish?" Jon asked.

Jenna smiled. "Of course not. Do you think you would have caught him otherwise? You've been favored, little man. And now you'd better take your prize around to the kitchen, then get cleaned up before you smell as fishy as the fish."

"Come on, Pudge," he said, levering himself and his

catfish up off the step. Suddenly he turned back around. "You're going to stay, aren't you, Jenna?"

His question surprised her, as did his perception. "I—"

"Please don't go," Beth pleaded.

"This isn't my home," Jenna said, trying to be gentle. "I have another place, another life."

"But why do you want to leave so quickly?" Jon asked. "We want to be friends."

Inexplicable tears stung the inside of Jenna's eyelids. Perhaps not so inexplicable; she'd never had a friend before. "I'll stay another day or so. Will that do?"

"Hurrah!" Jon cried. He ran off around the corner of the house with Beth in close pursuit.

Dorcas looked up at Jenna. "Thank you. They would have been very hurt had you refused."

"It might have been better for everyone if I'd gone."

"I'm not sure I agree." With her handkerchief, the nanny dabbed at the worst of the spots on her skirt. "That was quite a story you told. I thought for a moment it would end with the fish swallowing Jacques up, boat and all."

"So did I," Alan said from behind them.

Her pulse pounding wildly, Jenna turned to look at him. He'd changed into a pair of gray trousers and a crisp linen shirt. She liked him best this way, without the frills of collar and cravat to hide the strong, clean lines of his throat.

"I didn't know you were listening," she said.

"I'm glad I did." The sunlight struck obsidian sparks in his dark hair. "Dorcas, I believe Beth will need help with her bath."

"Yes, sir." The nanny rose, gave Jenna a hooded, incomprehensible glance, then walked past him into the house.

"Must she do what you say?" Jenna asked.

He smiled. "Dorcas humors me."

She studied him from beneath her lashes, annoyed by how unconsciously he expected obedience.

"Is the Grandaddy Catfish a common tale," he asked, "or did you make it up to entertain the children?"

"It's an old legend. There are many such about the Dismal. But many are too grim for children's ears."

"You'll have to tell them to me, then."

"I doubt they'd interest you."

"Everything about you interests me." His deep voice seemed to sink into her, flowing through her veins like dark wine.

"The legends are about the swamp," she pointed out. "Not me."

"That's not entirely true, is it?"

Her chin went up. "If it's lurid tales of the witch you want, you'll have to go into town."

Miranda's high voice speared out of the open door. "Alan! Where are you?"

"I'll be there in a moment," he called over his shoulder.

A chill settled around Jenna's heart. For a moment, she'd forgotten the other woman, forgotten everything but the stark masculine beauty of him and the way he made her soul leap just by smiling.

He leaned against the nearest column. His gaze was coolly speculative, and she realized with a swift flare of surprise that he expected her to react to Miranda's presence. No, wanted her to react.

Jenna didn't know why he'd chosen to play this game. But he'd made a serious miscalculation: the Llewellyns never played by the rules.

Her churning emotions crystallized into determination.

She rose with all the grace and dignity at her command. "Excuse me, but I'd better get out of these wet things."

Alan watched her come toward him, thinking he'd never seen a woman move with such coiled grace. Her wet clothes clung to her, revealing the sweet, flaring curve of her hips, the tiny waist, and high, full breasts. *Tigress*, he thought. She'd be like that in bed, he knew. All that grace and passion, it would be like getting caught in a whirlpool, plunging deep and deeper still and never wanting to come up again.

"You're not angry at me for dumping you into the water, are you?" he asked.

"I've been told that men can't help but be asses from time to time," she said with false sweetness.

Alan narrowed his eyes. He shouldn't have let her goad him. Wasn't he the man who'd always prided himself on his control? But the defiance in her eyes brought something hard and primitive roaring to life within him, and he acted from instinct, not intellect. Grasping the bottom edge of her shirt, he balled the fabric in his hands. The garment drew tightly across her breasts, outlining the ripe mounds even more.

With a defiant lift of her chin, she met his burning gaze and said, "Don't touch me."

"I'm touching your shirt," he growled.

Instinct hammered at her, urging her to flee. But she controlled it. She *would not* show weakness before this man.

"Alan!" Miranda called. "Where have you run off to?" Her voice grew louder as she came closer. "Oh, Alan!"

His midnight gaze bore into Jenna's a moment longer. Then he released her, slowly and grudgingly. "This isn't finished, Jenna."

Miranda appeared in the doorway, looking surprisingly calm after her hysterics such a short time ago. Despite her beauty, her eyes were restless and her mouth had an air of discontent.

"Oh," she said, her gaze frankly contemptuous as it came to rest on Jenna. "It's you. Don't you think you ought to run upstairs and do something with yourself? You look a fright, Miss, ah . . ."

As the other woman paused, waiting to be supplied with her name, Jenna smiled. The time had come to change the game Alan Langston had begun playing. He might not like this new one quite so well.

"My name is Jenna," she said, pulling the bonnet off so her hair would show. "Jenna Llewellyn."

Miranda's face went chalk-white. "The witch!"

Slowly, Jenna turned to look at Alan. He stared back at her, his mouth curved in an enigmatic smile. His eyes, however, were frankly admiring. He knew she'd thrown down the gauntlet and had responded in kind. Challenge accepted.

She answered his smile with one of her own, then stalked past him into the house.

Eleven

Jenna slammed the bedroom door closed behind her. She started across the room, then came back and turned the key in the lock. Faintly, she heard the sound of agitated female voices downstairs, then Alan's deeper tones as he tried to soothe his guests.

"You can find your amusement elsewhere, Mr. Langston," she muttered. "Bosoms, indeed!"

Then she saw a large metal tub sitting in the center of the room. Water filled it halfway, and a bucket of water for rinsing had been placed beside it. A set of clean undergarments lay on the bed, as well as a plain dark skirt and white blouse that looked like they'd come from Dorcas's wardrobe.

"As long as it doesn't come from him," Jenna said to herself, "I'll wear it."

She would have liked to linger in the bath; the soap smelled of roses, and it was a pleasure to wash the river-smell from her skin and hair. But a feeling of impending trouble nagged at her, a surety that there would be consequences to her actions downstairs. And she had no intention of dealing with Alan from a position of weakness, in which being naked in a bath surely would put her.

She'd just finished combing her hair when he knocked.

She knew it was him by the firmness of the knock and the way her heart leapt.

"I want to talk to you, Jenna," he called through the door.

"What would you say if I told you we had nothing to talk about?" she asked, instinctively covering her chemise-covered breasts with her hands.

"I'd say that I was going to break the bloody door down," he replied in a pleasant tone that didn't fool her at all.

Panic shot through her. "I'm not dressed."

"You have one minute."

She picked a stocking up from the bed, then discarded it over her shoulder. Swiftly, she donned petticoat, skirt and blouse, fumbling with unfamiliar fastenings.

"Time's up," he said.

"I'm coming, I'm coming," she panted, unlocking the door.

Alan strode into the room, looking rather dangerous with his swept-back hair and brooding scowl. Jenna met his bad humor with serenity, the fire in his eyes with tightly held coolness.

"Yes?" she asked.

His gaze raked her. "Those clothes are twenty years out of style."

"Beggars should be no choosers."

"I've never seen a beggar with such pride," he said, his eyes narrowing.

"You said you had something to say to me."

Alan walked around her slowly, both to disconcert her and to admire her. Her freshly washed hair lay in white-blonde coils along her shoulders and back, and her bare feet peeked out from beneath the skirt. Her toes curled into the carpet in a gesture that was both childlike and incredibly sensual.

He glanced beyond her, to the just-used tub, and his mind conjured up a luscious image of her bathing, that incredible hair floating around her, soapsuds gleaming on that satin skin, curves and hollows and sweet, shadowed places . . . "The perfume is wrong," he said. Which was not, of course, what he'd intended to say.

"What?"

"Honeysuckle," he said. "Your scent is honeysuckle."

It should have been amusing. But Jenna felt a crackle of danger on the air, a taut imminence that had to be averted. "You should be with your guests."

"They left, as you very well know."

"Am I a seer as well as a witch now?"

His brows contracted. "You knew exactly what would happen when you told Miranda who you were."

"Of course," she said.

Jenna watched his face tauten with surprise. He'd expected denial and had prepared himself for an argument. Triumph shot through her.

Then he smiled. Alarm replaced her triumph when she realized he was enjoying this. He liked the fact that she'd outmaneuvered him. But she also knew he wouldn't have liked it so much if he hadn't already found a way to counter her.

His grin widened. "They're coming back tonight for supper," he said.

"How did you manage that?"

"Langston charm."

"Is there such a thing?" she asked.

"So I've been told."

She studied him from beneath the veil of her lashes.

A picture swept into her mind, as sharp and visceral as if it were happening now: Alan hurling himself into the water in a curving dive, his hair slashing out in a black wedge behind him, the muscles standing out like cords in his arms as he swam toward her. A warrior come to save her.

"Why did you go diving into that water today?" she asked, horrifying herself. What had possessed her to say that?

He took a step closer, a new look coming into his eyes. "I didn't want you to get hurt."

"You, more than most, know I can take care of myself."

"You're not invulnerable, Jenna."

Without her willing it, her voice dropped to a whisper. "How do you know?"

"Because you tremble when I do this."

He skimmed his fingertips just above her cheek. Not touching, for that would break his promise, but near enough that every nerve in her body quivered in response.

She did tremble. She could no more have stopped it than she could have kept her heart from beating. He knew it, too. The awareness of it and his response was betrayed by the sudden darkening of his eyes.

He moved nearer, so that his mouth was as close as his fingertips had been. His breath mingled with hers, urgent and hot, and her lips parted involuntarily. Memories of what his kiss had been like wrapped her in a silken cloud of desire. Heat and more heat and a promise of unknown delights.

"I want you," he murmured.

His voice was stark with need. She closed her eyes against the sweeping response of her body, searching deep within for the strength to deny what her heart urged her to do. Bitter tears stung her eyes.

"You promised," she said, her voice breaking on the last word.

Alan saw tears glittering on the golden-brown sweep of her lashes, passion mingled with fear in the trembling of her full lips. Tenderness swept through him, tempering somewhat the savage firestorm of his desire. This wasn't any woman, eager for the taking. This was Jenna. Wood sprite, fierce of heart and passion, yet truly innocent.

He took a deep breath, searching deep inside for the strength to move away from her. Somehow he did it. One step, two, yet another, with body and soul aching from loss. She stood immobile for a moment, her eyes still closed, her breasts rising and falling with her rapid breathing. Barely, he managed to keep from groaning at the sight of her. Her lips were moist and slightly swollen, as though he'd been kissing her, and her nipples rose up in taut peaks beneath the fabric of her shirt. And he hadn't even touched her.

She looked the very image of passion, tempting, lovely, as lush and fragrant as a newly opened flower. So much woman, enough, perhaps, to ensnare a man and keep him forever.

"How long can you deny what you feel?" he asked hoarsely.

Her eyes opened. "I don't deny what I feel," she said. "I deny its possibility."

"Why is it so impossible?"

"Because you are of Orwell Stepton's blood and I am . . . who I am."

"You're no witch," he said, utter certainty in his voice.

"Go back to England. Take Jon and Beth with you and forget you ever saw Heronsgate."

"Why?"

"Don't you see?" She spread her hands in evocative appeal, wishing she could make him see what was so very clear to her. "If you're not the master of Heronsgate, the curse—"

"There is no curse!"

"How can you be sure?"

"Because I've lived on this earth for thirty years and have kept my eyes open throughout most of them. There are no such things as witches or fairies or other supernatural nonsense."

"You said you'd listen with an open mind."

"Ah, I see." He crossed his arms over his chest. "So this is what you had in mind when you agreed to come here."

"It's the only sensible thing to do."

"No!" he snapped. "It isn't sensible. It's insane. I worked all my life for something like this. Heronsgate is mine, and by God, I plan to keep it."

"Orwell Stepton said the same thing. But the curse took him anyway."

"I am no Orwell Stepton."

Jenna turned and walked to the window. She felt exposed, stripped bare by her own emotions, and didn't want him to see her face. "The curse was created in the aftermath of murder, born of a hatred that made it powerful. If I could stop it, I would. But I can't. You're in danger, Alan. You can't hear it or see it, but it exists nonetheless."

"I grew up knowing my brother would inherit Langston Hall. He had no talent for it, no love of the land or its people, and he beggared it. He all but beggared me, for I was the one who paid the Langston debts. Now I have Heronsgate and a future. America is a young land, a place where a man can build his empire with guts and

sweat and toil. And nothing, not devil nor man nor this
so-called curse, is going to stop me."

"I wish that were true."

"Damn your curse," he growled. "I won't accept it.
And I'll prove you wrong."

"You might not be like Orwell Stepton in some ways,"
she said. "But you have his arrogance. He paid the full
price for his o'erweening pride."

"I'll take the chance."

She turned, putting her back against the window. He
stood with his hands clasped behind his back, his jaw
set but no anger in his eyes. Rather, he looked silkily
determined.

"You don't deny the arrogance," she said.

"Would you concede the point if I did?"

"No."

"Are all wood sprites this stubborn?"

"I wouldn't know."

He ran his thumb along the edge of his jaw, his gaze
coolly speculative. "About supper—"

"I am not interested in spending my evening trading
insults with Miranda Carrew and her . . . mother."

"You were about to say bosoms."

"I—"

Suddenly he smiled, that reckless rogue's grin of his.
And there it was, the mercurial change of mood that always kept her off balance with this man. Delight bubbled
up inside her, and she threw back her head and laughed.

With a predator's speed, he moved close. He didn't
need to touch her; she could feel his heat and aggressiveness with every fiber in her body. Another change,
and this one more disturbing than the first. The air had

suddenly become thick with tension, the room fairly crackling with the intensity of his mood.

"You're too beautiful for your own good," he said.

Hiding her alarm, she tilted her head back to stare at him. "Is that what you say to every woman you meet?"

"Come to supper, Jenna."

"And be put on display for the entertainment of your bored, simpering friends?"

"No. In the hope that if they come to know you as you truly are, the hatred will stop."

"I don't need their goodwill.

He smiled, but there was a hard edge to it that boded ill for her resistance. "If you don't come to supper, Miranda will think she's beaten you."

Jenna stiffened. "I don't care."

"Liar. You ought to see the look on your face. You'd rather cut off your arm than give Miranda the satisfaction of knowing you're afraid of her."

Without giving her a chance to reply, he turned on his heel and walked out. Jenna was left with a retort unspoken and a very disturbing feeling in the pit of her stomach.

He hadn't listened. He didn't believe.

Suddenly cold despite the golden sunlight streaming through the window, she rubbed her arms in an attempt to dispel the heavy weight of her fear. Fear for Alan, fear for Jon and Beth . . . and fear for herself. For her destiny seemed tied with theirs. It had happened so quietly that she hadn't realized it. But she'd come to care deeply for the gray-eyed boy and the little girl with the smile that could melt the stoniest heart.

And what of the father? Don't you care for him as well? She closed her eyes against the seductiveness of the thought. He infuriated her, made her laugh, and filled her with sweet, aching desire all at the same time.

She didn't dare put a name to what she felt; acknowledging it would have made it real.

"It's only for another day," she said aloud. "Then I'll go home again and forget."

Jenna wore the green gown that night. She told herself it wasn't to please Alan or to displease Miranda but for herself. She paused outside the dining room, listening to the drone of voices inside. Miranda's rather shrill tones dominated the conversation, her mother adding a comment from time to time. But there were also two men besides Alan, something Jenna hadn't expected.

Suddenly intimidated, she turned to go. But at that moment the door opened, and Alan stood framed in the doorway.

"You look lovely," he said, extending his arm.

She wouldn't run. Not from him, not from anyone. With a lift of her chin, she laid her hand on his and let him escort her into the room.

Alan introduced her to his guests. Miranda was lovely as always, her lush figure set off to perfection by a russet gown. Her mother, Mathilde, was a stout, buxom woman with dark blonde hair piled high atop her head. She wore a diamond necklace and bracelet to match, and the stones' hard glitter reflected that of her eyes.

Glancing at Miranda's pinched, bloodless lips, Jenna guessed the Carrew women had come, not to socialize with the witch, but to protect Miranda's interest in the master of Heronsgate. Both stared through her, not acknowledging her presence in the least.

But the men rose, a courtesy she hadn't expected, and came forward to bow over her hand. She blushed, not knowing how to respond to their courtliness.

"This is Jameson Graeme and his son, Carlton," Alan said.

Jenna studied the men curiously. One was older, perhaps sixty, but hale and fit and very distinguished with his mane of gray hair. He studied Jenna with an intentness in his bright blue eyes that had nothing of disapproval or approval, either. It seemed as if he wanted to peel her away, layer by layer, and find what lay at the center.

Then his son stepped forward, breaking the contact between them. Carlton looked to be in his mid-twenties, evidently a child come late in his parents' lives. He seemed an amiable young man, with his father's height and bright blue eyes.

"It's a pleasure to meet you, Miss Llewellyn," he said. "We've heard a great deal about you."

"Then why are you here?" she asked.

"Well, ah . . ."

The older man came to his son's rescue. "Your bluntness is most refreshing, my dear. We came because the rumors are too fantastic to be true. So we wanted to meet the reality so that we could make our own judgment."

She nodded, accepting the fairness of that.

"Alan should have told us how lovely you are," Carlton said, still holding her hand. "So we wouldn't stutter and scrape and make fools of ourselves."

Jenna smiled at him, pleased that the evening she'd dreaded might turn out to be pleasant after all. "I think you've got a glib tongue, Mr. Graeme."

"Carlton, please."

"Carlton."

Alan was possessed by a wave of jealousy so powerful that he stepped forward and firmly removed Jenna's hand from Carlton's grasp. It betrayed his feelings, both to her and to the others, but he could no more have resisted it than he could have stopped breathing.

"Opal has outdone herself tonight," he said, drawing her toward the table. "We've got ham, steamed rice, and the most wonderful gravy you've ever tasted. And, for those of more adventurous tastes," he grinned down at Jenna, "a delectable catfish, caught this very morning by my son."

"Not that great, ugly thing!" Miranda exclaimed.

"Jon and Beth have already tried it and pronounced it delicious."

Miranda shuddered. "I'd almost rather eat the snake."

"That could be arranged," Jenna said, sotto voce.

"Little savage," Alan whispered.

She shot him a glance from beneath her lashes. "You have no idea."

He placed her to his right. Carlton took the seat next to her, Miranda directly across from Jenna. Jameson Graeme seated Mathilde Carrew beside his son, then smiled disarmingly at Miranda as he sat down beside her.

Jenna folded her hands in her lap and sat silently while Opal and Ulysses served. She saw Alan watching her, the corners of his mouth quirked upward in an enigmatic smile, and turned her own gaze downward.

"I understand, Miss Llewellyn, that you actually live in the swamp," Mathilde said.

"That is true."

"Isn't it a terribly hard life, living out there like a savage?"

Jenna's chin went up. "I don't know how savages live."

"Come now. Surely you have to admit that sleeping out in the open, eating whatever you can find, existing without so much as a tub in which to bathe—"

"And freedom," Jenna said. "The wealth of the Dismal is mine for the taking, and I answer to no man."

Mathilde sniffed. "Wealth! Mud and insects, snakes and leeches and stinking slime—those are your riches?"

"Are they less than the brick and wood you shut yourself in to hide from the world around you? Is a flower less precious than those cold stones you wear around your neck?"

The older woman reached up to touch the diamond necklace that encircled her throat. "Of course. It's ridiculous to assume otherwise."

"Is it?" Jameson asked, tapping Jenna lightly on the wrist. "Why did you make that particular comparison?"

"Because they're so different," she said. "If you measure the weight in gold of a diamond or a flower, you know which will be more valuable. But if you're ill, and the flower can be made into a medicine that will make you well, by that measure the flower is far more valuable than the stone."

"So wealth depends on your point of view?" the older man asked, leaning forward intently.

Jenna nodded. "If you were starving, would you value a gold coin or a piece of meat more?"

"That's an interesting point of philosophy," Jameson said.

"What is philosophy?" she asked.

He blinked. "Ah, it is a discipline that comprises logic, ethics, esthetics—"

"It's the way over-educated men try to explain life to themselves," Alan said.

Jenna tilted her head to one side, absorbing that, then turned back to the older man. "Truth is truth, Mr. Graeme. A hungry man will ignore the money and take the meat. Always."

"Good heavens!" Miranda exclaimed. "What a silly thing to talk about. Why don't we discuss something interesting?"

"But I thought it quite—" Jameson began.

"Let's move on, as my daughter suggested," Mathilde said. "Did you hear that Lew Edmunds's bull got loose and ran clear over to the Hadley farm, where he chased Emmaline up a tree?"

"No," Alan said, "we didn't."

Mathilde launched into the tale, seemingly oblivious to the flaming disinterest of everyone but her daughter. Alan found himself drifting off, lost in watching Jenna. He was proud of her for holding her own with the others, but then, he had the feeling she could hold her own with anyone.

Then he caught Carlton staring at her, frank admiration in his eyes. Again, jealousy stabbed deep into his soul, and for a moment he bitterly regretted bringing these people here. He wanted Jenna all to himself. *Damn* Carlton for looking at her like that; *damn* her for smiling at the awe-struck young man, and for being so lovely, so achingly mysterious and serene. A knot formed in his chest, hard and painful, and he clenched his hands into fists.

"Alan, what do you plan to do with Heronsgate now that you've settled in?" Jameson asked, unwittingly rescuing his son from a throttling.

Alan took a calming breath, then another. "There wasn't time to get a cotton crop in this year, unfortunately. But next year we'll plant on schedule."

"I do hope so," Miranda said. "This spring was a poor

one; it rained for weeks on end, turning the fields into vast pools of mud. Papa says the harvest will be scanty this year."

"That means the price of cotton will be high next year," Alan said.

"I hope you have some slaves left by that time," Mathilde said.

His brows went up. "Why do you say that?"

She smiled, a stretch of lips that had little to do with humor. "It's said that when the witch appears, slaves disappear."

"True," Miranda said. "Do you have anything to say to that, Miss Llewellyn?"

"When I meet people in the swamp," Jenna replied, "I never ask them where they've been or where they're going."

"I can attest to that," Alan said. "She asked me no questions; her only goal was to escort me out of her swamp as soon as possible."

Jenna glanced at him, grateful for his rescue. "Any who had to care for such an ill-tempered and uncooperative patient would have been eager to see him well."

Jameson laughed. "So, you were found out, Alan."

"I envy you," Carlton said.

"Indeed?" Alan's brows went up. "Some might call you daft for envying a man a snakebite."

"Ah, but to awaken and find oneself in the care of such a lovely nurse!"

"You *are* daft," Alan retorted. "She sewed me up with the same air of practicality she'd use in mending a torn handkerchief, and not a particularly favorite one at that."

"And never mind the howls of pain, eh?" Jameson asked.

Miranda's eyes chilled still further. "I thought you were bitten by a snake."

"I was. But I'd also managed to cut my leg as I bashed around the swamp."

"Where on your leg?"

Jenna opened her mouth to say something but closed it again when she saw Opal hovering just outside the doorway. The cook's manner bespoke something wrong. She beckoned Jenna urgently.

"Excuse me," Jenna said, pushing her chair back.

She saw Alan start to rise. But then Miranda put her hand on his arm, detaining him, and he turned with obvious ill-humor to listen to her.

Jenna stepped out into the hallway and closed the door behind her. "Opal, what's—"

"Hallie, her baby's comin'," the cook said breathlessly. "But she's havin' trouble—"

"Take me to her."

The door banged open behind them, and Alan stepped out into the hall. Miranda followed a moment later. She stood so close beside him that her breast was pressed to his arm. Jenna looked at the pair of them, so civilized and handsome, and had to swallow a sudden tightness in her throat.

"What's the matter?" he asked.

Jenna stripped off her gloves and tossed them onto a nearby table. "A childbirth."

"Are you a midwife?" he asked.

She glanced at him, then at Miranda. "Not exactly. But I'm a witch, aren't I?"

"I'll come with you," he said.

Miranda gasped. "Heavens, Alan! You must be daft. You've got guests—"

"Play hostess for me, then."

"But, darling, why? Let the Llewellyn woman take care of this. After all, it's only a—"

"Enough!" Anger darkened his eyes and put a granite edge to his jaw. Miranda met that blazing gaze for a moment, then turned and fled back into the dining room.

"What do you need, Jenna?" he asked.

Something warm and vital bloomed in her, born of his caring and the affirmation she read in his eyes. "My pack is upstairs. And I'll need clean cloths, a stack of them."

"Opal, fetch them. Meet us at the cabin."

"Yes, suh!"

Twelve

Alan led Jenna to the place where Heronsgate's slaves lived, a collection of tiny whitewashed cabins and well-tended gardens. Pens held chickens and an occasional hog. She was impressed by the neatness of the place; it looked like a thriving little community and not a place of misery.

"This way," Alan said, pulling her forward.

Light spilled from the open door of one cabin. A groan rose on the night air, a sound of inexpressible agony.

Jenna's throat tightened as she stepped through the doorway into the tiny, one-room house. It was painfully clean, the earthen floor swept, the few furnishings gleaming in the light of the single candle.

Hallie lay on the bed, writhing in the throes of a contraction so strong that Jenna could see it rippling across her swollen belly. A man held her hand, a tall, strong-looking man with tears running down his cheeks. Jenna knew him; he'd bowed to her out there in the swamp.

"Ben," she said. "You are her husband?"

"Yes, Lady."

Jenna moved to the bed and laid her hand on Hallie's forehead. Pain etched the woman's face, sent sweat running in streams down her neck. She groaned as yet another contraction ripped through her.

"How long has she been in labor?" Jenna asked.

"Since this mornin'."

Too long, Jenna thought. *Oh, much too long.* She watched Hallie's face relax as the contraction passed; pain turned to fear.

"I'm scared, Miss," Hallie whispered.

"Don't be," Jenna said. "We're going to stay with you through this."

Another contraction gripped the woman, and she bared her teeth from the pain of it. Jenna waited for it to pass, then slid her hand into Hallie's body as gently as she could. She found what she'd feared the most: a breech birth and one not going well. Hallie was exhausted from her long labor, so much so that she might not have the strength to endure the coming ordeal.

Jenna settled the woman as comfortably as possible. "Let's get some fresh air," she said.

Both men followed her out. She took a deep breath, then another, and met Ben's fearful gaze. "The child is coming out feet first," she said. "But one foot is twisted up in the womb, preventing it from coming any farther. If it is to be born, I'll have to push the child back into the womb and then turn it."

Ben opened his mouth to answer, but she held up her hand to stop him. "There are risks, Ben. I've seen this done, but I've never done it myself. I don't know if I can save the baby . . . we may lose them both."

"I trust you, Lady. You have the power."

She shook her head, desperate to make him understand the risks. Dread laid a cold hand on her heart. If she did this, she'd be responsible for Hallie's life in a way few people ever were; if she guessed wrong, pushed too lightly or too hard, she might lose both lives. "Ben, I—"

"I love her," he said, as though that answered everything.

Perhaps it did. With tears stinging the back of her eyelids, Jenna reached out and put her hand on his shoulder.

"Wait," Alan said. "I'll send someone to fetch the doctor."

Turning, Jenna looked up into his taut face. "It will take hours to go to town and back. Hallie doesn't have hours."

"Suh," Ben said, "We got to trust the Lady. She got the power."

"Power!" Alan snapped. "What power?"

"The power of healin'." Ben's shoulders were square, his face serene with the sureness of his belief. "The Lord give her the way of it; it's in her heart and her hands, better than any book-learnin'. If anybody can save my Hallie, she kin. Please, suh."

Astonishment swept through Alan as he realized Ben was asking for his permission. Why? Because he was the master. All of them, Ben and Hallie and the unborn child, were his property. No matter what they wanted, the decision was his. By right of ownership.

With a swift, hot rush of anger, Alan rejected it. "She's your wife. You're the only one who can decide."

The man drew in a sharp breath. "Then I choose the Lady."

"Very well," Jenna said, all business now. "Ben, get the kettle on to boil. As soon as Opal gets here with—"

"Here, miss."

The cook seemed almost to materialize out of the darkness. Jenna took her by the arm and drew her into the cabin. Alan followed, feeling helpless and frustrated with it.

He watched Jenna work. Her hands were steady, her face serene with a self-confidence that seemed to fill the room. She directed Ben and Opal in a quiet voice, asking once for more light, once for Ben to shift Hallie to a more comfortable position.

"Hallie," she said, leaning over to wipe the pain-stricken woman's face with a wet cloth. "Here's the problem. Your baby is stuck just now, and I'm going to have to move him around a bit so that he can be born."

Tears of pain and fear glittered in Hallie's eyes. But a trace of hope came into them, too. "Can it be done?"

"Anything can be done," Jenna said. "You have to believe that, and hold onto it very tightly. See, I'll have to hurt you, and you're going to have to trust me enough to let me do it."

The woman nodded. Suddenly her face crumpled as the terrible pain overcame her again. Jenna waited it out with her, gazing into her eyes as though giving her strength to endure it.

"Lady," Hallie gasped when it was over. "I trust you."

"Thank you." Jenna turned away to wash her hands in hot, soapy water. "Ben," she said. "Alan. Hold her."

Alan obeyed, moving to Hallie's left side when Ben took the right. He could feel the woman trembling beneath his hands. Life or death—in a few moments more, one or the other would be hers. He was certain the child was lost already. The intensity of what was happening made the air seem thick and cloying.

Then he saw Jenna watching him. For a moment her eyes looked like clear green pools, and he felt as though he could see straight into her soul. He saw fear there but also a commitment that was fine and sure.

For the first time, he understood the enormity of the

responsibility she'd taken. Of her free will, she'd accepted the weight of two lives. *Because she is a healer, and a healer . . . heals.*

With that understanding came the realization that she needed something from him. Not strength, precisely, for she had that in abundance. Perhaps it was the understanding itself that she needed. He didn't care; just now, he'd have handed her his soul had she asked it of him.

So he smiled at her, a smile as calm and assured as her manner. And she smiled back, accepting his gift, and the faint shadow of fear left her eyes. His chest tightened with emotion he didn't dare show—or dare examine too closely.

"Opal, her arms," Jenna said quietly.

The cook leaned over Hattie's chest, obscuring Alan's view of Jenna. "Ready," she said.

Hallie bucked against their restraining hands. A shriek ripped from her, a sound of such incredible agony that Alan closed his eyes against it. She bucked again, screamed again. A third time.

"Now push," Jenna said.

Hallie groaned, a low, animal sound of effort.

"Again."

"I can't," Hallie whimpered. "I'm so . . . tired."

"Push!" It was a command, sharp and imperative.

The woman groaned again. Her voice rose to a wail. No, Alan thought, opening his eyes. That wasn't Hallie; it was an infant's cry. Joy surged through him, a wild rushing tide of it that was almost painful.

"Praise the Lord!" Opal cried. "It's a boy!"

Hallie began to cry. Ben wiped the tears from her face and bent to kiss her.

"We got us a son," he murmured.

Jenna brought the baby to Hallie. The slave woman

hadn't the strength to hold her son, so Ben wrapped his arm around his wife and held them both. Alan watched the other man's face, seeing the pride and joy, the vast relief of tragedy averted. And then he looked at Jenna, who had accomplished this, and his heart beat so hard and fast he felt as though it might come straight out of his chest.

Jenna caught Alan watching her. She found herself smiling at him, responding to the reckless delight in his eyes. She was glad she could share it with him and glad he'd shared the fight that had gone before.

"Thank you," she said.

"You're welcome."

She tried to look away but couldn't. "You'd better get back to your guests."

"I'd rather wait for you."

"I'm spending the night here," she said. "I'm needed."

He strode to her. His hand trembled as he tucked a stray curl back behind her ear. "There are times when it's a comfort to be held in another person's arms."

Jenna could hardly breathe. "Is this one of those times?"

"For me, it is."

She moved closer. Winding her arms around his waist, she pressed her cheek to the crisp fabric of his shirt. His hands were hard and warm upon her back as he held her, just held her. Time seemed suspended, the world held at bay by the strong, steady beat of his heart. He drew a breath that was almost a shudder.

Then he stepped back, his eyes dark and fathomless with a stormwind of emotion. Without a word, he left her, striding out into the darkness.

She stared after him, as shaken as he.

* * *

The first violet streaks of dawn were staining the sky when Jenna returned to the house. She slipped through the quiet rooms, intending to go straight upstairs. But a sound drew her to the study, where she found Alan sprawled upon the sofa.

She paused in the doorway, watching him as he slept. His body lost none of its power in repose; rather, he looked like a great cat, relaxed now but able to spring into coiled action whenever necessary. The faint light cast shadows across his high cheekbones and highlighted the lean firmness of his chin.

Perhaps it was exhaustion, perhaps simple lack of will, but she found herself walking toward him.

His eyes opened. She stopped, but the time for flight had passed. "Good morning," he said.

"You were waiting for me?"

"Of course."

Of course. Inside, she trembled.

"How is Hallie?" he asked.

"She's doing well.

He sat up, then rose swiftly to his feet in a powerful, lithe movement. "And the child?"

"A strong babe for all he's been through."

"I'm glad of it."

Jenna's pulse pounded wildly as she watched him come toward her. His eyes were dark, unfathomable, and she felt as though she were about to fall into them.

"You're no witch," he said.

She blinked, disconcerted by the unexpected statement. "Ask that of your neighbors," she said at last. "And see what they say."

"I don't care what they say. I don't care what anyone says, because I looked into your eyes when you prepared to take that woman's life into your hands, and I saw the truth."

"Truth can be a changeable thing."

"No," he said. "Truth never changes. You were afraid last night, Jenna."

She opened her mouth to speak, but he shook his head, denying her. "You had no special powers," he said. "Only your hands and your caring, and your willingness to take two lives upon your soul."

She closed her eyes. He knew. He truly understood what she'd felt, the uncertainty, the terrible fear of being wrong and having Hallie and the baby pay the price for it.

"No wonder they bow to you," he said.

"They bow to the witch."

He shook his head. "They bow to the woman."

Hot tears spilled out. She had no control over them; she hardly even felt the wetness on her cheeks. Tears for her enemy, this man who stretched her heart ten different ways, tears for the curse she couldn't undo.

Alan reached out and caught one of those crystal droplets on his finger. "Why are you crying?"

"I . . ." She took a deep breath. "That was a fine thing you did last night, giving the decision to Ben."

"It was never my decision."

"Again, you should ask your neighbors. I think they'd disagree. After all, you own Ben and Hallie. You own the labor of their hands and even their children."

"You make it sound damned ugly."

"It is ugly." She reached out, almost touched him, then curled her hand into a fist and let it fall back to her side. "I learned something last night. You taught me that there can be beauty even in ugliness, kindness within the tragedy that is slavery. Last night, you gave Ben his rights as a husband and as a man. He will never forget it. Nor will I."

"Jenna—"

"Please, let me finish," she said, compelled to tell him the thoughts that had consumed her during those long, quiet hours spent watching Hallie sleep. "You made me realize that I've been guilty of the same blind prejudices I accused the townsfolk of having. Just as they were, I was raised to hate. But perhaps you're right. Perhaps I, too, can learn to set aside what I was told and try to see them not as enemies but as people."

"Ah, Jenna. You humble me." He moved closer, close enough to touch if he were permitted, close enough to smell the faint scent of honeysuckle that still clung to her skin. Reaching up, he pulled the pins from her hair. It cascaded over his hand and wrist in a silken flood, as pale and lovely as sea foam.

His need for her was as raw and earthy as nature itself, a wild clamor of the senses that brought his body to the edge of tightly held control. But his soul also hungered for her, wanting to dive into the fiery well of her spirit and never come up again.

"Jenna," he whispered. "I need you."

She couldn't move, couldn't breathe. Her ears thundered with a wild heartbeat, but she couldn't tell if it was hers or his. A strange languor overcame her even as heavy, liquid desire coiled in the depths of her belly. At that moment, she truly didn't know if she would have held him to his promise or begged him for what they both wanted so badly.

Suddenly he lifted his head. Frustration etched a line

between his brows, and he muttered a curse that echoed the unrequited ache in her body.

"Someone's coming," he said, moving away from her.

A moment later Beth appeared in the doorway. She was wearing her nightclothes still, and her hair was sleep-tousled. Alan went to her and swung her into his arms.

"What's the matter, sweet? Did you have a bad dream?"

She nodded. Sliding her thumb into her mouth, she regarded her father with wide eyes.

"Wasn't Dorcas up?" he asked.

Pulling her thumb out with an audible pop, Beth shook her head. "I wanted you. You weren't in your room, an' then I came downstairs to look for you."

"Well, you've found me. Does the dream seem so very bad now?"

She shook her head.

"Then I'll take you back to bed, and you can wait for a nice dream to come."

"I want to stay with you."

"I'm sorry, sweet, but I've got to leave in a few minutes to meet Mr. Porter and Mr. Graeme in town."

The thumb went back in, and a stubborn look crept into Beth's eyes.

"And then I'm going to buy that gray mare I promised you. Won't that be fun?" he asked.

No answer.

"You begged me for a horse of your own, sweet," he said, truly desperate now. "I have to go; it's all arranged."

Still no answer.

Jenna couldn't help but smile, thinking how like the daughter was to the father. *She'll lead him a fine dance when she's older.* Jon would be a high-spirited fellow, but he was straight and solid and would carry his responsibilities well. Beth, now . . . Beth would singe the world with her flaming spirit, and God help the man who tried to tame her.

But, as a charitable soul, she decided to go to Alan's rescue. "I'm just on my way upstairs for a nap, Beth," she said. "Would you like to lie down with me for a while? I promise to keep all the bad dreams away."

Without a word, Beth held out her arms. When Jenna took her, feeling that small, warm cheek nestle trustingly against her shoulder, another sort of ache came into being inside her. Raised by Roanna never to make her mother's mistakes, she hadn't thought to have a child of her own.

But now she wondered if that lesson had been as flawed as the one of hatred. Somehow, she didn't think Silvan would have considered her child a mistake, even at the price of her life.

"Don't worry about her," she told Alan. "She'll be safe with me."

Before leaving, Alan went upstairs to see how Beth and Jenna were faring. He found the door unlocked. Softly, he unlatched it and pushed it open.

They were both asleep. Side by side, a dark-haired angel and an angel of moonlight. Jenna wore only her chemise and petticoat, and a shaft of morning light slanted across her face and breast, limning her with gold. Faint violet smudges marked the skin beneath her eyes, making her look fragile and very lovely.

She turned onto her side. The petticoat draped itself alluringly over the flare of her hip and long, slender legs.

Sweat broke out on his forehead as he saw how tightly her chemise was drawn over her breasts.

His imagination ran wild, carrying his body with it. He was possessed with a desire so powerful he shook with it, his manhood rising so hard beneath his trousers that it was painful. He clenched his fists. Like a starving man denied the banquet, he studied her, his gaze moving possessively over satin curves and tantalizing hollows. His body in torment, his heart aching with loneliness. Denied, he could only look.

Watching her, needing her, beset and bereft.

It was then that he knew how far he'd fallen: had his daughter not been there, he would have taken Jenna. He would have forgotten his promise, ignored her if she'd reminded him. There would be only the two of them, a man and a woman and the delights they could create between them.

He would have taken her, pleasured her, possessed her completely, and the devil with the consequences. It was a staggering revelation to a man who'd lived his life under the rules of honor and the order of reason.

He wanted her. Beyond honor, beyond reason, he wanted her.

Somehow he found the strength to leave the room. Closing the door, he laid his forehead against the smooth coolness of the wood until some semblance of control returned to him. Then he turned away, his determination strengthened by the torment of his heart. He *would* have her. For the desire ran both ways. Male and female, townsman and wood sprite, they'd both been trapped by passion.

If this was his curse, so be it. For it was also hers.

Thirteen

Jenna and Dorcas walked along the edge of Heronsgate land, keeping a watch over the children who were exploring a short distance ahead.

"I must admit," Dorcas said a bit breathlessly, "that you look very comfortable in your trousers."

"They're the only practical thing for the outdoors."

"Being young helps, too," the nanny said. "I'm heaving along like a tired old horse, while you're not the least bit out of breath even though you're carrying the basket and everything else."

"As Miranda Carrew would say, savages never get tired."

"Humph. Miranda's got a tongue . . . Never mind. It's not my place to talk about my betters."

Jenna turned to look fully at her. "I'd hardly consider Miranda your better." Raising her voice, she called, "Jon! Beth! Here's the spot for our picnic."

"This *is* nice," Dorcas said.

Smiling, Jenna surveyed the spot she'd discovered earlier this morning. A huge old poplar spread thick shade upon the grass below, offering an attractive haven on this hot, humid August day. Late-summer flowers carpeted the ground, tossing their bright heads in the sultry breeze.

Jon and Beth came running back, faces glowing with

youth and exertion. They helped spread the cloth and set the dishes and tableware out for the picnic.

"What did Opal give us?" Jon asked, always practical.

"Let's see." Jenna delved into the heavy, cloth-covered basket. "We've got chicken and ham, corn and squash from the garden, and fresh, hot biscuits."

"Oh, look, there's Father," Beth said, pointing back toward the house.

Jenna stilled the sudden trembling of her hands as she saw Alan riding toward them on a big chestnut stallion. He rode as if he'd been born to the saddle, his hands easy and sure on the reins, his wide shoulders and wind-blown hair making him seem like some barbarian prince. A disturbing image, that one; he looked very much the conqueror. The closer he got, the faster her heart pounded. To hide her discomfiture, she busied herself setting out the food.

"Father, Father!" Beth cried. "Have you come to picnic with us?"

"After a morning talking about cotton, cotton and more cotton, I can think of nothing I'd rather do," he said, swinging easily down from the saddle. Knotting the reins to shorten them, he let the horse wander free. "Go, Hector. Amuse yourself."

Jenna watched the beautiful animal amble away, pausing from time to time to crop the vegetation at his feet. Then she frowned. "Alan, don't let him go that way. That area beneath the pines is full of jimsonweed. It might make him sick."

He whistled sharply. The stallion raised his head and whickered, then came trotting back toward his master. Alan tied him to the trunk of a nearby tree, giving him enough slack to graze but not enough to get in trouble.

"Thank you," he said, striding back to Jenna. "Jameson Graeme mentioned that he'd had some cattle fall mysteriously ill lately. Could this jimsonweed be the cause?"

"Perhaps. Years ago, my grandmother tried to tell them of the danger, but—"

"No one believed the witch."

"Or they believed the witch bespelled the animals herself and wanted to shift the blame. Ignorance, all of it. 'Tis strange that my medicines are called witchery, while some of the most useless concoctions—like drinking the sap of the bull nettle for potency—are considered wisdom."

"What's potency, Father?" Beth asked.

"It's something to do with your liver," he said without hesitation.

He hadn't looked away from Jenna and was rewarded by the look of consternation on her face. Innocent that she was, she hadn't considered the effect of her words. Then he saw amusement dawn in her eyes and hoped that sparkling warmth was tribute to his quick lie.

"How can you make medicine from plants?" Jon asked. "Do you use the leaves or flowers?"

Jenna smiled at him. "It depends on the plant, little man. Sometimes I use the root, sometimes the leaves and flowers. There are times when it's the bark that's useful. So many plants can be helpful if you know how to use them. Do you see that tree over there?" When he nodded, she continued, "That's a sweet gum. If you chew the twigs of that tree, you'll have good teeth all your life. Or boil Justice's weed to make a decoction for ague. Holly root tea helps a cough, Cherokee root is good for hives. Your father," she glanced at Alan, gauging his reaction, "knows well the usefulness of snakeroot."

"And I can also verify that it tastes as horrible as any medicine concocted by modern science," he said.

Jenna ignored him. "Many plants are useful as food. The root of the morning glory can be eaten, and the young shoots of the plant you know as smilax are very tasty."

"What I want to know," Alan said, "is how you always manage to smell of honeysuckle."

"No witchcraft there, either. I merely bathe with soap-root mixed with dried and powdered honeysuckle blossoms."

"Why honeysuckle?" Jon asked.

She smiled. "Because I like the smell."

Then she glanced at Alan. She froze, the stillness of her hands and body masking the sudden stutter of her heart. Something very intense had come into his eyes, and for a moment she was afraid she'd fall into those swirling blue depths and never come out again.

"Don't you get lonely living out there in the swamp with no one to talk to?" Jon asked.

It should have been a distraction but wasn't; Jenna couldn't seem to tear her gaze away from Alan's. "Yes," she said. "I get lonely sometimes."

"You know us now," Beth said. "We're your friends. You can visit us any time you like."

Dorcas frowned. "Beth, it's not your place—"

"She's right," Alan said, the intimacy of his voice running in a wave up Jenna's spine. "You're always welcome at Heronsgate."

Jenna looked away, her throat tight with emotion. Friends. During her childhood, growing up in Roanna's steady but rather grim care, she'd yearned for a friend. During that time when she'd blossomed into womanhood and wondered about the mysteries of men and women and love, she'd wanted one friend to confide in.

And now, when she'd given up being anything but the White Lady—hated by the townsfolk, revered and feared by the slaves, but always lonely—she'd stumbled into friendship. How had this happened? Why had this happened? Of all the people in the world, why these?

For the first time, she truly understood the tragedy of hate that had shaped all their lives. The curse didn't discern guilt or innocence or the worth of its victims; it merely was. It had struck down Orwell and his sons. Like a great, mindless killing machine, it would take Alan, and it would take his children.

Unless I find a way to stop it.

Impossible, Roanna had said. The curse was as inevitable as winter turning to spring, as unstoppable as the wind. Jenna watched Alan reach out to rumple his son's hair in a gesture rife with tenderness, and her heart turned over in her chest.

Lost in her thoughts, she absently accepted the plate Dorcas handed to her. She ate even more absently, her gaze lingering on Alan's strong, long-fingered hands as he spread blackberry jam on a pale, flaky biscuit.

He smiled at her, his gaze gentle and knowing, then spread his arms in an expansive gesture of content. "Truly, I'm a fortunate man," he said.

" 'Fortune makes a fool of him whom she flatters too much'," Dorcas quoted.

He laughed. "Perhaps. But that means it's all the more important to enjoy her favor while it lasts."

"Whose favor?" Jon asked.

"Fortune," Alan said. "Her majesty, Lady Luck. Our Jenna, now, doesn't believe in luck, only destiny."

Our Jenna. She shied away from the implications of that statement—and her reaction to it. "Luck isn't trustworthy," she said.

"Is destiny?" Alan asked.

She scowled at him. "You've been spending too much time with the Graemes."

He grinned at her, that impudent, wily smile that never failed to send heat surging through her. She felt too vulnerable just now, beset with the urgings of body and heart to the point that it was hard to think clearly when he was near.

"Who's that man?" Jon asked, pointing toward the pines.

Startled, Jenna turned and peered into the clustered trees. After a moment, she made out the figure of a man half-hidden among the trunks. He moved toward her then, walking with a loose-limbed stride that looked strangely familiar. "Jonas Rafferty," she said, placing him at last.

"Jon, take your sister over there to pick flowers," Alan said.

"But—"

"Stay where we can see you."

"Yes, Father." Jon's reluctance was obvious. But he took Beth by the hand and led her away, saying, "Let's see who can pick the most, Pudge. Winner gets an extra serving of pie."

The sun glinted off the barrel of Jonas Rafferty's flintlock as he walked out from under the trees. Jenna gathered herself, ready to run, but Alan grasped her arm and held her still.

"Steady," he said.

"He'll only cause trouble," she whispered.

A wolf could have envied Alan's smile. "This is my

world, remember? To use your own words, here he's a swamp rat and I'm the master of Heronsgate." His grip tightened slightly. "Let me handle this, Jenna."

She looked deep into his eyes. Slowly, her gaze still locked with his, she nodded. She couldn't help it, any more than she could help the leap of her heart when he smiled at her. Or the feeling of loss when he let go of her.

He rose to his feet as Rafferty approached. The slave hunter's eyes looked like hard blue pebbles amid a nesting of weathered skin. His gaze slid over Jenna with insulting slowness, then came to rest on Alan.

"What are you doing here, Rafferty?" Alan asked.

"I heered you had the witch stayin' with you," he said. "I jest had to see for myself."

Alan crossed his arms over his chest and leaned against the trunk behind him, but the tautness of his body belied his casual pose. "There's no such thing as a witch. That's ignorant superstition."

"You better live here more'n a couple of months afore you talk about ignorance, Englishman. We'uns have been livin' with one Llewellyn witch or another for nigh fifty years, and we know what they are and what they do. And folks don't like you bringin' her among us."

"Were you sent as their delegate to tell me?" Alan asked, his voice deceptively gentle.

"A wise man would heed the warning."

Alan's brows went up. "Warning?"

"We ain't about to tolerate a witch among us."

"No?" Five hundred years of privilege came rushing through on the heels of Alan's outrage. His anger turned cold, and so did his voice; a man who knew him better would have walked away then, while he had the chance. "And what will you do about it?"

"She's got you wound up tight as a tick, don't she?" Rafferty showed his stained teeth in a sneer. "All them Llewellyns have been good to look at, always drew the men like bees to honey. Beauty on the outside, Englishman, but their hearts are black as Satan's."

Jenna's temper flared. She'd had enough of this man. He made his living on the suffering of others; how dare he accuse her of having a black heart? She rose to her feet, facing Rafferty's hate with fiery disdain. "If I'm so dangerous, why do you dare stand here and insult me? Let's see, perhaps I could give you scabies to go with your lice, or perhaps shrivel your manhood—"

"Jenna, please!" Dorcas gasped.

"—if it weren't already—"

"Jenna!" Alan snapped.

She ignored him, instead closing the distance between her and Rafferty. "Remember, slave hunter, that whenever you walk in the swamp, you walk in my territory. A man could get swallowed up in there and never be seen again."

A shadow of fear came into his eyes, but it only intensified the blazing hatred already there. Suddenly, without warning, he struck at her. Jenna was caught off guard, unable to react quickly enough to get out of the way. Then Alan reached past her, his hand moving faster than she would have believed possible, and closed over Rafferty's fist, stopping it in midair. The flintlock fell to the ground with a clatter.

Muscles flexing, the two men strained against each other. Rafferty's teeth were bared, his face gleaming with sweat. Alan's mouth was set in a grim line, his eyes glittering with rage. Slowly, inevitably, he forced the slave trader's arm back. And still more. Rafferty's face creased with the pain of it, and finally he sank to his knees.

"If you so much as touch her, I'll kill you," Alan growled.

"You're a fool," Rafferty gasped. "Your mind's been turned by her spells—"

"Damn you." Alan increased the pressure still more.

"You're the one damned! She'll drain your soul and laugh while she's doin' it."

"Enough!"

Jenna stared at him, shocked by the barely leashed savagery in his voice. She realized the full depth of his anger and that Rafferty was in real danger. "Alan—"

"Stay out of this!" he blazed.

"I can't." She stepped forward and put her hand on his arm. "Please. Before you do something you'll regret."

"He tried to hit you."

"There are many in town who think the way he does and who would say and do the same things. You can't fight them all, and even if you could, would that stop them from hating?"

He looked at her for a long, frozen moment. A muscle twitched at the corner of his jaw. Then, with a muttered curse, he let Rafferty go.

Cradling his right arm against his body, the slave trader slowly rose to his feet. "You'll be sorry," he snarled.

Alan bent and picked the flintlock from the ground. With smooth, expert motions, he flipped open the cover of the priming pan and knocked the powder out. Then he tossed the weapon back to its owner.

"You're on Heronsgate land," he said. "Get off. If I find you here again, you're a dead man."

"Like a snake," Rafferty said, backing away. "Mark my words, Englishman. She'll turn on you.

Alan lunged forward. Jenna flung herself against him,

trying to hold him back. He could have tossed her aside easily, but as his hands settled on her shoulders, the violence suddenly drained from his eyes.

"You may regret stopping me," he said, curving his fingers possessively over her shoulders.

"You would have regretted it more had I not," she replied. "In a day or so I'll go back to the swamp. But you have to live among these people."

"I don't give a damn what they think."

"Well, you should," Dorcas said from behind him. "If you alienate your neighbors, it's the children who will suffer. Jon and Beth are young now, willing to let us be their world. But in a few years, they'll need more. Who will be their friends if they're ostracized by the community? Who will they marry?"

"I don't—"

"Stop." Jenna laid her fingers across his mouth, determined to make him understand the price he would pay for befriending her. "Years ago, my grandmother said much the same thing. Roanna is . . . was a very strong-minded woman. She ignored the rumors, ignored the dark looks and the conversations that died away when she came near. But hate is a heavy burden. Even she was driven away in time."

"But yet she bore your mother, and your mother bore you," he said.

"As Rafferty told you, we draw the men."

"Don't say that again."

His hands tightened. Not enough to hurt but enough that she knew the anger her words had caused. She tilted her head back to look more fully at him. "How do you know it isn't true?"

"I know," he said.

Certainty filled his eyes. She stared at him, shaken by his faith. He had no reason to trust her, but he did. It filled her with joy, a glorious bursting warmth that was almost too big to be held. His eyes reflected that warmth, turned it molten and cast it back to her. She felt her limbs weakening, as though her very bones had begun to melt. Her gaze dropped to his mouth. A sweet, aching hunger pooled in her belly, fueled by the desire she saw in him.

He held her a moment more. Then, slowly, he relaxed his grasp on her shoulders. Released from the haze of desire that had held her more securely than his hands, she went back to sit with Dorcas.

"I won, I won!" Beth cried, her pantalettes flashing as she ran toward them. She dumped an armload of flowers into Dorcas's lap. "I get an extra piece of pie."

Jon came to a halt in front of Jenna. Shyly, he held out a bouquet of flowers. "For you," he said.

"Thank you, little man." She brought them to her nose to savor their sweet scent. Then, smiling, she wove them into a crown and placed it on her head.

"Oh, it's lovely," Beth breathed. "Will you make me one, too?"

Jenna obeyed, placing the bright wreath upon the child's dark hair. Then, at Beth's order, she made a third for Dorcas, who submitted with good grace.

"What do you think, Father?" Beth asked, tossing her head to make the blossoms swing.

Alan looked at Jenna, who wore her flowery diadem with a queen's pride. A pair of dragonflies came darting around her head, their iridescent wings less brilliant than her clear green eyes. "I think Jon and I have become surrounded with fairies. What do you think, my son?"

Jon put his head to one side. "Two lady fairies and one small troll."

"Oh, you!" Beth tossed a buttercup at him.

Jenna, thinking that Alan would be watching his children, risked at glance at him. But he was staring at her, such heat and longing in his gaze that she began to tremble. She turned away from it, lest she fall into his arms in front of Dorcas and the children. Lest she beg him to hold her, touch her, despite all consequences.

And he knew. One corner of his mouth quirked upward, and his heavy-lidded gaze dropped to her mouth. Nervously, she licked her lips, then froze as she saw his hands tighten into fists.

"Who wants pie?" Dorcas asked, evidently unaware of the heavy tension.

"Two pieces," Beth demanded.

"Would you like some, Jenna?" the nanny asked.

"Yes," she replied, unknowing whether she were asking for pie or for the moon itself.

She took the plate Dorcas offered, feeling as though she'd fallen out of time; she ate blackberry pie and drank tea, even allowed herself to be persuaded to tell the story of Grandaddy Catfish once again. But inside, she was beset by something momentous and powerful.

She had to save this man and his children. Somehow she had to find a way to stop what could not be stopped, to make the impossible possible.

For their sakes, but also for hers.

Fourteen

Jenna spun in the grip of a nightmare, unable to chart the course of her own motion. It was as though she'd become a leaf on the breeze, carried along a path of another's choosing.

She heard a woman cry out, her voice harsh with anguish, and knew it was Roanna. *Silvan! Oh, my daughter, what have they done to you?*

The mist parted, and she saw her grandmother facing Orwell Stepton. Roanna was younger now, straighter, and her face was alight with terrible purpose. She raised her hand to point at Stepton, and then she cursed him. He and all his kin, doomed.

The mist swirled, hiding Roanna, then parted again, showing Jenna another scene. A carriage careened down the road, piloted by the Stepton boys, drunk and wild as they always were. Thunder crashed overhead suddenly, and the already skittish horse bolted, slamming the carriage into a tree.

She saw Orwell on his deathbed, his face congealed in a rictus of agony. The curse fulfilled; father and sons, all the masters of Heronsgate.

And then she saw Alan, his eyes alight with mischief as he smiled down at his children. She reached out to him, yearning. But the mist rose between her and them and slowly took them from her sight.

Noooo! The dream-Jenna cried. *Not them!*

Terror wrenched her from sleep. She found herself sitting up, her nightgown torn as she'd struggled against the dream. Her chest heaved as though she'd been running, and her hair straggled in a wild cloud around her shoulders.

Tears spilled out, running down her cheeks in a hot flood. Sobs tore through her, painful and hard, and she felt as though they'd rip her asunder. Stripping the torn nightgown up and over her head, she balled it between her hands and buried her face against it.

"Please," she moaned. "Don't let it happen."

Suddenly her door was thrown open. Light spilled into the room, silhouetting Alan's broad-shouldered shape in the doorway. Wildly, she snatched the bedclothes up to her chin. She stared at him, half-blinded by the sudden illumination.

"I heard you crying," he said.

"I . . . never cry."

He came in, closing the door behind him. "You were crying."

"No, I—"

With a suddenness that took her breath away, he opened the curtains over the north window, flooding the room with moonlight. Then he sat on the edge of the bed beside her, his face stark and tight-drawn in the pale light. His eyes were in shadow, hiding his thoughts from her.

"There are tears on your cheeks," he said.

She looked away, pulling the covers still higher. " 'Twas a dream, that's all."

"Tell me about it."

"I . . ." Her voice quavered for a moment before she got it under control. "It was about the curse. I saw too many deaths and too much hate. And I saw you."

He drew in his breath sharply. "Go on."

"I was so afraid." The words began to spill out of her, fear and longing pouring them out in a flood. "I don't want anything to happen to you or your children, but I don't know how to stop it. It just goes on and on and takes and takes, even the innocent, and I have to find a way to stop it before—"

"Shhhh." He cupped her cheeks between his hands, a gesture so tender that it brought fresh tears to her eyes. "Jenna—"

"It's like trying to stop the sea or the wind," she sobbed. "I haven't the skills to break it, but if I don't . . ." She broke off with a gasp when he lifted her into his lap.

Alan had meant only to comfort her. But he found himself with an armful of satiny naked Jenna, and was lost. Mind, soul, and manhood surged to urgent life, and rational thought whirled away on a stormwind of desire.

She tried to cover herself with her hands, but he shook his head.

"I want to look at you," he said.

Jenna gazed into his eyes and saw the raging fever there. Recklessness soared through her, deep and powerful, inevitable as the dawn. She let her hands fall to her sides.

"You're beautiful," he said, his voice reverent.

He looked at her slowly, hungrily. She was everything he'd imagined and more. Her breasts were full and high, the coral nipples already taut as though begging his touch. Her legs were incredibly long and graceful, her waist slender, her belly curving gently down to the pale thatch covering her womanhood. He'd never felt like this before. Never felt these staggering, almost violent emotions, the desire so powerful it felt like fate.

"This is destiny," he said. "Yours and mine, Jenna." His voice hardened suddenly. "And if it weren't, I'd find a way to make it so."

"You can't change destiny," she whispered.

"Nor can you."

Nor can I. She closed her eyes as his breath feathered over her temple and cheek, then brushed across her lips. He smelled of mint and brandy and desire.

"You say the curse was forged by hate," he said.

She opened her eyes. "Yes."

"But love is stronger than hate. Perhaps with our loving, we can break those bonds."

Love, she thought. Love. Was this it? This aching, bittersweet longing, this need to lose herself in him? God, she hoped so. "Even if it doesn't," she said, her heart beating frantically, "you said this was our destiny."

"From the moment we met."

If anything felt like destiny, this did. Jenna waited for doubt, for fear, but all she felt was rightness. And desire. This was her time—their time—and he was the only man who could ever touch her in this powerful way. Now, at last, she could understand her mother. Silvan had loved Rene Broussard; she had treasured their time together and the child who had come of it. And she hadn't regretted any of it. Of that, Jenna was very sure.

And now she knew: whatever came of it, tonight was hers. A special night. She looked at Alan, absorbing the lean male beauty of his face, the tenderness and need in his eyes.

He held out his hand. Trusting him, she placed hers in it.

She expected him to kiss her. Instead, he took her hand and brushed her own fingers over her lips. Startled by the sensation, she drew in her breath sharply. He smiled down at her, his eyes hot and urgent, his movements languid. Slowly, he slid her hand lower over the curve of her breast.

"Oh," she said, shivering.

"You're not afraid, are you?" he murmured. "There can be much gentleness between men and women, much pleasure."

He moved her hand lower still, bringing a trail of goose-bumps along her ribs and belly. She could feel his manhood beneath her buttocks, a brand that seared her even through his trousers. A wild tide of passion swept through her, bringing with it a throbbing ache and a rush of wetness between her legs. Mindlessly, she shifted to feel him better.

His eyes darkened. "Tell me."

Jenna let her head fall back against his arm as he slid her hand along the inside of her thigh. Lightly, teasingly, but oh, bringing unbelievable pleasure with it.

"Tell me," he said again.

"Tell you what?"

At that moment, he brought her hand to her throbbing woman's flesh, slid her fingertips in a trail of fire across velvet skin. She cried out, her hips bucking in response. But she wanted more. She wanted *him* to touch her. She wanted his hands, his mouth, his body.

"Please, Alan!" she gasped.

"Release me from my promise, Jenna. But before you do . . ." Gazing deeply into her eyes, he brought her hand to his mouth. She moaned sharply as he licked her essence from her fingers. "Before you do, remember that you can never take it back. Nothing on this earth can force me to make that vow again."

She was lost, lost. "I release you. Touch me, Alan."

"Ahhh, Jenna!"

He bore her down to the bed, his mouth claiming hers in a kiss that was savage and possessive and tender all at once. She gave herself up to it, moaning as he nibbled at her lips with gentle aggression, then delved deep into her mouth. A kind of fever settled in her, wild heat and yearning that only he could assuage. It was as though she'd been cast adrift on a sea of desire, bound for a destination to which only he could take her.

She ran her hands up the muscular length of his arms and along his shoulders, then explored the long, strong line of his back. Caught by a sudden fierce surge of desire, she sank her fingers into the thick hair at the nape of his neck. He shuddered.

"It seems like I've wanted you forever," he whispered. "Woman of moonlight, wood sprite—"

"No," she said, laying her hand over his mouth. "None of that. I'm only a woman. That's all I ever was, all I ever want to be."

"Then I'll worship you as a man." He drew her finger into his mouth, laving the sensitive tip with his tongue. "And we'll find the magic together."

A tear slid from the corner of her eye. Alan leaned forward and caught the droplet on his tongue.

"Why?" he asked.

"Because you make me feel beautiful," she said. "Because I've never felt like this before."

He smiled. Then he ran his forefinger down the slim

line of her nose and traced the fullness of her mouth. She parted her lips, taking his fingertip into her mouth the way he'd done hers. A flame leaped in his eyes—the heat of desire barely held in check. But it was a two-edged sword, this sultry play; her own passion surged as she watched the planes of his face tighten.

Slowly, he traced a line down her throat, lingering for a moment in the hollow at the base, then moved lower to the upper slope of her breast. She waited, breath suspended, her flesh seeming to swell beneath his touch. Then he circled her nipple, causing it to tighten into a hard little bud. A gasp escaped her, and she arched upward.

"Did you like that?" he murmured, knowing the answer.

"Do it again." It was only half a plea.

He obeyed. And again, reveling in her response. He'd never known such fire; something deep within him understood that he'd never know it in another woman. Only this one. His Jenna.

"More," she whispered. "Show me what to do."

"I'll show you everything," he promised.

Jenna sighed as he claimed her mouth again. It was a hard, intemperate kiss, but not an impatient one. She met him eagerly, her tongue playing with his, arching beneath him as he stroked her nipples with his thumbs.

He broke the kiss to run his open mouth along her throat and lower. She cried out when his tongue touched her nipple, coaxing it to tighten even more. Then he began to suckle. Something fierce and abandoned bloomed inside her, and she thrust herself up to meet his mouth. He turned his attention to her other breast, then back again and again until she was writhing beneath him.

Frantic to feel his skin against hers, she plucked at

the buttons of his shirt. He lifted himself with an impatient sound, stripping the garment off and tossing it away. She stopped him when he would have lain down again.

"I want to touch you," she said.

"I'm yours, my lovely wood sprite."

Her hands trembled as she explored the hard planes of his chest. Steel sheathed in satin skin, she thought, reveling in the power of him. She drew her breath in sharply as his flat male nipples stiffened beneath her hands, pleased that she had the same effect on him. His abdomen was ridged with muscle, taut with tight-held passion. She paused at his waist, her palm flat on the line of hair that arrowed beneath his trousers.

"Go on," he rasped, his eyes narrowed to slits. "You know you want to."

She did. Oh, she did. He was rock hard, frightening and compelling at the same time. She traced the length of him through the trousers, fascinated by the springing strength of him.

"Ah, Jenna." He took her hand from him, raising it to his mouth and kissing it. "I find I want you, too much. Later, you can touch me to your heart's content. Now . . . now, just let me pleasure you."

He wanted her. He wanted her as he'd never wanted another woman—mind, body, soul. Something deep within him roared to possess her. With an effort of will, he pushed it into abeyance. This wasn't just any woman. This was Jenna. He wanted this joining to be good for her. No, perfect for her, so that she would never want to leave again.

"Lie back," he whispered hoarsely. "Let me love you."

Caught by the raging storm in his eyes, she obeyed. He came back to her then, lightly brushing his furred chest over her breasts with a slowness that stirred the fires within her.

Her skin was so sensitive that she shivered as his trousered legs slid between hers. Pleasure rocketed through her as he settled in the cradle of her thighs, the potent promise of him still sheathed behind fabric. She slid her legs along the outside of his and was rewarded by his gasp. Boldly, she did it again. He kissed her deeply, savagely, his body mimicking the thrusting of his tongue.

"You're driving me mad," he murmured against her lips. He'd never felt like this before; he wanted to taste her, stroke her, kiss her, bury himself in her all at once. And he wanted to do it forever.

"Then we must be mad together," she said. "I'm burning, Alan. I need something, but I don't know what it is."

"Shhhh. I do."

His hand slid between them, delving beneath the pale curls of her womanhood. Jenna fell into a maelstrom of need as he stroked her, parted her, then slid his finger deep inside. Her body tightened with almost unbearable delight. It was stark and powerful, this ecstasy, and yet incomplete. Surcease lay somewhere beyond her grasp. She strove for it, gasping, crying out in an extremity of pleasure.

Alan felt her hands move upon his back, and knew she was ready. More than ready. She burned like a flame in his arms, in his heart. His control crumbled. If he didn't claim her now, this instant, he felt sure he would die of it. Freeing his manhood, he settled back into the sweet cradle of her hips.

"I'm going to take you now," he rasped. "Jenna, my Jenna."

Impatient to know him completely, she sank her hands

into his hair and pulled him down. His tongue slid into her mouth as his manhood sheathed itself in her body. She tore her lips away from his, gasping as pain stabbed through her.

"I'm sorry," he said. "It will only hurt this once, never again."

He held still above her, in her, gently kissing her eyes, her temples, the corners of her mouth. His hands were busy, too, stroking her breasts, skimming down to caress the smooth curve of her hips. Jenna looked up at him, seeing the raging fire in his eyes, and understood the iron will that kept him under control. For her.

Even as that realization swept through her, the pain began to subside. Instead there was only fullness and a coursing awareness of the hard shaft inside her. She slid her legs up alongside his hips, allowing him to sink deeper.

"God," he muttered. "Do you know what you're doing to me?"

"Yes," she said. "Yes, yes, yes."

He started to move then, withdrawing in an exquisite glide, then thrusting in again with a power that made her gasp. Not with pain. No. It was sheer pleasure that tore that sound from her. That and all the rest. Again she rode the slope toward that bright, beckoning something, borne by his strength and caring.

His strokes became deeper, faster. It was like riding a whirlwind; she let herself be carried with him, responding, lifting her hips to meet him. He buried his face against the side of her neck, calling her name, and slid his hands beneath her buttocks to pull her even higher.

A tiny shiver bloomed inside her. Tremors convulsed her, a shockwave of sheer wanton pleasure. She cried out in surprise and delight, her legs wrapping around Alan's hips. He groaned, driving into her with pistonlike thrusts. His face tautened as he arched his back, pouring himself in her.

She lay beneath him, listening contentedly to the beat of his heart. After a moment he roused, propping himself on his elbows to look down into her eyes.

"Are you all right?" he asked.

"Mmm-hmm." Really, she was more than all right; she was drifting in a haze of satiation, content to be held thus in his arms. "No wonder the girls like to show you their bosoms."

Astonished, he stared down at her open-mouthed. It was then that she realized what she'd said, and a blush heated her cheeks. "I . . . don't know what made me say that," she stammered.

He grinned. "I do. And I want you to know that I've never touched Miranda's bosoms, no matter how often she showed them to me."

"Then you should tell her to keep them in her dress," she said. "Better yet, let *me* tell her."

"Little savage." With a deft shift of powerful muscles, he rolled onto his back and brought her with him. They were still joined intimately, and the change of position brought renewed stirrings deep in her body.

"Oh," she breathed in surprise. "I thought—"

"You thought we were finished."

"Yes."

"I'll never be finished," he said. "Even if my body is sated, my heart still desires you."

"Then you . . . Ah!" The cry was wrung from her as he cupped her hips in his hands and surged upward with his body. Desire coiled through her with renewed force, and she spread her hands out over his chest.

He taught her the rhythm, sliding her upward along his shaft, then slowly, skillfully, sliding her down again. A fast learner, his Jenna. Soon she'd taken over, riding him at a pace that had him half-crazy with need. There was no coyness to her, no virginal hesitation; she braced her arms on his chest, letting him look his fill while she loved him. He cupped the sweet weight of her breasts in his hands, running his thumbs over the taut buds over and over until he heard her moan. Her unbound hair fell over her shoulder in a pale cascade, and he sank his hands into the shining mass of curls. It slid like cool silk between his palms and her skin. She threw her head back, and he could see her pulse hammering beneath the smooth, graceful curve of her throat. For a moment she seemed the embodiment of woman, of passion, a being of moonlight and fire created just for him.

Feeling her tighten around him, he slipped his hand between their bodies and found the small, erect center of her passion. He stroked it, and was rewarded by the sudden tension in her body.

"What are you doing?" she gasped.

"Pleasuring you," he said.

He continued stroking her, his fingers gentle and sure. Then he felt the first, faint tremors of her release, and drove up into her with a powerful thrust. She called his name when she climaxed, and he let her shudders pull him over the precipice with her.

When breath and reason returned to him, he rolled over onto his side, bringing her with him. She was crying again. This time, however, he knew it was not unhappiness. So he soothed her with gentle kisses and whispered endearments. Jenna. His wanton virgin, his wood sprite. His.

Certainty coiled within him now that he'd claimed her. It was a calm, powerful sureness: now that he'd made her his, he would never let her go.

Never.

Fifteen

Jenna woke as Alan left her bed in the soft violet light that came just before dawn. Rolling onto her side, she watched him pull his trousers on and button them, then reach for his shirt.

"Why are you leaving?" she asked.

He quirked one dark eyebrow at her. "Best that I return to my own room before the servants are about."

Realization shot through her, and it wasn't a pleasant one. She sat up, clutching the bedclothes against her. "This is to be hidden?"

"People do, if they're not married."

"You're ashamed because—"

"No!"

He strode to the bed, stripping the covers away from her in one savage wrench. Jenna found herself flat on her back, staring up into eyes that had turned the color of a stormswept sky. His wide shoulders blocked her view of the room as he propped one hand on either side of her. His expression was one of pure male aggressiveness, tumultuous desire and possession so fierce it made her pulse hammer in her ears.

"Now tell me, Jenna, about shame."

"I—"

"Do you truly think I could feel regret for what happened between us? And do you think I give a bloody damn for what anyone thinks of me?"

"Well, I—"

"Do you think I care about anything but protecting you? This is my world, Jenna. I know how wagging tongues and pointing fingers can hurt. They call you witch. If they learn about this," he swept his hand down her side, bringing her body to sudden, swift arousal, "they'll brand you a whore, too."

She slid one hand along his shoulder and cupped the back of his neck. "Do you always argue like this, without giving the other person a chance to speak?"

"Always. Although I suspect that now that you know my method, it won't work any longer."

"You're right."

"Then I'll just have to find another way."

Warmth spread through her body, and she looked up at him with eyes that had gone slumbrous with desire. "Such as?"

He slid one trousered knee between her thighs, spreading them wide. She gasped as he lay fully on her, his groin pressed to hers, his furred chest against her breasts. He took advantage of her open mouth, thrusting his tongue deep into her honeyed sweetness.

Arousal swept through her in a hot, liquid tide. Her tongue boldly played with his, and she slid her hands down the hardridged length of his back to grasp his taut male buttocks and pull him still closer.

"Ah, Jenna," he whispered into her open mouth. "You touch me like fire."

He kissed her again, fiercely, then heaved a sigh and sat up. Sorely disappointed, she made a soft sound of protest.

"Another moment, sweet, and I won't be able to stop. Think of the shock it would be for poor Maisie to find us cavorting on the bed in mad, flaming passion."

"I like mad, flaming passion."

"I'll come back to you tonight."

"Sure?"

Alan studied her, this woman who'd ensnared his soul. Her lips were slightly swollen from his kiss, parted as though begging for more. Her coral-tipped breasts were full and taut, her legs only partially concealing her satin woman's flesh. And although he'd loved her over and over the past night until he thought he'd die of pleasure, he wanted her all over again. Of its own volition, his hand stroked downward along the silken curve of her hip, coming to rest finally on her thigh. His fingers spread out across her skin possessively.

He narrowed his eyes, shaken by the power of his feelings for her. There was nothing rational in them, and very little of civilization. No, this was pure instinct, the primal urge of a man to claim his woman—and to hold her.

"No power on this earth could keep me away from you," he growled.

"That almost sounds like a threat."

"Take it for what you will," he said. "It's the truth. If you fled to the end of the world, I'd come after you. No matter how far you ran or how well you hid, I'd find you."

Gazing into his eyes, Jenna shivered. There was utter certainty in those midnight depths, certainty and ada-mantine will. It was a bit frightening to be the focus of that determination. But exciting, too—almost like being swept away on the arms of the stormwind. Reckless desire coiled through her.

"Until tonight," she whispered.

It took an act of will for Alan to take his hand from her, an even greater one to get off the bed. Even while he dressed, he couldn't take his gaze from her. She lay before him like a sumptuous feast, unembarrassed by her nakedness. His heart tightened. Always, she was unique. There was no coyness in her, no thought of being anything but herself. Sweet, sensuous, and oh, so inviting.

He finished dressing. Returning to the bed, he brushed his open palm across her thrusting breasts. Her nipples pouted. He did it again, savagely pleased that he could evoke such fiery response from her. His breath rasped as he fought the raging need to possess her again.

Jenna saw it in his eyes, and her body responded in kind. She shifted her legs, smiling as she saw his gaze follow. Truly, she didn't care whether the household knew they'd become lovers; the Llewellyns had never held to any rules save their own. But his care pleased her . . . and perversely, made her want to break his self-control.

"Do you have to go?" she murmured.

"Yes," he said. "For your sake. Oh, God, Jenna! Do you have to look at me like that?"

"It's the only way I know to look at you."

He sighed, wanting her so badly his body shook with it. But time had run out. So he backed away from her beauty, away from the lush invitation of her lips and breasts and curving hips. It took more will than he'd thought he possessed, but he did it. Not trusting himself to touch her again, he put his hands behind his back.

"Go to bed early tonight," he said.

Jenna smiled, knowing the power she had over him. "Shall I plead illness?"

"Plead anything you bloody well please, just be ready for me when I come."

He turned on his heel and walked out, closing the door softly behind him. Jenna pulled the covers back over her, thinking that this business of love was very nice. So very uncomplicated once the trappings of the outside world were torn away.

As she drifted off to sleep, she almost thought she heard her mother singing.

A tap on the door woke Jenna again. She sat up, surprised to see that the golden light of full morning flooded the room.

"Who is it?" she called, reaching for the robe hanging on the chair beside the bed.

"Opal, miss."

"Come in."

The cook pushed the door open and walked into the room, a large package held in her sturdy arms. "This came from town for you."

"For me?" Jenna swung her legs over the side of the bed. "What is it?"

"I don't know. Master Alan said to bring it up, so here I am."

Urged by a sudden, strange excitement, Jenna tore the package open. It held a gown made of a delicate white muslin, trimmed with yellow ribbon at the sleeves and the base of the high bodice. With it were underclothes—a beribboned silk chemise and a petticoat so rich with lace it was almost a shame to hide it.

"How lovely," she said.

"He said for you to wear it today," Opal said. "He's gettin' more clothes made for you, but it do take time and—" She broke off so abruptly that Jenna swung around to look at her.

The cook was staring at the bed. Following her gaze, Jenna saw the stain of her own virgin's blood upon the sheets. She saw the older woman's mouth press tight, her brow crease with concern.

"Opal—"

"Ah, Lady. Do you know what you be doin'?"

"I love him."

Opal heaved a sigh. "I knows you ain't one to follow other folks' ways. But I got a daughter of my own, and I knows your dead mama would want me to tell you to be careful."

"Careful of what?" Jenna asked.

"He be a man, and men be hard for us women to understand. Now Master Alan seems t'be a good man and honest. But you comes from different worlds, Lady, and you might find there ain't no place in either of them for the pair of you."

"I can't believe that." Jenna held her joy close and hard, refusing to think that anything could shatter it.

Opal sighed and took Jenna's hand in both her large, capable ones. "Never mind, child. There ain't changin' what the good Lord set to be. But remember: you need something, you come to old Opal, hear?" Then, suddenly brisk again, she said, "Let's get you cleaned up and in this pretty gown, hmmm?"

"Now?" Jenna asked, surprised. "I thought I'd take Jon fishing again—"

"Oh, no you ain't. That Miranda Carrew came driving up jest after breakfast, and I don't think you want her havin' Master Alan all to herself."

Jenna frowned. "No, I don't think I do."

A short time later, she headed downstairs. The lovely dress seemed to float around her as she walked, pale gossamer draperies almost as light as mist. She knew Alan had chosen it for her because of this.

She followed Miranda's voice outside to the veranda, where she found its owner ensconced beside Alan on the wide stair. Jenna's gaze was all for him. His shoulders strained the seams of his crisp white shirt, and his hair swung like black silk over the collar of his shirt. Now that she'd tasted his sensuality, she knew him for what he was: a jaguar posing as a gentleman. Leashed power hovered beneath that veneer of civilization, needing only her touch to be released. Her breath quickened.

Then Miranda laughed, sending the sensual spell crashing down in shattered pieces. Jenna's gaze focused on the other woman's hand, which had dropped to Alan's knee. She stared at those greedy white fingers spread so possessively on the fawn trousers, and a wild, streaming rush of jealousy shot through her. It wasn't a pleasant emotion, but it was a powerful one. She stood rooted to the spot, hating herself for feeling like this, hating Alan for letting it happen.

Miranda laughed again. "Alan, darling, you can be so droll sometimes," she said.

"I was being perfectly serious," he replied. "You should know me by now."

"Should I?" she murmured, leaning so close that he'd only have to bend his head to kiss her.

"Careful," he said, his tone coolly polite as he set her upright, "you don't want to tumble off the step."

Relief replaced the hot swell of jealousy in Jenna's heart, and the hovering threat of disappointment turned to joy. She'd been a fool not to trust him, even more a fool to judge him by a townsman's standards. He deserved better from her.

Softly, she cleared her throat. Alan swung around, surprise evident in his movement, then rose to his feet. He surveyed her slowly from head to foot.

"You look lovely," he said.

"It's the dress."

"A moonlight gown for a moonlight lady." He smiled lazily at her, his eyes hot with appreciation and desire. "But it's the woman who lends beauty to the clothing."

Suddenly flustered, she dropped her gaze. And happened to look straight into Miranda's furious aquamarine eyes. The hate in them was staggering in its intensity. With a dart of surprise, Jenna realized that Miranda didn't hate the White Lady, she hated *her*, Jenna, and only because Alan looked at her so hungrily.

A novelty, she thought, being hated just for herself.

"My goodness," Miranda breathed, her voice sweet and her eyes spiteful, "you walk as quietly as any red Indian."

"And as gracefully," Alan said. "Shall we take a stroll in the garden?"

"I'd love to." Miranda rose to her feet, managing to wiggle the bodice of her sea-green dress down another inch in the process. "I do love your garden, Alan. It's so private."

Her tone insinuated many things, chiefly that she'd experienced that privacy before and had enjoyed every moment. But Jenna's moment of jealousy had passed; she didn't intend to play Miranda's malicious game.

Or so she told herself. But a pesky little demon whispered inside her head, making her realize that whatever mystical creature the townsfolk thought her to be, she was all too human, subject to jealousy, dislike and anger like the rest of them. So, when Alan held out his arm to her, she took it, preferring Miranda's company to giving him up to another woman even for a moment.

"Oh, dear," Miranda murmured. "Just a moment, Alan. My stocking has come loose. Would you be a darling and take my slipper off for me?"

She raised her skirt, blatant invitation in her face. Alan bent and pulled her slipper off. His hand didn't linger, but Jenna felt such a tearing surge of fury that she thought she'd burst.

Alan placed Miranda's slipper on the railing beside him, then took Jenna's hand and returned it to the crook of his arm. Gazing at Miranda with cool, hooded eyes, he said, "You'll catch up with us, right?"

Then he stepped off the veranda, bringing Jenna with him. And leaving Miranda standing open-mouthed on the steps.

"You're being unkind," Jenna murmured.

"It's only what she deserved," he replied. Then, with a grin, he added, "Besides, after seeing the look in your eyes, I was beginning to fear for my safety."

"The slipper was her doing. But," she added, "you're fortunate you pushed her away instead of kissing her earlier."

Alan grinned, thinking how delectable she looked this morning. She'd pinned her hair in a braided coronet around her head, and other than those fiery green eyes, she looked as cool and regal as a duchess. But he knew her secret now. All her secrets. "And what would you do to me, wood sprite, if your eavesdropping had found me untrue? Would you give me scabies or lice, or perhaps shrivel my manhood as you threatened to do to Rafferty?"

Jenna studied him from beneath the feathered veil of her lashes. "Oh, I think I'd leave you your manhood."

"So that you can enjoy it?"

Warmth spread through her, the memory of what had happened a few hours ago and the expectation of what would happen a few hours hence. "I—"

"Alan!" Miranda cried from behind them. "Wait!"

"Hell and damnation," he muttered.

He turned, bringing Jenna around with him. Miranda hurried across the lawn, breasts jouncing as she moved. He couldn't help but compare her with Jenna. Bird of paradise opposed to dove, an overblown, over-perfumed rose opposed to the sweet perfection of the lily—no, Miranda didn't fare well in the comparison.

She teetered to a stop beside him, her chest heaving, and took possession of his free arm. "You've never given me that ride you promised," she said. "Why not now?"

He turned to Jenna. "Shall we?"

"I don't ride," she said.

His eyes danced with laughter—and heat. They made Jenna remember that she did indeed know how to ride, although not horses. She smiled and knew by the look on his face that she'd conveyed her thoughts perfectly.

He glanced at Miranda, then spread his hands. "I'm afraid I can't. I can't leave my houseguest, you understand."

"Of course," she said, looking as though the words tasted foul in her mouth.

They rounded the corner of the house and entered the garden, where paths curved serenely amid well-tamed boxwoods brought all the way from England. It was too ordered for Jenna. She would have let the shrubs grow free, as God intended, and allowed flowers to riot along the paths.

"Such a *lovely* garden," Miranda breathed.

"Thank you," Alan said. "It went rather wild after Orwell Stepton died, but we're getting it back in order now."

Spotting a brush of color at one side of the path, Jenna pulled away from Alan and went to investigate. There, tucked between two cone-shaped boxwoods, she found a single cardinal flower blooming far later than the norm. Perhaps the protected spot had given it this long life. She smiled, crouching to touch its delicate scarlet petals. This was Nature's gift to her, given so that she wouldn't be blind to the beauty of this spot.

"What have you found, Jenna?" Alan asked.

"A small treasure." She straightened as the others came up beside her.

"Oh, look," Miranda said. "Isn't it lovely?" She bent and plucked the blossom, pulling it with a harsh tearing sound that made Jenna's throat tighten in distress.

Miranda tucked the flower into her hair. A single petal, loosened by the rough grasp that had shorn the bloom from the stem, fluttered to the ground. "There," she said. "A rose would have been prettier, I think, but this will do."

Jenna turned away sharply. This shouldn't bother her so deeply; after all, it was only a flower. Jon and Beth had picked many more yesterday. But the children had done it in joy, Miranda in spite. One was an innocent acceptance of Nature's bounty freely given, the other a violation.

With all her heart, Jenna wished she could escape this woman, her hate and her malice. But Alan caught her hand, keeping her beside him.

"Goodness, it's getting hot," Miranda said, fanning herself with her hand. "Why don't we have something cool to drink on the veranda, where it's shady?"

Alan's brows went up. "But we just got here, Miranda."

"You know I can't stay in the sun too long, darling. Skin like mine just won't bear it. And—Oh!" With a squeal of alarm, she stumbled, falling to the ground in a welter of blue silk.

"Are you all right?" Alan asked, going down on one knee beside her.

"Yes, I think so." She tried to rise but sank down again with a moan. "It's my ankle. I think I've broken it."

Jenna crouched in front of her. "Here, let me see it."

"Don't touch me," Miranda cried. "Alan, don't let her touch me!"

"She knows twice what I know about broken bones," he said, scowling.

"No!" The tawny-haired girl flung herself into his arms with sobbing frenzy. "Please, I'm frightened."

So it was Alan who drew Miranda's skirt up, Alan who gently probed her ankle. He glanced up at Jenna, disgust plain on his face. She nodded in silent understanding; no one with a broken ankle could possibly throw herself around with such abandon. Miranda's injury was pure theatrics, nothing more. Judging by the expression on Alan's face, he thought so, too.

"It's not broken," he said. "A sprain, perhaps."

"It hurts terribly." Miranda's eyelids fluttered. "Oh, I think it's beginning to swell."

Jenna saw no sign of swelling, other than the overblown bosom. "You'd better take her up to the house,

Alan," she said, keeping her voice carefully inflection-less. "That ankle should be soaked in cool water."

"Oh, yes, that sounds wonderful." Miranda's eyes had gone smoky with satisfaction.

Alan shot Jenna a glance that should have dropped her where she stood. Disengaging himself from Miranda's clinging arms, he rose and came to her, his broad shoulders blocking Jenna's view of the other woman. "You're coming with us."

"No," she said. "I'm not."

"Jenna—"

"My presence will only upset Miss Carrew more." *Or I'll strangle her.* As though sent by heaven itself, Beth's high, clear voice rang out from somewhere near the river. "Besides," she said, "I think I should check on the chil-dren. They shouldn't be playing so near the water."

"Dorcas is bound to be with them," he said.

"You never know," she replied.

He grasped her wrist. "You really are a savage," he muttered, "leaving me to that woman's mercy."

"She has no mercy," Jenna murmured, meeting his burning gaze levelly. "So watch yourself; I could change my mind about your manhood."

"Say that later." His grip turned warm, intimate.

She smiled at him, a seductive, wanton smile that seemed to sink deep into his body. He growled low in his throat, tempted beyond words to throw her over his shoulder and carry her up to his bed.

"Alan, please," Miranda moaned. "The pain . . ."

Gritting his teeth, he turned back to her. As he scooped her into his arms, she wound her arms around his neck and squashed her breasts against his chest. He wished he weren't a gentleman; he'd like to drop Miranda straight on her pampered derriere. But he was a gentle-man, much as he regretted it sometimes.

Turning, he strode toward the house. In his arms was a woman who interested him not at all; behind him, her hair gleaming like molten silver in the bright sunlight, was the woman who was the focus of all his desire.

"Bloody damn," he muttered.

"What did you say, darling?" Miranda asked.

His gaze skimmed her, then returned to the house. "I said I wished it would rain."

"Do you?" She laid her head on his shoulder. "I hate the rain, especially those great, thrashing storms we get this time of year. But perhaps you might persuade your guest to use her . . . power to make your wish come true."

He grinned, his ill humor vanishing at the thought of getting what he really wanted: Jenna in his arms. *If wishes were horses, then beggars would ride.*

"That's an excellent suggestion, Miranda," he said. "I think I'll do just that."

Tonight.

Sixteen

Jenna walked through the gathering dusk, her bare feet silent on the lawn. Just ahead, the whitewashed walls of the slave cabins gleamed palely in the dimness. She made her way to the one occupied by Ben and his family and tapped lightly on the door.

Ben opened it. Seeing her, he swung it wider and stepped back to let her in. "You be welcome, Lady."

Jenna smiled at him, then glanced over at Hallie, who lay propped up in the bed, her new son beside her. "How are you feeling today, Hallie?"

"Better. Little by little, I'm gettin' better."

Ben dipped a cup of water out of the bucket beside the door and offered it to Jenna. "The master, he said she can stay in bed as long as she needs, and no field work until she gets her full strength back."

"That's very kind of him," Jenna said.

"Master Orwell sent the women back to the fields one week after birthin', easy or not." Ben clasped his big hands together. "We named him Lew, for Llewellyn."

"I'm honored," she said, and was.

Husband and wife exchanged a glance full of hidden meaning. Then Ben closed the door and set his back against it, as though to keep out the rest of the world. "Are you goin' to stay with us for long?"

Jenna didn't know how to answer; she hadn't planned beyond tonight, beyond being in Alan's arms. "I can't see the future, Ben. Why? Is something wrong?"

"Folks has been talkin'," he said.

Uneasiness sank cold fingers into her stomach. "Townsfolk?"

"It ain't pretty talk, Lady. Most don't like you bein' here. And those Carrew . . . ladies been the worst of all. They sayin' you bewitched Master Alan and the children, and that you goin' to do somethin' terrible to them. And Rafferty, he been gettin' the white trash worked to a lather over it."

"How do you know all this?"

"We hear everythin' that goes on. You don't know these folks like we do. You're gentle, Lady. You stay here, they goin' to rip your heart to pieces. And there ain't nobody can protect you, not even Master Alan. You'd best get back to the swamp where they can't hurt you."

Jenna tried to imagine walking away from here, never to come back. And she couldn't. Never see the children or Alan again? Never lie in his arms again, never know the sweeping pleasure of his lovemaking? Her spirit shrank from the thought.

Her thoughts must have shown in her face, for Ben sighed. "You ain't goin' to go, are you?"

"I'll be careful," she said, impulsively reaching out and laying her hand on his arm. "Thank you."

He moved away from the door. Jenna smiled at him, then at Hallie, and slipped out into the late-summer night. The air felt tense and suddenly chill, a promise of rain, or danger. Perhaps it was only the realization of how much she was hated that gave her this feeling of foreboding.

You will never belong. They will never let you belong.

So leave, the practical part of her mind urged. The swamp was the only home she'd ever known, the only safety. But it was also a prison of sorts, a cage forged by the town's refusal to see anyone named Llewellyn as anything but evil. And in it she would be alone.

She tipped her head back to look up at the sky. Dark clouds were beginning to pile up around the moon. Even as she watched, a thick tendril moved across its glowing face, extinguishing its brightness. Plunged suddenly into thick darkness, Jenna shivered.

The house loomed ahead, dark and silent. The night hadn't claimed Heronsgate yet, however; inside, its master waited. Jenna could feel him, his desire like a tangible force.

Alan. The only belonging she'd ever have was in his arms. Could she leave him, knowing now how pale and lonely her life would be? Could she abandon him to the curse, could she walk away without fighting to save him and the children she'd come to love?

"No," she whispered.

She started walking toward the house. To Alan. She could feel him waiting for her, feel the surge and flow of his desire. As she got nearer, her steps became faster and faster. His arms would be her home, her haven.

Her breath coming in quick pants, she rushed up the back stairs. As she turned the corner, strong arms caught her up. She didn't struggle; even in the dark, she knew him.

"Alan," she breathed.

"You're shivering," he said.

"The night laid a cold hand on me, that's all."

"Why?"

Refusing to give in to the chill feeling of foreboding, she slipped her arms around his neck. He would keep her safe. He would warm her and banish the dread hovering at the back of her mind. "Because you weren't with me," she murmured.

His breath went out with a sharp sound. Turning, he carried her down the hallway to her room. Setting her on her feet, he locked the door and went to light the lamp on the bedside table.

"To banish the darkness," he said. "And so that I can see your face while I love you."

She held out her arms. He came to her swiftly, his face taut with desire. Sinking his hands into her hair, he pulled her head back and kissed her. Tenderly, yet fiercely, mastering her mouth with a hunger that matched her own.

Jenna ran her hand up the strong column of his throat, her thumb rasping along the faint stubble on his jawline. His scent filled her senses, a heady mixture of musk and leather flavored with brandy. Fascinated, she explored the granite hardness of his shoulders and arms, the long arc of his spine.

A groan rose in his chest, a smoky male sound of arousal. He slid one hand down her back to her buttocks, then grasped her thigh and pulled her leg up against his hip. She sighed, letting her head fall back as she was pressed intimately, thrillingly, against the long, thick ridge of his manhood.

"This has been the longest day of my life," he murmured, raising his head to look down at her with eyes darkened nearly to black with desire. "I thought I would go mad with wanting you."

"Even with Miranda's bosom as compensation?"

He slid his hands beneath her bodice, cupping her

breasts in his large, warm hands. "No woman on God's green earth can compare with you."

She closed her eyes against the sweet rush of arousal. Her body surged in response, desire pulsing through her veins with every beat of her heart. The world fell away. Had she been standing in a driving rainstorm, she wouldn't have felt anything but his touch. Her passion flared hotter than ever before, for now she knew the way of it, the incredible, peaking pleasure, the tumultuous culmination. She wanted it. And she wanted Alan, the only man who could give it to her.

"So hot," he whispered. "You burn my very soul."

He swung her into his arms. Without taking his gaze from hers, he carried her to the bed. But he didn't lay her down; instead, he turned her, letting her slide downward against his hard body until her feet reached the floor.

She was frantic to reach his skin, aching to feel him on her, in her. So much so, that she tore buttons from his shirt as she opened it.

"Little savage," he said. "Do you want me?"

"Can you doubt it?"

Alan took in her eyes, heavy-lidded with flaring desire, her moist, parted lips, the erect nipples that strained at the fabric of her dress. Such a creature of contrast, he thought, with that moonlight hair and passion that burned like the sun.

"No," he said, his voice hoarse, "I don't doubt it."

Slowly, with deliberate wantonness, she unbuttoned her bodice. He reached for her, but she said, "Wait."

He obeyed, his eyes raging. She loved seeing that heat in him, loved knowing she'd put it there. She loved *him*. There was no shame in her, no reticence. Letting the dress slide down her body, she untied the ribbons of her chemise. Her breath caught in her throat as his hot blue gaze traveled the length of her body.

"Go on," he said, his voice taut. "Don't stop."

She did, slowly removing her underclothing until she stood naked before him. Proudly. Unashamedly. He reached out with hands that trembled and loosened her hair from the braid. As the shining mass cascaded around her shoulders, he smoothed it over her skin.

"You're made of silk and satin and mother-of-pearl," he said, sliding his hands down her sides in a caress that was achingly tender. Still keeping her hair between her skin and his, he brushed his palms upward over the straining peaks of her breasts.

Jenna gasped. "Alan, don't play with me. Not tonight."

"Love should never be rushed." His hands moved around her, spreading across her back, and he pulled her against him. "Tonight is mine. I'm going to touch you, taste you to my heart's content. I want all of you, Jenna. Every inch of that marvelous skin will know the touch of my mouth, my hands. I'm going to do everything I've dreamed about in these past weeks."

"Dreams?" she whispered.

"Didn't I tell you I've been dreaming about you since the moment we met?" His hands delved into her hair, combing through it as though fascinated with the feel of it. "Fevered dreams, Jenna. All night, every night. I've made love to you every way a man can love a woman, over and over, and it was never enough. I'd wake from those dreams in a burning sweat, my soul aching because I thought it could never be."

"And now?"

"And now I find the reality more sensual than any dream," he said. "Everything about you arouses me. The way you look, the way you smell, the way you curl your bare toes into the carpet . . . Yes, I noticed that, my lovely, wanton wood sprite. I want you more than I've ever wanted a woman, more than is reasonable."

She let her breath out in a long sigh. To be wanted like *that* . . . Stirred immeasurably by his words and by the flaming hunger in his eyes, she sank her hands into his hair and pulled him down.

He swept into her mouth like a conqueror, a fierce kiss, a claiming. But tenderness tempered his strength and aggression, turning what might have seemed like submission into sharing. He gave as much as he took, and because of that, he made his possession into something achingly lovely.

If such a thing as magic existed, it was in this room, in this man's hands, in her heart.

Rising up on her tiptoes to reach him better, she let her tongue dart forward to play with his. Their mouths slanted and clung, seeking more heat, more sensation. A sigh rose on the air, and Jenna didn't know if it was his or hers. She didn't care; mind and body, she'd set out on a journey of inexpressible delight.

Sliding her hand between them, she undid the buttons on his trousers. His maleness sprang free. She explored the springing length of him, fascinated and a bit awed by its strength, iron sheathed in satin skin.

"Jenna," he groaned, burying his face in the curls at her temple. "Oh, God, woman, what you do to me—" He broke off abruptly, his body drawing as tight as a bow. "Stop. I want to go slow. If you keep this up—"

"I want to pleasure you."

"Ah, Jenna. You pleasure me beyond words." He took her hand from him and drew it up behind his neck.

She sighed as he kissed her temples, her brows, her closed eyes, the corners of her mouth. His tongue traced the line between her lips. Boldly, she opened her mouth and took him deep inside.

His skin was hot, and his chest heaved as though he'd been running. Still, she wanted more. Pressing her body against his, she trapped his maleness between them. He pulled her in tighter, higher. His hand stroked along the cleft of her buttocks, searching for the source of heat. Her body opened, welcoming him, and he stroked the desire-swollen flesh of her feminine core. He slid his knee between hers, opening her further to his exploration. One long finger slid into her sleek hot passage, stroking, withdrawing, stroking deep again in an exquisitely torturous glide. She arched her back, gasping.

"Yes," he muttered. "For me, Jenna. For me."

He found the small, erect nub that was the center of her desire. He stroked it with a smooth, expert rhythm that soon had her crying out in sheer voluptuous pleasure. She arched her back as the clenching waves of release caught her, overwhelming her with tumultuous sensation.

The world tilted and spun. It took her a moment to realize he'd tipped her back onto the bed. Dazed, she watched through her lashes as he divested himself of trousers and boots. Lord, but he was beautiful! A stark male creature of hard planes and taut muscle, his midnight eyes flaring with hunger, the jutting manhood a fierce, primitive symbol of his need—her lover, her love. The one man who could possess her utterly.

Her heart ached with love for him. She sat up, clasping her arms around his waist and laying her cheek against his chest. His hips bucked, pressing his erection like a steel bar against the sensitive skin of her breasts. She raked her nails lightly along his back, then clasped his hard male buttocks.

"You're so much woman," he whispered.

"Only for you."

"Yes," he agreed, his eyes slitted with tightly-leashed passion. Only for him. It was a gift more precious than anything he'd ever been given, more, surely, than any man had a right to expect. Only for him.

Jenna felt his manhood stir against her breasts, as though it had a life all its own. Every muscle in his body tensed as she swayed her chest, stroking that importuning hardness.

"You're . . . Jenna," he groaned, his hands sinking into her hair. He wanted her now, this instant, and yet he wanted this surging, exquisite sensation to go on forever. "You're driving me mad."

"I want to," she said. "I love driving you mad."

And then she did it again. With a muffled sound, he pressed her back against the coverlet. Pinning her hands over her head, he loomed above her in primitive need. His eyes had gone feral, the look of a man who'd passed beyond the limit of his will. Triumph shot through her. This was what she'd wanted; the surrender of that iron control of his, just for this, just for her.

"Open for me," he rasped.

She obeyed, able to do nothing else but welcome him. He surged into her body with a power that took her breath away. "Alan," she whispered, arching to meet him.

He withdrew almost completely. Then, when she was ready to beg for him to return, he slid home to the hilt. Passion surged through her like sparking gunpowder, and all centered in the spot where they were joined. Gone was her need to tease, to test the limits of his will. Gone was the thought of anything but him, and the lovely, lovely possession that tugged at her very soul.

"Love me," she cried, as lost as he. "Oh, love me!"

He drove his mouth down on hers, even as his body began to move with awesome power. He pleasured her with long, liquid strokes, growing deeper and deeper until she thought she'd go mad from it. She wrapped her arms around his neck and her legs around his driving hips; he responded with a thick male groan and deepened his thrusts still more.

She plunged off the edge of the waiting precipice, falling straight into a multicolored ocean of sensation.

"Jenna," he groaned, shuddering like a man possessed. "Oh, God, Jenna."

His back arched as he pressed deep and long, and she felt his essence pour out into her. She looked up at him, this man she adored, and saw the tight-drawn planes of his face, the way his chest heaved with every ragged breath. She felt the trembling of his arms and understood that he'd surrendered wholly to the wildfire of their loving. And she knew this had never happened to him before. It staggered her and humbled her just a bit.

She gentled him, stroking the hair back from his forehead with trembling hands, pressing light kisses over his mouth and the lean angle of his jaw. Slowly, his breathing grew steady again.

Propping his weight on his elbows, he kissed her, a sated, tender kiss. When she opened her eyes again, she saw that he'd slipped back behind the adamantine veil of his control. Ah, but for one glorious, stunning moment, she'd held him in a way no one had ever held him before. She'd never forget it.

"That was nice," she said.

"Nice!" Mingled amusement and outrage swirled in his eyes. "That, my dear Miss Llewellyn, was much more than nice."

"Forgive me, but I've not been tutored in the proper things to say to a man after making love."

The corners of his mouth curved upward. "I'd teach you myself, but there are many, many other things I'd like you to experience first."

"Tonight?"

"We can get a good start on it."

"Mmmm. Are you like this with all your women?"

He tilted her face up, probing her eyes with a gaze that had suddenly gone very serious. "From the moment I met you, my beautiful wood sprite, I haven't thought about another woman. In fact, I've hardly thought about *anything* but throwing myself into the flames of your passion. And now that I have you in my arms, I intend to make the most of it."

"But there are things we must discuss. You can't continue to flaunt your wishes in the faces of your neighbors—"

"Yes, I can."

"You're arrogant."

"I'm besotted."

Placing her hands flat on his chest, she levered some space between them. "This does not only affect you, Alan."

"Forget the bloody neighbors," he said.

"But—"

He laid claim to her mouth again, a staggering, skillful kiss that started her blood heating again. It occurred to her that he was using sensuality to keep from discussing the future with her, but she could feel him stirring within her, filling her, heavy and hard, once again. Rational thought spun away in a riptide of renewed desire.

"Again?" she murmured, sliding her hands up the hard muscles of his arms.

His teeth flashed white as he grinned. "I feel no reluctance in you," he said, lifting her hips with his hand as he pressed deep within.

"No," she whispered, arching beneath the fierce upwelling of sensation. "No reluctance."

"This is all that matters. Nothing else."

She closed her eyes. "Nothing else."

And she sailed off on a sea of blazing passion, so bright and beckoning that she had to close her eyes against it. She let Alan be her guide through those uncharted waters, surrendering to his strength, his tenderness, and the firestorm of his desire.

Something pulled Jenna from sleep. It wasn't a sound, precisely; it was more an awareness of the soul that was stronger than slumber, stronger than the desire to remain in the warm safety of Alan's arms.

She sat up, careful not to rouse him. Padding to the window, she drew the curtains aside. The night was as thick and soft as velvet, lit only by the waning moon. Movement caught her attention, focusing her gaze on the trees that separated Heronsgate from the swamp.

Something pale moved down there in the blackness under the leafy canopy. Jenna's heart contracted with fear.

"Grandmother," she whispered.

She glanced back at the bed, where Alan sprawled like a great sleeping cat. Silently, she drew on her trousers and shirt, then slipped out of the room. The house seemed abnormally hushed, as though it knew something she didn't. But she pushed that notion aside; surely it had been born of the darkness and her surprise at Roanna's coming.

Once outside, she broke into a run. Roanna stepped out of the trees to meet her. The moment Jenna saw the grim anger that etched the old woman's face, her stomach clenched.

"Grandmother, you shouldn't be here," she said. "You know what the townspeople will do if they know you're still alive?"

"They'll hunt me down like a dog and kill me with no mercy," the old woman snapped.

"Then go," Jenna urged. "Before someone sees you!"

Roanna smiled, a baring of teeth with much pain in it. "Did you think I wouldn't find out you'd come here?" she asked.

"Grandmother—"

"The slaves know. They always know. And they tell their brethren in the swamp."

"I didn't try to hide it from you."

"Nor did you tell me, either."

Jenna nodded. "I doubted you'd approve."

"You fool!" the old woman spat. "Have you lost your wits entirely, to dwell in the house of our enemy?"

"I—"

"Stepton blood runs in their veins, and Orwell's fate runs in their future."

Jenna shook her head. "They're good people. They shouldn't have to pay the price of Orwell's sins."

"The curse cannot be broken," the old woman said. "No matter what you think or do, it cannot. And don't be fooled by their pretty ways; they're townsmen, blood and bone and heart, and there is no love in them for such as us."

"That's not true."

"It is!" Roanna blazed. "I've fought them for nearly fifty years. Do you think I came by this mistrust for no reason? Look you, Jenna; I've been reviled, betrayed, convicted without trial, hunted like an animal. You'll learn, just as I did, that you can expect no different from any of them."

"I don't believe that," Jenna said.

"You'll learn. Remember this and remember it well: a time will come when these 'good people' will call you witch. Like all the others, they'll point their fingers to blame you for everything from bad crops to mosquito bites."

Jenna met the old woman's obsidian gaze with outward calm, but inside, her heart thudded painfully in her chest. "I love him, Grandmother."

Roanna staggered backward as though she'd been struck. "You love . . . the master of Heronsgate?"

"Yes."

"You've given yourself to him?"

With a lift of her chin, Jenna said, "Yes."

"Ahhh!" Roanna moaned. "Do you know what you've done?"

"Only what any woman in love would do."

"Fool!" The old woman chopped at the air with her hand. "A witch who loves a man loses her powers."

Mingled astonishment and dismay clutched at Jenna's heart, and she groped for some meaning amid the turmoil of her mind. "It can't be true. You bore Silvan—"

"It's the love, not the giving of your body!"

"I don't . . . I haven't lost my knowledge of plants,

Grandmother. I still know how to set a bone or sew a wound or cool a fever."

"The magic of the healing is in your hands, not your head. At a time when you'll need it most, it will fail you. *That* is the price of loving a man. It happened with Silvan and it will happen with you."

"I don't believe you," Jenna cried.

"I speak the truth!" Roanna hissed. "And I—" She broke off suddenly, her lips bloodless, her face convulsed with terrible pain.

Jenna leaped forward, catching her grandmother's slight weight before she hit the ground. Terror beat black wings in her mind as she felt frantically for the old woman's heartbeat.

"Grandmother! Grandmother, talk to me!" she whispered. "Dear God, not like this. Oh, please, don't take her from me!"

After a seemingly endless time, Roanna's eyelids fluttered. Jenna sobbed in inexpressible relief, lifting the old woman into her arms and holding her close.

"Don't crush me, child," Roanna said, her voice weak but gruff. "And help me up."

Jenna obeyed, keeping one arm around Roanna's waist to steady her. "Grandmother—"

"I'm fine," the old woman snapped. "Just get me to my boat. I want to go home."

She didn't look fine; her face was still ashen, and her eyes were filmed with pain amid the nesting of wrinkles. Jenna tried to calm the fear coursing through her.

"I'll take you," she said.

"Go back to your lover. I can make it on my own." Roanna pushed her away, straightening with a visible effort.

Jenna grasped the old woman's arm, resisting her efforts to free herself. Even at her best, Roanna would be no match for Jonas Rafferty. Should she meet him now, weak as she was . . . With a shudder, Jenna pushed from her mind the thoughts of what the slave trader would do to her grandmother if she fell into his hands.

"I'll take you," Jenna said. "Willingly or not. I won't have you fainting on the way and drowning yourself."

"And what about Heronsgate's master?"

Jenna thought about Alan lying so peacefully in her bed. She hated to leave him without warning, but the explanation would take too long. And the longer Roanna stayed here, the more likely it was that she'd be seen.

Alan would never understand that while the townsfolk might tolerate—almost—Jenna Llewellyn's presence for a time, they'd come howling for Roanna's blood. For nigh fifty years, they'd called her witch, madwoman, Devil's mistress; since the Steptons died, they'd added murderess to her titles.

With a sigh, Jenna turned toward the swamp. "It will be all right, Grandmother. Alan trusts me."

Seventeen

"Come on, Pudge," Jon said, leading his sister toward the river. "Let's get into the trees before Dorcas wakes up and finds us gone."

"We're going to get into trouble," she said, yawning.

"We're going to get in trouble anyway," he countered. "So I'd rather catch my fish first, if you don't mind."

"I don't know why we had to come out so early. The sun's hardly up."

"You know what Jenna said about early morning being the best time to catch fish." He brandished the supple willow branch that held his line. "I'm going to surprise her and Father with fresh-caught fish for breakfast."

She laughed. "All right. And I'll gather plants and berries to go with it, just like Jenna does. It will make her feel at home, too."

"D'you think she misses the swamp?"

"I hope not. I hope she stays with us forever."

As she moved away from him, gaze fixed on the ground, Jon called, "Now stay away from the water, Pudge. If one of us falls in, we're going to catch it for certain."

"I'm not going to fall in, nit."

"Goose."

"Addlepate."

With that rejoinder, Beth flounced off. Jon baited his hook with a great, wriggling worm and dropped it into the water. Within a few minutes, he had a pair of fine perch flopping on the riverbank.

Beth returned just as he added a third to his catch. "Bravo," she said. "You've got nice fat ones."

He turned to look at her. She'd collected a mound of greenery, using her skirt as a makeshift basket to hold it all. Her pantalettes were filthy. Jon tallied the damage with an expert eye, deciding that it would be hidden once her skirt was down again.

"What've you got?" he asked.

She pulled a pale green shoot out of the pile and held it up. "This is the one Jenna said was good to eat. Smilax, she called it."

Jon took it from her, dangling it between thumb and forefinger. "Are you sure?"

" 'Course. Jenna said."

"Jenna said, Jenna said," he echoed. "Are you sure she really said that, or is this one of your tricks?"

"What tricks?"

"Let's see . . . What about the great black spider you put in the tutor's cravat?"

She giggled. "Oh, that. Remember how he jumped?"

"I thought he was going straight out the window for a moment." Jon studied his sister's face, gauging her mood. She seemed sincere enough; besides, while Pudge was as capable of as good a prank as anyone, he didn't think she'd deliberately give him something that would make him sick. "So, what does this one taste like?"

"Try it."

He did and found that he rather liked it. It was cool and somehow clean-tasting, and he took another bite.

"Hmmm. Not bad, Pudge. Do you know what the rest are?"

" 'Course I know. I paid good attention when Jenna told us about plants; when I grow up, I'm going to be just like her. We're going to live here for the rest of our lives; don't you think we'd better learn to live off the land like she does?"

"Do you think she's a witch, like people say?"

"Oh, yes. But she's a good witch. She only wants to help people. Now, I heard her grandmother wasn't so nice, but I don't think that should have anything to do with Jenna, do you?"

"No." He poked amid the greenery. "What's the rest of this mess you've collected?"

"This and that. Most of them are plants Jenna said were good to cook."

He grimaced. "How're we going to cook them?"

"Well . . ." She tapped her foot on the ground, her small, soft face turning thoughtful. "What do you say we borrow a pot from the kitchen? Opal isn't up yet. We can slip in and out again before anybody knows better."

"All right. But you'd better let me do the fire." Bending, he scooped his fish up and turned toward the house. Suddenly he stopped. "You didn't get any of that plant that Jenna said makes the horses sick?"

"Of course not," Beth said. "I know what's what."

Alan rolled over, instinctively reaching for Jenna in that fuzzy state just before wakefulness. Finding only an empty pillow, he opened his eyes.

The light of full morning lay in bright window-pane squares on the floor. He slid out of bed and reached for his clothes; the servants had been up and about for a while now, and it was a wonder Maisie or Opal hadn't caught him sprawled in Jenna's bed. Careless of him not to leave before dawn as he'd intended.

Ah, but he'd spent the night to good purpose. Very good purpose.

She'd become part of him, so quickly that he'd hardly noticed it happening. He didn't know what name to put on his feelings for her; his love for Helena had been a gentle thing, born of respect and caring and growing up on adjoining estates. They'd lived in the same world, known the same people, believed the same things. His feelings for Jenna, however, were anything but gentle. It seemed as though Nature itself had come to roost in his heart, bringing rain and tearing wind, winter storms and searing summer heat all at the same time.

I will hold her.

Wood sprite, fairy princess, healer, passionate woman—all were Jenna, and all elusive. He knew she had no concept of home and marriage. Born and bred in the Dismal, raised to wild lore and even wilder freedom.

I will hold her.

Jenna, whose passion burned bright and hot as the sun, whose touch he felt deep in his soul. Somehow he had to hold what could not be held, bind what could not be bound.

"I will hold her," he said aloud, as though speaking the words would make them possible.

A tap sounded at the door, startling him from his reverie. Silently and with haste, he buttoned his trousers and shrugged his shirt over his shoulders.

"Master Alan, it's me, Opal. I got to talk to you."

Alan sighed; servants always knew. "Come in."

The cook obeyed. Closing the door behind her, she set her back against it as though barring his way. "Don't worry, suh. You can trust me; I ain't goin' to tell anyone about this."

"For Jenna's sake?"

"And yours. What do you think the rest of the towns-folk goin' to say about you takin' a Llewellyn as mistress?"

"What do *you* say?"

She met his gaze levelly. "I says you is playin' with fire. I says you got a fine, fierce hawk in your hands and you goin' to try to cage it like some fancy songbird, and you goin' to hurt yo'self and the Lady whilst you does it."

"Would you have spoken to Orwell Stepton this way?"

"No, suh. He'd have whipped the hide off me."

"Aren't you afraid I'll do the same?"

"No, suh," she said with infuriating placidity. "You ain't the type—unless the other fella's got a whip, too."

He sighed. "Is that a compliment?"

"Depends on who you is."

The front door banged loudly, and a moment later footsteps clattered on the stairs. Such urgency pounded in that quick tattoo that Alan strode to the hallway to meet whoever was coming up.

Dorcas turned the corner and came running toward him. Her hair had come loose, straggling around her face in sweaty bands, and terror marked her features.

"Dorcas!" Alan called, his heart thumping with sudden alarm. "What's the matter? Did something—"

"Oh, sir!" she gasped. "It's the children, the children!"

He grasped her by the elbows as she all but fell into

his arms. His hands felt unnaturally cold, his skin clammy, as though his life were draining out through his pores. "Tell me."

"They're ill, sir, terribly ill. Oh, dear God in heaven, don't let it—"

"Stop!" Alan shook her, hard enough to get her attention. "Where are they?"

"Near the river. The men are bringing them up to the house now."

Setting her to one side, he flung himself toward the stairs. Not this, he prayed. Not this. Not my children. As he ran from the house, he saw Ben and Ulysses carrying the two small forms. Alan's heart stuttered as he rushed forward to meet them. Jon was moaning steadily, curled around his abdomen as though it hurt him, but Beth lay like a rag in Ben's arms.

"Jon," he whispered. "Beth."

His daughter's eyes fluttered open. "Father. Oh, I feel so . . ." She moaned, her forehead beaded with sweat.

Alan took her from Ben. She retched weakly, and he cradled her against his shoulder and turned toward the house. "Bring my son," he said. "Ben, go fetch the doctor."

But the comfort of the soft beds did nothing to relieve their discomfort. Alan washed their faces with cool water, but they only moaned and thrashed even more. Their pain tore at him, ripping great gashes in the fabric of his soul. He looked up at Dorcas and Opal and Ulysses, and saw equal helplessness in their faces.

"Someone find Jenna," he said over his shoulder. "She'll know what to do until the doctor gets here."

"No!" Dorcas's voice lashed out at him sharply. "Ulysses, bring what we found with the children."

Silently, he left the room, returning a moment later with a small cookpot.

"That's one of mine," Opal said. "What you doin' with that there pot, Ulysses?"

"It weren't me," he said.

"The children had it. We found it in the bed of a dying fire." Dorcas pointed at the seemingly innocent-looking iron pot. "Look inside, Mr. Langston."

He obeyed, frowning when he saw a dark-green mess inside. "What is it?"

"Some kind of greens, looks like," Opal said.

Alan's chest clenched. Slowly, he turned back toward the bed and put his hand on Jon's shoulder. "Jon, did you eat anything you weren't supposed to?"

The boy shook his head from side to side fretfully. "Jenna said . . . Jenna said . . ." And then his eyes closed, and consciousness slipped away.

Alan squeezed the towel out in fresh water and replaced it on his son's forehead. His mind whirled madly, torn between what seemed to be and what *couldn't* be.

"There has to be an explanation," he said.

"Mr. Langston," Dorcas said softly. "You just heard the explanation. 'Jenna said.' "

He shook his head, a gesture born of automatic denial. But the nanny reached out and gripped his arm, her nails digging into the muscle.

"It's time to leave the fantasy behind," she said. "Time to look beneath the beauty and see the darkness within."

"No!" Opal cried. "The Lady is good, she's good!"

Dorcas drew herself up and pointed to the children's pain-filled faces. Then she turned away sharply, her thin shoulders heaving with silent sobs.

Alan didn't offer comfort; his own pain was too great.

Jenna said. Working automatically, he rinsed out Beth's towel and draped it gently over her sweaty forehead. *Jenna said.* Had she loved him all night, then roused in the morning to do something terrible to his children? His heart cried no. But the calm, calculating mind that had kept him alive and also brought him a profit in the rake-hell shipping business urged him to look at this more carefully.

"Where is Jenna?" he asked.

Dorcas sat on the edge of Jon's bed and took his hand in hers. "No one has seen her this morning."

"Ulysses." Alan didn't turn his gaze away from Beth's small face. "Find her."

His attention focused completely on the children. He sat between them, jaw set, hands clenched into fists as though he could make them better by just willing it. From time to time, he got up to rinse out the towels, to hold the children when their pain made them curl up, and sometimes just to talk to them to let them know their father was near.

He lost track of time completely; there was only his children's pain—Jon's gasps, Beth's ragged crying. He felt so bloody helpless. Jenna could have done something, he knew. She had the knowledge, the skill.

Ulysses came back into the room, Opal with him. Alan's eyes narrowed as he noticed the man twirling his hat between his hands in obvious nervousness.

"What?" Alan snapped.

"The Lady, she be gone," he said.

Alan clamped his hand on the arm of the chair. Wood creaked and groaned as he put pressure on it. "Where?"

"Back to the swamp, suh. I found the tracks myself, and the mark of a boat pulled up on the shore."

"I knew it," Dorcas said. "A leopard doesn't change its spots."

Opal stepped forward. "It be a mistake to judge the Lady. She come and she go, but she never hurt no one."

"Didn't you hear that boy?" Dorcas raged. " 'Jenna said, Jenna said!' Who else knows plants?"

"Medicine—" Opal began.

"If she can make medicine, then she can make poison," the nanny hissed. "Am I right?"

"Yes, ma'am. But—"

"If she were innocent, she wouldn't have sneaked away like a thief in the night."

The sound of wood snapping brought them all around. Alan rose, tossing the shattered remains of the chair arms on the floor. Rage coursed through him in a bitter rush, and for a moment he felt capable of tearing the very walls down around him.

Then the sound of a carriage outside speared through the red haze of violence that ensnared him. "That will be the doctor," he said. "Ulysses, bring him up."

The man scurried out. Opal hesitated, opened her mouth as though to say something, then turned and walked from the room.

"She is afraid for the witch," Dorcas said. "Such loyalty is commendable but misplaced."

Alan whipped around to face her. "Did you hate Jenna so?"

"Actually, I rather liked her. But I never trusted her."

"I did," Alan said, his voice as heavy and cold as his heart. "I did."

Hearing footsteps, he turned toward the door. He'd never met the doctor before, but Lewis Culhane seemed a pleasant enough sort with his round face and body and balding head. His eyes were clever and yet sympathetic, his handshake firm as he greeted Alan.

"I'm sorry to hear of your troubles, Mr. Langston," he said, his gaze going to the beds. "May I see the patients?"

Alan nodded. The doctor bustled past him, sitting on each bed in turn as he examined the children. Then he asked to see the pot of cooked greenery.

"Is this what they ate?" he asked, sniffing the pot's contents.

"We think so," Dorcas said. "Do you know what it is?"

He shook his head. With a sigh, he set the pot aside and raised his gaze to Alan's. "May we talk in the hallway outside?"

Alan led the way out, closing the door behind him. "Can you do anything for my children, doctor?"

"I . . . No. I'm sorry, Mr. Langston."

"You have to." Without quite realizing what he was doing, Alan grasped the doctor by the front of his coat and pulled him closer. "I can't believe you'll stand there and tell me there's nothing to be done."

Lewis Culhane's eyes didn't change, nor did he show the fear another might have done in his situation. "I'm sorry. But they appear to have been poisoned by that green . . . concoction."

"Surely you can do *something*—"

"This is beyond my knowledge, sir."

"I refuse to sit back and just let them die!"

"Would you have me treat them willy-nilly and perhaps kill them while trying to help them? There's a chance they might throw this off on their own, you know."

With a sharp exhalation, Alan let the other man go. "How much chance?"

"I can't even tell you that. Perhaps your houseguest—"

"Gossip travels fast."

"Always, Mr. Langston. And especially gossip of that sort. I don't want to pry into your private affairs, but perhaps the, ah, young lady might know something about that green mess."

Oh, yes, Alan thought. *Perhaps she does.* "She is no longer with us."

His voice was harsh with pain and revealed more of his feelings than he would have liked. He saw the awareness of it in the doctor's eyes.

"Ah, yes," Culhane said. "I'm sorry, Mr. Langston, if I've touched on an uncomfortable subject. And since the . . . lady is no longer here, then she couldn't have had anything to do with this situation. Whatever those children ate, it doesn't seem to be a very quick-acting poison, or they would already have . . ." He broke off, his eyes full of compassion. "We can only watch and wait, Mr. Langston."

Black rage clenched Alan's hands into fists. "Is there nothing else I can do for my children?"

"Pray, Mr. Langston."

"God seems very far away right now."

Culhane met Alan's gaze calmly. "Keep them as comfortable as you can, and see if you can get some liquids into them. I have to attend another patient, but I'll be back this evening to look in on the children." He turned away, then swung back around to meet Alan's gaze steadily. "If they begin to have trouble breathing, send for me immediately. My wife knows my schedule."

Alan went back into the sickroom. His children's faces

looked so pale and tiny against the pillows that he had to turn his back on the sight lest he burst asunder from his fear for their lives and his anger at the one who had done this to them.

Jenna said. Jenna said, and now his children might be dying. Innocents. They had only loved her.

He went to the window, bracing his hands on the frame as he glared out over the swamp. Watch and wait, the doctor had said. Sit by the bedside and watch them suffer, helpless to do anything to save them? Alan shook his head.

That wasn't his way. He *would* do something to save them, or he would die trying. There was only one person who could take away the poison: the one who had given it. Wood sprite, healer . . . witch.

"To the ends of the earth," he rasped, a quiet vow that held all his rage, despair and determination in it. "Run as far and as fast as you will, witch, but I will find you. As God is my witness, I will find you."

Eighteen

"Drink this, Grandmother," Jenna said.

"What is it?"

"Decoction of elderberry root, just like last time."

"Last time you added a bit of loosestrife," Roanna said. "Just to make me sleep."

"Not to sleep," Jenna said. "To stop you from complaining."

The old woman scowled at her. "Can you blame me? I find that my granddaughter has fallen in love with my mortal enemy, and not only do I have to be carried like some helpless townsman, I'm not even allowed to go to my own house."

"My cabin was closer," Jenna said.

"Hmph."

Jenna held out the cup. I'm glad you're feeling better. Now, drink."

"Not if there's—"

"There's no loosestrife in it, you have my word," Jenna said.

Roanna drank. Then she turned over onto her side, presenting Jenna with her back. Jenna smiled; her grandmother was a difficult woman sometimes and always a stubborn one. But her love had been a constant in Jenna's life; grim, gruff as the old woman might be, the love was there.

Her collapse at Heronsgate had frightened Jenna badly. But Roanna seemed stronger, as though the return to her beloved Dismal had restored some of her vitality. A night or two of rest, and she should be back to normal.

"Did it occur to you that you might already be with child?" Roanna asked without turning around.

The unexpected question brought images flooding Jenna's mind: a little girl or boy with Alan's midnight eyes, or perhaps with Jon's cool gray ones. "Oh, I'd like that," she said.

"Would *he?*"

"I . . . hope so." It bothered her that she didn't know the answer. But she hadn't looked beyond the wondrous passion they'd shared; the future, like the world, seemed to melt away in his arms.

"Doesn't matter." Roanna yawned loudly. "We always take care of our own."

Her acceptance warmed Jenna. For three generations the Llewellyn women had borne their children alone, raised them alone, taught them the lore of survival. It was as good a legacy as any: a kingdom called the Dismal. But the thought of ruling it alone, without Alan, seemed a very lonely one just now.

Folding her hands in her lap, Jenna sat silently at her grandmother's bedside. Soon, the tempo of the old woman's breathing changed as sleep claimed her. A smile tugged at the corners of Jenna's mouth; the loosestrife hadn't been in the elderberry decoction, but it certainly had been in the tea she'd given Roanna an hour ago.

"Lost my powers, indeed," she murmured. "All a healer needs is to be cleverer than her patient."

She rose and walked out into the thick, humid darkness. A day and half another night had passed since she'd left Alan, and her heart ached with the need to see him again. Once again she regretted the necessity of keeping her grandmother's existence a secret. But it was a necessity; the only real safety Roanna had was the townspeople's belief that she was dead.

A familiar scent floated on the quiet air. Jenna's nostrils flared. Wood smoke.

She glanced over her shoulder to make sure everything was quiet in the cabin, then followed that elusive scent into the woods. An owl glided ahead of her on soundless wings; following, she made no more noise on the spongy turf.

Little light came from the scrap of moon overhead. But this was her territory; she knew every tree, every bush, every smell. She traveled nearly a mile before she saw the glow of the fire. It glimmered yellowly through the trees, the small, contained blaze of a human encampment.

Her breathing quickened. Humans almost always meant danger in this part of the swamp; danger from the intruders themselves or from those who hunted them. She approached cautiously, silently.

A lone person bent over the fire. In silhouette, his form was distorted against the leaping flames. Then he straightened. Jenna gasped; she knew those wide shoulders, the arrogant carriage of the head.

"Alan," she breathed.

She stepped out from the screening bushes. He stiffened as though she'd touched him, then swung around to look at her. His eyes caught the light oddly.

"Jenna," he said.

She could hardly contain her joy at just seeing him

again. With her heart leaping like the flames, she walked toward him. "So you found me again," she said.

He moved then, surging toward her like a great, night-bound cat. She gave a gasp of surprise and welcome, expecting him to sweep her into his arms.

But his hands clamped down on her wrists painfully. Before she had a chance to react, he'd bound her wrists together, dragged her to the ground, then tied her ankles as well.

"What are you doing?" she demanded. "Have you gone mad?"

"No," he said. "I've regained my senses." Then, in a tone as sharp and deadly as a rapier, he added, "Witch."

She drew in her breath sharply. He'd meant it to hurt, and it had. More than she would have believed. Her joy shriveled and died as she stared up into his eyes. They looked black in this light and as hard and cold as stone.

"You called me witch," she said.

"Aren't you?"

"Why?" Her voice was a whisper; she couldn't force anything louder through a throat that had gone tight with tears.

"Jon and Beth have been poisoned," he said.

She shook her head, speechless with horror. *Not the children!* "We have to do something—"

"They cooked up some plants and ate them. All they've been able to tell us is 'Jenna said, Jenna said'."

His voice stabbed at her cruelly, relentlessly. Her spirit cringed under the lash of what he said, what he believed. "And you think I did it," she said.

"Tell me the truth about what happened."

I love them! That's the truth, the only truth! "What do you think happened?"

"Tell me!"

She brought her feet beneath her, rising despite the bonds. And then she looked deeply into his eyes. Her heart seemed to congeal in her chest; he believed she'd poisoned his children. It was there in his eyes, in the burning rage and betrayal she saw in their depths. She turned away, unable to bear the sight of it.

"Have you nothing to say?" he growled.

"Everything has already been said." That word "witch," uttered in a tone full of spite, had shattered the world they'd built between them. He'd had no faith in her. His loving had been shallow, born of the flesh and not of the spirit.

Grandmother had been right. She'd said that the master of Heronsgate would call Jenna witch one day, and she'd been right.

"What will you do now?" she asked. "Is it burning at the stake that's your pleasure, or do you prefer a rope?"

He clamped his hands on her shoulders and swung her around. She hung in his hands, limp and defiant, expecting him to strike her. But he didn't. He merely held her in that iron grip, his eyes reflecting the firelight, his mouth pressed in a grim line.

"Aren't you going to hit me?" she taunted.

"I don't hit women," he said.

"Not even witches?"

"Not even witches."

Small mercy, that, she thought. He'd already struck her in a way that hurt far more. She wished she had the ability to wall her feelings away like he did; her heart felt as though it had been torn asunder, the life draining out of it with every beat. She wanted to run, hide, forget she'd ever set eyes on this man. But she couldn't, for that would mean turning her back on Jon and Beth.

"Take me back to Heronsgate," she said. "I want to try to help them."

He laughed, a harsh sound. "Of course you will. That's why I came after you. You know what they were given; you can counter it."

"Indeed." She tilted her head back to look at him. "I will do my best to help your children. But not because you demand it. There's no pain you can inflict on me to *force* me to do it."

"Don't be so sure," he said.

"Then begin," she challenged.

With a muttered oath, he flung her away. She teetered on the brink of falling. Just as she thought she'd tumble straight into the fire, he grabbed her arm and pulled her back.

"I'll be watching you every moment you're with them," he growled. "One false move, and I'll make you wish you'd never been born."

She drew herself up stiffly, pulling her battered emotions inside the cool, contained mask that was the White Lady. His hate might tear her soul asunder, but he wouldn't have the satisfaction of seeing it.

"Hadn't we better get started?" she asked, glad that her voice was as chill as she wanted. "While you're standing here threatening me, your children are suffering."

"Damn you," he hissed.

With a smile as full of bitterness as her heart, she offered him her bound hands. "Do you intend to drag me? I assure you that will take much more time than if I walk."

He took her knife out of its sheath and slit her bonds,

then turned and hurled the blade far out into the brush. "If you try to run—"

"I assume you have a boat?"

"Yes. Just over there."

She watched as he doused the fire and collected his gear, knowing she could have slipped into the trees so quickly he'd never have caught her. Without him, however, she'd never get to see the children. So she waited, hating him, hating herself for having been foolish enough to have loved him.

Once he looked up at her, a raging glare that should have set her afire where she stood. She met it levelly, absorbing it into that vast, cold calmness that filled the place where her heart had been. As soon as he was ready, she turned and led the way to the river.

He'd brought one of her boats. She stepped into it, moving directly to the bow and sitting down cross-legged. He took the pole, shoving powerfully out into the current.

"I trust you haven't disposed of my pack?" she asked.

"No one has touched your things," he said. "No one would."

"Ah, yes. They're tainted."

He poled steadily, the muscles of his arms bulging and relaxing, bulging and relaxing. The boat moved forward jerkily at first, then steadied as he settled into a smooth, powerful rhythm. An hour passed, then another. Still, he kept it up. Another man would have had to rest, but Alan pressed on, driven by that same determination that had first attracted her to him.

Jenna closed her eyes, pushing that thought aside. "What are their symptoms?" she asked.

"Cramping, violent nausea, weakness—"

"Difficult breathing?"

He gave the boat a particularly violent shove forward. "Not when I left."

"Which was?"

"This morning."

She opened her eyes and looked at him. The healer in her struggled with the woman betrayed, and finally the healer won. She saw him as a father whose children might be dying. Saw and responded. Even after the terrible hurt he'd brought her, she would have said something to comfort him if she could. But there were no words powerful enough to give comfort in this, even if he would have accepted them.

So she clasped her hands in her lap and fixed her gaze on them, harboring her strength for the fight ahead. For it would be a fight; from Alan's description of the children's symptoms, they were very sick indeed.

And had he known as much as she about the number of poisonous plants about, he would have been even more frightened than he was.

Night turned to dawn, dawn to the full light of morning. Jenna dozed fitfully, lulled by the motion of the boat, roused by the roiling pain in her heart. And always her gaze went to Alan. His face showed the strain of hours of poling; exhaustion had turned to pain, pain to numbness. But he didn't stop. She had the feeling he would have died on his feet, his hands locked to that pole.

She didn't want to admire him. But she did. Despite the fact that he'd savaged her heart, she had to acknowledge the iron will that kept him going. Again, for his children. Whatever else he was, whatever else he did, this one thing shone pure and untrammeled.

"Let me take a turn," she said.

He didn't seem to hear her. She understood that he'd passed beyond hearing, locked as he was in the fight to continue. Rising, she went and grasped the pole. For a moment she thought he'd keep working, ignoring the drag of her weight. But then he stopped, awareness of her coming into his eyes.

With awareness came cold anger. She ignored it, saying only, "Sit down. We're only a short distance from Heronsgate."

With an obvious effort, he unclenched his fingers from the pole. He took Jenna's place in the bow, sitting down rather abruptly. But he didn't relax his vigilance; that burning midnight gaze never left his face.

Soon the wildness of the Dismal paled as they neared the cultivated land of Heronsgate. A few hundred yards farther on the chimneys of the house came into sight through the trees. Jenna steered the boat toward the riverbank, tied it up, and turned back to Alan with her hands outstretched.

"Do you want to bind me again?" she asked. "Just for effect?"

"Get out," he said.

With a smile that surely must look as fierce as she felt, she sprang from the boat and ran toward the house. She wasn't sure why she did it; perhaps it was sheer perversity in wanting him to know he could neither stop her nor catch her. But it might have been more an attempt to show him that he had no power over her and that she'd come because it was what *she* wanted.

She heard him cursing behind her, and it gave her a

great deal of satisfaction. The moment she entered the house, however, lesser things became lost in her urgency to see the children.

Opal met her at the bottom of the stairs. Tears ran down the woman's face, and she twisted her apron between her hands. "I tried to tell them you wouldn't—"

"It's all right," Jenna said, pausing to stroke the back of her hand down the other woman's face. "Are they still . . ." She couldn't finish the sentence.

"They hangin' on, Lady. But it's bad, real bad. The doctor moved them down to the room beside the master's, said the air was better for them than that hot upstairs room."

"A man of some sense, then. I'll need hot water and cloths, plenty of them. But first I want to see whatever it is you think they ate."

"Yes, Lady."

Alan's boots racketed on the veranda. Jenna hurried upstairs, only to be barred from the bedside by Dorcas.

"What are you doing here?" the nanny snapped.

"I've come to help."

"Or finish the job, most likely."

Jenna met the older woman's glare without flinching. "Who else do you have? Obviously the doctor can do nothing."

"Stand aside, Dorcas," Alan said from behind Jenna. "I brought her here to undo whatever has been done."

"But, sir! How can you even consider it—"

"Dorcas!" His voice wasn't loud, but it lashed like a whip.

Slowly, with obvious reluctance, Dorcas moved aside. Jenna bent over the children's small, still forms, and her heart raced with dread. They were so ill, so terribly weak.

"Hello, Beth. Hello, Jon," she crooned, stroking the hair back from each sweaty forehead. "It's Jenna. I've come back."

Jon moaned. Beth made no sound, but her eyelids fluttered. Jenna drew a breath that sounded like a sob. Hearing Opal come into the room, she turned away from the bed and grabbed the small cookpot the woman held.

Dipping two fingers into the green mess inside, she scooped a bit out and held it to her nose. Then she tasted it.

"Pokeweed," she said, spitting the small portion out.

"But I've ate pokeweed myself," Opal said.

"And how do you cook it?"

"Well, you pick the young shoots, an' then you boil them twice."

Jenna nodded. "You throw out the first water."

"Yes, Lady. My grandmamma showed me how."

"The poison, which is much less in the young shoots, leaches out into the first water," Jenna explained.

Dorcas frowned. "But why would a person eat something they know is poisonous?"

"Do you eat potatoes?" Jenna asked.

"Of course. What has that to do with it?"

"The potato is cousin to deadly nightshade. If you eat the green plant or the shoots of the unripe potato, you could die."

Leaving the nanny to digest that information, she turned back to the bed. Alan moved to the other side of the bed, fixing her with those baleful, burning eyes of his.

"What do you think?" he asked.

She laid her hand on Jon's forehead. "By morning, we should know."

"The doctor said the crisis would be tonight," Dorcas said.

"What are you giving them?" Jenna asked.

"Tea, but they haven't been able to hold much down."

Jenna shook her head. "Opal, bring me my pack. I'll need hot water—a teapot will do—and fresh, cool water."

"What are your plans?" Alan asked as the cook hurried from the room. "I won't allow you to give them any more of your concoctions."

"I'm going to try to save your children. Despite what you may think, I cannot do that by waving my hands around and chanting. Besides," she added, looking at him from beneath her lashes, "If I possessed true powers of magic, I would have lost them the moment you took my love."

Dorcas gasped. Alan didn't react in any way; his gaze remained fixed on Jenna's.

"As it is," she continued, "I've been told that I've lost the special power that made my healing work."

His mouth curved in a smile that had nothing of humor in it. "Then you better find it again, and quickly. For your own sake."

"No," she said, refusing to be drawn into his game. Reaching down, she clasped Jon's pale, flaccid hand in both of hers. "For theirs. Pray, Alan, that the person who told me that was wrong."

Nineteen

Jenna slid her hand beneath Beth's head and lifted it a few inches above the pillow. The child moaned, and her back arched as spasms of nausea racked her body.

"Easy," Jenna murmured, squeezing a few drops of water from a clean cloth into the child's mouth. "Take a bit of this, dear. That's it," she added, as Beth's parched little tongue moved at the touch of the moisture.

"Jen . . . na?"

Jenna's gaze went to Alan, who'd risen from his chair at the sound of his daughter's voice. Hope blurred the stark line of his jaw and softened the deep lines bracketing his mouth.

"Beth," he said. "Talk to me, sweet. Can you talk to me?"

"I'm afraid she's drifted off again," Jenna said.

Alan flung himself away from the bed to lean his weight against the window frame. Rage filled him at the sight of the plantation's activities going on outside. Illogical to begrudge the rest of the world normalcy, but he did. How dare the sun rise in the sky with Beth and Jon at death's door?

"Tell me the truth," he rasped. "Are they going to make it?"

Jenna studied him, saw pain in every line of his powerful body. On the one hand, she loathed him for what he'd done to her. On the other, well, he was just a man who was afraid his children would die. For their sakes, she must deal with him as she would anyone who came to her for help.

Setting Beth gently back against the pillow, she went to stand behind him. "I don't know what will happen. But they're fighters, your children; they won't be taken easily."

Alan was astonished by his own eagerness for good news. No, his desperation. "Why aren't you doing anything for them?" he snarled.

"I'm doing everything I can. Do you think I have some sort of magic potion to give them to make it all right?"

"One concoction made it all wrong. As you very well know."

The statement was uttered in such a tone of contempt that she nearly flinched before she got her reaction under control. *Don't let him see. Don't let him think he can hurt you, or he'll tear you apart.*

Likely, he'd tear her apart anyway. But he wouldn't see. No townsman had ever brought a Llewellyn to her knees, and it wasn't going to change now.

"If I had treated them from the beginning, I would have been able to do more," she said. "As it is, the poison has had enough time to get a good hold on them; I can only treat the things I see as they happen."

"I don't want to hear excuses," he growled. "I only want my children to get better."

Jenna turned back to the bed, determined to ignore him. How could she have been so wrong about him? *Because you let your body run away with your head, and you saw things in him that weren't really there.*

The sunlight waned, died. Opal came into the room, protecting a taper with her cupped hand, and lit the candles. Jenna stood vigil at the side of the bed, watching the children, being watched by Alan.

Shortly after, Dorcas came in, bringing a stranger with her. Alan greeted him, then, crossing his arms over his chest, nodded toward Jenna. "And this, Doctor Culhane, is our resident witch, Miss Llewellyn. She's come to cure my children."

The doctor's jaw fell as he stared at Jenna with obvious horror. Then he swung around to his host. "You can't be serious."

Alan's mouth twisted. "I don't think the situation could be *more* serious, Doctor. Do you?"

"But, but . . ." the man sputtered. "But how can you put your children's lives in her hands? How do you know she won't kill them instead of helping them?"

Jenna went cold, then hot, then cold again. She opened her mouth to protest, but the words sank razor claws into her throat and refused to come out.

"Her life is my children's bond," Alan said.

"What in Heaven's name do you think she's going to do for them?" Dorcas demanded. "Wave a chicken bone over them and conjure them well?"

Alan swung around to look at the nanny. "Have you an alternative?"

"No." She glanced at the doctor, then dropped her gaze to the floor.

"Then this is the only chance my children have," Alan said. "And I intend to take it."

The doctor raised his hands, his face creased with obvious distress. "This is insane!"

"If madness will save my children, I welcome it."

Alan's eyes glittered as he looked from Dorcas to the doctor and back again. "If witchcraft will save them, I welcome that, too."

"It's on your head," the doctor said. "Much as I hate to watch this, I expect I'd better. I've just come from several calls; could I impose on you for something to eat?"

Alan nodded. "Just go downstairs. Opal will fix you whatever you want."

As soon as the doctor left the room, Dorcas fixed Jenna with a glare ugly with dislike. "Be careful, witch," she said, dragging a chair to the foot of the bed. "I'm watching you. One false move—"

"And you'll kill me where I stand."

"I'd like to kill you now. You'll never understand what it feels like to have to watch you touch those children, knowing what you did . . ." Dorcas's voice broke as she struggled for control. "If you wanted to hurt us, why did you have to do it like that?"

The grate of Alan's teeth was loud in the room. "Because hurting the ones I love was the surest, most painful way to strike at the master of Heronsgate. And everyone knows the feud between the master of Heronsgate and the Llewellyn witch. Isn't that right, Jenna?"

She raised her chin, hiding with defiance the pain his words caused. She'd given this man the most precious thing she owned—her love. And more, her trust. She'd set aside everything she'd ever been taught to love him, believing him when he told her it might break the cycle of hate that had scarred so many lives. In return, he accused her of poisoning his children. *Children!*

Alan, Dorcas, Doctor Culhane—coldness in their eyes, hate in their hearts. Three different people, but they might as well have been poured from the same mold.

Hate. Anger. Mistrust. The townsfolk were all the same, would always be the same. Had she pulled the moon down from the sky and given it to them, they would have damned her for it.

Witch.

She'd been a fool to think she could find something common between them. For the first time, she understood why and how Roanna had become so grim; hate could only be deflected so much, so often, before a heart became calloused.

Defiantly, she met their gazes one by one. "Think what you will of me. You cannot touch me with your hate."

It was a lie, of course. But she'd had to tell more lies than one since she'd met these people. *Damn them. Damn them!*

Suddenly the rhythm of Jon's breathing changed, and Jenna forgot everything but him. She rushed to his side. Holding his hand, she watched his face contort as his chest rose and fell, rose and fell.

"Don't let her touch him!" Dorcas cried.

"I have to," Alan said. The taut anger in his voice showed he liked the idea as little as Dorcas. Striding to the door, he flung it open and shouted, "Doctor! We need you now!"

Jenna bent over the children, only to be brushed aside a moment later as the doctor rushed back into the room.

Culhane examined them, glancing up at Jenna with an enigmatic gaze, then straightened.

"What is it?" Alan demanded.

The doctor sighed. "The crisis has come."

"Beth, too?"

"Yes," Jenna said. "Soon. Do you want me to tend

them, or will you interfere every time I try to touch them?"

Alan looked at the doctor, who spread his hands. Then he impaled Jenna with a gaze filled with icy dislike. "Do what you can," he said. "But be very careful."

Her attention on her patients now, she hardly registered the threat. It was Jon and Beth who were important here, not Alan, not her own fate. Moving swiftly, she propped another pillow behind the patients to raise their upper bodies from the horizontal.

The children grew quickly worse. Their small chests strained as they struggled to draw air into their lungs. Jenna breathed in time with them, willing them to fight.

Dorcas began to sob. "I can't bear it, I can't!" she wailed. "Doctor, do something!"

"I cannot." His shoulders slumped. "I'm sorry. Terribly, terribly sorry."

Jenna looked from one to the other, registering Dorcas's grief, Culhane's resignation, Alan's burning outrage. They'd given up, all of them.

Perhaps she should, too. Perhaps Roanna had been right; in loving Alan, she'd given up her healing talent. Slowly, she balled her hands into fists. It couldn't happen like this! She wouldn't let it. No longer a healer? No!

These are the same hands I had before. With an effort, she relaxed her fingers, letting warmth run through them again. *This is the same heart I had before, bruised, perhaps, but still there, still able to care, to risk, to be willing to fight old man Death himself for a human life.* No man had taken her ability to care from her; no man could, unless she let him.

Whirling, she walked to the bedside table and poured a cup of flagroot tea. Then, returning to the bed, she lifted Jon from the pillow and tipped a few drops into his mouth. He didn't react. The tea dribbled out the corner of his mouth. She tipped another few drops in.

"Swallow," she commanded.

Still he didn't respond. She stroked his throat with her fingertips, seeking the reflex. After a seemingly interminable moment, he obeyed.

"Again," she said.

And again she had to stimulate his swallowing reflex. But he got another few drops down.

Dorcas gasped. "Stop her, for God's sake!"

"They're dying, woman!" the doctor protested. "Leave them in peace."

Jenna looked up. "As long as they're drinking, as long as they're doing something, they're alive. They're fighting."

"But—"

"Dead people don't swallow," she said. Suddenly, with a flare of emotion that surprised even her, she let her own anger burst out into the open. "I won't follow your rules, nor am I bound by your limitations! For as long as I can hold them, these two lives belong to me. To me! And if I can make them swallow, they won't die."

Alan stared at her, seeing at last why the townspeople called her witch. Something powerful blazed in those pale-jade eyes, something as deep as the ocean and as hard to contain. For a moment, he almost believed that if she willed Jon and Beth to live, they would.

Perhaps self-preservation motivated her, perhaps something else. He didn't care; if it worked for his children, he'd accept it. Striding to the table, he poured another cup of tea and brought it to the bed. Pulling Beth into his arms, he supported her against his chest.

"Drink, Beth," he said, stroking her throat the way Jenna had Jon's.

Rewarded by the child's response, he did it again. And again.

Jenna held Jon in her arms, matching the rhythm of his breathing with her own as though that alone would keep him there. Every few minutes, she forced him to drink more tea. His eyelids fluttered.

"Jon," she said, her voice sharp and imperative. "Stay with me. You're going to have to drink this whole cup of tea before I let you rest."

She looked over at Alan. He fought the same battle with Beth, and she knew he was as determined to win as she. As though drawn by the touch of her gaze, he glanced up. Jenna had never seen such a look in a human being's eyes. Grief, outrage, an anger as hot as the midsummer sun—he was a man on the brink of exploding. She understood; here, in the lush green luxury of the bedroom with its gilded looking-glass and polished, expensive furnishings, this rich, powerful man suddenly realized his helplessness. Here, with his children's lives in the balance, there was no logic, no privilege, none of the safe boundaries within which townsmen so liked to box themselves. This was the world of faith, of the human spirit, where nothing made sense but anything was possible. He was alien here, cast adrift in things he couldn't understand.

But the Llewellyn witches dwelled in this world. For her, there was nothing to fear.

Holding his gaze for a long, frozen moment, she said, "Hold her, Alan. Keep her with your voice and the touch of your hands."

"Are you so sure?" he rasped.

"I am sure of nothing. But," she paused to raise the

cup to Jon's lips again, "Neither am I willing to just sit back and let them drift away. Are you?"

"What do you think?"

"I think that if tearing out your own heart would save them, you would do it."

He nodded. "So, Lady, shall we fight? For their lives . . . and yours?"

"We shall."

And so they fought. They fought with all the power and the passion that had once brought them together, all the determination that would surely keep them apart afterward. Two people at odds on almost everything but this, enemies by birth and by betrayal, but joined by the need to save these children. Jenna knew he believed that she'd caused this and that her devotion was prompted by the desire to save her own skin. It might matter an hour from now or perhaps tomorrow, but just now, only Jon and Beth mattered.

She forced Jon to drink the last of the cup of tea, then began on another. Sometimes he swallowed, sometimes he sputtered, but he kept it down. So did Beth. Dorcas sat in the chair at the foot of the bed, her long face drawn with worry, her gaze going from one child to the other and back again. She rose once only, to bring a fresh teapot.

Jenna moved like an automaton, ignoring fatigue, then ignoring exhaustion. She glanced at the doctor, who sat, head bowed, in the armchair beside the fireplace. For a moment she thought he was praying, then realized he'd fallen asleep.

So she prayed. Prayed for the children's lives and for the strength to bear it if they died. Another woman had borne them, but she, Jenna, loved them as though they were her own.

The memory of Roanna's voice hovered like a vulture in her mind. *They're doomed, all of them. The curse cannot be stopped. Cannot be changed. And by loving the master of Heronsgate, you have lost the power to heal. Lay them down. Let them go, for it's their destiny.*

Anger bloomed hot in her chest, banishing the pain of her cramped and aching muscles, her burning eyes and fatigue-numbed mind.

I am a healer. In mind and in heart, nothing else. In all the madness of this world, that at least remains. I've held them this long. I'll hold them longer.

"Drink, Jon," she said, holding the cup to his lips. "Yes. More now. Good."

As the night went on, the rectangle of moonlight on the floor shifted. Gradually, so much so that she was only vaguely aware of the change, she realized that the color of the light had changed from silver to gold. Morning had come.

Jon's breath brushed the side of her neck. Stronger than before and steady. Jenna didn't dare look, didn't dare hope. She just sat still, her heart seemingly frozen in her chest, and counted each exhalation as it came. Her gaze went to Alan, who still held Beth. The child's eyes were still closed and her face pale, but her breathing had strengthened like her brother's.

"Drink a bit more," Alan urged.

"No."

It was barely a whisper, but so inexpressibly Beth that Jenna drew in a long, shuddering breath. Joy flooded her. They'd won. Jon and Beth had won! Feeling moisture on her face, she reached up with her free hand and found tears.

Her gaze locked with Alan's, found it a match for what she was feeling inside. For one glorious moment, it was like the beginning. Before the loss of trust, before, before, before. Then it seemed as though a shutter had dropped down over those beautiful midnight eyes, leaving them only mirrors of cold disdain.

The sight brought numbness crashing down in her heart. With hands that shook, she gently laid Jon back onto the pillow. To sleep, not to die.

"Wha . . . ?" Dorcas, who'd fallen asleep in her chair, jerked awake. "My babies! Did no one think to call . . . They're still . . . Still . . ."

"They live," Alan said, holding his daughter close against his chest. "They live!"

Awakened by their voices, Doctor Culhane came rushing to the bed. He examined the children, then turned to Jenna. She levered herself upright, holding the bedpost for support. If he—or any of them—started in with their hatred and prejudice, she'd damn well curse them herself.

"I don't know how you did it," he said. "Magic or miracle or sheer stubbornness, you did it. My congratulations."

To her complete astonishment, he bowed to her. She stared at him, unable to speak, unable even to move. Suddenly, the world tilted around her. She swayed. Then the floor came up and hit her hard, and she slid into a vast, roaring blackness.

Jenna awoke to the steady thump-thump of someone's heartbeat against her ear. She didn't have to open her eyes to know who held her; she knew by his scent, the hardness of his body, and the sudden race of her own pulse. Outrage sent flames licking through her chest. How dare he touch her!

Her eyes flew open. She realized he was carrying her, his long strides bearing her toward the open doorway of her old room.

She pushed at his chest, wanting anything but to see that place again. "Put me down."

Ignoring her, he turned sideways to fit her through the doorway, then strode toward the bed. She began to struggle in earnest. Against him, against the memories of passion and promise they'd shared beneath those covers.

"No!" she gasped.

His jaw tightened. "I'm not about to ravish you, witch."

The last word was spoken like an epithet, and he couldn't have hurt her worse if he'd slapped her. She lay stiffly in his arms, unresisting as he placed her on the bed.

"Let me go," she said. "You have your children, your money, and your hate. Just let me walk away."

"That was not part of our agreement. My children's lives for yours, that's all."

"Why will you hold me?" she cried.

A wolf would have envied his smile. "Because there is still another bewitchment to be dealt with."

"The curse?" She sat up, shoulders straight and square with cool dignity. "I can do nothing about that."

"Not that!" he hissed.

"Then what?" Her voice rang with frustration.

"The spell you laid on me. To make me want you."

Jenna stared at him, completely dumbfounded. "Spell?"

"Don't lie to me any longer." The words were spoken in a whisper, but the low tone did nothing to mask the barely leashed violence in him. "You ensnared me with your power, your beauty, and the fire inside you. You betrayed me, striking at me in the most vicious and cowardly way possible, through my children, and I find that I still want you."

"You're mad!" she gasped.

His eyes narrowed. "Perhaps I am. If so, it's your doing. You ought to be happy with what you've wrought."

"Your malice is all your own, *townsman*."

Like a cat pouncing, he leaped upon her, bearing her backward to the mattress. Truly frightened now, she fought him, biting, scratching, kicking. But he smothered her struggles with his strength and weight, pinning her wrists in one big hand, her legs with his.

"You might as well have called me bastard," he said.

" 'Tis the worst insult I know."

" 'Tis also dangerous to bait a Langston."

She surged futilely against his weight. "You don't frighten me," she panted. "You will never hold me, never!"

"A rash declaration, considering your present position."

She glared up at him, wishing she had some of the powers he thought she did. Their gazes locked with volcanic intensity. Then, slowly, reluctantly, as though his hand worked at odds with his mind, he brushed her hair back from her face. His fingers speared through the satin thickness of it, separating the strands, releasing the scent of honeysuckle into the air.

"Stop," she said. "You have no right."

"Don't I?"

Trapped, she stared up at him like the mouse waiting for the cat's final cruelty. Then the fierce Llewellyn pride brought her chin up in cold defiance. "Why don't you just kill me and get it over with?"

"Because I doubt that would free me," he said.

He shifted, keeping his grip on her wrists as he dragged her to a sitting position. Before she could react, he pulled a set of iron fetters from beneath the coverlet and snapped one end around her ankle, the other around the bedpost.

"No!" she cried.

"This is only for today," he said. "My children need me, and I don't want you running off."

"You can't do this to me." Frantically, she tore at the restraints with her hands. "If there's any mercy in you at all, you won't do this to me!"

His gaze turned glacial. "I left mercy in that room where my children almost died. Now get some rest. We'll speak again later."

"I will never forgive you for this, never!"

Turning on his heel, he left the room. Jenna heard the key turn in the lock. Her breath went out in a sound that might have been a wail if she hadn't gritted her teeth against it. Chained and caged like an animal, she who'd had all the freedom of the Dismal. Her chest heaved with deep, shuddering breaths as she struggled for control.

This, *this* was the price of loving the master of Heronsgate. Not her healing ability but the most precious thing she possessed: her freedom.

Then her eyes narrowed. It wasn't going to be that easy for the master of Heronsgate. By his own words, he'd called himself ensnared. And as long as he kept her here, he would share the prison with her. Alan Langston was a hard man, a warrior, a nobleman and a pirate. But until now, his enemies had been men. Never a Llewellyn.

"And the Llewellyns never play by the rules," she said aloud to the quiet room. "In love or in war."

Twenty

Jenna woke to a darkened room. For a moment she lay disoriented, then abruptly remembered where she was. She sat up, accompanied by the clink of chain. Reaching down, she felt along her ankle until she found the encircling band of iron.

"Damn you, Alan Langston," she muttered.

"I was damned the moment I met you," he said, his voice drifting out of the darkness at the far end of the room.

She gasped in surprise, then pressed her lips tightly together as he stepped out into the faint moonlight cast by the window. He looked again the conqueror—broad-shouldered, aggressive, implacable. His face was half il-lumined, half in shadow, which only accentuated the bold lines of his jaw and the starkly sensual curve of his mouth.

"What do you want here?" she asked. "Isn't even my sleep to be inviolate?"

"You didn't ask how the children are," he said.

"I don't need your words to tell me how they are. I felt them reach for life, Mr. Langston. And I felt them grasp it." Tossing her hair back with a flick of her head, she added, "Besides, if they'd taken a turn for the worse, I'm sure you would have stormed in here threatening to kill me if I didn't do something for them."

Light shifted on his face as his jaw tightened even more. "I'll take your word that you won't try to escape."

"The word of a witch?"

"The word of a Llewellyn. I've heard it is reliable, whether for good or bad."

She turned her back on him. "I'll give you nothing. Chain me, nail me to the headboard if that's what pleases you, but I'll not willingly stay here."

"Release me from your bewitchment, and you won't have to."

"There is no bewitchment."

"No curse?"

"There is a curse."

"Then," he said, "there is a bewitchment."

She remained silent; there was nothing she could say that he would believe, nothing that could touch that granite heart of his. So be it. Crossing her arms over her chest, she waited for him to leave. Of course he didn't. Wouldn't. She knew this implacable side of him, the part that never gave up, never let go. Until now, she hadn't realized what a terrible thing it was to be the focus of it.

"Go away," she said.

"I haven't finished talking to you," he snapped.

She lay down, still keeping her back to him. "And I would prefer that you torment me tomorrow, when I am not so tired."

"I did not come here to torment you."

"Why, then?"

"To thank you for the lives of my children."

There was no softening of his voice. She didn't turn, knowing there would be no softening of his face or his feelings toward her.

"I know your reasons were selfish," he continued.

"But still, I treasure the lives of my children. As a gentleman, I must offer my thanks."

She raised her fettered ankle. "Is this the act of a gentleman?"

"You left me no choice."

"There is always a choice."

"Then you admit that poisoning my children was no accident?"

"I did not poison them."

"I heard it from their own lips. 'Jenna said.' My daughter spoke those words to me as she lay helpless in my arms. I asked her what she had eaten, and she whispered 'Jenna said'."

She closed her eyes. He didn't know her. He'd never known her. She'd been a pretty doll he'd played with, dressed and petted and bedded. He'd never looked to see Jenna herself, the woman who loved both him and his children, the woman who'd never hurt another human being in her life. To think that he believed she could deliberately feed those children something that might kill them, and do it for *revenge?* No, he hadn't known her.

"I did not poison your children," she said again. "But I advise *you* not to eat in my presence."

"I used to think you were jesting when you said things like that. Now I know better."

"You will never break me," she said, her voice calm and steady. "You can keep me here until hell freezes over, but you cannot break me."

"Jenna—"

"I know who I am and what I am, and there is nothing you can do that will change that."

"Unfortunately for you, I also know who you are and what you are."

She opened her mouth to reply, but a knock at the door stopped her.

"Who is it?" Alan barked.

"Opal, suh. You asked me to bring supper for the Lady."

With a muttered curse, he strode to the door and wrenched it open. Opal came in, a tray balanced in her hands. She looked at Alan, speculation in her dark eyes, then to Jenna. Her gaze lingered for a moment on the shackle, and grim disapproval hardened her normally good-natured face.

"And what's the matter with you?" Alan asked silkily.

"Why are you askin' me, suh?"

"Because I know you'll give me an honest answer."

"Hmph. You don't want to hear what I got to say."

He raised one dark eyebrow. "Which is?"

"All men is fools. And all women is fools for puttin' up with them."

"Thank you for your observation," he said. "You may put the tray on the table beside the bed."

It was a dismissal, a firm one. She obeyed without protest, but the sway of her hips and the indignant angle at which she held her head spoke her thoughts better than words.

Jenna waited until the door closed behind the cook, then said, "I won't eat your food."

"That is your choice."

"I won't stay in your house."

"Now that," he said, "is not your choice."

"I hate you," Jenna said, clearly and calmly.

"You know what you have to do to be rid of me."

Everything that had happened the past few days crashed in on her. Her temper flared white-hot. Leaping to her feet atop the bed, she grasped the chain and wrenched it savagely. "You're mad if you think you can keep me here like this!" she hissed.

"Heronsgate is mine," he retorted. "I can do anything I want here. And as you pointed out before, no one will say nay to anything I do to the witch."

Snatching up the tray, she hurled it and its contents straight at his head. He ducked, cursing. Dishes, utensils and food smashed against the wall behind him.

Alan straightened, turning to survey the damage. Shards of broken china littered the floor, and a dollop of corn pudding slid wetly down the wall like a huge snail. "You've got a hell of a temper for a woman of such cool beauty," he said. "But then it matches the other fire within you."

"I wish I were a witch! I'd . . . I'd . . ." Unable to think of anything horrible enough to suit her, she snatched the pillow off the bed and hurled it at him.

He dodged, a grin of unholy joy curving his mouth. After all the torment he'd been through, he welcomed a good, walloping fight. And damn him for a fool, Jenna in a full, flaring temper was a magnificent sight. Wild, beautiful woman, with that hair swinging around her like pale seafoam and those green eyes full of fire.

"That was a waste of perfectly good food," he said, knowing it would goad her further.

"Damn your food! Damn your suspicion, your arrogance, and damn *you!*"

"As I said before, I was damned the moment I met you. I should have listened to Rafferty."

"Rafferty!" She gave the chain another yank, scoring ragged white patches in the wood of the bedpost. "I would rather you gave me to him!" she shouted. "At least he was honest about his hate!"

"Shall I?" His voice turned dangerously soft. "Shall I give you to Rafferty?"

"Anything to get away from you!" she shouted. "Anything and anyone! I wish I'd given myself to anyone but you!"

Absurdly, that reckless statement made him angrier than anything she'd said before. The thought of another man touching her sent a wild torrent of jealousy crashing through him. Consumed with fury, he hurled himself toward her.

Jenna flung herself to one side. But the chain jerked her foot out from under her, and she sprawled facedown upon the mattress. Alan's hands closed on her shoulders, rolling her over roughly. She found herself gazing into a pair of furious indigo eyes as he leaned over her.

"Watch your tongue, madam," he growled. "I am not a man you can push too far."

"Get off me!"

She raked at his face with her nails. Cursing, he grabbed her wrists, pulling her up toward him as he tried to restrain her. She twisted frantically. Panic closed in on her; it seemed as though if she lost this battle, somehow she'd lose everything.

"Stop it," Alan panted. "Bloody hell, Jenna!"

He managed to wrestle her back down. Unwilling to hurt her to subdue her, he absorbed her struggles, using his greater weight and strength to wear her out. But damn, she was a handful! Worse, his body was reacting to her nearness. Her hips bucked and twisted beneath him, and her shirt had come loose from her trousers, exposing the smooth flesh of her abdomen.

With a grunt of effort, he forced her arms up over her head and pinned them there. His lower body rested upon her thighs, stilling the movement of her legs. Panting from exertion, he raised himself enough so that he could look at her.

Prisoner she might be, but she certainly wasn't docile; if looks could kill, those blazing green eyes would have taken him down instantly.

"Are you going to shackle my arms as well?" she hissed.

"I don't need to, do I?"

"You can't hold me forever. The instant you relax, I'll go straight for your throat."

"Bloodthirsty little savage that you are."

What had once been an endearment had become an insult. He saw it hit, saw it hurt, and strangely, felt emptiness instead of triumph.

Suddenly she arched, a convulsive movement that very nearly dislodged him. He shifted, coming down more fully upon her.

"Stop fighting, damn it," he muttered.

He noticed that her shirt had drawn up farther still. He could see the gentle ridges of her ribs, and above that, the beginning underswell of her breasts. The sight jolted him powerfully. His mind conjured up the memory of those lovely, pale mounds, rose-tipped and eager. The nipples had responded so beautifully to his hands, his mouth. So visceral was the picture that he could almost feel them, taste them.

"You're not wearing anything beneath your shirt," he said.

Jenna froze, staring up at him. The flame of rage had

faded, but heat of another sort flared in his eyes. And this heat was far more dangerous than anger.

"Let me go," she whispered.

"I can't."

Jenna shook her head, denying what she knew was about to happen. Wrenching one arm free, she pounded at his shoulders and back.

"Damn it to hell," he growled.

He trapped her wrist again, then plunged his mouth down on hers. It was a bruising kiss, a savage male attempt to dominate on the most primitive level. His body pressed her deep into the mattress, his muscled thighs spreading hers wide beneath him. Even through his trousers and hers, she could feel the blatant rod of his manhood.

No! Please, not this! This was a violation she couldn't bear, this assault from the man she'd once been eager to love. She fought to turn her head, to escape his plundering tongue and hands.

To her horror, she realized that her own body had begun to react to his carnal touch, his scent, and her memories of what had once been. It seemed as though her skin, her flesh had taken on a life of their own—at his behest.

Suddenly the kiss changed. His mouth softened, even as his body grew still harder. And the hands that had caught her wrists gentled, then drew her arms up around her neck. It was the tenderness that was her undoing.

For it was a lie. If she let him, he would pleasure her. He would take her to the height of passion, and then afterward . . . afterward he'd drop her straight into hell. No caring warmed his hands or his heart, only lust.

His mouth left hers to nibble a path along her jaw to

her throat. She squeezed her eyes closed, fighting the clamor of her body. Her heart beat a wild tattoo in her chest, even as rich, liquid heat pooled in the center of her body. Her belly tightened. Anticipating. Wanting. Needing.

A shiver went through her as he brushed her shirt upward, exposing her breasts. He stared at her for one flaring moment, then bent his head to trace a wet, hot circle around her nipples with his tongue. Her protest died in a moan of pleasure. He began to suckle her, nipping gently, tugging, sending waves of need spearing through her.

It had always been like this between them. Flesh calling to flesh, desire igniting desire. He was the only man who had ever touched the passion in her, the only one she'd ever wanted. Her lover. Her . . .

He thinks you poisoned his children. But she knew that if she didn't stop him, didn't stop herself, that wouldn't matter. A moment more, and she'd drop into a maelstrom of desire from which there was no escape.

No escape. Trapped. Chained. If he'd taken the shackles off, she still would be chained by what she felt when he touched her.

"No!" she gasped.

He looked up at her, his eyes nearly black with desire. "What?"

"Stop. Please, stop."

"Tell the truth, Jenna." Clasping her breasts gently, but with infinite possession, he ran his thumbs across her taut nipples. It had to be bewitchment, this obsessive need for her. But knowing it didn't help; his body seemed to have a life of its own, all centered around this woman. "You don't want me to stop."

She didn't. She did. She wanted him to take her in love, in trust, and that could never be. Looking directly into his eyes, she asked, "Will you take me by force?"

With a groan of irrepressible frustration, Alan sat up. He had to close his eyes and take several deep breaths before he could get his emotions under control. Finally, he dared look at her. She'd pulled her shirt down. Tears leaked out from her tight-closed eyes and ran down to soak the hair at her temples. She was achingly lovely, and it took an effort of will not to touch her again.

Damn. He knew he could seduce her. He could make her writhe, he could make her beg for his touch. And he knew it would be the worst thing he could do to her.

This is your chance to hurt her as much as she hurt you. Do it. Another man would.

But he was not other men. Call him the bloodiest fool to have been born in the past century, he found himself incapable of doing what another might have done in his situation. With a groan of mingled frustration and anger, he levered himself off the bed.

She lay before him, as beautiful as a dream. Tears glistened like quicksilver on her cheeks, matching the wild cascade of hair spread out around her. He wanted to hold her, keep her and escape her all at once.

If only he weren't plagued with memories of her writhing beneath him in the throes of her passion, those long, long legs wrapped around his hips, her body inciting him to more. If only he could look on it as a mere physical coupling.

"You're fortunate I'm an honorable man," he said.

Her eyes opened, clear green pools deep enough for a man to get lost in. He expected to see anger there, or perhaps loathing. But he saw only sadness. His heart twisted in his chest.

Bending, he unlocked her shackles and tossed them aside. He'd detested the necessity of them, but he'd had to make certain she couldn't get away from him. She retreated to the head of the bed, tucking her legs beneath her as though expecting him to change his mind.

"I told you it was only for the day," he said.

Jenna gathered herself, ready to try for the door. If she could get a few yards' start, he'd never catch her.

"Do you think you can make it?" Alan asked, as though he'd been privy to her thoughts. "If you don't, it's the shackle again."

Jenna decided caution was the better part of valor—not because she feared the shackle, but because she couldn't risk another physical encounter with him. Besides, he might lock the door, but there was always the window. So she relaxed, folding her hands upon her lap like any demure young lady.

"You ought to see the look on your face," Alan said.

"And how do I look, pray?"

He came toward her, and it took all her courage not to move. Feeling like a mouse about to be gobbled up, she tilted her head back to look at him.

"You look like a very pretty lady cat who has gotten into the larder," he said. "And who thinks no one knows."

For a moment she thought he'd try to kiss her again, but he only ran his forefinger lightly down her cheek. She pulled back from his touch.

"Don't get cocky just because your fetters are off," he said, with a smile she didn't like at all.

"And you should remember that cats have claws," she retorted.

He met her gaze, accepting the challenge. "I'll send someone up to clean up the mess," he said. "Don't try any tricks." Then he turned and strode out of the room.

Jenna waited until she heard the key turn in the lock before running to the window. She tried to lift the sash. And failed. Pulling the curtain aside, she found that the window frame had been nailed shut. She wasn't much surprised; Alan had been much too pleased with himself.

But at least the shackles were off. Moving to the pile of shattered china, she picked through the mess. There was no knife, of course, but she did find a spoon.

Smiling, she ran her finger down the handle. "Meow," she said.

Twenty-one

Roanna woke to the sweet, high trill of a bird as it sang to greet the dawn. She sat up, stretching hard enough to make her old bones remember to move.

"Jenna?" she called.

Only the bird answered her. Tossing the blanket aside, she rose from the pallet and unbraided her long, white hair. She felt much better this morning, much. The shock of hearing Jenna profess her love for the master of Heronsgate had laid her low, wrapping an iron band of pain around her heart.

"Ah, youth," she muttered, taking the liberty of borrowing Jenna's brush. "You're just like Silvan, child. Too much. Your heart is far too open for your own good."

The golden morning light drew her outside. She'd never been one to stay indoors, not with all God's green beauty at her doorstep. Jenna's doorstep, rather. She hadn't approved of her granddaughter living apart from her, but it had turned out well enough; Jenna wanted to be accessible to those who needed her help, and Roanna wanted only to be left alone.

She pushed the veil of brush aside and stepped into the tiny clearing which served as nursery, hospital, and boardinghouse for Jenna's animal patients. She walked along the line of cages. Much of this was the work of

Man: a hawk, one wing shattered by a hunter's shot, a fox that had chewed its own foot off to escape a trap, a duckling whose mother had gone into some townsman's stewpot.

"Had your run-ins with the bastards, too, didn't you?" Roanna asked.

The fox watched her with round, avid eyes. Suddenly she stiffened, realizing with a jolt that the animals had not been fed. Jenna had said she planned to feed them before coming to bed. The old woman stood for a moment, considering this, then abruptly turned back to the cabin.

"I have a bad feeling about this," she muttered. "She would never forget you, not even for a tumble with the man of her dreams."

She fed the beasts before she left. Then she trudged off toward the river, knowing that the only way a townsman could get this far into the swamp was by water. She found the dead campfire only a short time later. As she neared it, she saw the tracks Jenna had made, and also the larger ones left by a man.

"Came straight toward the fire," she said. "Knew him, didn't you?"

Then she discovered a place where the scurf had been disturbed, and violently.

Roanna closed her hands into fists. For the moment, anger overshadowed age. "She knew you, trusted you, and you jumped her." She circled the campsite, her gaze fixed on the ground. Finding the cut pieces of rawhide, she said, "You tied her, then untied her. What did you say to her to make her go with you without a fight? Was it a threat, or a lie? Ah, Jenna, child!"

Ugly memories stabbed through her mind. She'd run

from them for years, had even managed to hide them away for a while. But now they returned in a black flood: Silvan's pale, crumpled body, blood covering her chest and loins, the pain of feeling her daughter's life slip through her hands, the loss of the kindest, gentlest soul that had ever walked this earth. And the song, the beautiful, beautiful voice that turned the swamp into heaven, forever stilled.

But not Jenna. No. It wouldn't happen again. She hadn't protected Silvan properly, but she wasn't about to make the same mistake with her granddaughter.

She'd lost Silvan to the hatred, but she wasn't about to lose Jenna. Not if she had to pull the town down plank by plank, stone by stone, and cast the remains to the wind.

Lifting her face to the sky, she cried, "I'm coming, Jenna! I'm coming!"

Using the spoon, which she'd sharpened against the chain of the shackle, Jenna dug carefully at the wood around one of the twopenny nails securing the window. She'd worked all night, and had nearly freed the head enough to pull the nail out.

But the house was beginning to stir. Scooping up the sawdust from the sill, she moistened it with water from the ewer and patched the hole she'd made.

"One night, one nail," she said, impatience settling over her in a smothering cloak. At this rate, it would take four days to get out. Roanna would have awakened this morning to find her gone, and unless she missed her guess badly, the old woman would be up and looking for her.

Roanna possessed great wisdom, but the one thing she'd never learned was fear. She would come to Heronsgate. Even knowing it could mean her death, she would come.

Hearing the rattle of a key in the lock, Jenna ran to the nearest chair and sat down. The door swung open, revealing Alan's lean, broad-shouldered figure.

The sight of him jolted her. She wished it weren't so, that she didn't find him so compelling and so disturbing, that she could look upon him with the disdain he deserved. But her heart leaped, ignoring the dictates of her mind, and she seemed incapable of keeping her gaze from roaming the broad expanse of his shoulders and chest, the trim waist and hips, the long, strong stretch of legs beneath his trousers. He'd freshly bathed; his hair, still wet, slicked smoothly back from his forehead, and he'd shaved—rather hastily, judging from the three dabs of plaster that marked his jaw.

"Too bad the razor didn't slip a little lower," she said.

"Such as right over the jugular vein?"

She nodded. "That would have been nice."

He smiled at her then, a grin that spoke of plans she was sure she wouldn't like. Here in the flood of golden morning light, his eyes looked like dark sapphires. And as hard. "Did you sleep well?" he asked.

"Well enough. May I see the children?"

"No."

She scowled. "So that I won't have a chance to poison them again?"

"Wouldn't you do the same if you were me?"

"I find it hard to imagine being without trust or compassion, and so completely arrogant that I assumed the world revolved around my concerns."

His brows contracted, and she knew that one had struck home. Good. He'd find her a most disagreeable prisoner.

"You've quite a way with words, madam," he said with patently false pleasantness. "But you should remember that every one of them will cost you."

"Is it your plan to wear me down by ruining my appetite before every meal?"

"Not at all. It would be a shame to starve such a lovely body." If his eyes hadn't remained so glacial, she might have taken it for a compliment. "I've merely come to escort you down to breakfast," he said.

Honestly surprised, she asked, "Downstairs?"

"Do you prefer to eat alone?"

"Not at all. May I suggest a picnic?"

"In the swamp, perhaps?"

"Perhaps."

He smiled. Grimly. "I think you've a natural talent for cynical drawing-room conversation."

"I wouldn't know."

"I would."

Crossing her arms over her chest, she matched his smile. "You could have spared yourself this conversation by merely saying 'please come down to breakfast'."

"Very well. Please come down to breakfast."

"Are you planning to shackle me to my chair?"

"No."

"Aren't you afraid I'll run away?"

"No. You see, I plan to be your constant companion everywhere you go."

"I'd almost rather stay here."

"Almost?"

She cocked her head to one side. "I'll take the chance that you might blink."

"So will I." With an ironic bow, he extended his arm. "Shall we?"

She didn't want to touch him. Head high, she stalked past him, only to have him hook his arm around her waist and draw her back. She drew her breath in raggedly as she felt the hard plane of his chest against her back.

"Don't you want to change?" he asked, his breath warm against the back of her neck. "There are some gowns in the armoire that should fit you."

Shivers ran through her, only partly from fear. "I'll wear nothing of yours."

He held her for a moment, his fingers spread out across her hip as though to assess the gentle curve of flesh. She closed her eyes as his breath brushed along her ear, the side of her neck. Desire coiled like hot smoke through her veins, and with it, panic.

That's what he wants. He can't affect you any other way, so he does this.

This man was no friend, no lover, but her sworn enemy. He didn't want her; this was just a coolly calculating probe for weakness. If she showed it to him, he'd attack it without mercy. So she ignored the flutter of her pulse and the softening of her body and stood stiffly against the restraint of his arm.

After a moment, he let her go. But he'd made his point; when he offered his arm once again, she took it. Her fingers trembled a bit as they settled on his hard-hewn forearm.

"And you intend to carry out this nonsense every day?" she asked, keeping her tone quite reasonable.

"Every day," he said.

Alan watched her profile as they walked. He'd expected her to be much more annoyed at this. But she looked cool and self-contained, as though nothing he said or did could shake her.

He couldn't help himself; the more she wanted to get away from him, the more he seemed to want to keep her. Obsessed, that's what he was. Ensnared body and soul. Had she tapped him this instant with a magic wand and announced him free, he couldn't be sure he'd be able to let her go even then.

Witch. Poisoner. Betrayer. All true. But still, seeing her move with such unconscious grace, that pale hair flowing down her back in a moonlight froth, he wanted her.

"You didn't braid your hair this morning." He said it because he had to; by saying it, he could control the urge to sink his hands into that shining mass of curls.

"My comb is in my pack."

"I'll see that it is returned to you."

"My pack?"

"Your comb."

Jenna felt more than a little sick inside. "Do you think I'm going to use my herbs to murder you all in your beds? Or perhaps I'll conjure myself right out of that locked room?"

"A week ago, I didn't believe in witchcraft at all. Now, the world has twisted halfway around, and I intend to be cautious until I learn the new rules."

She fell silent and remained so until they reached the dining room. But her docility was only on the surface; inside, she seethed with indignation. When Alan opened the door for her, she stalked in ahead of him, head held high.

He followed her in, leaning one hip upon the corner of the table and studying her with an impassive gaze.

She felt as though he were stripping her, layer by layer down to her soul and that he didn't much like what he found.

Lifting her chin up another notch, she went to the sideboard and began to fill her plate. Opal had obviously cooked for her; from the delightful, deep-smoked ham to the cornbread and blackberry jam, the dishes were Jenna's favorites. It was a kindness and much appreciated just now.

"We'll want fresh tea," Alan said, reaching for the bell cord. "Or would you prefer something else?"

"Tea is fine."

As she passed the window, she spotted a familiar, lanky form standing in front of the trees that separated Heronsgate land from the swamp. Rafferty. His hat hung low over his forehead, making him look even more sinister than usual. She stopped, plate in hand, and watched as two other men came out of the trees to stand beside the slave hunter. Perhaps she should have been afraid, but she'd much rather have them here, and after her, than roaming the swamp and finding Roanna.

"What are you looking at?" Alan asked.

She shrugged. "The vultures are beginning to gather."

He moved closer to the window, his expression turning cold and somehow secretive. "I suppose he's waiting for you to leave."

"So I should be wary of escaping."

"That would be wise."

Jenna thumped her plate down on the table. "His presence here couldn't have been more convenient if you'd arranged it yourself."

"True," he replied, moving toward the sideboard.

She stared at his broad back, then picked up her knife

and fork and cut a piece of ham. "A less arrogant man would hesitate to give his prisoner a knife and then turn his back."

"I'd call it confidence, not arrogance."

"You're confident, then, that I am not the sort who'd stick a blade between a man's shoulder blades?"

Turning, he fixed her with a stone-cold indigo stare. "I'm confident that I could stop you before you could."

Her hand tightened on the knife, and for a moment she wished, truly wished, that she were a violent person.

He sat down across from her. "Pass the butter, please."

She let go of the knife and handed him the butter dish. It seemed a strange scene, two bitter enemies sitting across the breakfast table, so cozy and civilized on the outside, so angry beneath.

"I wish I'd never met you," she said.

"Too bad you didn't know who I was when you found me that day."

"Yes. Too bad."

"I'm sure you would have done things very differently."

"You're right." Slowly, she spread jam on a steaming half of biscuit and took a bite. A dollop of sweetness clung to her lower lip, and she licked it off. Then she saw Alan's gaze drop to her mouth. A hot little flame sprang to existence in the depth of his eyes, and she froze.

Desire. It flared as hot as the anger, and not only in him. She hated herself for being so weak and him for being able to do this to her. Jonas Rafferty might be dangerous as a rat when cornered, but Alan Langston was far more deadly. Corner a rat and it would surely bite; corner a wolf and it would tear your throat out.

It should have frightened her. But it was desire, not fear, that made her pulse quicken and brought molten heat swirling through her body. She'd loved this man. He'd initiated her to the pleasures of the body and the anguish of the heart.

And she loved him still. Even after his betrayal, his insults and his accusations, she still loved him.

You're doubly a fool then. Once for falling in the first place, twice for not having the strength to despise him now.

She closed her eyes, unable to bear his too-knowing indigo gaze a moment longer. Her being centered on that place deep inside her that ached and desired, needed and wanted and cried out in despair. Even when she heard his chair scrape back, felt him take the biscuit from her lax fingers, she didn't open them.

"Look at me," he said.

"No."

"Damn it, Jenna—"

"Oh, Alan!" Miranda Carrew's shrill voice rang from the front of the house. "Yoo-hoo!"

"Bloody hell," he muttered. Raising his voice, he called, "I'm in the dining room."

A moment later, Miranda hove into the doorway. She looked like an exotic bird in her burgundy riding habit, Jenna thought, a creature of perfumed lushness and perfect uselessness. All show and no substance. What would Grandmother have said about this? Ah, yes. She would have lifted one pale eyebrow in perfect cynicism and said, "What makes you think men want substance, girl?"

Miranda rushed forward, hands extended, as Alan came to meet her. "Hello, darling!" Then her gaze went to Jenna, and her mouth thinned. "I thought she ran back to the swamp."

"Hello, Miranda," Jenna said.

The other woman ignored her. Gazing up at Alan from beneath her lashes, she said, "You've been neglecting me, Alan, dear."

"Sorry," he said, although he wasn't. "Tea's on its way. Why don't you join us?"

"Why, thank you, darling."

She sat down with elaborate grace. Jenna refused to look at the handsome couple across from her, for then she'd have to recognize the emotion that made her heart feel so cold and heavy. Alan Langston was no longer any concern of hers, after all. The man who had captured her heart had been only a lovely dream; the reality was the cold-eyed aristocrat who'd accused her of poisoning his children.

Then why does it bother you that she puts her hand on his arm with such familiarity? Why does it bother you to see him smile so beguilingly at her?

Because she loved him. She loved the dream *and* the man. With all his faults and arrogance, she still loved him.

She glanced up at him and found him watching her. His eyes were speculative, his mouth a chiseled curve with all the beauty and hardness of a marble statue. Clasping her hands in her lap, she fixed her gaze on them.

Enos entered the room, bearing the tea things on a large silver tray. He busied himself serving, his hands moving with grace and gentleness among the delicate porcelain. Then he stepped back from the table.

"Thank you, Enos," Alan said. "That will be all."

Jenna kept her hands in her lap, ignoring the steaming cup of tea in front of her. She felt Alan's gaze on her, as real as if he'd reached out and touched her, but stubbornly refused to look at him.

"You promised to take me riding days ago, darling," Miranda said.

"I've been busy."

"Ah, yes, the poor children," she said, pressing her hand to her bosom. "I was so worried about them." Leaning close, Miranda asked, "Are you coming to the ball Saturday night?"

"What ball?"

"You've forgotten already? I don't know what to do with you, darling. It's the Carrew autumn ball. We host it every year, and everyone so looks forward to it. Do say you'll come."

Alan glanced at Jenna and saw a flicker of emotion in her eyes. Jealousy, perhaps? Triumph shot through him at the thought; he'd break that serene, caring facade of hers. Perhaps then he could hate her. Perhaps then he could sleep without seeing her face, feeling her skin beneath his hands, waking to the raging torment of his desire for her. And always, waking and sleeping, the haunting fragrance of honeysuckle.

He looked into Miranda's eyes. "Of course I'll come."

"Good. It just wouldn't be any fun without you."

"Now that," he said, "I find hard to believe. Rumor has it that a dozen or so suitors descend upon your house nearly every day."

"Oh, them." With a flick of slender white fingers, Miranda dismissed them. "They're boys. Fun, in a way, because they're so terribly eager for attention. But I want a man."

Jenna felt sick, her body clenching around the sudden swift pain in her heart. It wouldn't have been so bad if Alan hadn't looked at Miranda with that rakish half-smile on his face. As though he liked her. As though he were looking forward to being with her, to being the "man" she wanted.

Pushing her plate away, Jenna stood up. "I have to go upstairs."

Alan rose with her. "You haven't drunk your tea yet. Sit down."

"I'm not thirsty, thank you."

"Sit down. Please." The last was no request but an ironic play on her studied politeness.

Jenna saw the untrammeled arrogance in his eyes and realized he'd be quite impossible to deal with just now. Another woman might have deemed acquiescence the better part of valor. Not, however, a Llewellyn.

"Sit down," he said again, not quite as politely.

She smiled. "No."

For a moment she thought he'd spring on her and wrestle her into submission right on the table amid the plates and glasses. Suddenly he grinned, a piratical flash of strong white teeth that sank straight into her heart and made her limbs go weak.

"Very well," he said. "I'll escort you upstairs."

"It would be rude to leave your guest."

He walked around the table, taking her by the arm in a grip that numbed it to the elbow. "But doubly rude to let you walk all the way upstairs with that ankle you sprained this morning. Let me carry you—"

"I'll walk," she said.

"Then I'll help you." He glanced at Miranda. "Excuse me for a moment."

Looking as though she'd swallowed something sour, she said, "Of course, darling. Hurry back."

Jenna didn't begin to pretend she had a limp. Alan, apparently unconcerned that his lie had been found out, kept his grip on her arm as she strode out of the dining room.

"Your ladylove is bound to be angry at you," she said, striving for a cool tone and demeanor to match.

He made an impatient sound. "Miranda doesn't give a damn whether I lie."

"Only that you make love to her."

"Does that bother you?"

Yes, yes, yes! "Of course not."

"Then why are your eyes shooting green fire at me?"

"Perhaps because you're being obnoxious."

"You're jealous."

"I am not."

"Liar."

Jenna pressed her lips tightly together and remained silent as they walked up the stairs and down the hallway to her room.

A bath had been brought in while she'd been gone. Water steamed in the metal tub, and towels and soap sat on the stool beside it. Alan's gaze lingered on the scene for a seemingly endless moment, then returned to Jenna.

"Perhaps now is the time to exercise my rights as constant companion," he said.

"Is that why you had the bath brought up?"

"I merely told Opal to take care of you as she would any guest."

"But I'm not a guest, am I?"

His jaw hardened. "That was your choice. And continues to be."

"Why must you do this?" she cried. "Why are you so certain I'm some sort of ogre?"

"Ogre?" His brows went up. "Hardly, madam. Enchantress, siren, wood sprite—"

"Witch," she finished.

"Witch," he agreed. Closing the door, he leaned his back against it and watched her. "Had an ogre come roaring out of the swamp, I would have known its danger. But you, in your freshness and beauty, lured me into your web."

"I release you," she said.

He pushed away from the door and strode to her. Jenna stood her ground as he came, her gaze fixed on his.

"If you meant it, I'd be free," he said. "I wouldn't want to touch you." He grasped her shoulder, his fingers curving over her firm flesh. Then, slowly, he ran his hand up her neck, spearing his fingers through the heavy silk of her hair. "I wouldn't want to kiss you."

Jenna fought the sweet, treacherous tide of desire running through her. "Don't."

"Don't?" He tightened his grip, enough to pull her head back but not to hurt. Her eyes had turned smoky, answering the heat blazing inside him. "You don't mean that."

"You hate me." She closed her eyes, forcing the lie. "And I hate you."

"Ah, but our hate burns hot," he whispered. "Doesn't it?"

She shook her head. His hand gentled, then slid slowly down her arm to her wrist. The caress wasn't lascivious, just . . . possessive.

"Oh, Alan!" Miranda called.

"Blast," he growled. "Where is she, do you think?"

"At the bottom of the stairs. A moment more, and she'll come in here looking for you."

He let his breath out in a harsh sigh. "You look damn pleased with yourself. I'll wager you never thought to be grateful to Miranda for anything."

"I'll be even more grateful to her if she keeps you away permanently."

"I would never be so accommodating,"

Turning on his heel, he stalked out and slammed the door behind him.

Jenna sank to her knees, hands pressed to her chest. "Dear Lord, why must I love him?" she whispered, while hot tears spilled down her face. "Why?

Downstairs, Miranda laughed.

Twenty-two

Jenna watched dusk spread its violet cloak over Heronsgate. The shadows of the trees seemed to spread and soften until they blended with the onrushing darkness. The sight should have brought her contentment; now, it only underscored the tumult in her heart.

She slept little, instead working at the nails that secured the window. The nights seemed ages long. She seethed with worry that Roanna would come back looking for her, seethed even more with fury and frustration because of Alan. Alan, Alan, Alan. It was a terrible thing to love someone so deeply and to want so badly not to.

True to his promise, he'd spent every waking moment in her company. Brooding, cynical, as handsome as Lucifer himself, he'd made her days a hell. He kept her trapped with his gaze, with his smoldering desire and even hotter anger. She'd managed to meet it all with serene self-confidence, but inside she ached to the depths of her soul.

It might not have been so terrible if she hadn't wanted him in return. There were times when she nearly cried out for him to hold her, simply hold her, so that she might remember for a moment how it had once been.

"You're a fool," she said aloud. True. But no truer than her weakness where Alan Langston was concerned.

She looked down at the sharpened spoon in her hand. It had become badly worn in the past three nights. Three nights, three nails. Tonight was the fourth. Alan would go to the Carrews' ball, and by the time he got home, his prisoner would have flown.

Never, never would she leave the swamp again. This world was not for her; it held too much pain and too little understanding.

She looked up, startled, as someone knocked at the door, then hid the spoon and moved away from the window. "Who is it?" she called.

"Opal, Lady."

"You know I can't open the door."

The key rattled in the lock, and a moment later the cook came into the room, carrying the enormous iron teakettle from the kitchen. Ulysses and Enos followed her in, one bearing the tin bathtub, the other holding a pail in each hand.

"I got your bath," Opal said.

Jenna couldn't help but smile; the cook's kindness had been steadfast and very welcome. "You're trying very hard to spoil me."

"Ah, Lady, I wish—"

"That will be all, Opal." Alan's granite tones came from the hallway outside.

He stepped into the doorway. Dressed in his evening clothes, he looked imposing and incredibly handsome. Again, Jenna got the impression of a leopard disguised as a gentleman, an impression heightened by the stark ferocity of his eyes. He'd obviously come prepared for a battle—nay, eager for one.

Without looking away from her, he held his hand out

to Opal. She placed the key in his outstretched palm, then stalked out of the room.

Jenna put her hands on her hips, regarding Alan with narrowed eyes. Better to meet the challenge head-on; it wasn't her way to step back from a fight. "What do you want?"

Instead of answering, he stepped back into the hallway. He reappeared a moment later, a cascade of brilliant scarlet silk in his hands. Jenna's breath caught as she realized it was a gown—a beautiful, elegant garment meant, she knew, for a ball.

"You can't be serious," she said.

"I am."

"I won't go."

"Yes, you will." He closed the door. And very deliberately, locked it. "I'm perfectly willing to strip you naked, bathe you, and then dress you again."

She stared at him, frightened by his polished looks and raging eyes, and by his capacity to hurt her. How could he force her to attend that ball, knowing that everyone there thought her a witch and a poisoner?

"Are you dissatisfied with punishing me yourself, that you must throw me on the pyre of your neighbors' hatred?"

"I merely want to go to the ball and don't trust you here alone."

"Even locked up?"

"Even then."

She crossed her arms over her chest. "Don't you trust your own household?"

"Actually, no. The servants are in complete awe of you. I think they'd risk a whipping to let you go."

"And would you whip them?" she asked softly.

His brows contracted, a dark flare of annoyance above his eyes. "What do you think?"

"I no longer know what to think."

"Indeed." He closed the door and leaned his back against it. "Even Dorcas thinks I should let you go. She has been most persistent about it."

This surprised Jenna; she'd never thought Dorcas her friend. "Why don't you, then?"

"Because I can't."

"You won't."

"No." Pain made his voice harsh. "I can't."

"Why do you blame me for your own simple lust?" she asked in exasperation.

"This . . . thing between us is hardly simple, madam. Nor would I call this lust. *That* I'm familiar with. It would have been sated the first time I had you, and I could have walked away without a thought."

Jenna let her breath out sharply. She'd hit that adamantine wall within him; nothing she said or did was going to change his mind. He didn't believe her. He was never going to believe her. As long as he desired her, he'd think it was because of her spellcasting, not the simple passion of a man for a woman. And why? Because she was a Llewellyn, and Llewellyns were witches.

He was like all the rest. Prejudiced. Blind. Unwilling to accept anyone different, anyone who didn't fit their idea of what a woman should be and how she should act.

Unwilling to love.

Alan took her silence as acquiescence. He filled the bath for her, setting out the towels and rose-petal soap that should have been honeysuckle.

"There you are," he said. "I've played ladies' maid thus far. Do you need my help further?"

Jenna looked deeply into his eyes, reading the desire there. It simmered in those indigo depths like red-hot coals, ready to burst into incandescence at the slightest provocation. She had the feeling it would always be like this between them.

"Jenna?" he prompted, daring her.

Ah, she thought, *'tis a game with him, this sensual play.* He used it to keep her off balance. Perhaps it worked with the simpering females he was accustomed to. But not Jenna Llewellyn. She'd been confused by the unfamiliar urgings of her body and her heart and had allowed him to take the upper hand. No more. She would not be bound by his rules.

"I can manage," she said. "Do you intend to watch?"

The heat in his eyes flared. "Do you want me to?"

"It matters not, one way or another."

"Then, madam, no power on this earth could drag me away."

Meeting his gaze levelly, she unbuttoned her shirt and shrugged it off. Then she unfastened her trousers and pushed them down over her hips, stepping out of them gracefully.

"Are you going to continue?" he asked as she hesitated.

"Do you want me to stop?"

"No."

The hoarseness of his voice betrayed him. Jenna almost smiled, her heart soaring with triumph at the effect she had on him. She untied the ribbons of her chemise and let it fall, then removed her drawers. Magnificently, unashamedly naked, she walked toward the bath.

His gaze burned a path along her flesh, and it almost felt as though he'd caressed her with his hands. She ignored him, even as she fought to ignore the frantic rush of her pulse, the quickening of her body.

Alan stood poised at the edge of control, honor struggling with the powerful, primitive urge to take her here and now. Sweat broke out on his forehead as he studied the seductive curves of her hips and taut breasts, the pale thatch of woman's hair covering the sweet delights below.

For a moment he thought he might die with his need for her. He repressed a groan as she paused beside the tub to wind her braid into a platinum coronet around her head, lifting her breasts as though offering them to his mouth.

"You're taunting me," he muttered.

Jenna didn't deny it. Without looking away from him, she stepped into the tub and began to wash. The soap slid slickly over her skin, bringing a rush of goosebumps in its wake. Alan's hot gaze followed the movement of her hands. Boldly. Hungrily, as though he wanted to consume her then and there.

This, she thought. *This is a woman's power.* A man had strength and boldness and the law on his side, but a woman wielded something infinitely more powerful. Slowly, she scrubbed the soap between her hands, working up a rich lather. She washed her neck and shoulders, then ran her hands over the taut curves of her breasts. Her nipples peaked in involuntary response. But not to her touch. No, *he* engendered that reaction in her, with the thick sound of passion that he seemed unaware of making.

Repressing a smile of triumph, she lifted one leg clear of the water, propping her foot on the top of the tub to wash. Which she did, slowly and tantalizingly, gazing at him all the while.

It was hardly a one-sided torment, however; her own body ran hot with desire, frissons of arousal spinning like foxfire along her nerves. Emptiness dawned inside her, emptiness that only Alan could fill. Her eyelids lowered as she remembered the flaring pleasure they'd shared, the feeling of possessing and being possessed as he loved her, hard and long and tender, the way he'd called her name when he'd climaxed.

Her whole body seemed centered around that coiling, liquid arousal. The water felt cool against her fevered skin, the sensation of soap bubbles as they slid down her body almost too much to bear. She watched him from beneath her lashes, seeing his need, feeling her own. It was a kind of madness, this desperate, fathomless wanting. Beyond reason, beyond distrust and betrayal—a primitive drive for completion.

Her hands trembled just a bit as she began to rinse. It was tempting, so very tempting. All she had to do was ask. He would please her, pleasure her, take her spinning into a vast, soaring ocean of voluptuousness. He could, he could. Only he.

But then he'd fling her away in cold arrogance, accusing her again of poisoning his children. Without a thought, he'd tear her heart out and stamp it beneath his feet. No one else could touch her like this, hurt her like this.

The price was too high. Alan Langston had cost her far too much already; self-respect was the only thing left for her. She would keep it. Regaining control of her careening emotions, she leaned against the back of the tub so that the water lapped at the undersides of her breasts.

Her nipples tautened still further, a fact that didn't go unnoticed, judging from the look in Alan's eyes.

"You're playing a dangerous game," he said.

She smiled. "You can leave any time you wish."

Alan clenched his fists, knowing her words were a lie, knowing she realized it as well as he. He couldn't leave. Even if he'd had the strength of mind to order it, his body wouldn't have obeyed. Now he understood the full extent of the disaster that had struck him. He'd been trapped by her beauty and his desire for her, equally trapped by his distrust. By imprisoning her, he'd only bound himself; if he let her go, something vital within him would go with her.

Cursed. Like Orwell Stepton and his sons before him, cursed. But his affliction was of the heart and not the body, for he'd been damned to desire the witch forever, knowing it could never be, knowing he could never be free.

He watched her hands move over the sweet curve of her lower leg, then slide upward along her thigh. He wished he were the one washing her. Ah, to have the freedom of that exquisite body, to touch her, taste her, plunge deep into her tight, hot depths . . . Like a starving man forced to watch the banquet but not partake, he longed, he suffered, he regretted what he could not have.

She shifted position, leaning forward so that he could see the upper slopes of her buttocks. His whole body felt like one pulsing heartbeat, and he was so hard that it was actually painful.

"Get out of the tub," he rasped, knowing it was capitulation but unable to bear it any longer.

"Excuse me?"

"Get out of the tub. Now."

Jenna obeyed. Ah, triumph was sweet! She stood for a moment to let the water sluice from her skin, ignoring the sharp inhalation that was torn from Alan's throat.

"Is that better?" she asked.

He closed the distance between them. The flaring aggression in his eyes daunted her for a moment, but then temper and defiance brought her chin up.

"Don't even think about touching me," she said.

A muscle jumped at the corner of his jaw. "After watching that display a moment ago, most men would think they had a right to touch."

"You have no rights," she said. "The only thing you'll get from me is what you take."

"That might be enough."

Unafraid, she met his gaze squarely. "Would it?"

Alan let his breath out in a harsh sigh. She had him there. He'd never be satisfied with what was not given freely; only Jenna herself, offered in joy, would ease the grinding ache in his body and his heart.

"You're fortunate I am who I am," he said. "Another man would take you here on the carpet."

"Other men be damned," she retorted. " 'Tis your own honor you struggle with here."

"Get dressed."

"And if I don't?"

His voice turned silken. "I'd like nothing better than an excuse to get my hands on you. Do you think you could stand cold beneath my touch?"

"Undoubtedly."

"Shall we try?"

"Do you intend to force me?"

"Not if you dress yourself."

Fury beat white-hot wings in her chest. Always this!

She got out of the tub, stepping so close to him that her pointed nipples grazed the front of his jacket. The contact sent a storm-wind of sensation through her, desire and anger and frustration so intense she nearly cried from it. Bending, she snatched the towel from the floor and wrapped it around her.

She marched to the bed and lifted the gown. It was a beautiful thing, made of silk as thin and lustrous as the night breeze, a red as pure and brilliant as heart's-blood. Holding it to her, she spun to face him.

"Why red?" she asked.

"Isn't it fitting?"

"For a witch?"

He shook his head. "For passion. Does it surprise you, Jenna? It shouldn't. You burn like a flame for all your paleness. A man could be consumed if he didn't guard himself."

Alan tensed as he saw the towel slither downward, exposing most of her breasts to his gaze. Her skin glowed like mother of pearl against the scarlet gown, pale, sumptuous flesh finer than silk could ever be.

"A man can never guard enough," she said.

He showed the edges of his teeth in a grin that had no humor in it. "I'll take the risk."

She matched his smile. Smoothing the gown with her palm, she said, "Yes. You will."

Roanna walked the streets of Old Lebanon, her hair covered with a bonnet she'd filched from someone's windowsill. The town had changed little in the years she'd been gone. The raucous sounds of revelry floated from the places that catered to the bawdy men who came to

drink and fight the nights away. Rogues all, from the
captains and crews of the shingles that plied the canals,
to the lumberjacks who raped the riches of the Dismal
and the motley hangers-on who feasted on the leavings
of more successful parasites.

The stink of civilization hung all around her: burned
grease and open privies, smoke and rum and unwashed
human flesh. Laughter gusted from a doorway nearby,
the shrill screech of a woman's voice underscored by the
deeper tones of lewd, drunken men.

The old woman shivered, pulling the hood of her cape
further around her face. "If I had half the power rumor
gave me, I'd blast the lot of you off the face of the earth,"
she said.

Getting here hadn't been easy; bands of swamp rats
prowled this section of the Dismal. She'd had to dodge
and hide and circle far out of her way to keep from being
discovered.

Ah, but she was here now. Memory chose her path
for her, past the noisy taverns and bawdy houses, past
the piles of fresh-cut cypress, maple, and juniper, past
the place where docks stretched out into the river like
many-legged insects. Everywhere she went, she watched
and listened in vain for some sign of Jenna.

She made her way to the tiny cypress house that had
once served as her prison many years ago. It hadn't aged
well. Poorly built to begin with, it had darkened almost
to black from smoke and age and sagged like a spavined
horse.

"Just like me," she muttered, with the ghost of a
chuckle.

Stretching up on tiptoe, she peered in one of the high,
glassless windows. Jenna was not there; the only occu-

pant of the single room was a blowsy woman with hair
an improbable shade of red. She lay on the bed, her abun-
dant flesh clad only in chemise and pantalettes.

Roanna blew her breath out in frustration. She hadn't
been able to get close to Heronsgate; even more men
prowled the edges of the plantation than this section of
the swamp. Men! she thought disdainfully. Packs of
wolves, rather. If she'd been twenty years younger, she
could have ghosted through them like smoke on a winter's eve. But not now.

A hand fell heavily on her shoulder, spinning her
around to see a man's bearded face looming over her.

"You gettin' impatient for . . . You ain't Marta," he
said, enveloping her in a cloud of rum-scented breath.
"What are you doing skulking around here, you?"

"Take your hands from me," she snapped. "Or you'll
be licking Satan's boots this very night."

Still holding her with one hand, he snatched her hood
back with the other. "Who the hell . . ." He recoiled, his
face turning pasty white under his beard. "The witch!"

"Say a word about this, and you'll share Stepton's
fate."

"I wouldn't . . . I couldn't . . ." He all but swallowed
his beard in his terror.

He took to his heels. The sound of his footsteps faded
rapidly in the distance. Roanna smiled grimly.

"You wanted a witch, gentlefolk," she said. "Now
you've got one."

And perhaps a bit more of one than they'd bargained
for. Leaving her hood down, she turned and walked into
the darkness. She had work to do.

Twenty-three

Alan watched the people turn and stare as he escorted Jenna into the Carrews' spacious drawing room. Not that he blamed them; she was more than breathtaking. Had she been wearing rags, she would have easily eclipsed the other women. In the sumptuous scarlet gown, she shone like the sun.

"Come, Jenna." He drew her into the room, straight toward Mrs. Carrew.

The older woman stared with open hostility in her eyes. The sight lifted Jenna's chin and helped her walk toward her enemies as though it didn't matter.

Alan bowed to the dowager. "Good evening, Mrs. Carrew."

The older woman gave a stiff little nod of her head. "Mr. Langston."

"You remember Miss Llewellyn, of course."

"Yes."

Mrs. Carrew started to turn away, but someone trod on her train and she stumbled gracelessly. Jenna reacted instinctively, catching her by the arm and steadying her. The woman drew herself up, glaring at Jenna with such intense disgust that she released her immediately. Without a word, Mrs. Carrew turned and walked away.

Jenna felt the blood drain from her cheeks. Turning,

she looked at Alan, only to find him in conversation with someone else. He hadn't seen the ugly little exchange; probably wouldn't have cared if he had. And these people talked about manners! After a moment he turned back to her, as though her gaze had been a physical touch demanding his attention.

"I want to go now," she said.

"We just got here, Jenna."

"You've had your fun. Now take me back."

Alan studied her, admiring the contrast between the brilliant silk of her gown and the pale ivory satin of her skin. The chandelier cast shards of rainbow light over her hair. His gaze dropped to the lush double curve of her mouth, then lower, to the even more luxurious flesh of her breasts.

He wasn't the only man to notice those swelling curves, he noted, and many of those glances were more than admiring. A rush of sheer male jealousy shafted through him. *Damn* her for being so beautiful!

"Why do you want to leave so soon?" he asked.

"I didn't want to come at all, if you remember."

"I remember." He laid his hand over hers, a gesture of possession that seared her even through her glove. "But you have no more choice now than you had before."

She stared into his eyes, and a shiver ran up her spine when she saw the rapacious hunger in them. If she relented one moment, if she showed one morsel of weakness, she'd be lost. He'd take her, burn her in the pyre of his hate and his passion, and leave only ashes in her heart. Most frightening of all . . . she wanted it. She wanted him.

The spacious room suddenly seemed too small. Her

breathing quickened as she fought to escape the illusion that the walls and ceiling were moving in on her. She wanted to run and run and never stop . . .

"Jenna," he said, his voice sharp for all that it was a whisper. "Are you all right?"

She drew a breath that hurt. "I . . . I'm fine."

He drew her closer against his side. Strangely, the gesture offered comfort, anchoring her in a world that had begun to spin. She squared her shoulders, forcing the terror into abeyance. He held her a moment more. Then he released her, his hand sliding away with what might have been reluctance.

"All right?" he asked.

Nodding, she glanced at the people around her. Some were watching her openly; more studied her out of the corners of their eyes. Frightened, perhaps, to stare at the witch.

"They're all looking at me," she whispered.

"The men in awe, the women in despair," he said.

"Rot."

Against his will, Alan found that he was very proud of her; she'd walked into a roomful of people she considered her enemies and managed it with a grace and pride a queen might have envied. Only he had known her fear.

They had shared something, just the two of them, that had nothing to do with their difficult situation. It wasn't trust; that had become an impossibility between them. But it was a sharing nonetheless, and the realization of it sent a storm of emotion surging through him.

"That bodice is too bloody low," he growled, surprising himself immensely.

Jenna blinked. "You chose it yourself."

"I must have been insane. Or rather, I must have been insane to let you wear it out in public."

Outrage shot through her. "You've got a bloody lot of gall, is what I say."

"Jenna—"

"Alan, darling!" Miranda's high-pitched voice cut through the background drone of conversation.

He muttered something Jenna didn't quite catch, for her attention had focused on Miranda. She looked quite lovely in a gown of golden silk, with a bodice cut so low it was almost indecent. Her breasts bounced precariously as she made her way toward them.

"Talk about bodices," Jenna muttered. She opened the fan Alan had given her, a silly thing made of silk and lace that did little to move air made stifling by the press of bodies. But it gave her something to do with her hands, which twitched with the urge to throttle someone. Alan perhaps, Miranda more likely.

The tawny-haired woman reached them, latching immediately onto Alan's other arm. "Why, Alan," she purred. "I didn't know you were bringing a guest."

"It would be rude to leave her languishing at home, wouldn't it?"

"Of course, darling." Her eyes looked as though they'd been chipped out of glass as she studied Jenna from head to toe. "That is a most . . . interesting color."

"Alan chose it for me," she said.

"Indeed?" Miranda's tone could have frozen the river.

Without the slightest change in expression, Jenna continued, "He has quite a talent for picking out women's clothes. Why, he even knew my sizes. Except for the slippers."

Miranda looked her up and down. "Indeed. Perhaps

you should have shown him your feet along with the rest."

"Really?" Jenna asked in a falsely sweet voice she didn't know she possessed. "That's an interesting observation from a woman whose gown is cut as low as yours. And he hasn't even *asked* to see your breasts."

Meow! Alan thought, watching twin spots of color appear in Miranda's cheeks. Dangerous thing, crossing swords with a Llewellyn.

Evidently left without a suitable retort, Miranda turned to him. "Darling, you've never come to take me riding. Have you forgotten?"

"I've been very busy with the children, you know."

"Good Heavens, what's the nanny for?"

"To be a nanny, not a father," he said.

Jenna watched Miranda's face change as she realized her mistake. The tawny-haired woman was quick to correct it. "Oh, I didn't mean that you shouldn't spend time with your children, of course. It's just that a man needs, well, other things in his life. Doesn't he?"

"Yes," he said, his gaze caught in the spun-moonlight depths of Jenna's hair.

"See?" Miranda murmured, pressing herself so tightly against his arm that her breasts were dangerously close to overflowing her bodice. "I finally got you to admit it."

Jenna felt suddenly tired. Goaded by her own ridiculous jealousy, she'd allowed Miranda to draw her into a malicious game she'd never have bothered playing before. And Alan stood there, watching her with those cynical, too-knowing eyes, as though he shared every thought, every dart of possessiveness.

She longed for the Dismal and the uncomplicated life

she'd lived there. Her gaze went to the open door that led to what must be the garden. Freedom. So intently did she yearn for it that she almost welcomed the distraction when Miranda moved around in front of Alan, ostensibly to fix his cravat but really to press her breasts against his chest.

Casually, Jenna turned away. "I think I'll take a walk in the garden while you two talk."

"Yes, do," Miranda said.

Taking advantage of the woman's resolute grip on Alan, Jenna slipped through the crowd. But a moment later, Alan appeared at her side. He took her hand and tucked it in the crook of his black-clad arm, his smile hard and devastatingly rakish.

"Won't work," he said with annoying cheerfulness.

"Why don't you just let me go?" she asked. "Jon and Beth are safe, and you only want—"

"Of course I want you." He raised her hand to his mouth. His lips were hot, even through her glove.

"That wasn't what I was going to say."

"You've ensnared me, lady witch. How could I let you go?"

She gritted her teeth, trying unsuccessfully to pull her hand free. " 'Tis no spell, just simple male lust. And stubbornness."

"I wonder how long it takes for 'simple' lust to burn itself out? Shall we test it, beginning tonight?"

"Why don't you test it on your lady bountiful?" She tried again to pull free and failed.

"Miranda?" he queried. "As you so succinctly put it, I've been offered things in which I have little interest." His gaze slid to Jenna's mouth, and hunger gnawed at his vitals. He wanted to snatch her into his arms and kiss her until the world faded away. Until he could pretend she was what he'd thought her at first, his innocent, sensual wood sprite, his moonlight woman.

He slid his arm around her waist, drawing her closer. She resisted him, stubborn chit that she was, but he could see response in the clear green depths of her eyes, feel it in the subtle softening of her body.

"Well, hello, you two." Carlton Graeme asked from behind them.

Alan swung around to see Carlton grinning at him. Then the young man's gaze swung to Jenna, and his eyes sparkled with what looked like mischief.

"Evening, Miss Llewellyn." Carlton bowed over her hand. "It's a pleasure to see you again."

Jenna was astonished to see honest friendliness in his eyes. It confused her; she'd expected to be vilified by everyone here. "Hello, Carlton."

"You look especially lovely tonight," he continued without relinquishing her hand. "I hope you'll honor me with the first dance."

"She's promised that to me," Alan said, annoyance getting the better of him. Gently but firmly, he removed Jenna's hand from the younger man's grasp.

Carlton only smiled. "The second, then."

"That, too," Alan said.

"Alan, you have to share," Carlton protested. "The lady is simply too beautiful for you to be so selfish."

"I do not have to share."

Jenna turned to look at him. Ill-temper darkened his eyes, and he wasn't making the least effort to hide it. *Why, he's jealous!* she thought. She took a deep breath. Instantly, his gaze snapped to her breasts, and she realized the source of his irritation; Carlton's gaze followed the same path. Barely, she repressed a smile. "Hoist with his own petard," as Roanna would have said.

It was bound to be a very long evening for Mr. Langston, indeed.

Jenna fanned herself. The fan didn't cool her a whit, but it did seem to give her movements an air of exotic languor. *Ah,* she thought. *That's what the dratted thing is for.* "I'd very much like to dance with you, Carlton," she said.

He bowed. "The third dance?"

"You will find me?"

"Like a bee to honey."

He bowed over her hand again, then grinned at Alan before moving off into the crowd.

"Interfering pup," Alan muttered.

"I think he's nice."

"You're enjoying this, aren't you?"

She fanned herself leisurely. "And why shouldn't I? It's my first ball."

Alan drew a sharp breath. Her statement had been very matter of fact, but he saw through it to the stark loneliness of her life. He imagined the girl she'd been, picturing her growing up without toys or friends or pretty clothes. And he hurt for her. It was a softness he didn't expect to feel, and it made him angry.

"Don't play games with me, Jenna," he growled.

"This is no game," she said.

"Call it what you will, but I intend to win."

Jenna tilted her head back to look more fully at him. Moved by an urge too powerful to resist, she discarded the clever reply she could have made, choosing instead the bare, bald truth. "We've already lost, Alan. Both of us."

He drew his breath in sharply. She watched his eyes change as he registered her words and her meaning. Yes, and she saw her own loss reflected in those indigo depths.

"Ah, Miss Llewellyn. I'm so glad you decided to join us tonight." The voice was a familiar one. She glanced over her shoulder to see Dr. Culhane standing behind her, arm in arm with a pleasant-faced woman.

"Hello, Doctor," Jenna said.

He bowed. "This is my wife, Emmaline."

"Pleased to meet you," the woman said.

Jenna blinked in surprise; she hadn't had much luck "pleasing" civilized women so far. "You are?"

Emmaline laughed. "Don't judge us all by Miranda, dear. Or by men like Jonas Rafferty. My husband told me how you saved those children's lives, and I think that was a wonderful thing to do."

"Thank you," Jenna said. It was a gift, this kindness from a stranger.

"Will you be staying with us long?" Emmaline asked.

"No."

"Yes," Alan interposed smoothly.

"Ah, I see," the doctor said.

"See what?" Alan demanded.

Culhane grinned, tucking his wife's hand securely against his side. "Come, my dear. Let's let these two young people have some time alone. I fear Mr. Langston will be rather occupied fending off the competition once the dancing begins."

"Yes, my love." Emmaline smiled once again at Jenna. "Do have Alan bring you by for a visit. We'd love to have you."

Jenna stared at them as they moved off into the crowd. Again, she'd been surprised to find honest friendship in the midst of her enemies. Then realization burst in her mind. Alan hadn't told them that he believed she'd poisoned Jon and Beth. He hadn't told anyone.

Startled, she swung around to stare at him. The man always seemed to turn the tables on her just when she thought she had the way of it. Her heart leaped with the hope that he'd cared enough for her to protect her from his neighbors' inevitable reaction to that news.

Fool, she thought, even as treacherous warmth flowed through her, moving slowly but steadily. Sweet betrayal, it coursed into her limbs, weakening them, and set up a dark, molten place deep in her body.

"Why are you looking at me like that?" he asked.

"Like what?"

"Like you want me to kiss you."

"I do not want you to kiss me." She did, she did.

"No?"

He slid his hand up her arm, coming to rest on the skin just over her glove. Reaction sizzled from that contact point and ran in darting quicksilver streaks through her body.

She took a step backward, using the fan to create an illusion of a barrier between them. Useful things, fans. "I thought you would have told them."

His eyes betrayed his understanding. Strange that even now, in the extremity of their distrust, he should be able to read her so easily. Then she caught her breath as he recaptured the lost space, very nearly trapping the fan between their bodies.

"Why didn't you?" she whispered.

"I'd rather deal with you myself," he said.

His words had to do with punishment and revenge; the look in his eyes promised something else altogether. She could deal with the first adequately enough. But the second was infinitely dangerous because she wanted it so much. Ah, to be so weak that the desire in his eyes could tempt her to forget all that had passed between them.

She stood silent in the midst of the chattering crowd, lost in the midnight depths of his eyes. And he . . . he drew her in, submerging her in the surging torrent of his need. No man had ever touched her like this, no other man ever would. She would flee Heronsgate tonight and never come back, but she would leave her heart behind.

Her gaze was dragged away as the crowd began to eddy and shift. She caught a glimpse of a trio of musicians climbing up on the low wooden platform that had been set out for them.

"Shall we?" Alan asked, offering his arm.

"I don't know how to dance."

His brows went up. "Just follow my lead, and you'll do fine."

"That hasn't worked so well for me up to now," she murmured.

"Very amusing." He gave her a sharp-edged smile, then took her hand and placed it in the crook of his arm. As he led her toward the section set aside for dancing, the musicians broke into a lively reel.

Jenna found herself paired with Alan, completing one corner of a square of four couples. At first she was nervous. But soon her attention was focused on the dance. She and Alan moved as though they possessed a single pair of feet. Sidestep, sidestep, turn to center. Then promenade, her hands held securely in Alan's strong, warm ones. She ceased to think about what she was doing; her body moved to the music and to the man who danced with her as though their bodies were joined with a cord.

And then she did the most foolhardy and dangerous thing she'd ever done: she allowed herself to sink into the fantasy. The hate and betrayal, the shattered trust all belonged to another time, another world. She would enter that world again. But for this brief, precious time, there was only Alan.

The illusion was so seductive that she lost track of when one song ended and another began. Then Carlton Graeme claimed her for the promised dance. Alan gave her up with obvious reluctance and considerable ill-humor.

Jenna watched him surreptitiously as he walked away. Instead of taking another partner, he stood at the edge of the dance floor to watch, hot-eyed, as she danced with the younger man.

"Our friend seems rather annoyed at having to give you up," Carlton said.

" 'Tis good for him," she said. "A man shouldn't live his life thinking everyone is going to do what he wants."

He laughed. "I have a feeling your visit at Heronsgate has been an interesting one."

"Interesting was not exactly the word I would have used," she said, perhaps more tartly than she would have liked.

"Father wants a dance, too," Carlton said, grinning at Alan over her shoulder. "Do you think it'll be safe?"

"I . . . Oh!" The cry was torn from her as something

caught the hem of her gown, almost pulling her off balance. A sharp ripping sound cut through the music.

Carlton caught her arms to steady her. Out of the corner of her eye, she saw Miranda twirl away.

"Drat the girl," Carlton said. "Is your dress torn?"

She twisted around, and her heart sank when she saw that the delicate silk had been ripped from the hem almost to the waist. The train lay like spilled blood on the wooden floor behind her. She glanced at the people around her. Most, she thought, approved of Miranda's action. Tears stung her eyes, but they were caused by anger, not sadness.

Suddenly Alan appeared at her side. "Let's get you out of this crowd. Carlton, take her arm while I hold the gown—"

"I don't need your help," Jenna said.

She scooped the red fabric up and draped it over her arm, an action that exposed her legs to the knees. Then, with her chin held high, she stalked toward the door amid a flurry of turning heads and whispered comments. Alan and Carlton walked with her, one on either side, tall, dark-clad frames for her defiance.

Once out of the room, she faltered to a stop. Defiance could only take one so far.

"Jacob, the carriage," Alan called to the servant tending the front door.

Carlton took Jenna's hand and bent over it as though she were a duchess. "We're not all like that, you know."

She took a deep breath. "I know," she said. "Thank you, Carlton."

He turned back to the drawing room, leaving her alone with Alan. His face was composed, his eyes shuttered, but a muscle throbbed at the corner of his jaw.

"I expected worse," she said.

A group of women emerged from the drawing room. Alan turned and regarded them as they whispered among themselves. Then he bent and lifted Jenna into his arms. A chorus of shocked gasps followed them out to the veranda.

Jenna was nearly as shocked as they. "Your reputation will soon be as bad as mine."

"A nice, juicy scandal will give them something to do."

The carriage rolled around the corner of the house, driven by one of the Carrew slaves. The man jumped down and waited while Alan placed Jenna in the vehicle, then handed him the lines.

Alan drove expertly but absently. His thoughts were in a tumult just now, and he knew he wouldn't be able to make sense of them as long as she was near. His gaze kept going to her shapely ankles and calves, a sight made more erotic by the pale, sheer stockings she wore.

Damn but she'd been magnificent, tossing her gown over her arm and marching out of there as though she didn't have a care in the world. He ought to hate her; he'd tried very hard to do so. But her courage touched something deep inside him, turning the desire to hate into another kind of desire entirely.

"I lost your fan," she said.

The simple statement touched him profoundly, for she had so little. All her life, so little. "It is *your* fan, and I'll send someone over for it tomorrow."

"I doubt I'll have need of it again."

She shifted position, and he caught a glimpse of pale skin above the stockings. Arousal shot through him in a white-hot flare. He didn't understand why he had so little control over his feelings for her and hated being bound to her so powerfully.

"Cover yourself," he said, his tone as fierce as his mood.

Surprised by the sudden, unexpected savagery in his voice, she let the gown fall. "What's the matter?"

"I shouldn't have brought you there."

Her heart clenched. "You're ashamed—"

"No, damn it!" He swung around to glare at her, his knuckles whitening as he gripped the lines. "That's not it at all."

"Then what?" she cried.

He pulled the horse to a halt so suddenly that she was flung from the seat. But he caught her in his arms, levering her back into the seat and then pinning her there with a hand on either side of her body.

"It's unnatural to want a woman as much as I want you," he rasped. "I consider myself a rational man. Or used to. I was married to a woman I loved. I gave her two children. I expected to live the rest of my life with her."

"Alan—"

"Let me finish." Pain bracketed lines on either side of his mouth. "I felt all the things a man feels for a treasured wife, the mother of his children and the keeper of his future. All those things, Helena was to me. But they're nothing, *nothing* compared to what I feel for you."

"I—"

"Let me finish. This must be said here, tonight, or it may never be said." His voice grew still more grim as he continued. "It's not love. It can't be love. But when I touch you, it's like heaven and hell, thunder and lightning and brimstone all at once. It hurts to bloody damnation, and I only want to do it again and again and again."

The stark pain in his eyes staggered her. Everything in her that made her a healer—and a woman—responded to it. If he would only believe in her, she could take that pain away. Almost, she reached for him.

Touch him, and you're lost! cried some last, remaining shred of reason.

She closed her eyes, staggered by the power of her love for him. Towering, passionate . . . and so very futile. He was a townsman, born and bred. He couldn't be anything but, couldn't believe that they could share anything but pain.

It was sad, so sad. More so that even now she wished there was a way to change his mind. If she stayed with him much longer, she might even be willing to sacrifice her pride to give him a few moments of peace.

And it wouldn't be enough. She loved him too much to take less than everything, for she didn't know how to give less than everything in return. Looking away, she retreated from the raw pain and even rawer need in his face.

"You've had your say," she whispered. "Now take me back to my prison and lock me up."

He drew in his breath, then turned away from her with a sharp, angry movement. The carriage swung into motion again, soon gaining a speed that might have been reckless with less sure a driver. Jenna welcomed it, welcomed the violence of her hair whipping around her as the wind scoured the pins from it.

The sound of the wheels echoed through her mind, becoming a paean of mingled hope and despair. *Run while you can. Run while you must,* they seemed to say. *For your pride, for your soul, for what's left of your heart.*

Twenty-four

Alone in her room, Jenna stripped off the ruined scarlet dress and donned her old blouse and trousers. Then she sat down in the chair near the window and waited. She could hear the sound of Alan pacing his room for a long time, but finally the house returned to silence.

Moving swiftly and silently, she removed the nails from the window and slid it upward. Outside, a cottonwood tree stretched its branches high above the house. The breeze stirred the leaves, making them look like a sparkling silver sea as their paler undersides caught the starlight.

She climbed onto the sill. This wasn't going to be easy; the nearest branch that would hold her weight was a good six feet away. Gathering her strength and her courage, she sprang out over empty space. Her hands skidded painfully over the fissured bark as she hit, teetered, and then held.

It took but a few moments to reach the ground. She headed toward the swamp, keeping to the shadows lest Rafferty and his men be lurking nearby. Freedom beckoned. Soon she'd be safe in the haven of the swamp, away from Alan, away from all the heartbreak of her sojourn there.

She ought to be glad. "I *am* glad," she whispered.

Then why did her steps slow? Why did her heart seem to hang back, urging her to listen to something on the night air? A lifetime of believing her instincts brought her to a halt. It almost seemed as though someone was calling her. A small voice, made powerful by its innocence.

"Bloody damn, as Alan would say," she muttered.

Turning, she headed back to the house. Not, however, to the room she'd just fled. She went around to the other side, where the children slept. A tree grew very near the half-open window, an easy climb. Crouching like a cat on the sill, she peered inside. Jon and Beth occupied the bed, Dorcas a cot near the door.

Just one moment, she thought. Just enough to stroke their hair and perhaps place a goodbye kiss on their cheeks.

She eased the window open and slipped inside, her moccasins silent on the oak floor. Still, Beth awoke. She nudged her brother, who sat bolt upright, his eyes widening when he saw Jenna.

"Shhh," she whispered.

She held out her arms, and the children tottered into them. Something bright and fine bloomed in her heart as she held them close. If nothing else good came of her visit there, these two small lives would be enough.

"I missed you," Beth whispered. "I waited for you to come."

"I couldn't, love. But I'm here now."

After shooting a swift glance at Dorcas, Jenna sat down cross-legged on the floor, drawing Jon and Beth with her. Her spirit cringed away from the coming separation.

"We ate the wrong thing," Jon said, his voice low.

"Indeed you did," Jenna agreed. "Never, never eat any wild thing unless you know exactly what it is. And one casual conversation on a day's outing does not make you an expert. There are things, you know, that can make you much sicker than the pokeweed."

"Much?" Beth asked, her eyes round with awe.

"Much, much sicker. Promise me you won't be so foolish again."

"I don't want to be that sick again," Jon said. "Ever."

Jenna nodded in feigned severity. "Then let it be a lesson to you."

"Yes, ma'am." The whispered chorus was no less fervent for its lack of volume.

"Very well," Jenna said. "Now give me a hug. I've got to go."

"You're never coming back." Jon said. His face was as set as a man's.

"No," she said, unable to lie. "I am not."

Glancing up, she saw that Dorcas's eyes were open. Panic assailed her. She started to rise to her feet, only to be bowled backwards when Beth's small body hit her amidship.

"I don't want you to go!" Beth sobbed.

"Ah, sweet, I haven't a choice." Jenna was dangerously close to tears herself.

The nanny rose from the bed. Gently, she disengaged the girl's arms from around Jenna's neck.

"Dorcas!" Beth cried, burying her face against the older woman's neck. "Dorcas, she's leaving us!"

"I know, darling. Don't make it worse for her."

Startled, Jenna looked deep into the nanny's eyes. No hatred lurked there, only understanding and an abiding sympathy.

"I've been awake since you came in," Dorcas said. "And I heard what you said to the children."

"But you were so sure—"

"I was wrong. I've been struggling with this for days now, once they were safe and I could think clearly again. It was your love that held them. No magic. Love. I saw it in your eyes and in your hands as you tended them. You could no more hurt them than I could."

Jenna didn't try to stem the flow of tears that coursed down her cheeks. "Thank you."

"Will you forgive me?"

"Of course. If only . . ." she broke off, unable to finish.

"I'll talk to him, tell him what—"

"No. Every moment I stay, I die a little more inside. He thought I , . ." Glancing at the children, she chose not to finish the sentence. "I cannot abide that."

"But you forgave *me*," the nanny said.

"I don't require as much faith from you."

Jon stepped forward to take Jenna's hands in his. "Will you remember us?"

"Ah, Jon. All my life I'll hold a spot inside me that will have your name on it. And Beth's." Her voice caught. *And his. Oh, and his.*

Leaning forward, she kissed his cheek. "Goodbye, little man." Then she embraced Dorcas and Beth in one quick, hard hug, kissing the child with lips that quivered with barely held sobs. "Goodbye. Be good for Dorcas and your father."

Before she lost her resolve, she ran to the window and swung out into the tree. It felt as though her heart had remained behind, held by the family she'd come to love. Terrible things, goodbyes; no wonder Roanna preferred to remain always separate from other people. It hurt too much.

As she reached the ground, an awareness of something wrong pulled her into the deep shadows at the tree's base. She searched the night with eyes and ears and a woodsman's nose. The birds were silent in the woods at the edge of the swamp, and there, just within the edge of her perception, was the faint scent of tobacco.

"Rafferty," she murmured.

When one door closed, it was best just to find another. If she could slip around the house and through the garden, she could approach the swamp from another direction. Before the watchers realized what was happening, she'd be past them and into the Dismal.

She kept to the shadows as she made her way around the corner of the house. Without her quite realizing it, tears welled into her eyes and spilled down her cheeks. She stumbled once, then dashed the wetness from her eyes with the back of her hand and continued on her way.

The garden seemed a sterile, colorless place in the starlight. Too much of civilization dwelled here, too many straight lines and clipped hedges. If she had a free hand here, she'd plant flowers everywhere.

She moved deeper into the garden, her attention focused on that telltale scent of tobacco. So much so that she never sensed another presence until a hand fell heavily on her shoulder.

"Going somewhere?" Alan asked.

Jenna didn't know how he'd found her; all she knew was that her freedom had been snatched from her. Desperation beat frantic black wings in her mind. She'd been so close! And now, to be dragged back and locked away

again . . . Her reaction was instantaneous, a purely instinctive drive to escape at any cost. Whirling as far as
his iron grip allowed, she drove her elbow into his chest.
His breath went out in a rush, but he didn't let go.

"Little savage," he growled. "How did you get out of
that room?"

"I flew out," she said. "We witches do, you know."

Alan pulled her closer. The scent of honeysuckle surrounded him, seeming to sink straight through to his
soul. If he hadn't taken a walk in the garden to try to
relax the tumult in his mind, he'd have lost her. Rage
burst like hot lava in his brain.

"You're coming with me," he said, turning toward the
house and pulling her with him.

"Let me go!" she panted, jerking wildly against his
grasp.

"Never."

A whirlwind seemed to explode in his grasp. She
fought with skill and determination, and for the first time
he realized just how strong and agile a woman could be.
It was all he could do to keep her from hurting him, and
to keep from hurting her in the process.

"Damn it, Jenna!" Barely, he deflected her knee from
his groin. "I'm going to pretend that was an accident.
But if . . . *Oof!*" The gasp was wrung from him as her
fist connected with his belly. Bloody *hell* that a woman
knew how to hit like that.

Instead of driving him back, the blow only brought
the battle-rush surging through his veins. He no longer
felt pain; the only thing registering now was the need to
stop her. It was a primal, powerful need to dominate, to
capture. To possess.

"Let . . . me . . . go!" she gasped.

"Stop fighting me."

"I'll never stop fighting you, never!"

He spun her around, looping his arm around her waist and bringing her against him. She kicked backward. He countered by lifting her off her feet, taking her leverage away. She flailed futilely as he carried her into the house.

"I'll scream," she cried.

"Scream all you want."

"I'll scratch your eyes out."

"Now, *that* I believe."

Jenna tried to catch the banister as he headed upstairs, but he foresaw that and held her away. She couldn't stop fighting. It seemed almost as though some demon had hold of her, driving her to this frantic effort.

"Damn it," Alan panted.

He tucked her beneath one arm and unlocked her door, moving with swift efficiency despite her struggles. Still carrying her, he turned the key in the lock again, then strode to the open window. He closed it with a bang that echoed through the room.

"Flew out, eh?" He flung her unceremoniously on the bed. "It's a shame you fought me so hard down there; I might have believed that branch too long a jump for you."

"Go to hell."

Turning, he examined the window frame, his long fingers running over the spots where she'd gouged the wood in her effort to get the nails out.

"Very interesting," he said. "What did you use?"

"A sharpened teaspoon," she retorted, all defiance.

"You have my admiration, madam. Your inventiveness amazes me."

She rose up on her knees amid the rumpled bedclothes. "Well, what are you going to do now? Shackle me, perhaps, or lock me in the smokehouse?"

He came toward her, pure male arrogance in every line of his body. Her heartbeat broke into a gallop at the sight. Wide shoulders, powerful arms, the deep chest with its furring of dark hair, the lean, ridged belly, the long, muscled legs—he was everything she hated, everything she loved.

"The only prison you'll have," he said, "is my arms. I can't leave you now, even for a moment, or you'll fly from me."

"No," she whispered.

"Yes. I was wrong ever to have allowed you to stray from my arms. Whenever you were there, things were all right."

"This is insane."

He shook his head. "The only insanity was our meeting, and that was arranged by a force more powerful than either of us. Since then, we've both been trapped. Cursed."

"Not I," she said, her chin going up.

"You as much as I," he said. "For I will not let you go. You belong to me as surely as the sun rises in the morning, and I will keep you."

His eyes darkened to midnight pools of desire. Sharpened by anger and by their days apart, that desire had grown like a brush fire. Building with every passing moment, it burned high and hot. Jenna found herself spinning down into those fiery depths, a helpless sacrifice on the altar of passion.

She couldn't deny him. Despite everything he'd done, despite everything that had gone between them, she loved him still. There was precious little peace outside his arms, and none at all within them. But her body and spirit didn't care. There was only him, only now, only this. She started to tremble.

"God help me," she whispered. "For I cannot help myself."

"God help me," he echoed, "neither can I."

He took her chin in his hand and tilted her face upward. A protest rose to her lips but died unspoken as he claimed them. Of their own volition, her arms crept around his neck; without willing it, she parted her lips to allow him entry.

"Jenna," he muttered, biting gently, voraciously at her mouth. After all the days of wanting her and being unable to touch her, he felt like a dying man given respite.

Wild, passionate, stubborn, clever enough to counter him at every turn, she was the essence of everything he wanted in a woman. But she was also a will-o'-the-wisp, a woodland sprite who could never be held. His mind knew it; his heart did not.

Jenna moaned as his hands speared into her hair. That small, muffled sound seemed to affect him powerfully, for an answering groan rumbled deep in his throat. She ran her hands down the strong, flexing line of his back, her fingers digging into the firm muscles in a gesture rife with need.

"I'm tired of seeing you in this," he growled, winding his hands in the neckline of her blouse.

With a single, sharp movement, he tore the garment downward. Buttons popped free to roll along the floor. Jenna didn't care; all she knew was the incredible sensation as he brought her to him, brushing her sensitive nipples against the crispness of his chest hair.

"Yes," she gasped, arching into it.

Slivers of delight shot through her. The world narrowed to this one bed, this one man. She wound her fingers into his hair, as possessive as he. He drew in his breath sharply, then claimed her mouth with a burning ferocity that only stoked the leaping fires within her. She pressed still closer, her tongue darting forward to spar boldly with his.

She sighed as his hand slipped beneath the waist of her trousers. His fingers skimmed the curve of her hip, then cupped the smooth, firm silk of her derriere. Unable to do anything else, she slid one knee up along his thigh. Inviting him. No, demanding that he do what they both wanted. Instead, he slid his hands around to the front of her trousers to unbutton them. Then he pushed them down, lifting her so that she could kick them off.

Then, *then* he obeyed. His hand caressed her hip with firm possession, then slid down the long slim line of her thigh. She raised her knee eagerly when he urged it.

She sank her nails into his back as he traced a path to the hot, sweet cleft between her legs. He explored her tenderly, expertly, gliding along flesh that heated and swelled to welcome him. She swayed in the age-old dance of arousal, wanting more, wanting everything.

"It's like being burned alive," she moaned. "Oh . . ."

Alan's chest heaved as he struggled for control. He'd never been a man to take a woman in a rush, but oh, Jenna tempted him! She was hot and open and ready, her need like slick satin. His body throbbed as she swayed again, pressing her woman's mound against his rigid erection. If he didn't get some control over this, his body was going to take over.

Adamantine will wrestled with the heady carnal excitement that threatened to carry him away. He wanted to tease, to bring her to the edge again and again, until he impressed himself upon her soul as deeply as she was on his.

"Tell me what you want," he said into her open mouth.

"You," she whispered.

"But you have me." He slid one finger into her tight, hot depths, then slid his thumb upward to rub the small, erect nub that was the center of her desire.

Jenna closed her eyes as a fiery torrent of arousal coursed through her. He slipped another finger into her, stretching the throbbing flesh. Their mouths slipped and caught and sighed as they kissed. His tongue flickered against hers, perfectly mimicking the thrusting of his fingers. She quivered in total, wanton need.

"I have to touch you," she said.

"Later."

Unwilling to let him take complete control, Jenna ran her hands between their bodies, tracing the long, thick ridge of his erection. He shuddered beneath her touch. Heady with her own power, she unbuttoned his trousers and slipped her hands inside. He was powerfully aroused, his iron-hard shaft lengthening under her touch.

She reveled in his response, the involuntary tightening of his big body, the gasps that were wrung from him, the way his eyelids drifted downward in immense desire. When he dragged her hands from him at last, she couldn't stop the moan of protest that came unbidden to her lips.

He bore her back to the bed. For a moment he leaned over her, his eyes glittering into hers. Then he bent and reclaimed her mouth in a hot, tempestuous kiss. It assailed her, demanding submission. Her mind recognized this even as her heart redefined it. He could take only what she gave . . . and she gave everything. For tonight, everything. It was pure recklessness, perhaps, but she had no choice but to accept its inevitability.

She arched her back as he broke the kiss to slide his open mouth down her throat, shivered as his tongue dipped deliciously into the hollow below. He licked a wet path over her nipple to the underswell of her breast. Then up again, to flick over the pointed, throbbing peak.

She caught his head, afraid he'd leave her. He laughed then, a triumphant male sound, and took her nipple into his mouth. A wash of heat ran from that spot to deep in her belly, tightening her loins into one throbbing pulse-point. He caressed her other breast with his hand, lifting its sweet, firm weight, pebbling the tip with his thumb.

Love and longing, desire and despair coursed like dark honey through her veins. She spun away on a whirlwind of sensation, her being centered on the man who caressed her so tenderly. Frantic to love him as thoroughly as he did her, she rose up and pressed him onto his back.

Alan obeyed her heated command, his eyes smoky with the knowledge that she wanted him as much as he did her. In a world that seemed to have lost all sense, only this mattered. He surrendered to this woman who'd shattered his peace.

Raging desire brought everything to diamond-sharp clarity, and he understood at last that he had to shrug off all his preconceived notions of men and women. Jenna was unique, as precious as a moonflower blooming in the light of day. His surrender had to be as profound as hers.

As she slid his trousers down and off, he learned just how easy surrender could be. And pleasurable.

"I never thought a man could be so beautiful," she said when he lay naked before her.

"A man is all angles and hardness and hair, sweet," he replied. "It's you who's beautiful, with your luscious woman's curves and those bold eyes."

Bolder still, she straddled his legs and looked at him. So hard, so rampantly masculine, from the aggressive line of his jaw to his leanly muscled chest and arms, and finally to the upstanding shaft that so blatantly bespoke his arousal. It pulsed with the beat of his heart. And hers.

"Do you want me to touch you now?" she asked.

"I'm in your power," he said, his voice hoarse with anticipation. "I couldn't stop you if I wanted to."

She loved him then, with hands and lips and tongue. He groaned, balling the bedclothes in his hands, arching beneath her in a pleasure that seemed sharp enough to be torment.

With a savage, muffled sound, he pulled her up along his body. His hands trembled as he lifted her, trembled even more as he slowly, exquisitely, impaled her on his shaft. Her flesh welcomed him. Bracing her hands upon his chest, she began to move upon him. He filled her, bringing fullness and delight, and a sense of completion. They matched, she and he. Male and female, master of Heronsgate and Llewellyn witch, they matched as nothing else in this crazy world could.

She closed her eyes against a sudden upwelling of tears; she'd remember the beauty of this joining as long as she lived. And miss it. Oh, and miss it.

"Jenna," he said, clasping her hips to stop her movement.

"Please," she moaned.

"Do you want me?"

"Yes." Intimately aware of the heat and hardness she held deep in her body, she writhed beneath the restraint of his hands. "Now."

He growled deep in his throat, a thick, animal sound of arousal. "You belong to me," he rasped. "You've always belonged to me."

"I've always belonged to you," she said, in final, complete surrender.

With a smooth, powerful movement, he rolled over, placing her beneath him. He thrust into her in fierce, driving passion. She cried out, wrapping her legs around his hard waist.

"That's it," he gasped. "Perfect. Ah, Jenna . . ."

His breathing grew ragged. Jenna watched his eyes close, the lean planes of his face tauten. The sight brought her own passion raging out of control, brought her knees higher and higher as she sought more of him.

She arched her back as the first quicksilver tremors began. Then a tremendous, shuddering climax caught her, ripping her into a place where there was only heat and light and Alan.

He called her name hoarsely as he followed her into that world, and for a moment they cleaved together in perfect unison. Then he collapsed upon her, shuddering, his hands still moving over her sweat-slick skin as though he wanted to memorize the feel of her.

"Alan," she began.

"Shhh. Don't talk," he whispered. "Don't break the spell."

She opened her mouth to protest, but he moved in her again, stopping her breath in her throat. At another time, she would have thought it too soon, but her body roused in immediate response to his touch.

"Again?" she murmured.

"I'm a greedy man, at least where you're concerned."

He made love to her again, his caresses as fierce and tender as the first time. Even as she spiraled off on a stormswept sea of passion, she felt the desperation in him. As though he had to make the most of this night, this fragile, glorious truce.

I'm as greedy as he, and as desperate.

So she let herself go with desire's tide, fearing, like him, that the magic might fade in the morning light. Leaving her with nothing.

Twenty-five

Alan woke in the velvet hush just before dawn. Jenna lay on her side, cupped in the curve of his body. *So beautiful,* he thought, lifting a pale, satin curl of hair with his finger.

"Alan," she sighed.

Even in sleep, she called his name. It stirred him immeasurably. Despite the frenzied night of pleasure they'd just shared, he wanted her all over again, and with the same volcanic intensity.

Witch she might be, but one thing was certain: she'd ruined him for any other woman. He had the feeling he was going to spend the rest of his life haunted by the scent of honeysuckle and the memory of the touch of a woman of cool moonlight beauty and a spirit of fire.

He slid his hand lightly along the graceful line of her waist and hips, then leaned forward and traced the curve of her ear with his tongue.

"Good morning," he murmured.

Jenna slid into wakefulness, and the awareness of him pressed against her, hard and hot and eager. Her body responded instantly.

"It's not morning yet," she said.

"Close enough."

She was willing to concede the point, particularly as his hands were beginning to roam. His tongue dipped into her ear, causing a frisson to run up her spine.

"Are you cold?" he asked, feeling the shiver.

"What do you think?" she countered.

"I think . . ." He ran his palms lightly over her nipples, which instantly drew up into tight buds. "That touching you is like holding flame in my hands."

She arched her back, caught by the pleasure his touch elicited in her. Ah, she should be sated after a night like the one past. He'd pleasured her again and again; she'd been astonished that her body could respond so many times, equally astonished that there were so many ways a woman and a man could love each other.

And now, again, she was willing. Nay, eager. Her pulse hammered in her ears. Suddenly she stiffened, realizing that the pounding wasn't her heart at all but the sound of a fist knocking heavily on the front door.

"Alan—"

"I hear it." With a groan, he rolled away from her and reached for his pants.

"Who could it be at this hour?" she asked.

"Whoever it is, he'd better have a bloody important reason to have come here at this hour."

She watched him as he buttoned his trousers. His eyes had turned suddenly, completely cold, as though the wonderful, magical night had never been.

Her heart clenched in agony. The night, the wonderful, magical night had ended. He was once more the master of Heronsgate and she the witch. One cursed, the other reviled. Her soul wept for the loss of what had been.

"Get dressed," he said. "Quickly."

"You tore my shirt."

The pounding began again. Muttering imprecations under his breath, he strode to the armoire and pulled out an azure silk dressing gown. He tossed it to her. "Put this on, then."

It was a lovely thing, one she might have enjoyed wearing in other circumstances. Now, it had become one more luxury in the gilded cage in which she'd been locked. Her hands trembled noticeably as she tied the sash.

He grabbed her by the hand and swung the door open. Dorcas stood in the opening, a candle in one hand, her other hand raised to knock. Jenna wished she had his aplomb; caught in the act of leaving his lover's bedroom, he merely lifted one flaring dark eyebrow while she and Dorcas both blushed furiously.

"Er, ah . . . It's that scoundrel Rafferty and his men," the nanny said. "I peered out the window at them. They're up to no good, sir. You can wager on that."

"I never take a losing wager," he said. "I'll handle them. Make sure the children don't become alarmed."

"Yes, sir."

She glanced at Jenna once, her eyes troubled. Then she turned and walked away.

Alan headed for the stairs, pulling Jenna after him. His eyes had the flat lucid gleam of a purpose she couldn't define, and her heart thudded with sudden dread. Why was he bringing her with him if he intended to send Rafferty away?

She could see the shapes of men silhouetted in the windows, and knew from their position that they were trying to peer into the house. Although her mind knew they couldn't see in, not with the growing dawn at their backs, her skin crawled with the instinctive feeling of being watched.

Rafferty. She had seen the cruelty and the simmering hatred in his eyes. Her fate at his hands would be worse than anything Silvan had suffered.

It couldn't be that Alan intended . . . No, she thought, with a shudder that ran straight to her soul. She couldn't have been wrong about him; hard, ruthless man that he was, he couldn't make love to her one moment and throw her to the wolves the next.

But that single moment of doubt sent a wave of clenching horror washing through her, an emotion so powerful that she cried out when Alan touched her shoulder.

"Are you thinking that I'd toss you out to them?" he asked, his gaze hard on her face. "I see that you do." A muscle in his jaw jerked spasmodically, and he took his hand from her as though she'd burned him.

She backed away from the raw fury in his eyes. But she couldn't deny the accusation.

"I'm sure they have someone watching the back door," he said. "If you try to run, it will be your life."

"If I run, it will be in a direction they don't expect."

His eyes hardened, and he took a step toward her. Before he could take another, however, Jon came pelting down the stairs. Dorcas, her face red with exertion, hurried after him, Beth cradled in her arms.

"What the hell is going on here?" Alan demanded.

"I couldn't stop him, sir," Dorcas panted.

Jon ran straight to Jenna, placing his small body between her and the door. His face was white with fatigue but also taut with determination. "They can't have her," he said.

"Damn it!" Alan pointed toward the stairs. "Back up-stairs, all of you."

Beth wriggled out of Dorcas's arms and rushed to Jenna on unsteady legs. Drawing a breath that sounded suspiciously like a sob, Jenna swung her up.

"No!" Beth said, the expression on her small face star-tlingly like that on her father's. "We're staying with Jenna!"

Although Jon remained silent, his spread-legged stance was just as determined as Beth's declaration. This was full-blown mutiny, and Alan's eyes reflected his awareness of it.

"Get in the drawing room," he snarled.

Jenna caught Jon's shoulder and drew him into the other room. Dorcas caught up the voluminous skirts of her dressing gown and followed. The four of them hov-ered just within the doorway, out of sight of the front door but within easy hearing distance.

"Langston!" Rafferty shouted, pounding again with his fist. "Open up. We got to talk to you!"

Instead of moving toward the door, however, Alan strode to the small desk in the corner and unlocked the center drawer. Jenna gasped in shock when she saw him take a pair of pistols out and shove them into his waist-band.

"He's going to fight them," Jon said, straining against Jenna's restraining hand.

"Stay," she said, even as she tried to control the frantic beating of her own heart. "You'll only distract him."

"What do you want, Rafferty?" Alan called.

"The witch was sneakin' around town tonight, scared the bejesus out of Fred Mullins. She admitted her witch-ery, man."

"Nonsense."

"Tell him, Fred."

Another man spoke—a different voice, but the hate was the same. "I saw her, I tell you. That white hair of her'n marks her as the Devil's own, and them eyes burning at me like black coals while she called on her unholy master."

Alan drew in his breath sharply, struck by the untutored imagery of the man's words. "When was this?"

"Nigh midnight."

Jenna closed her eyes. She'd been locked in her room at the time, but Alan wouldn't know that. All he knew was that she'd gotten out; she could just as easily have been coming back to Heronsgate as leaving it.

It had been Roanna in town, of course, come to frighten the townspeople into freeing her granddaughter. Jenna couldn't tell Alan the truth, couldn't defend herself in any way; she'd rather be burned at the stake than set these men after the old woman.

"Jenna was locked up at midnight," Alan said.

She stared at him in astonishment. She didn't question his reasons for saying that and didn't want to. All that mattered was that he'd acted to protect her when she needed him most. Whatever happened between them, she would treasure this moment for the rest of her life.

Then Rafferty laughed, and the harsh sound brought her crashing back to reality.

"She's a witch, Englishman," he said. "Lock the door, she goes up the chimney. Or through the keyhole, if'n that's the only way. Give her to us. We'll take care of her."

"No," Alan said.

"You're a fool, Englishman! Haven't your own children sickened since she came?"

Jenna peered around the doorjamb. Alan stood in the foyer, his hair gleaming in the soft-filtered light of dawn, his muscles bunched with violence barely held in check. If he hadn't had to protect his children, she had the feeling he'd be happy as sin to walk straight out into a fight, pistols blazing. He looked like a pagan prince, dark and wild and fierce, and her heart beat faster at the sight.

"My children are my concern," he said, the urbanity of his tone a stark contrast to the savagery that glittered in his eyes. "And so is Jenna Llewellyn."

"Make it easy on yourself. Just toss her on out. If you don't, we'll have to come in and get her."

With a sharp-edged smile, Alan drew the pistols from his waistband. He fired the left one straight at the door, filling the room with a thunderous crack and the acrid smoke of burnt gunpowder.

A howl of alarm rose from the men outside, then a series of thumps as they hurled themselves flat. More noises ensued, and Jenna knew they were crawling off the veranda.

Finally, Rafferty shouted again, but from a distance, "You'll be sorry! Folks around here ain't about to let this go. The witch needs to be stopped, and fer good."

"If you're not off my land in thirty seconds, I'm going to shoot the lot of you," Alan called.

"We'll be back." Rafferty's voice grew steadily more faint. "You can be sure of that, Englishman. This ain't over."

No, Jenna thought. But at least for now, battle had been averted. Her breath went out in a long sigh of relief as Alan went to put the pistols back into the locked drawer.

"Good heavens," Dorcas said into the smoky silence.

Alan turned to face her. His eyes still raged with pent-up savagery, and he seemed even larger and more arrogant than usual. "Get the children upstairs, Dorcas. I want to talk to Jenna alone."

"But, Father—" Beth protested.

"Now!"

His voice cracked like a whip, lashing Jenna into motion. Setting Beth on her feet, she gently pushed her toward Dorcas. "Go on, both of you. You protected me bravely, and I'm proud of you for it, but the danger's passed now." She wasn't quite sure of the last, but the children had dared enough for one day.

Alan's smoldering gaze snapped to her, and Jenna wouldn't have been surprised had her dressing gown burst into flame.

Dorcas shepherded the children toward the stairs but stopped and turned back to Alan. "She came to say good-bye to the children tonight," she said. " 'Twas about half-past twelve."

"Thank you, Dorcas," he said without looking away from Jenna.

"And I don't believe she had anything to do with the children being poisoned. Beth and Jon were just experimenting, as children do."

"That's right, Father," Jon said. "Jenna never told us to eat anything. Beth was so sure she knew one plant from another—"

"Thank you."

Alan spoke the phrase in a voice that had gone deadly soft. Without another word, Dorcas and the children fled upstairs. Left alone with him, Jenna quailed inside but forced her chin up in a show of defiance.

She stood her ground as he stalked toward her. He stopped a scant foot away, gazing down into her eyes as though to bore straight through to her soul.

"It doesn't surprise me that my children championed you," he said, "but Dorcas seems to have come around as well."

"She doesn't approve of me, but she's fair-minded enough not to think me capable of killing a child."

"Neither do I."

Astonished, she gaped at him. He laughed, but there was little humor in it, and no capitulation.

"Poisoning the children would have been the act of a coward," he said. "And whatever else you may be, you're not a coward."

Relief warred with an outrage so powerful that she had to force the words out. "And when did you realize this?" she asked, jamming her fists on her hips.

"While listening to Rafferty's accusations."

"I see. So it's all right for *you* to accuse me of attempted murder but not anyone else?"

He smiled. "You're very beautiful when you're angry."

"And you're awfully damned slow coming to conclusions."

"I've been distracted."

She turned her back on him, too furious to speak. Damn him for putting her through this! He didn't even say he was sorry.

"Now," he said, moving close enough that his bare chest brushed the silk of her dressing gown, "Tell me about this trip to town."

Her breath went out in a gasp. She whirled to face

him, ready, at that moment, to curse him herself if she'd known how to go about it. "How dare you ask me that?"

"I dare anything," he shot back.

She beat her fists on his chest, once, twice, again. He didn't even step backward, just grabbed her wrists and imprisoned her hands against him.

"There are no rules between us," he said. "There never have been."

"Liar!" she panted. "You've been quick enough to punish me when you thought I didn't abide by what you thought I should do and be."

"True. I'm sorry."

A simple apology. But her anger drained away, leached by those simple words. It left her vulnerable to her own feelings and those she read in his eyes.

"I'm not sure I can forgive you," she said.

"Try."

"Why should I?"

He raised her right hand to his lips. She shivered when his open mouth brushed the pulsepoint in her wrist. "That's why. There's magic between us, Jenna. There always has been."

"Lust."

"Magic."

She pulled her hands from his and put them behind her. But there was no escape for her; the pugnacious thrust of his jaw told her he wasn't about to let her go.

"Now," he said. "I want to know what happened in town last night."

"I refuse to explain myself to you."

"I might believe you, if you did."

"Might!"

He closed the distance between them. She took another step backward, then found herself up against the wall. With a smile reminiscent of the one he'd held as he fired point blank at the door, he asked, "Don't you think it strange that Mullins described your eyes 'burning at him like black coals' when they happen to be a most striking shade of green?"

"He said I fly up chimneys, too." Fear sank frigid claws into her chest. Alan was treading much too close to the truth, one that could hang Roanna.

"Perhaps it was a trick of the light, hmmm?"

"Perhaps."

He leaned forward, placing one hand on either side of her head. When he spoke, his mouth was so near hers that she felt the mint-scented heat of his breath. "You're not going to tell me, are you?"

"Tell you what?" she whispered, trying to ignore the swift stirrings of her body. Of their own volition, her eyelids drifted downward.

"Tell me . . ." he paused to kiss one corner of her mouth, "who went into town last night."

"Mullins himself pointed the finger at me."

"I don't believe him."

"You didn't believe me, either."

"Then tell me how you managed to get to town and back in less than two hours."

Her gaze dropped to his mouth. The hard sensuality of it mesmerized her, making it difficult to concentrate on the conversation. "I . . . flew. Isn't that what witches do?"

"That's what some people say." He seemed as distracted as she. "How long did it take you to dig those nails out of the window frame?"

"Four days," she said, too surprised by the question to ponder his reason for asking it.

"A great deal of time to spend when there's a nice, large chimney in the offing, don't you think?"

"I'm . . . having some difficulty thinking just now," she murmured.

"So am I."

A shiver went through her as he came fully against her, his heat searing her through the delicate fabric of the dressing gown. Her being centered around him, her body responding with all the passion he engendered in her. She sighed his name as his lips brushed hers with exquisite softness.

"Jenna—"

She couldn't help herself. Boldly, she raised up on her tiptoes and ran her tongue along the hard curve of his lower lip. A ragged groan rose in his chest, and he sank his hands into the silken wealth of her hair as he plundered her mouth in a kiss as torrid and wild as a summer storm.

Alan sank deep, deep, wanting her all over again. His very soul craved her. If he hadn't been sure his children were lurking just out of sight upstairs, he would have taken her here on the floor. And she would have been willing. More than willing.

A small, rational corner of his mind prevailed, giving him the strength to break the kiss. But not enough to stop him from smoothing the dressing gown over her breasts so that he could see her response in the luscious, thrusting peaks. So much woman, he thought. Enough to keep a man in thrall to the end of time.

His hands shook as he released her. God, this was torment beyond what any man should have to bear. But the time and place were wrong, and there were a bloody lot of questions to be answered.

"Tell me the truth," he said.

Jenna shook her head. She wouldn't lie, but for Roanna's sake, neither could she tell him the truth.

His jaw tightened. "Very well. But you'll have my company day and night until you do. I will know the truth."

"Let me go."

"No."

"You have to," she whispered. "It's important."

"To whom?"

Tell him. She didn't have the right. Not with Roanna's life at stake. The old woman didn't have the strength to carry the battle she'd begun, and there was too much bad blood between her and the town for her to get any kind of mercy from them.

"I have to go," she said.

"Not until I have the truth."

"You didn't give a tinker's damn about the truth before. Why is it so important now?"

"Because, as you say, I'm an arrogant man." He cupped her chin in his hand, his thumb straying over the lush curve of her bottom lip. "If I let you go, I'll be letting you walk straight into danger. I find that I have a powerful interest in keeping that lovely hide of yours intact."

"So you can enjoy it."

"That is but one of the reasons."

She made a sharp sound of exasperation. "You can't hold me forever, Alan."

"I can bloody well try."

Jenna met his slashing indigo gaze levelly, accepting

the challenge. *He has to sleep sometime. No one, not even he, can hold a Llewellyn for long.*

But, as she gazed into his iron-hard eyes, she wondered.

Twenty-six

Jenna stalked up the stairs, seething with indignation. How dare he demand trust from her when he'd all but torn her heart out with his oft-declared suspicions? Even if she weren't determined to get to Roanna, she would have done everything in her power to escape him.

She stopped as she saw Jon and Beth peering through the posts of the banister above her. "You weren't eavesdropping, were you?" she asked.

"We're too well bred to eavesdrop," Jon said.

"Rot." Jenna climbed the last few stairs and bending to embrace them both in a quick, hard hug. "That's to thank you for defending me so bravely," she said. "I should chide you for putting yourselves in danger—"

"Father will do that soon enough," Beth said.

Jenna heard Alan's firm tread on the staircase behind her. A moment later, he stepped onto the landing. Hands on hips, he stood and regarded her with an inscrutable indigo stare.

"Children," he said, "on your feet."

They scrambled up, small faces full of apprehension. Jenna rose, too, placing herself between him and the children.

"Don't be angry with them," she said. "They only acted out of concern—"

"This is between me and my children."

She took a step forward. "No, it isn't."

"It's all right, Jenna." Jon moved past her, his jaw as hard-set and stubborn as his father's. "I did what I thought was right."

Alan's face betrayed nothing of what might be going on in his thoughts. "Don't you realize that by running downstairs the way you did, you endangered all our lives?"

"But—"

"With you standing almost at my back, I couldn't fight and protect you at the same time."

"Yes, sir, but—"

"I had but two pistols, two shots. What do you think might have happened if those men had charged the door? I couldn't leave the foyer, couldn't get you out in any way. With you upstairs, I would have had more options."

"Yes, sir." But the boy neither dropped his gaze nor apologized.

"However," Alan continued, "I'm proud of you. Damned proud of you."

Jon drew his breath in with a hiss. His face went pale, then flushed crimson. He rushed to his father, embracing him. Beth hurled herself after. Alan didn't try to extricate himself; he held them both close, his dark head bent solicitously over theirs.

Jenna swallowed hard against a sudden lump in her throat. Here, with his children in his arms, he'd become once again the man she'd fallen in love with. His eyes had turned gentle, and the cynical hardness had left his mouth.

She didn't want to see it. She hadn't yet learned to protect herself from this. Her treacherous memory called up pictures of him as he taught her to laugh, to trust, to hope there might be a place for her outside the Dismal. And most dangerous of all, the remembrance of how he looked as he made love to her, the passion burning like wildfire in his eyes, the hard planes of his face and the gentleness of his hands, the urgency of his deep voice as he called her name.

Suddenly he looked up at her as though her thoughts had been a physical touch. She saw echoes of her own memories in his eyes and trembled at the deep, visceral reaction the sight kindled in her. She loved him. Loved even the man who had hurt her with his mistrust and his betrayal.

She turned away, striding to the far end of the hallway to stare unseeing out the window. Her skin prickled when she heard his footsteps behind her.

"Looking for a way out?" he asked, his low voice keeping their conversation private from the children behind him.

"Always."

He leaned over her shoulder, trapping her between the window and his body. She stood stiffly, not wanting to feel the things his nearness engendered in her, yet overly aware of the sudden swift heat coursing like wine through her limbs.

"You really would have to fly from here," he murmured.

"And you're standing too close."

"We can never be too close."

With a hiss of indrawn breath, she slid away from him. His eyes had turned dark and moody, but to her relief, he let her go.

"Come, my children," Alan said. "Opal said she'll

have some nice, hot biscuits for us in a few minutes. Ben happened to find some wonderful honey in the woods yesterday. Clover, I believe."

"I *love* honey," Beth said.

"Well, climb aboard," he said, bending his knees.

The girl swarmed to a perch on his broad shoulders, taking a double fistful of his thick dark hair for security. Jon looked a bit wistful but brightened when his father laid a hand on his shoulder.

"Come, Jenna," Alan said.

"Thank you, but I'm not hungry—"

"Then you can keep us company."

He took hold of her arm, his hand warm even through the sleeve. She made one futile attempt to free herself, then gave it up. But she held her arm stiffly out from her side so that he couldn't touch her any more than what was absolutely necessary.

As he drew her down the stairs and along the hallway to the dining room, she felt as though she walked into a trap from which she'd never escape.

"I want to sit beside Jenna," Beth announced the moment they entered the dining room.

"So do I," Jon said.

"Does no one want to sit with me?" Alan asked with patently false mournfulness.

"Oh, Father." Beth patted him on the head with the same affectionate thump with which she caressed her dog Boswell. "We can sit with you anytime. Jenna's *special.*"

"That she is," he agreed.

He looked at Jenna with such mischief in his eyes that she had to turn away. She didn't want to laugh with him, didn't want to acknowledge the side of him that could bounce Beth on his shoulders and ruffle Jon's hair . . .

and make her own heart do flip-flops in her chest. So she went to the table and sat down, choosing a chair that would enable the children to sit on either side of her.

"Put me down, Father!" Beth commanded.

Alan obeyed, then took his place at the head of the table. He watched every nuance on Jenna's face as she explained to the children that there was no difference in favor between her right side or her left, calmly averting an argument before it quite got started. Her eyes were soft, her mouth curved in a smile he would rather have kept for himself alone.

He didn't begrudge the children her love, for love it was. As he watched her with them, he couldn't understand how he could have imagined for one moment that she might have harmed them. He owed her much for that one.

So let her go. It's what she wants.

He couldn't. There was a puzzle to be solved, one that had to do with black eyes and green ones, the present and the past. Perhaps, too, their future.

And Jenna held the key; he knew it as surely as he knew his own face. She glanced up at him, a slow, unconsciously erotic perusal that traveled from his eyes to his mouth. His breath caught in his chest.

He hardly noticed Opal come in with tea and biscuits, hardly tasted the food his hands automatically lifted to his mouth. His whole being was centered on Jenna as he watched her smile and laugh with his children and watch him back with those slumbrous pale jade eyes that fanned the flames inside him to a fever pitch.

Fire spirit that she was, she seared him with her courage, her untrammeled passion, her flaming independence. She didn't need him. Truly, she didn't even need his world; driven from it by an accident of birth, she'd made her own world. And he knew that if he let go of her for one moment, she'd disappear forever.

I will hold her. Somehow, I will.

A knock sounded at the door. Welcoming the distraction, he went to answer it. Ulysses stood outside, his silver-shot hair gleaming in the morning light.

"Mr. Graeme is here to see you, suh."

"The elder Mr. Graeme?"

"No, suh. The younger."

Alan scowled. "I suppose we'll have to see him, then."

"Yes, suh."

Alan stood in the doorway, waiting for his guest. He glanced over his shoulder at Jenna. Slim, straight, proud, her hair flowing like seafoam down the back of her chair, she was much too beautiful to share, even for a moment.

But civilized men did not turn their neighbors away because of jealousy, and he'd always thought himself a civilized man. He'd never regretted it more, however, and the feeling grew as he watched Carlton stride down the hallway toward him.

"Good morning, Alan."

"Good morning."

He stepped aside to let his guest enter the room ahead of him. Then Carlton stopped, and Alan saw first surprise, then amusement, and finally admiration cross the young man's expressive features.

It was then that he saw the scene from Carlton's perspective: the children still in their nightclothes, bare feet swinging beneath them. And Jenna in her dressing gown with her hair flowing around her, looking like an angel come to earth. An intensely intimate picture, the sort rarely offered to visitors.

Jenna glanced over her shoulder. "Why, hello, Carlton," she said, obviously pleased to see the young man.

Alan knew he shouldn't mind that she was happy to see Carlton, who'd always been a pleasant fellow. He shouldn't mind that she rose from her chair to greet the visitor or that the dressing gown clung to her curves like a second skin.

"Would you like some tea and biscuits?" she asked.

"No, thank you, Miss Jenna. I've come to ask you to take a look at some of my people who've fallen ill. Doctor Culhane isn't available; he left for Richmond this morning."

Jenna rose to her feet. "Does your father know you've come here?"

"He insisted I ask you."

"I'll come," she said. "Can you tell me their symptoms?"

"Flu, nausea, headache."

"Fever?"

"Not yet."

She took a deep breath. "Skin eruptions?"

"No." His face paled. "It's not pox. I know pox."

Inside, Jenna's thoughts spun helplessly. Those symptoms could belong to a number of illnesses. But then, they could just as easily have been caused by an overdose of eyebright, elder, water hemlock. Not Roanna, surely. But a nugget of doubt remained; the old woman wasn't completely rational when it came to her hatred for Old Lebanon. And if she'd come to stir up mischief . . .

There was only one way of finding out. If Roanna had done something unconscionable, then only Jenna herself could counter it.

"We'd better hurry," she said.

Alan caught her arm as she tried to walk past him. He studied her for a long, frozen moment, then glanced over her shoulder at his children. "Take your sister upstairs," he said.

They left without protest, although Jon shot an inquiring glance over his shoulder as he steered his sister out of the room. Alan waited until they were out of earshot, then turned to Carlton.

"There's danger in Jenna leaving Heronsgate just now," he said.

Carlton's brows went up. "Does this have something to do with that ball buried in your front door?"

"Rafferty and his men came here this morning, demanding that I hand Jenna over to them," Alan continued. "I fired a warning shot to run them off."

"Indeed. Then perhaps—"

"Enough," Jenna said, jamming her hands on her hips. "It's my decision, not yours."

"But, Miss Jenna—"

"You couldn't stop her," Alan said.

Startled, she looked at him. She'd expected a fight over this, but she should have realized that he wasn't the sort of man to deny help to another person.

And that was why she loved him. He wasn't a simple man, one who could be loved safely and comfortably. No, he confused the mind and stirred the soul, a wild, reckless tempest of a lover, kind and courageous, arrogant and honorable and insufferable all at once. She realized now that this was the only kind of man who could have captured the heart of the Dismal's White Lady.

"Of course, I'm coming along," he said.

"Of course," she replied.

Carlton cleared his throat. "Don't you think you ought to get dressed first?"

Jenna glanced down at her dressing gown, then at the furred expanse of Alan's chest. She'd forgotten their state of undress. At another time, she might have been embarrassed.

"Give us five minutes," she said.

Jenna pulled the blanket up around the sick man's shoulders, tucking it in gently. He'd been the first of the Graemes' slaves to fall ill. He'd spent the afternoon racked with alternating chills and fever, his symptoms soon mirrored by the others. All were very sick and were bound to get sicker before this was over. The only bright spot in the situation was the fact that Roanna had had nothing to do with this. No, this affliction was Nature's . . . and perhaps all the more deadly for that.

She straightened, her gaze going to the man's wife. The woman might have been pretty at another time, but just now her face was a mixture of concern for her husband and fear of the witch.

"What is your name?" Jenna asked.

"Thalia, Lady."

"Make sure you keep giving him liquids, Thalia. It's very important. Water, tea, anything he can keep down."

"Yes, Lady."

"If his fever goes up, you must bathe him in lukewarm water. Just sponge him down as I showed you. That pot over there contains medicine. Give him a half-cupful every few hours. Remember: bathing to keep the fever down and make him take liquids."

"Bathing and liquids," Thalia repeated. "And the

medicine every few hours." Clasping her hands in front of her, she asked, "Lady, will he be all right?"

Covering the slave woman's tightly held hands with hers, she said, "He's a strong man. With God's grace and our help, he'll recover nicely. And be sure you take care of yourself," she added, glancing down at Thalia's pregnancy-swollen belly. "The baby needs you to be strong, too."

She turned toward the door, needing to escape the dark, reeking interior of the hut. But the sunlight didn't warm her; this chill had been caused by dread, not darkness. She took a deep breath, then another.

Her gaze went to the stolid brick rectangle of the Graemes' main house. With its thick walls and sturdy shutters, it had protected its inhabitants from Indian attacks and British muskets, but it couldn't protect the Graemes from this new threat. Master and slave, rich man or poor, all were vulnerable.

Her head came up as she saw Alan and Jameson walk toward her from the direction of the fields. Alan had doffed his cravat and rolled his shirt sleeves up; his tanned, sinewy forearms and sturdy neck showed dark against the white linen.

His gaze met hers across the intervening space, and for a moment it seemed as though the rest of the world dropped away. She needed him. Needed the comfort of his presence and the buttress of his strength. Awareness flared in his eyes, and she knew he'd somehow sensed her distress. He strode toward her, the older man following in his wake.

"Ah, Miss Jenna!" Jameson called, apparently unaware of the emotions coursing beneath the outward scene of sun and lush greenery. "You are indeed a ministering angel. I can't tell you how grateful I am that you came."

"You should send someone to scrub out the cabins with lye soap to counteract the stench of illness," she said. "And I need someone to go into the swamp and collect the inner bark of the swamp willow so that I can make more medicine."

"Whatever you say," Jameson said. "We'll have this set right in just a few hours, and then—"

"Wait." Alan laid his hand on the smaller man's shoulder. "What is it, Jenna?"

"Influenza."

Jameson gasped. His eyes echoed the dread that chilled Jenna's heart, and she knew he was thinking about other times when influenza had raged through the community.

"Then more of my people will fall ill. And others."

"I hope not," she said, although there was nothing in her that felt like hope.

He squared his shoulders. "We'll deal with it, as we always have. If God is willing, this will be an isolated outbreak."

"If He isn't," Alan said, "there'll be bloody little cotton picked around here. I never thought I'd be glad that there wasn't time to get a crop in at Heronsgate this year. As it is, I'll be able to lend you my field hands . . . those that are healthy."

"Thank you," Jameson said. "And if there's anything we can do for you—"

"Just pray. For all of us."

The older man bent over Jenna's hand with a gallantry that brought a tightness to her throat. "Thank you for your help, Miss Jenna. No wonder they call you 'Lady'."

"They only do it because they're afraid to call me 'witch.' "

He looked up at her, surprise plain in his eyes. "You should listen better when they say it, then. I . . ."

His voice trailed off oddly, bringing her attention to sharper focus. "Is there something more?" she asked.

After a moment's hesitation, he shook his head. Then, with another courtly bow, he turned and strode toward his home.

Jenna glanced at Alan. "Walk with me."

He fell into step beside her, watching her elegant profile from the corner of his eye. She seemed tired, but he didn't think it was the work itself that had put that strain in her face. Rather, it was a weariness of spirit weighing on her.

"You know what this means," she said.

Yes, he did. "You can't be sure they'll blame you."

"Of course they'll blame me. They blamed Grandmother for everything from miscarriages to hangnails, and they're just looking for an excuse to point their fingers at me."

"Influenza existed long before there were Llewellyns."

She shrugged. "So they'll call it a curse, and blame me anyway. Let me go, Alan."

"So Rafferty and his men can run you down like the dogs they are?"

"Don't you think I can handle them?"

His hands came down on her shoulders, compelling her to turn toward the Dismal. "Look."

She saw an oily-looking column of smoke rising into the sky over the spot where her cabin lay. And another column of smoke, made darker and hazier by distance.

Roanna's cabin. They'd found it. They'd burned it. Jenna's breath went out sharply, as though she'd been struck.

"I'm sorry," Alan said. "But you see that even the swamp is no longer safe for you."

Grandmother. There was no longer anywhere for Roanna to run, nowhere to hide. *Grandmother! I'll come for you. Just hold on, stay hidden, and I'll come.*

But how soon? And would it be soon enough? Panic fluttered like a trapped bird in her chest, and she cried out when Alan's hard hands closed on her upper arms and pulled her close.

"Why two?" he asked.

"Two what?"

"Two bloody columns of smoke, Jenna."

"How should I know?"

His grip tightened. "I can't help you if you don't tell me the truth."

"Which truth?" she retorted, tilting her head back to stare at him defiantly. "The real truth, or the truth you want to hear?"

For a moment she thought he might shake her, then his grip shifted, one arm coming around her in an embrace whose comfort she couldn't let herself feel.

"We'd better get back to Heronsgate," he said.

To prison.

Twenty-seven

He'd nailed the windows shut again. Jenna stood for a moment, holding the curtains bunched in her hands, and counted at least twenty nails.

"I intend to keep you," Alan said from the doorway behind her.

She turned to look at him, only to be rewarded with one of his unreadable stares.

"You truly belong in New Lebanon," she said.

His brows went up. "Somehow I don't think you meant that as a compliment."

"Even your language mirrors theirs: keep, take, possess, own. Hold the slaves because there are none to tell you nay, hold the witch simply because you can."

Alan leaned his shoulder against the wall, studying her with an equanimity that was only outward. Inside, he was assailed with many emotions, most of which were uncomfortable.

But time had run out for him, for he read desperation in her eyes. Whatever her secret might be, it had suddenly turned very dangerous. And now that he'd lost her trust, she wouldn't let him help her.

And then he realized what his heart must have known from the beginning: he loved her. It had confused him, battered him, this love, but it was as real and strong as

the ocean itself. So different from what he'd felt for
Helena: a wild tropical gale as opposed to a placid
breeze, a riotous tangle of wildflowers instead of a dainty
English rose, a windswept night sky against a gentle
dawn. Ah, but the power of it! It could stretch a man
ten different ways, yet endure a lifetime.

Somehow, he had to convince her of it. For he had
the terrible feeling that if he did not, he couldn't save
her from the danger gathering around them like piled-up
stormclouds.

"Jenna—"

But she turned away, her hair swirling in a moonlight
fan around her. He closed the distance between them in
a few long strides, catching her by the arm and swinging
her around.

"More taking?" she asked, her chin lifted in that defiant gesture he'd come to know so well.

Alan went down on one knee before her, shifting his
grip so that he clasped both her hands in his. "If anyone
is enslaved, it is I."

"Magic," she scoffed.

"Yes!" He lifted her hands to his mouth and ran his
lips over the smooth, cool skin. "But it's the magic of
men and women, the simple human need to be touched,
to be held, to be cherished. To be loved. I love you,
Jenna."

She stared down into his eyes. His large, strong hands
held hers with an ineffable tenderness that struck to her
soul, and it was all she could do not to fall to her knees
with him.

"Why now?" she whispered.

"Because I've been too great a fool to see it. I called
it one thing or another but never love. Not until now."

She tasted salt on her lips and only then realized that her cheeks were wet with tears. She'd waited so long to hear it, wished so hard, prayed and dreamed and hoped for it. Joy swept through her, but it was a bittersweet joy, for it had come at a time when she couldn't embrace it. She *had* to leave now, for Roanna's sake. And for his.

There could only be disaster between them. Love wasn't enough to overcome the barrier of who they were; master of Heronsgate and Llewellyn witch. Cursed to love one another, and fated to lose that love in the miasma of hate that had followed her family for so many years.

Gently, she extricated her hands from his, intending to step away from him. But somehow, her feet wouldn't move and her hands, instead of pushing him away, sank of their own volition into the satin darkness of his hair.

"Tell me again," she said.

"I love you." It burned in his eyes, in the hard line of his mouth, and in the lean-cut planes of his face. "I love you."

She sobbed in joy and despair and sharp, surging passion. He pulled her down, enfolding her against him. His mouth brushed her temples, her brows, the wet spikes of her lashes, then settled with hot finality on her lips.

They feasted on one another, tongues darting, toying, teasing in sensual play. His hands moved over her body with an almost reverent tenderness that brought still more tears to her eyes.

He broke the kiss, moving away just enough so that he could see her. "What? Still crying?"

"It's happiness," she said, sliding her fingertip along his lower lip, then shuddering as he drew it into his mouth and sucked on it.

Alan closed his eyes, awash in an extravagant sweep of sensation. It was always like this between them and always would be. She was moonlight, she was flame, she was everything he'd ever wanted. He ran his hands restlessly along her back, drawing her nearer still, wishing he could pull her straight into his soul.

"I want you," she whispered.

"You have me," he replied.

Jenna unbuttoned his shirt and pulled it off with a sharp, impatient movement. Nothing mattered but this. It might be only a few precious moments in a world of pain, but she wanted it. Nay, she had to have it. For it would give her the strength to go on. They could make a lifetime's worth of memories in this brief, glorious time, joy forged in the heat of their bodies and the sweet blending of their hearts.

"Love me," she cried. "Oh, love me!"

He obeyed, stripping her clothes from her. She undressed him in turn, her hands shaking with impatience. And then she pulled him down on the pile of tumbled clothing.

"Shhh. We've plenty of time," he murmured.

"Do we?" she asked, a bit dazed. "I think I might die if you don't take me right now."

"No one dies of impatience, my love."

Jenna wasn't so certain. But she had no choice in the matter; laughing, he pinned her roaming hands over her head and held her still while he plundered her mouth. Breaking the kiss, he ran his open mouth down her throat and lower. She arched her back, offering herself. He took her gift, suckling her until she cried out in pleasure, then soothing her gently with his tongue.

He let go of her hands, but she no longer had the

strength to hurry him. She'd slipped effortlessly into a brimming haze of desire. He was her guide, her only guide, and pleasure the path along which he led her. Every touch of his hands, his mouth, even the sensation of his hair-roughened chest moving along her skin took her to new heights.

She moaned deep in her throat when he moved down her body, sliding inch by inch along her over-sensitive skin. He dipped his tongue fleetingly into her navel, then explored the delicate slope of her belly. She obeyed mindlessly when he urged her legs apart, moaning yet again when his hands teased the swollen flesh between. He slid one finger into her, then another, driving her to distraction with his smooth, surging strokes. She cried out, wanting this, wanting so much more.

"Alan, please," she gasped.

He raised his head to look at her, and the love in his eyes made her tremble even more. "Trust me," he said. "I'll give you everything you want, and more."

She couldn't refuse him. If it had cost her life, or even her soul, she couldn't have refused him. "I trust you."

Alan closed his eyes, driven almost over the edge of control by those three simple words. He'd needed them so very badly. With an effort of will that brought beads of sweat to his forehead, he pushed his own clamoring desire aside and concentrated on her.

Truly, she was magnificent in the extremity of her desire. Her lips were parted, her eyes slumbrous, and the peaks of her breasts stood high and proud. Beneath his hands, she was slick and luscious and eager, more woman than he'd ever known. And she was his.

Jenna cried out in sheer wanton pleasure as his tongue slid through the nest of pale curls at the apex of her thighs, cried out again as he found the small nub and worked it. And his fingers, sliding in and out of her in matching rhythm . . . She had never felt anything like this, never.

Sensation exploded through her body, a clenching, shuddering wave that made her hips buck wildly beneath him. For a moment, she thought, actually thought, she'd touched heaven. And then she came spiraling down.

"That was . . ." she murmured, closing her eyes to savor the small, pulsing aftershocks that still coursed through her body. "That was . . . wonderful."

"There's more," he said.

He slid upward along her body. Upward and in, with a driving force that took her breath away. She opened her eyes and looked up at the man she loved. His eyes were raging midnight pools of desire long-withheld, and the planes of his face were even more tightly drawn than usual.

Propping himself over her with braced arms, he withdrew almost completely, then drove deep again. She gasped as her desire burst into smoldering life once again. Alan felt it happen to her; the awareness of it was in his face, and triumph along with it.

She wanted to rip him out of his self-imposed prison of control. She wanted to set him free, and herself. So she wrapped her legs around his hips, pulling him even deeper into her. Inciting him with her heat, her passion, and her love.

"Jenna," he groaned. "Ah, Jenna!"

And then she saw him give in to her. Surrender. She arched her back, welcoming his driving thrusts, letting him pull her back up the slope toward completion. Higher. Harder. Someone moaned, him or her. She didn't know, didn't care. All that mattered was that he held her in his arms, loving her. They strove and gasped and clung, passion matching passion, limbs twining until she didn't know which were hers and which were his.

The tremendous, wrenching climax caught them both. Jenna clung to him, her only anchor in a multicolored sea of sensation. He cried her name, shuddering, as he poured himself into her depths.

"I love you," he groaned. "I love you."

Slowly, he collapsed upon her, propping himself on one elbow to kiss her with such tenderness that it brought tears to her eyes. She wrapped her arms around him and held him close.

Thank you, Lord, she thought, feeling the rapid thump-thump of his heart against her chest. It had been so very beautiful, this sharing, and she would treasure the memory of it for the rest of her life. If she were so lucky as to bear a child of this night's joining, she would raise it to know how strong and special the love had been between them.

"Alan?" she asked softly, feeling him relax against her.

"Mmmm." He rolled onto his side, bringing her with him. Cupped against the warmth of his body, she lay still and listened as his breathing slowed.

"I love you," she whispered. "More than my freedom, more than life itself."

But he'd fallen asleep. It didn't matter, really; he knew what she felt. She'd shown him in ways far more powerful than words could ever be. She hoped it might be some compensation.

She waited for perhaps a quarter of an hour, then, to be sure, another. He was deeply asleep now, his arms and legs lax, his chest rising and falling with deep, regular breathing. With tightly held breath, she slid out of his embrace and stood up.

It took her but a moment to don her old trousers and shirt—with the buttons neatly resewn. Opal, probably. Moving with sure-footed silence, she went to the door. Alan had forgotten to lock it earlier. He'd been too busy to notice the omission, but she had.

She opened it but paused for a moment in the doorway. "I have to do this," she murmured under her breath. "Someday, I hope you will understand. Remember me, my love."

Then she slipped out.

Alan pulled the curtain aside to watch Jenna leave. She moved with the fey, swift grace of a deer, flitting from cover to cover. Her ash-blonde braid caught the light once, like a silver flash from a river's surface.

He'd let her go.

It was the hardest thing he'd ever done. But his love for her had taught him something he would never have understood on his own: to hold her, he had to set her free.

Something drew her away from him tonight, something so important that she would leave the man she loved. Oh, yes, he'd heard her. He'd heard the tearing emotion in her voice, the desire to stay warring with the necessity of going. If it were any other woman than Jenna, he would have forced the confession and then taken the task upon himself. Helena would have been grateful to let him. But not Jenna. She was unique, and he loved that more than any other quality she possessed.

He loved her. Of all the women in the world, only her. And so he let her go.

It wasn't easy to set his own nature aside for someone else's needs. But he'd forfeited her trust when he'd accused her of harming his children; this was the only way to gain it back.

A corner of the curtain tore away from the supporting rod. He looked up, surprised; he hadn't thought his grip quite so tight.

"I think you're being wise," Dorcas said from behind him.

He swung around to stare at her. "How the devil did you know?"

"I heard her leave."

"You didn't warn me?"

Her expression saddened. "She had to go, sir. Something is wrong; I could see it in her face. And she believes that whatever it is, she's the only one who can fix it."

"I love her, Dorcas."

"You did the right thing in letting her go."

He let his breath out in a long sigh. "It's hard, Dorcas. Bloody hard. Come, watch with me. Pray that she is able to fix what she needs to fix without anyone being the wiser."

"I'm sure she can."

He thought about Mullins's description about those 'eyes black as the pit of Hell.' And he wondered. For Jenna had a secret. And there were some kinds of secrets that could be more important than one's own danger . . . perhaps more important than one's own life.

* * *

Jenna kept to the shelter of the trees beside the road as she made her way toward town. The air was cool and very still, as though the night held its breath in anticipation of what might come.

She tracked Roanna as much by instinct as by woods' lore; the only trace of the old woman's passage was a single white hair caught on a branch of a holly bush. But something kept drawing Jenna on, a sixth sense of presence honed by a lifetime in the trackless swamp.

Suddenly she stopped, going down on one knee to brush fallen leaves away from the ground. A depression had been made in the humus here, just the size and shape of a human body. Roanna had slept here. Jenna drew her breath in sharply at the thought of the old woman sleeping on the damp ground.

"Oh, Grandmother," she whispered. "You'll do neither of us any good by dying for this."

She laid her palm flat on the ground, her head coming up sharply when she felt the faint residual warmth against her skin. Roanna had left only a few moments ago! On hands and knees, Jenna searched the area all around. She found the first track a few yards farther on. It wasn't much, an almost invisible mark in the earth that could have easily have been made by a stick or small animal, but then she found another a short distance away, a small, roundish hole that could only have been made by the tip of a stick with some weight behind it.

Roanna's leg must be giving her trouble; only once before had the old woman bowed to her pain enough to use a stick to walk.

Jenna started forward again, following that faint, intermittent trail. Several times she lost it and had to swing around in wide loops to pick it up again. The woods were getting thicker, too, the moonlight dimmer. Then, off in the distance ahead, she saw a golden-yellow glow that bespoke human habitation.

Roanna's trail led straight toward that house.

On intuition—or perhaps faith—Jenna gave up the trail and headed for the house as fast as she could. It turned out to be the right decision; a few hundred yards further on, she picked up a clear trail again. Roanna was no longer trying to cover her tracks.

"Oh, Grandmother," she whispered. "What are you doing?"

The glow resolved itself into many separate rectangles. Every window in the house, it seemed, poured light out to fight the darkness. When she grew closer, she caught the hum of several voices. None, however, was Roanna's.

She took cover at the edge of the woods, watching, waiting. This was one of the large frame houses that had sprung up near Old Lebanon in the past few years. Her nostrils flared. Despite the fact that their comfortable lives had been built with riches from the Dismal, she'd wager that no one in that building had ever set foot in the swamp.

A trio of carriages waited out front, their drivers talking together in hushed tones. So, the visitors must be getting ready to leave. And Roanna was getting ready to do whatever mad thing she planned . . . Jenna peered into every shadowy place near the house, looking for any kind of movement. But Roanna knew the art of stillness as much as she; who, after all, had taught her to sit motionless in a thicket while hunters or loggers tramped past only a few inches away?

But she knew Roanna was somewhere nearby. Like the cool brush of air upon her cheek, she could feel the old woman's presence. Impatience dug chilly claws into the back of her mind; logic told her to wait, that the encounter with Mullins had been an accident and that Roanna had far too much sense to let herself be seen again.

But that was hope, not expectation, and fear trilled cold fingers across her heart.

The front door opened, spilling a wedge of light across the porch. A man and woman emerged, then two other couples, all calling gay greetings to someone behind them. They were well-fed, well-dressed, well-spoken.

The couples separated then, each moving to one of the waiting carriages. With their passengers comfortably inside, the drivers urged their horses into motion. Laughter floated like wine upon the air.

And then Roanna stepped out into the moonlight. A gusting breeze lifted her pale, moon-shot hair into a cloud around her head and sent her cloak whipping upward like black wings.

She lifted her hand in a flaring, dramatic gesture that sent her cloak billowing outward again.

"It's the witch!" a woman shrieked.

One of the horses reared, its cry as shrill as the woman's. Then it bolted down the drive, dragging the careening carriage and its screaming occupants behind it. After a moment of churning chaos, the other two drivers whipped their horses into a gallop and followed.

Roanna stared after them, her arm still raised. "I won't rest until I get my granddaughter back!"

Only Jenna heard, and that vaguely; she'd burst into a run the moment the woman had screamed. She reached the old woman just as a man pelted out onto the porch. Grabbing Roanna around the waist, she dragged her into the dense shadows from which she'd come.

"Jenna!" Roanna gasped in a high, breathless voice that didn't sound like her at all.

"What the devil are you doing?" Jenna demanded.

"Scaring the earbobs off them, that's what."

"Come on," Jenna hissed. "Let's get out of here."

She led the way back into the woods but stopped again when she realized how badly Roanna was limping.

"Go on," the old woman snapped. "I can keep up."

"It doesn't look that way to me."

"Hmmph. Silvan never spoke to me the way you do."

"Silvan never had to rescue you from your own idiocy," Jenna said. Using the knife she'd taken from Heronsgate's kitchen, she chopped through the base of a nearby sapling. A moment more and she'd stripped it of leaves and cut it to length.

"Here," she said, tossing it to the old woman.

Roanna took it without further protest, which didn't bode well; had she been feeling stronger, she wouldn't have accepted it so docilely.

Jenna led the way onward. Behind her she heard hoofbeats. These woods would be crawling with men before too long. She kept going at the only pace Roanna could manage, a pace that was far too slow.

The glow marking the house faded. Only the breeze stirred the quiet of the woods now, and the velvet arms of the night enclosed the women in a deceptive illusion of safety.

"We'll never make it," Roanna said.

"Of course we will." They wouldn't. They couldn't.

"Don't be a fool. It's already too late."

Jenna stopped. Closing her eyes, she let herself become one with the earth, the sifting breeze, the smells and sounds of the world around her. And there, drifting upon the breeze, was the scent of tobacco.

"We have the Lord to thank for creating stupid men," Roanna said, sniffing. "But they're between us and the swamp."

"We'll find a way," Jenna said.

She moved forward again, navigating by the wind and that drifting of tobacco smoke. Behind her, she could hear Roanna moving, her steps halting and pained, so different from the fluid, powerful stride that had once been hers.

Suddenly the old woman stumbled. Jenna rushed to lift her from the ground. "Are you all right, Grandmother?"

"This damned leg—"

"Here. I can carry you. You don't weigh more than a—"

"Idiot!" Roanna's voice was a hiss of pain and anger. "When the day comes that I can't carry myself, then I'll lie down and let them have me."

"Grandmother—"

The old woman swung the stick in a whistling arc that passed a scant inch over Jenna's head. She ducked instinctively, then deflected the next blow with her forearm. "Stop it! Have you gone mad?"

"Yes! I'm mad, that's it." Roanna swung again.

Jenna caught the stick this time, caught it and wrenched it away. She stood, chest heaving with shock and exertion, and stared down at her grandmother. Then she saw tears glistening on Roanna's cheeks. Her breath went out in a long sigh as she went to her knees beside the old woman.

"It won't work, Grandmother. If you stay, I stay."

"You can't carry me—"

"Of course I can. You raised me strong, Roanna Llewellyn. I can do anything I have to do."

"They burned our homes," the old woman said.

"We'll build new ones."

"I'm too old to start over again."

"Then you can sit in the sun and knit while I do the work."

"Ahhh," Roanna sighed, bowing her head. "You're an idiot."

"It's only what you taught me. Get up, Grandmother."

Jenna rose to her feet and held her hand out. The old woman's head came up. Their gazes warred for a moment, obsidian dark and clear green, then Roanna reached up and grasped Jenna's hand.

Without a flicker of expression, Jenna turned, bending her knees so that the old woman could climb up on her back. She straightened slowly, testing the weight and her own strength, then set off again.

"It's a good thing you're so scrawny," she said over her shoulder.

"You'd have carried me anyway," Roanna said. "Save your breath, girl."

Jenna knew she was leaving a trail; with the burden she carried, there was nothing she could do about it. A few hundred yards farther on, she had to change direction to avoid a brace of men questing through the woods.

"That's east," Roanna muttered. "And the tobacco to the north. West is the road, which will put us straight into their laps."

"So we'll go south."

"To Heronsgate."

"Toward Heronsgate," Jenna amended.

"You still love him."

"I always will."

She stopped talking then; breath was becoming much too precious to waste. More men had come into the woods, summoned, no doubt, by those Roanna had terrified. Jenna trod a dangerous path among them, slipping from bush to shadow to tree, unable now to walk openly at all. With growing despair, she realized she was being forced farther away from the swamp.

"Put me down," Roanna murmured, her voice the barest breath of sound. "You can make it on your own. You know you can."

"I'll not leave you."

"Fool."

"We'll find a way. There's always a way."

The old woman sighed. "Tell that to Silvan."

"The road's just ahead. We'll cross it and see if we can't find a place to hide until they get tired of swanning around in the dark."

"Rest. You'll need your strength."

Jenna glanced around, finally deciding that it would be safe enough, at least for a minute or two. She needed to rest; her back and legs burned as though a fire had been lit in them, and her heart pounded so hard that it had become difficult to hear what was going on around her. So she let Roanna down but turned to pin the old woman with a forbidding stare. "Stay with me, Grandmother."

"I'll not endanger you, twit."

With a smile that trembled just a bit, Jenna laid her

hand on Roanna's cheek. A suspicious moisture gleamed in the old woman's eyes.

"Time to go," Jenna whispered.

Roanna grabbed her wrist in an iron grip, holding her down when she would have straightened. "Horse coming," she said. "No, two."

Jenna tried to hear over the still rapid beating of her heart, but everything seemed to blend together. Fear hammered at her as she watched the bend in the road for the riders to appear.

A moment later they pounded into sight. A big horse led the way, the white of its rider's shirt reflecting the pale hide of the horse that followed. Something about the way the man sat triggered recognition in Jenna's mind.

"Alan," she gasped.

All unexpected, the decision had come. Time seemed to stand still as she wavered between head and heart, trust and remembered betrayal. Decision. Finally, irrevocably, with Roanna's life in the balance.

Suddenly the night seemed very clear. She stepped out of her hiding place to stand in the center of the road to wait.

"Are you mad?" Roanna hissed.

"Perhaps," she said. "We're about to find out."

Twenty-eight

The wind tore at Jenna's unbound hair as she watched Alan ride toward her. Savior or betrayer, enemy or lover, it would all be resolved now. He was close enough now to see her, and it registered like lightning on his face.

With a suddenness that sent dirt spraying out from beneath the horses' hooves, he pulled to a halt. He stared down at Jenna for a moment, his eyes glittering with some unidentifiable emotion, then tossed her the reins of the spare horse.

"So," Roanna hissed. "This is the master of Heronsgate."

He gazed at her for a moment, his eyes inscrutable, then turned back to Jenna. "This is your great secret?"

"My grandmother. Roanna Llewellyn."

Again, that bland midnight gaze examined the old woman. "Well, come along, Roanna Llewellyn. You can ride with me."

"Stay away from me!"

"I'm trying to save your bloody life, woman!"

Roanna's hands came up, nails ready to strike. "I'll claw your eyes out."

Alan dug his heels into the stallion's sides, sending the big horse lunging forward. Scooping the old woman up before him, he turned his horse and headed back toward Heronsgate.

For a heartbeat, Jenna could only stare. Then she leaped astride the other mount's bare back and followed them. Her heart sang in rhythm with the pounding hooves. He'd come for her. Come for *them*. He'd defied his neighbors, his friends, his entire world to do it.

Alan adjusted the old woman's slight, squirming weight. She seemed both furious and terrified of him. Considering the connection between them, he didn't blame her overmuch. But she was making things difficult.

"If you don't stop struggling," he said, "Hector will buck us to kingdom come, and Jenna will stop with us. They'll catch her, and you know more than any of us what will happen."

She stilled. Without having to fight her, he was able to glance over his shoulder at Jenna. She lay low over the horse's neck, riding with instinctive grace. Her hair rippled like liquid moonlight on the wind.

It was as though everything that was wild and free in the world had crystallized in one lovely woman. He drank in the sight, knowing it would stay with him for the rest of his life. She'd trusted him. She'd offered her life, if he chose to take it. Risked the old woman's, because she believed he would not take it.

He turned back to find Roanna staring at him. Her time-etched face and pitch-dark gaze might have disconcerted another man. But he'd already stepped into the whirlwind; what disaster could even a witch bring him now?

A half-mile further on, he caught the gleam of Heronsgate's white walls in the distance. To him, it seemed so friendly and welcoming, but he felt the old woman stiffen in his arms.

Ben came running out to take their horses the moment they cantered up the drive. He flinched a bit when he saw Roanna but recovered quickly enough to bow.

"Thought I was dead, eh?" the old woman asked as he lifted her down.

"Everyone did," Ben replied.

"Well, what about it? Are you as frightened of me as you look?"

He glanced at Jenna, then met the old woman's gaze levelly. "I ain't scared of nobody who comes with the Lady."

Alan offered his arm to Roanna. She shot him a glance from under her brows, then accepted his help. Jenna smiled; the old woman couldn't have made it up the steps without him, but she managed to make it seem that she was doing him a favor.

She tilted her head back to look up at the house. "I hate this place."

"It's only a house," Alan said. "It's the people who make it good or bad."

Suddenly, the old woman's leg buckled beneath her. As Jenna sprang forward to help, he bent and lifted Roanna into his arms. He was surprised at how little she weighed.

"Your skin is like ice," he said, carrying her into the house. He was aware of Jenna hovering behind him and knew she was very concerned about the old woman's health.

"Take her to my room," Jenna said.

"I'll not lie down in this house," Roanna snapped.

Alan smiled, meeting her indignant dark stare. "Are you afraid of Stepton's ghost, perhaps?"

"Nay. But I'll damned well meet it sitting up."

Jenna sighed. "The drawing room."

Alan muttered something dire under his breath, saw the old woman register it with grim humor. He carried her into the drawing room and gently set her down in the armchair beside the fireplace. He laid a good fire, leaving Jenna to deal with her grandmother's boots and things.

"I wish I had my stick back," Roanna snarled, slapping at Jenna's hands. "Stop fussing, girl!"

"You're chilled to the bone," Jenna said.

"I've lived outdoors all my life."

"Put your feet closer to the fire, Grandmother."

"I am *fine.*"

Completely out of patience, Jenna looked up at Alan. "Alan, do something."

He crossed his arms over his chest and considered her request for a moment, doubting she'd approve anything he had in mind just now. It was the challenge in the old woman's face that made the decision for him.

Bending, he lifted Roanna and the chair and put them closer to the fire. "There," he said, gaining much satisfaction from the surprise on her face. "You might as well get used to such heat."

"Hmph. If you weren't already cursed, I might be tempted to turn you into a toad." But her voice lacked animosity, and he realized she was too exhausted to fight any longer.

As her eyes fluttered closed, he slid another log on the fire, then turned and took Jenna's hand.

"But—" she began.

"Shhh. Let her sleep," he murmured. "She needs that more than anything else just now."

Jenna let him lead her down the hall to his study. She'd never been in this room before, but she liked the burnished paneling of the walls, the creamy richness of the carpet and the deep wine-colored carpet that echoed the ruddy glints in the polished mahogany desk. It was an intensely masculine room but also a warm and intimate one.

"Where are the children?" she asked.

"Before I went looking for you, I sent Dorcas with them to the Graemes'. They'll be safe there."

She nodded, glad that he'd slipped Jon and Beth away from the struggle that was to come. "You shouldn't have brought us here. It will cost you much."

"Your grandmother is ill, Jenna," he said, keeping a firm grip on his burgeoning temper. Too much had already been lost because of it, and he wasn't about to lose any more. "You wouldn't have gotten a quarter of a mile more with her, and I know bloody well you'd never leave her. Even if I weren't madly in love with you, I'd have humanity enough not to toss an old woman out to be killed."

"Don't scowl, Alan. I wasn't trying to be insulting."

"Well, you bloody well were. Not," he added, "that I don't deserve your lack of faith, considering my own." Turning sharply away, he raked his hand through his hair. "You're chilled through, and I'm trying to keep my temper. I think a brandy will do us both good."

"I've never drunk brandy."

"Ah, yes. Your taste runs to elderberry wine."

For a moment she didn't understand. Then she remembered that time they'd spent together at her cabin. Those hours had been steeped in sensuality, of desire admitted but still unexplored. And they had been strangely innocent, as well, for they had truly believed that tiny, verdant corner of the world belonged only to them.

"Actually," she said, "I hate elderberry wine. But you were my guest, and I felt I had to offer you something special."

He stared at her for a moment, remembering how he'd choked down the awful stuff just to have the privilege of dwelling in her eyes for a time. He should have realized then that he loved her to distraction.

Suddenly, his ill humor vanished. Nothing else mattered except that she'd trusted him when it truly mattered. So much time had been wasted in mistrust and arguments. He'd never get it back, but he could learn from his mistakes and treasure what he had now.

Raising her hand to his lips, he murmured, "Let me have the honor of introducing you to something new."

"As you've introduced me to so many other new things?" she asked with a seductive half-smile that set his pulse racing.

It took an effort of will to move away from her. He poured two brandies at the sideboard, watching her in the mirror. There was just enough tension in those lovely features for him to know that she realized this was just an interlude in their troubles. But she seemed willing, as he was, to accept it for the precious thing it was.

"Here you are," he said, coming back to her, glasses in hand. "Take it slowly."

Jenna took a sip. For a moment, just a moment, alarm spread through her at the potency of it. But it was a smooth sort of power, heady and warming at once. When the first tingle subsided, she dared another sip.

"I like this," she said.

"I should think so. This is the noblest of spirits known to Man."

Jenna lifted her glass, drinking with more boldness. She held the last few drops on her tongue to let the taste linger. Warmth spread through her body, but she wasn't sure whether it was from the brandy or from his eyes.

"Why did you come after me?" she asked.

"Would you rather I hadn't?"

"That's not it at all," she said. Moving closer, she put her free hand flat on his chest. "Please, Alan. I have to know."

He grasped her wrist lightly, feeling the rapid kick of her pulse against his palm. "I let you go, knowing you had to do this yourself. But when I heard the riders shouting along the road, I knew you'd been found out."

"She was only trying to help me—" She broke off, suddenly registering what he'd said. "You . . . let me go?"

"I wasn't asleep, you know. Before you left, you said, 'Some day, I hope you understand. Remember me, my love'."

"But . . . why?"

"I knew you were protecting someone and that someone was very important to you."

"I—"

"Bloody hell, Jenna. I knew you hadn't gone into town. But you were willing to be branded a witch to protect the person who had. Who else could it be but your grandmother? And I knew that I had to let you go if you were ever to trust me again. It was bloody hard, I won't do it again."

Repressed violence darkened his eyes. Jenna reached

up, smoothing the grim lines bracketing his mouth. "I didn't think Roanna's secret was mine to tell."

"And yet you did, in the end."

She nodded. "We were both terribly foolish."

"I for not knowing love when it was staring me straight in the eye—"

"And I for not letting myself see that you would help me . . . or mine."

"I'd fight the Devil himself for you."

Joy crashed through her in a hot, blinding tide. He'd taken that last, great step into faith. This was the greatest gift of all, the one that tore away the last of the barriers between them. She took a step closer, coming against him completely, and slid her hand up to the strong, warm column of his neck.

"I'm glad you came," she whispered. "I needed you."

He pulled her against him with sudden fierceness. The glasses fell to the carpet, unheeded by either of them. Holding her face between his hands, he looked deeply into her eyes and said, "Marry me, Jenna."

"What?" She couldn't have been more astonished had the moon fallen out of the sky and landed at her feet.

"Marry me. I want to spend my life with you."

"But—"

"I love you, my children love you. And we may already have begun another life to share," he said, sliding his hand down to her flat belly.

"And the curse?"

"No one but God has the power to punish Orwell Stepton and his sons for what he did to your mother. If a curse existed, it was His."

"Grandmother believes she killed him."

"Your grandmother is a tired old woman who has believed in her hate for so long she can't see another way. But we found the way, Jenna. You and I. Hate made Roanna's life a prison; love set us free."

His eyes drew her. Deep indigo pools of flaring desire and unwavering purpose, they pulled her in and wrapped her up in a shimmering cloak of tenderness and need. For the first time, she dared believe that this was no shackling, no prison, but the doorway to a world in which they both could live.

"Will you?" he asked.

"Marry you?" With her forefinger, she traced the hard line of his mouth. "Ask me tomorrow, if it comes."

"Jenna—"

"Shhh. At this moment, there's only one thing that matters." She sank her hands into his hair and pulled his head down for a kiss. At first he resisted, wanting more from her. Then his mouth softened as he accepted her answer. For now, for now. She knew this man of hers better than to think he'd given up for a moment.

The kiss changed, turning from a gentle exploration into a heated possession, a sighing, intemperate embrace that became hotter and deeper every moment.

He tugged her shirt out of her waistband, and his hands felt wonderful on her skin. A shiver went up her spine, following the brush of his fingertips. He broke the kiss, lifting his mouth just enough to speak.

"You're still cold," he murmured. "I'll start the fire."

"I only need you."

"I've always wanted to make love to you in the fire-light."

His voice was as warm as his hands; his eyes held such infinite promise that she nodded. But her body

ached with loss when he left her to strike flint and steel
into the already prepared kindling.

As the flames began to lick hungrily at the wood,
Jenna unbuttoned her shirt and shrugged it off. Alan
looked over his shoulder at her, his body turning as
though helpless to do aught but follow his gaze. Ruddy
light from the fire danced in his eyes and cast flickering
shadows over the planes of his face.

"Don't stop," he said hoarsely.

She kicked off her moccasins, then unbuttoned her
trousers and let them fall. Reaching up with a movement
that lifted her breasts high, she unbraided her hair. His
chest rose and fell with breathing that had suddenly become very ragged. Smiling, Jenna shook her hair free,
letting it flow like satin mist around her shoulders.

"Is this what you wanted?" she asked.

"Yes."

Alan held her gaze as he removed his own clothing.
Then, naked and gloriously aroused, he crouched. The
firelight played across the stark muscular beauty of him,
and he looked primitive and feral—a powerful male creature that called to everything female in her.

"Come here, Jenna."

She obeyed, sinking to her knees in front of him. He
trailed his finger along her cheek and down her throat,
where the pulse throbbed frantically, then traced a teasing
circle around her nipple. The sensitive flesh reacted powerfully, the coral peak tightening to a taut nub.

With a hiss of indrawn breath, Jenna moved his hand
to her other breast. He kissed her temple, her ear, the
sweet, firm line of her chin, then nibbled at her mouth,
encouraging her to open to him. This, too, she obeyed.

His fingertips found her nipple at the same time his tongue touched hers.

Love. Passion. A woman's need for the only man who could claim her, a man's need for the only woman who could touch his soul. So simple now that she knew the truth of it.

She spread her fingers out across his chest, savoring the hard maleness of him. And then she slid her hands down his body, registering the differing textures of skin and muscle and hair. A groan rumbled deep in his chest when she clasped his jutting manhood. He swelled in her hand, and she reveled in the power she held over him.

"Jenna," he gasped. "Stop."

"I don't want to stop."

The world tilted suddenly as he lifted her and laid her down on the carpet. Heat from the fire coiled out over her body, but his hands were hotter. And his mouth. Oh, his mouth. Her awareness narrowed until there was nothing but the feel of his hands stroking, his kisses, the searing glide of his tongue along her skin.

She wrapped herself around him as he settled between her legs, so near and so very potent. But he held himself back from her, probing, teasing, sliding with torturous promise along flesh that ached for more.

"Are you trying to drive me mad?" she asked.

"No." The rasp in his voice betrayed his wavering control. "I just wanted to savor loving you."

"Then love me completely," she said. "I want all of you."

Alan closed his eyes. With a gasp of irrepressible desire, he slid into heaven. Her slick, hot depths closed around him like a tight, velvet glove. Keeping their intimate joining, he rolled over onto his back.

"You wanted me," he said. "I'm all yours, Lady."

"All?"

"Body and soul, heart and hands and . . . Ah, Jenna," he sighed as she began to move. "Oh, God."

The passion in his voice excited her immeasurably. Spreading her hands out over his chest, she rode him to a rhythm that soon had him gasping beneath her. But it was not one-sided, this immoderate pleasure; desire pulsed through her veins in a sweet, hot torrent.

She watched his face as she loved him. His eyes were slitted, his features taut with immense, uncontrolled passion. He belonged to her, his heart hers as truly as the part of him sheathed so deeply in her flesh.

"This is magic," he whispered. "The real kind."

"Yes," she whispered back. "The only kind."

With a powerful surge of muscles, he lifted his upper body so that he could tongue her nipples. She flung her head back in exquisite, surging pleasure, holding his dark head against her. Sensation ran in rippling sparks from her breasts to her groin, making her contract around him.

Suddenly she found herself on her back, staring up into his raging indigo eyes. Her body was empty, bereft. She cried out with the loss, but cried out again in pleasure a moment later when he reclaimed her in a powerful thrust of magnificent male possession.

Taking. Giving. Sharing. A love that seared the flesh and plumbed the depths of the soul; together, only together, they had it all. Jenna arched into his driving strokes; he plunged deep, deeper, lifting her hips so that she could feel all of him. She gasped, straining toward the completion that hovered just out of reach. And then it took her, casting her out into a whirlwind of sensation.

She heard Alan call her name as he fell with her. For

a moment, one, glorious moment, they spun together in an incandescent burst of shared glory. As she spiraled down into a haze of satiation, she knew that if she lived a thousand years, the memory of this night would stay with her. Tears slid out from beneath her closed eyelids.

"Crying?" Alan murmured, touching his tongue to one of those crystal drops.

"It's only because I love you so much."

"Good. I thought for a moment I'd made you un-happy."

She opened her eyes and looked straight up into his. "You're the only thing that makes sense in this madhouse of a world. Don't ever forget that, Alan Langston."

He rolled onto his side, bringing her with him. She wriggled so that she could hear the comforting thump-thump of his heart.

After a moment, she said the thing both of them were thinking. "They'll come looking for me," she said.

"I'll make them understand."

"They will never understand."

His arms tightened around her. "I told you before, Jenna. I intend to keep you. They will either accept you or they and their world can go to the Devil."

"And Grandmother?"

"She can go to the Devil, too. But they won't touch her. I promise you that."

"Alan, I can't let you—"

"Shhh. I ask you again: trust me."

Turning in his arms, she looked into his eyes. He wasn't tamed, this man of hers; he never would be. But then, neither would she. And if she was sure of nothing else in this mess, she knew he could be trusted.

"I trust you," she said.

The look in his eyes was enough to set her blood heating again. He brushed her hair away from her face, then traced the delicate curve of her ear with his fingertip. "There's still an hour or so until dawn, and that leaves us with a choice, my love. We can sleep here on the carpet like a pair of contented cats or we can make love again. Which appeals to you?"

"Well," she said, "it *has* been a long, tiring night . . ."

He surged against her, his satin hardness sliding with delicious demand against her thigh. She turned toward him, trapping that importunate heat between them. Truly, there was no decision but one; she would always choose him.

"Exactly how tired are you?" he asked, his breath warm on her ear.

She slipped her arm around his neck. "Well, if you asked properly, I might be able to find just a bit more energy . . ."

"Like this?"

"Mmmm," she murmured. "Yes. Just like that."

The first rosy streaks of dawn stained the eastern sky when they returned to the drawing room. Roanna didn't rouse, even when Alan bent to stir up the fire. Jenna frowned in concern; usually the old woman was the lightest of sleepers.

She brushed her fingertips across her grandmother's forehead but found her wrist caught and held before she could draw back.

"I may be old," Roanna said, "But I'm not so senile that I couldn't tell whether or not I had a fever." Her gaze shifted to Alan. "You look mighty pleased with yourself, Master of Heronsgate."

"You may call me Alan, or, if you'd prefer, Langston. And I *am* rather pleased with myself."

"Enjoy it while you can."

He smiled at her, genuinely enjoying the moment. "I don't feel particularly doomed today, Grandmother."

"You ought to."

Alan held out his arm, and Jenna moved to stand beside him. "I've asked your granddaughter to marry me."

"And?"

"She hasn't given me an answer yet. But I plan to convince her."

"Llewellyns don't marry," the old woman said.

Jenna watched her grandmother's face. Fear etched those wrinkled features, and anger, too. But concern overshadowed everything else. It wasn't the hate that Roanna was holding onto; she truly thought that only disaster could come from this. Glancing at Alan, she saw that he realized this as well. Some of the granite hardness left his jaw.

"There is no curse," he said. "It's time you did something with your life besides hate."

Roanna's chin went up, a gesture of defiance so much like her granddaughter's that his heart ached at the sight of it. "I spoke that curse myself. How can you say it doesn't exist when Stepton and his sons paid its price?"

"Coincidence."

"Nay. Magic. Llewellyn magic."

"Then do it now," he said. "Turn me into a toad, and I'll believe. Better yet, prove it to me by curing the ills of your own body and walking out of here."

Roanna scowled. "You tempt me sorely."

Someone rapped sharply on the door, and a moment later Opal leaned into the room. "There's a rider comin'," she said, her voice and expression urgent.

"Stay here, both of you," Alan said. "For your lives."

Twenty-nine

Alan stepped out onto the veranda. A cloud of dust hovered above the road, moving steadily closer. His neighbors, come to judge the woman he loved. Fury beat in his veins and curled his hands into fists.

"Damn them for this," he muttered.

A soft footfall on the veranda behind him brought him swinging around. Ben stood just outside the open front door, his thick arms crossed over his chest.

"Folks used to say to their children, 'ole Roanna's goin' to git you if you don't act right'," he said. "And that was about as potent a threat as callin' on Lucifer himself. But somethin' happened out there in the swamp the day she cursed master Stepton; I ain't never seen an innocent man so scared."

Alan nodded. Guilty or innocent, Stepton, by his living and his dying, had set the stage for this. "How many do you guess, Ben?"

" 'Bout a dozen riders, three, maybe four carriages. That ain't countin' the men who been watching the house since before dawn. I got the back of the house fixed up—door barred, shutters closed."

"Good. If they come, they have to come straight over me."

Ben took a deep breath. "Can't you get the Lady out?"

"Roanna can barely walk, and it would take a stronger man than I to get Jenna to leave her behind. Besides, this hatred has to stop."

"People been hatin' since Cain slew Abel, suh."

"I *will* stop it."

Alan knew how arrogant it sounded. But he couldn't help it; this feud had gone on too long and had cost everyone involved far too much. He wasn't going to pay the price for it, nor would his children.

He pulled his pistols out from his waistband and checked the priming. "You'd better get clear of this, Ben," he said. "Make sure our people are safe."

"I hope you got more than a pair of pistols, suh."

"I've got my wits and the knowledge that most of those are decent people." Hefting the guns with the expertise of long use, he smiled grimly. "I've got enough here to handle Rafferty, and that pleases me well enough. Go on. Do what I told you."

"Suh."

The big man left so noiselessly that Alan had to look to make sure he'd really gone. Then he thrust the pistols back into his waistband. He intended to try reason first. If that failed, well, so be it.

"I *will* hold her," he said.

He could see faces in the crowd now. He'd expected to see the owners of neighboring plantations but not Miranda Carrew and Lisa Tollerton. The women had come in Jameson Graeme's carriage. Their identical expressions of self-righteous outrage were almost balanced by the older man's calm eyes and steady hands.

Alan's shifted as Jonas Rafferty and his men came out of the woods. Someone had lent the slave hunter a mount, one which he had a bit of trouble controlling. He cradled his flintlock awkwardly as he fumbled with the reins.

Carlton Graeme dismounted and came to stand in front of Alan. "Father and I tried to stop this," he said. "I'm sorry."

"So why are you here?"

Carlton smiled. "I've come to protect the Lady."

"This isn't your fight."

"I was raised to do what I thought was right. And if Jonas Rafferty has his way, a very great wrong will be done here today. I can't allow that to happen."

"Get back on your horse," Alan said. "I won't have your blood on my hands."

Instead of answering, the young man stepped up onto the veranda. Alan saw the flash of metal as Carlton pulled a pistol out of his pocket and held it with elaborate casualness.

"I just want to make sure this is fair," he said.

"Two against twenty isn't fair."

"It's fairer than one against twenty."

Alan looked over the younger man's shoulder, realizing that the time for getting Carlton out of danger had passed; Rafferty and his men had reached the clustered townsfolk. Alan was struck by the difference between the two groups; on the one hand, the civilized men with their honest—if misplaced—outrage, on the other, human wolves with eyes that glittered with bloodlust.

"You're protecting the witch," Rafferty said.

With an arrogant lift of his head, Alan replied, "I know of no witch. But Jenna Llewellyn is under my protection. Go home, all of you."

"You can't turn us away so easily." That was offered by a portly man whose mount and dress proclaimed him a prosperous fellow. His broad face was flushed and sweaty, his hands shaking upon the reins. "You, sir, may have ruled your little corner of England, but this is America, and here we listen to our neighbors. We don't want the witch among us."

"There is no witch," Alan said. "Only a woman."

"Pshaw, man. People are falling sick even as we stand here."

Alan measured the man with a deliberately cold gaze. "Have you ever heard of influenza?"

"And I've heard of witchery, too. We've suffered much at the Llewellyns' hands. You can't walk in here and start telling us that fifty years of strife just isn't so."

"Just step aside," Rafferty said. "We'll do the rest."

Alan smiled. "No."

"Then we'll come through you."

"Come, then," Alan said. "Try."

Jenna peered out through the drawing room curtains. She didn't like the glitter of recklessness in Alan's eyes; at this moment, he was capable of almost anything. Anything, that is, but backing down. She knew Rafferty would challenge him, knew with equal certainty what his response would be.

"I've got to get out there," she said, flinging herself away from the window.

Roanna caught her by the arm. "Are you mad?"

"Rafferty's going to goad him into fighting. And then they'll have an excuse to kill him."

"And what do you think they'll do to you?"

"I won't stand here and let him be hurt."

"One less townsman."

With a sharp exclamation of disgust, Jenna pulled away. But Roanna limped hastily after her, grasping her by the shirt in a grip as determined as it was desperate. "I'm sorry, Jenna. I didn't mean that, truly. But you can' go out there. I saw what they did to Silvan. I know wha they'll do to you."

"You know what Rafferty will do. But other people are involved in this.

Roanna snorted. "They're all the same."

"They're not." Jenna grasped the old woman's shoulders as though she could convince her with her touch "All these years, I listened to you, believing withou question what you told me about them. But you're as wrong to lump them all under one name as they are to call us evil simply because we're different."

"Fine. Then *I'll* walk out there."

Jenna's eyes widened, then narrowed as she realized how neatly she'd been caught. Roanna would sacrifice herself, knowing there could be no mercy for the woman who'd cursed Orwell Stepton and his sons. "No, you won't."

"If they're so willing to accept a Llewellyn witch, why not me? You stay here, and I'll go say hello to the neighbors."

Roanna tore free and hobbled toward the front door Whirling her back around, Jenna balled her hand into a fist and struck the old woman square on the chin. She caught Roanna as she crumpled.

"I'm sorry, Grandmother," Jenna murmured, laying the old woman's slight form on the sofa. "But I can' let you do that."

She smoothed her tumbled hair and headed for the front door. Inexplicably, her racing pulse slowed and serenity flowed over her like cool spring water. She wasn't afraid any longer. As long as Alan stood at her side, she could do anything, face anyone.

Conversation ceased when she stepped out onto the veranda. Rafferty shifted his flintlock higher but lowered it again after a glance at the pistol that Carlton now aimed at his head.

"Get back in the house," Alan hissed, his hands hovering near his own weapons.

"For years I've been unable to defend myself against their vicious tongues," she said. "Now, I intend to look my accusers in the eye."

Although he raged inwardly, Alan knew he had to support her in this. Bloody hell, but he wished she'd do what she was told for once.

But then, he knew, she wouldn't be Jenna.

Moving in perfect, silent agreement, he and Carlton shifted so that they were standing shoulder to shoulder, creating a solid barrier between her and the others. After looking into Rafferty's coldly burning eyes, Jenna accepted it. But she faced the townsfolk with her chin raised and her stubborn Llewellyn pride flaring high.

"What are the charges against me?" she demanded.

"Witchcraft," a tall, balding man said. "Like all your kin."

"Thank you, Reverend Grey," Alan said in a voice drier than tinder. "It's always a comfort to know one's clergyman is at work protecting his flock's souls."

"Don't listen to him," Rafferty spat. "He's just tryin' to shake you with those high-and-mighty English ways of his. But he ain't no better than the rest of us; worse, even, fer beddin' the witch."

Jenna's gaze was drawn to Miranda. The tawny-haired

woman's face had turned pale; jealousy turned her eyes into hard, aquamarine pebbles, her mouth into a tightly pinched line.

"And have you indeed bedded the witch?" Reverend Grey asked.

Alan showed the edges of his teeth in a smile a tiger would have envied. "That is not a question a gentleman would ask, or answer," he said. "I plan to marry the lady, if she'll have me."

A collective gasp went up from the crowd. Miranda's hands clenched and unclenched on the side of the carriage, her knuckles showing white in the bright morning sun.

"He's been bespelled!" she cried.

Alan didn't even look at her. "If I was bespelled," he said, "then it was by the simple love of a man for a woman. Nothing more, nothing less."

"No!" Miranda's voice rang over the muttered conversation around her. "He doesn't know what he's saying. She put a spell on him, making him desire her. We all know how the Llewellyn witches lure the men with their bodies and their magic."

" 'Tis true," someone cried.

"Yes! Yes! 'Tis bewitchment for sure!" shouted another voice.

Alan came up on his toes. Jenna clamped her hand on his shoulder, exerting pressure. If he reached for his pistols, all talking would be over.

Jameson Graeme stood up. Arms outstretched like some Biblical prophet, he called, "Calmly, my friends, calmly! We are civilized men, are we not?"

The shouts dropped to a mutter. But Jenna could tell

the mood of the crowd was still ugly. A portly man urged his horse a step ahead of the others.

"Tell us, woman, about the illness that is striking us and our slaves," he said.

"It's influenza," she replied. "Surely some of you have experienced it before."

"Many times," Reverend Grey said. "But how do we know—"

"We don't." Miranda flounced down from the carriage and stood, arms akimbo, to face the others. "Don't you think it strange that people are falling ill not two days after she came to our autumn ball?" With sweeping, dramatic flair, she whirled to point at Jenna. "That night, she touched my mother. I'm not the only one who saw her do it, believe me. And now Mother's sick in bed, afflicted with this . . . so-called influenza. If you ask me, the witch has cursed us just as her foul grandmother cursed Orwell Stepton. Will you wait until people start dying before you do something about it?"

"You're a liar," Alan snapped.

She smiled. "Am I?"

He stared at her, realizing at last why Jenna had held so little hope that these people would accept her. There was nothing she could do, nothing she could say, that wouldn't be misinterpreted or misrepresented. Once a witch, always a witch.

"I *will* hold her," he muttered under his breath.

Lisa Tollerton was the next to stand up. "She nearly killed the lot of us last night at the Masons'. Bewitched our horses and made them bolt. I saw her with my own eyes, and so did three other people."

"How can you be sure it was she?" Carlton demanded.

"Look at her!" the woman said. "Do you think anyone could mistake that hair?"

Alan glanced over his shoulder at Jenna. His dilemma showed clearly in his eyes: he could help her only by incriminating Roanna.

Jenna smiled at him. "I love you," she said.

"Then get back in the house."

Still smiling, she shook her head.

Miranda's eyes narrowed, and she took another step forward. "She doesn't deny the charge! What reason did she have for sneaking around the Mason place, if not to sow a spell to make more people ill? We don't need her kind here; let's get rid of her before she breeds more like herself."

A murmur went through the crowd like a wave, then swelled and grew into a shout.

"She's right!" one man said.

" 'Tis long overdue," another cried.

"Take the witch!" called a third.

"Wait! This isn't the way!" Jameson Graeme tried to quell the din, but they shouted right over him.

Alan stood unmoving, his eyes as cold as a winter sea. With a smooth, practiced movement, he pulled the pistols out and aimed them at Rafferty and his men.

"I'll take two before I go down," he said. "Who wants the dubious honor of dying with Jonas Rafferty?"

The other men hesitated, more intimidated, Jenna thought, by his reckless disregard for his own safety than by the pistols. Without taking his gaze from Rafferty's cold killer's eyes, he whispered, "Get her inside, damn it!"

Carlton took a step backward, pushing Jenna with him. She shoved clear and went to stand at Alan's side.

"I'll stay with you," she said.

"Get!" he hissed.

She looked up at him, possessed by a wave of tenderness so powerful it almost brought tears to her eyes. He'd tried. For her, he'd challenged his friends, his enemies, and the conventions of his world. He'd risked enough.

"Alan has nothing to do with this," she said. " 'Twas all my doing—"

"No!" he raged.

"Yes," she said, putting all her love in her voice. "Your children need you."

With a sweep of his arm, he flung her back. Her arms windmilled frantically as Carlton caught her around the waist and dragged her toward the house.

"Alan!" she cried.

Time stuttered and slowed as she watched Rafferty bring the flintlock up. The slave trader's mouth stretched wide in an ugly smile of triumph. Then his jaw sagged, and he lowered the weapon again.

Jenna gasped as Ben led Heronsgate's slaves around the corner of the house. Armed with axes and hoes and rakes, men and women both came to stand behind the slave trader and his men.

"What the devil are you doing?" the portly man snapped.

"We come to defend the Lady," Ben said.

"Get back to your cabins!"

Opal shook her head, her kerchief a bright splash of color against her dark honey skin. "We may be slaves, but we be *Heronsgate* slaves. And we don't take orders from nobody but Master Alan."

"Thank you, Opal," Alan said. Keeping his pistols

trained on Rafferty's belly, he addressed the townspeople. "What do you say we talk some more?"

"That . . . would be acceptable," Reverend Grey said.

"Good. Now, you've had plenty of opportunity to air your grievances. But Jenna has something to say, too."

Lifting her chin, she studied each face in the group. "I, too, have reason to hate."

"We've done nothing to you!" called one of the men.

"Twenty years ago, four townsmen murdered my mother. Brutally, horribly. So terrible were the things they did to her that my grandmother's hair turned white overnight. So terrible that she's never been able to tell me what they did."

Miranda laughed raucously. "Only now, twenty years later, you tell the tale. And who's to say you nay, witch? Orwell's dead and can't defend himself. The old woman laid that curse out of sheer evil, and you know it."

"Why the Steptons?" Jenna asked. "Out of a whole town, why them?"

"It doesn't matter!" Miranda shouted. "What matters is that she did it! And you're just as bad as she ever was, with your love potions and spells and philters."

"Indeed?" Jenna lifted her hand and pointed at the portly man, who flinched away as though she'd aimed a pistol at his head. "Then why am I standing here at the risk of my life, instead of turning the lot of you into snakes and spiders and croaking toads?"

Reverend Grey spoke up then. "What about your powders and potions?"

"Herbs and medicines, clergyman. Have you never drunk horehound tea when you've got the sniffles?"

"Well, yes, but—"

"Then you're guilty of the same sort of witchcraft you're accusing me of."

"What of all the slaves you've helped escape?" A tall, well-dressed man pushed to the front of the crowd.

"I help anyone who comes to me. I don't ask who they are or where they're from."

"You know they've escaped," Rafferty said. "The Llewellyns been many things, but stupid, they ain't."

Jenna raised her chin another inch, staring down her nose at him. "Very well. I choose not to know. Am I on trial for hating slavery or for witchcraft?"

"Don't listen to her!" Miranda cried, her voice shrill with malice. "We all knew Orwell Stepton and his father before him. There's no truth to the charge that he killed the Llewellyn witch. Why did this man, this fine, good man we've known all our lives, commit murder?"

"Because he could," Jenna said. "Because there are men who hold a fine face up to the public and hide the blackness of their souls."

"You Llewellyns ought to know all about that," Miranda retorted. "An outsider would look at your face and see only the beauty, but we know you have Satan's own heart inside. And we know that your grandmother cursed Orwell Stepton and his sons; she killed them as surely as if she put a pistol to their heads."

Alan hardly heard her, caught as he was by the look in Rafferty's eyes. Fear had replaced the hate in those pale depths; a flicker only, but it had definitely been there. More revealing was the sheen of perspiration beneath the scraggly beard.

"Why does the mention of the curse bother you, Mr. Rafferty?" he asked.

"It don't bother me."

"Then why are you sweating?"

Jenna swung around to look at Rafferty. A shiver ran up her spine as a cloud slid over the face of the sun. Perhaps the chill had been created by the sudden drop in light, or perhaps a terrible sort of prescience that sent a frisson running through her body.

There had been four men that day. Four. And Rafferty with his hate and his conscienceless eyes . . .

"Did you enjoy yourself?" she asked.

"I don't know what you're talkin' about," Rafferty said. But his gaze flicked away. Just a little, and just for a moment, but he might as well have sounded a trumpet.

Jenna knew. As surely as she stood here, she knew. Rage shot through her veins in cold, darting rivulets. "You're one of them."

His eyes changed suddenly, profoundly; it was like watching a veil stripped away, taking the vestiges of humanity and revealing the beast below. Jenna realized then that he was mad. Born or made or cursed, he was mad. And he'd die before he let her get away from him.

"Do you think to escape the curse by killing the last of the Llewellyns?" she asked, pushing him yet further. "Do you truly think you can free yourself so easily after what you did to my mother?"

His teeth shone yellow as he snarled. "Bitch! She was fair game, ours by right. 'Twas Orwell's idea. 'No different than killin' a deer,' he said. And it wasn't." He jabbed his thumb toward the clustered townspeople, whose faces had gone blank with shock. "Look at them. They don't give a damn about it. Never did."

"Now, just a moment," Jameson began.

"Shut your mouth, old man. The Llewellyns are a pox

on the world, Satan's own brood. We did this town a favor, and they know it."

Jenna pushed against Alan's restraining arm. "You're doomed, Rafferty! Twenty years is a long time to be afraid, isn't it? Do you dream about it at night? Do you look over your shoulder every day, wondering if the curse has caught up with you at last?"

His mouth twisted. "They ain't a Llewellyn born who can scare me." Reaching into his pocket, he drew out a pipe and a small leather pouch. He filled the pipe, tamped it down with a stained forefinger, then lit it. The scent of tobacco coiled upon the air. "See this?" he asked, tossing the pouch to Jameson. "I tanned it myself."

"So?" the older man asked, his voice cold.

" 'Tis a trophy taken the day we caught the witch out in the swamp. Look careful, now."

Jameson turned the pouch over and over in his hands. "I don't understand."

"It's the witch's breast," Rafferty said. "Cut it from her myself."

"Good God in heaven!" Jameson dropped the pouch.

Rafferty looked around at the appalled faces of the townsfolk. Even his own men drew back as though unwilling to stand too near him. He turned his gaze to Jenna, meeting hers in defiant hatred.

And then he laughed.

Jenna cried out with a fury too large to contain, a wild tearing passion of anger that flung her past Alan and across the lawn toward Rafferty.

Thirty

Jenna heard Alan's shout of warning behind her, but she had no thought for her own safety; all she wanted was to get her hands on the man, even for an instant.

Then something pale seemed to materialize out of thin air in front of her. Roanna! Jenna made a wild grab for her, intending to toss her out of harm's way, but the old woman spun out of her grasp and stumbled almost into Rafferty's mount's chest.

The animal reared. Rafferty dropped his flintlock and grabbed for the reins. One of his men fired a pistol at Alan, much too near the already frightened horse. With a squeal of fright, it put its head down and bucked its rider straight into the air.

Roanna fell, and Jenna flung herself over the old woman's prostrate body to protect her from the flailing hooves. She felt more than heard the thump of those iron-shod feet hitting the ground a few inches from her head. Then Alan snatched them both up and slung them to safety.

Jenna landed hard. Gasping for breath, she sat up in time to see Alan hanging upon the horse's head, using his weight to bring those front hooves down. A moment later he'd gained control over the animal, soothing it with voice and hands until it calmed.

"Help me up," Roanna ordered.

That iron-tempered voice brought Jenna to her feet. She lifted the old woman from the ground, supporting her slight weight as she limped toward the people who surrounded Jonas Rafferty's sprawled form.

Roanna jabbed at the nearest back, and the crowd parted to let her through. Jenna stood looking down at the man who had cost them so much. He glared up at her, spittle running unheeded from the corner of his mouth.

"I can't feel my arms or legs," he gasped.

"A pity," Roanna said. "Then you can't feel pain, either."

Jenna bent and ran her hands along the fallen man's neck and back. Then she straightened. "His neck is broken."

It was a death sentence. And one not given by a Llewellyn. Glancing around at the townspeople, she saw little pity. Rafferty's hate had been too deep, too brutal, for them to condone what he'd done.

His eyes began to glaze. Roanna bent over him, leaning close to be certain he heard. With a smile that made Jenna shiver, she said, "I hope your master holds a fine, hot place for you in Hell."

The light in Rafferty's eyes dimmed and died. Jenna sagged, found Alan's arms waiting for her. She leaned against the solid warmth of his chest, exhausted now that the ordeal was over.

Despite her frailty, Roanna still had plenty of fight left. She faced the townspeople squarely, defiance lighting her eyes. " 'Twas I who came into town the other night, not Jenna," she said. " 'Twas I who frightened your horses last night. 'Twas I who cursed the animals who killed my daughter. If you want to kill a witch, take me."

Miranda Carrew swooped forward like a lovely, bitter vulture eager for death. "Take them both," she said. "The old one admits her witchery; by her own words, she brands the young one the Devil's get."

"Nay," Jameson Graeme said. "Carlton, help me down."

The young man helped his father from the carriage. Jameson held onto his son's arm as he came to stand before Roanna. "It's time to set things right, Roanna."

Her head came up sharply. "I never asked it of you. Never wanted it."

"So you didn't. But it's time nonetheless." His shoulders seemed even more stooped as he faced his neighbors. "The Devil did not father Roanna Llewellyn's daughter. I did."

Jenna studied Carlton, wondering if his astonishment matched her own. She had never expected to know the man who'd fathered Roanna's child; her grandmother had guarded that secret well.

"Was this . . . alliance before or after you married Mother?" Carlton asked.

Jameson's shoulders straightened, and he met his son's gaze steadily. "After."

"And don't start your prattle about a witch's spells," Jameson said, looking straight at Miranda. "There was no enchantment in it; Roanna was a beautiful, vibrant woman, and I a man who wanted her. I could have told the truth many years ago and perhaps stopped this talk of the Devil—"

"Hah," Roanna snapped. "They wouldn't have believed you."

Jameson shook his head. "I told myself I was protecting my wife, that she was too sickly, and the shock of learning that her husband had been unfaithful would kill her. But it was cowardice, not concern for her, that kept me silent. Why not let the witch take the blame, as she'd taken the blame for so many other things. Roanna was strong enough, more than strong enough. And then I thought she was dead, and none of it mattered any longer. I was wrong. It does matter, for lies and hatred grow stronger and stronger until they consume everyone."

. Tears stung Jenna's eyes as she watched the young man take it in and master it. It made her glad that Roanna had chosen so well. With gallant courtesy, Carlton bowed to the old woman.

"Our family shares the guilt for what happened. I'm sorry."

"Keep your guilt," she said. "No one made Orwell and the others into the beasts they became that day. They chose their path. So did we all." Her obsidian dark gaze raked the watching men and women.

Alan took a step forward, keeping his arm around Jenna's waist. Anger still coiled inside him, but it was cold now, chilled by the waste of human lives. He pointed to Rafferty's sprawled corpse. "There's your curse, and its name is hate. You laid it, you kept it alive." He pointed to each of them in turn. "You and you and you. And if you don't let it go, it will swallow you up as it did Jonas Rafferty."

More men were looking at their boots than not. Alan studied them with narrowed eyes, but they turned away, unable to face him.

Jenna felt more sadness than contempt; their part in this had been prompted by ignorance. So many lies, she thought, watching the people turn their horses and carriages around and depart. So many years of hate and betrayal. And this was the result.

Finally, the only ones left were Reverend Grey and Miranda. The man stood facing them as steadily as he'd done when accusing her. A great sadness had come into his eyes, however, and Jenna knew he regretted the hate perhaps more than any of them.

"Shame is a beginning," he said. "And I believe we will all do a great deal more thinking in the future than we've done in the past."

"Hmmph," Roanna muttered.

The clergyman ducked his head. "I don't blame you for your lack of belief, Mistress Llewellyn. But hate and mistrust can only be broken if both parties agree to try. Will you give it a chance?"

The old woman stared at him, her gaze seeming to sink straight through to his thoughts. Then she let her breath out in a harsh sigh. "If it were only me, I'd tell the lot of you to go to the Devil. But my granddaughter wants to live among you, so I will try." Crossing her arms over her chest, she glared at Jenna from beneath her brows. "And yes, I'll admit that even I am tired of hating. Been tired for a long time."

"Isn't this sweet," Miranda snapped, her eyes scathing as she stared straight at Jenna. "Well, I for one am not sorry for any of it. You walked in here and took what was mine—"

"You cannot *own* love. It comes to you freely—given, not taken," Jenna said. "I feel sorry for you, for you will never understand that."

Miranda stared at her, looking as shocked as if Jenna had struck her. Then her gaze lifted to Alan, and an ugly, mottled flush crept into her cheeks. Jenna saw in his eyes a contempt icy enough to freeze Hell itself. Pure Langston arrogance, she thought, and more effective than words could ever be.

Slowly, as though her body hurt her, Miranda turned and began walking down the drive.

"I'll pick her up on my way back to town," Reverend Grey said. "And now, Miss Llewellyn, is there something I can do for you before I go?"

"Marry us."

His jaw dropped. "Now?"

"Now."

"But what about banns and—"

"Civilized tripe," Roanna said.

Jenna smiled. "I have my family and my friends," she pointed to Ben and Opal and the others who had risked their lives to protect her. "I have my love, and a beautiful morning as well. Don't you think God has blessed this match already?"

"Marry us, Reverend," Alan said. "I've pursued her long enough, and I'm bloody well going to claim her now before she changes her mind."

"If I'm allowed, I'd like to give the bride away," Jameson said.

"Interfering already," Roanna muttered.

Carlton offered her his arm, a gallant gesture: "Allow me, er . . . With our rather convoluted association, I don't know what to call you. Step-Grandmother, perhaps?"

The old woman bared her teeth. "Try Roanna."

"Roanna, then," he said.

With a snort, she took his arm. "Well, Grey, get it over with." Before the clergyman quite got his Bible open, however, she added, "Shouldn't be *too* bad. There's good blood in the Llewellyns and Graemes. And once the stuffing's knocked out of Langston a bit, he might even be tolerable."

"Why, thank you, Grandmother," Alan said.

She looked him up and down, her eyes alight with mischief. "A fine, randy buck you've caught for yourself, Jenna. I expect you'll throw sturdy children."

"Madam!" Grey exclaimed.

Alan laughed. "Hurry up, Reverend. I'd like to get started on those sturdy children as soon as possible."

Jenna smiled at the now speechless clergyman. It was nice that her husband and her grandmother got along so well. It wasn't every day that a witch married into a fine old English family; rarer still that a townsman married into a family of Llewellyns.

"Wait a moment," Alan said.

She stared at him, completely astonished. He stepped back from her but retained his grip on her hands. "I've some unfinished business to take care of. Ben!"

"Yes, suh?"

"I have a problem and need your help in solving it."

Obviously perplexed, Ben said, "I'll do what I can."

"Good. You see, I want to give my bride a wedding gift, but she is appallingly uninterested in gowns and baubles and such things."

"Well, suh, that's the way of the Llewellyns."

"Yes, I understand that now." Alan's gaze softened as he looked at Jenna. His wood sprite . . . keeper of his heart. "So the only thing I can possibly give her that would adequately convey how deeply I treasure her is your freedom."

"I suppose . . . What did you say?"

"You're free. All of you."

A wail rose from the newly-made freedmen, Opal's voice rising high above the rest. With a cry, Jenna flung her arms around Alan's neck. "Oh, Alan!"

He looked over her head at Ben, who stood tall and proud, tears glistening on his cheeks. "You stood by me when I needed you most. Of your own free will. So, for as long as I hold Heronsgate, no slave will walk here."

"And how will you plant your crop?" Reverend Grey asked.

"I'll hire these good people, if they'll accept the task."

"Thank you, suh," Ben said simply.

"It will never work," the clergyman protested.

Alan smiled. "I think it will. What about you, Ben?"

"I expect we can make anything work we wants to."

"There you go, Reverend."

Jenna kissed her lover. He caught her to him, claiming her mouth in fierce possession and sweet tenderness. Her awareness of the world faded; there was only Alan, his scent, his passion, the feel of his hands hard upon her back, his mouth tender upon hers.

"Thank you," she whispered when he finally let her go. "You could have given me no more precious a gift."

"Enough to keep your love for a lifetime?"

"More. I will love you forever, Alan Langston."

He kissed her again. "I told you I'd hold you."

"So you did." But she realized now that this holding was no trap. Together, they'd found true freedom. Together, they would build a good life with love, with joy, and with all the passion they'd found in each other's arms.

"Marry me now," he said. "I can't wait another moment."

Nor could she. There, in the golden Carolina sunlight, she pledged her troth to the only man she'd ever love.

Epilog

Jenna, Alan, and the children walked down to the river to see Roanna off. Autumn had crept in on sly, frosty feet, sending the birds wheeling south in great flocks.

"I wish you'd stay the winter with us," Alan said.

The old woman snorted. "I've spent fifty-odd winters in the Dismal. Now that my cabin is finished, I'm ready to spend another. Besides, this soft living isn't my way."

"Besides," Alan said, his smile turning mischievous. "Jameson Graeme is showing signs of wanting to come a-courting."

"Perish the thought." Roanna shuddered with fine dramatic effect.

"Aren't you tempted, just a little?" Jenna asked. "After all, you found him appealing once."

"Finding a man appealing for a month or two and living with him for years on end are very different. I'd end up poisoning him."

"Pokeweed," Beth said.

"You've learned well, my girl."

"Toadstools are better," Jon said. "Faster."

"Excellent." The old woman glanced up at Alan. "Don't scowl so, Langston. I'm only jesting."

"Just so they are."

"Of course they are," she said. "Aren't you, children?"

"Of course, Great-Grandmother," they chorused.

"Good. Now run back up to the house and get warm," she said.

"You'll come back for Christmas?" Beth asked.

She sighed. "You've my word on it. And—"

"A Llewellyn never goes back on her word," Jon finished for her. "Are there any male Llewellyns?"

"Not in *my* swamp."

The children hugged her, then hurried back toward the house. Roanna stared after them for a moment, then turned her gaze on Jenna. "Have you told him yet?"

"I haven't even told *you.*"

"A witch knows these things."

With a smile that seemed to come straight from that warm, loving place deep inside her, Jenna thought about the tiny life now growing in her belly. "This one will be a Langston, not a Llewellyn," she said.

Roanna snorted. "Whatever you call it, it's bound to be stubborn."

"Wait," Alan said.

"Too late for that," Roanna said with a grin.

He ignored her, instead catching Jenna against him. The look in her eyes told him everything. Joy crashed through him in a blinding quicksilver tide.

"It's true?" he asked, although he knew what she'd say.

"It's true. You're glad?"

"Glad! I hope it will be a little girl with hair just like yours—"

"Or a boy with your indigo eyes—"

"Perhaps one of each," Roanna interjected. "The Llewellyns run to twins."

"Twins," Jenna echoed, dazzled by the possibility. "Oh, that would be—"

She stopped talking because it was impossible to talk while being kissed with great thoroughness by the love of her life. When she came up for air again, she saw that Roanna had already cast off, heading upriver in her sturdy, flat-bottomed boat.

" 'Til Christmas!" Jenna called.

"Christmas," the old woman echoed.

A moment later she'd disappeared around the bend. Jenna sighed. She wished Roanna had been happier at Heronsgate, but the old woman had lived too long alone to do anything else now.

"She still thinks of herself as a witch," Alan said.

"The curse *was* effective."

He swiveled to stare incredulously at her. She grinned in pure mischief. "Jon and Beth would be most disappointed if she didn't have special powers."

"Why?"

"It's not every child who can claim a real-life fairy grandmother as his very own."

He threw back his head and laughed, long and joyful. "God, I love you."

"Still?"

"Always."

She watched him as the wind ruffled his hair. He wouldn't be easy, this man she loved, but he was all she ever wanted. He'd called their joining destiny, and surely it was; from the moment she'd met him, their lives had been intertwined. Forever.

"Let's go in," she said. "I've got a . . . fire that needs stoking."

His eyes turned molten. "Now?"

"Now."

SURRENDER TO THE SPLENDOR OF THE ROMANCES OF F. ROSANNE BITTNER!

CARESS	(3791, $5.99/$6.99)
COMANCHE SUNSET	(3568, $4.99/$5.99)
HEARTS SURRENDER	(2945, $4.50/$5.50)
LAWLESS LOVE	(3877, $4.50/$5.50)
PRAIRIE EMBRACE	(3160, $4.50/$5.50)
RAPTURE'S GOLD	(3879, $4.50/$5.50)
SHAMELESS	(4056, $5.99/$6.99)

Available wherever paperbacks are sold, or order direct from the Publisher. Send cover price plus 50¢ per copy for mailing and handling to Penguin USA, P.O. Box 999, c/o Dept. 17109, Bergenfield, NJ 07621. Residents of New York and Tennessee must include sales tax. DO NOT SEND CASH.

WHAT'S LOVE GOT TO DO WITH IT?

Everything . . . Just ask Kathleen Drymon . . . and Zebra Books

CASTAWAY ANGEL	*(3569-1, $4.50/$5.50)*
GENTLE SAVAGE	*(3888-7, $4.50/$5.50)*
MIDNIGHT BRIDE	*(3265-X, $4.50/$5.50)*
VELVET SAVAGE	*(3886-0, $4.50/$5.50)*
TEXAS BLOSSOM	*(3887-9, $4.50/$5.50)*
WARRIOR OF THE SUN	*(3924-7, $4.99/$5.99)*

THE FIERY PASSION, EARTHY SENSUALITY, AND THRILLING ADVENTURES OF THE McLOUGHLIN CLAN